# ORGANICS

## MIKE TINGLE

Ten-Strikes *i*MH Press

TS*i*MH@TS*i*MH.com

WRONG WORLD®

REGISTERED TRADEMARK-MARCA REGISTRADA

ISBN-13: 978-0615588193
ISBN-10: 0615588190

# DEDICATION

For my pal Doc Brian

# TABLE OF CONTENTS

DEDICATION ............................................................. iii

ACKNOWLEDGMENTS ................................................ ix

PROLOGUE ............................................................... 1

CHAPTER 1 ~~ James and Kara ................................... 5

CHAPTER 2 ~~ Dr. Kate Lambert ............................... 21

CHAPTER 3 ~~ Found Lost ........................................ 28

CHAPTER 4 ~~ On The Beach .................................... 29

CHAPTER 5 ~~ The Midas Six .................................... 32

CHAPTER 6 ~~ Sheriff Renner McCauley .................... 34

CHAPTER 7 ~~ Josh, Erin and the FBI ....................... 40

CHAPTER 8 ~~ Jurassic Lark ..................................... 42

CHAPTER 9 ~~ BB & Puck .......................................... 47

CHAPTER 10 ~~ Dora the Explorer ............................ 49

CHAPTER 11 ~~ Worse Worser Worst ........................ 53

CHAPTER 12 ~~ Continuums ..................................... 56

CHAPTER 13 ~~ The Arrival ...................................... 60

CHAPTER 14 ~~ The Secret ....................................... 67

CHAPTER 15 ~~ Sweet Baby Genius ........................... 71

CHAPTER 16 ~~ Monsters in Waiting ......................... 82

CHAPTER 17 ~~ Doc Karl ........................................... 84

CHAPTER 18 ~~ Hunter's Morn ................................. 99

CHAPTER 19 ~~ Life Rising ...................................... 100

CHAPTER 20 ~~ Machine Rising ............................... 104

CHAPTER 21 ~~ Midas Six.......................................................106

CHAPTER 22 ~~ First Kills......................................................111

CHAPTER 23 ~~ Legend of Ol' Snatch.......................................117

CHAPTER 24 ~~ Poacher Poaching on Cruel Lake ...................122

CHAPTER 25 ~~ Missing Persons.............................................125

CHAPTER 26 ~~ Curtis Judy ...................................................127

CHAPTER 27 ~~ Routine Illusion.............................................130

CHAPTER 28 ~~ Curtis On the Rocks ......................................132

CHAPTER 29 ~~ Call for Chooke Cooke ..................................133

CHAPTER 30 ~~ Civic and Sick...............................................135

CHAPTER 31 ~~ Dead Men Don't Melt....................................138

CHAPTER 32 ~~ Alien Recon..................................................142

CHAPTER 33 ~~ Poacher Bird Feed.........................................145

CHAPTER 34 ~~ Alien Battle Plan ..........................................147

CHAPTER 35 ~~ To Love, Cherish and Honor Secrets..............148

CHAPTER 36 ~~ Alien & Hippie Go Hand-to-Hand ..................155

CHAPTER 37 ~~ Back in Time From Dead and Back .................159

CHAPTER 38 ~~ Ominous & Anomalous..................................177

CHAPTER 39 ~~ g'Hhol-deune ...............................................180

CHAPTER 40 ~~ Evidence of What?........................................186

CHAPTER 41 ~~ The Crawling Wounded .................................189

CHAPTER 42 ~~ Fried Mind Confession...................................191

CHAPTER 43 ~~ ATTACK! ......................................................194

CHAPTER 44 ~~ Boys Get Out Night.......................................200

CHAPTER 45 ~~ Behind Enemy Lines ........................................ 207

CHAPTER 46 ~~ Science Fiction Not ......................................... 210

CHAPTER 47 ~~ Terrorists Gang? ............................................. 213

CHAPTER 48 ~~ Gone-Down-Out ............................................. 221

CHAPTER 49 ~~ Killer Water Jugs ............................................ 229

CHAPTER 50 ~~ I Can Hear You! .............................................. 238

CHAPTER 51 ~~ Recon ........................................................... 246

CHAPTER 52 ~~ It is Them! ..................................................... 249

CHAPTER 53 ~~ Tyrannosaurus Rats ........................................ 253

CHAPTER 54 ~~ Shocked and Awed ......................................... 263

CHAPTER 55 ~~ Casualties ..................................................... 277

CHAPTER 56 ~~ Failsafe ......................................................... 290

CHAPTER 57 ~~ Bait .............................................................. 308

CHAPTER 58 ~~ Into the Breach .............................................. 315

CHAPTER 59 ~~ Kar Ver $2^{2867473247913577275968375838284832848282815}$ ... 319

CHAPTER 60 ~~ The One Is Here ............................................. 325

CHAPTER 61 ~~ Leaving Kilpatre ............................................. 327

CHAPTER 62 ~~ Hobo Immortal .............................................. 330

CHAPTER 63 ~~ Ghost Miner ................................................... 344

CHAPTER 64 ~~ Call For Hoop ................................................ 347

CHAPTER 65 ~~ Would the Real Cyril Hoop Please Stand? ....... 349

CHAPTER 66 ~~ Organics Offensive ......................................... 354

CHAPTER 67 ~~ Kar Offensive ................................................ 357

CHAPTER 68 ~~ Divide and Hide ............................................. 358

CHAPTER 69  ~~  Hunters Hunted ..............................................366

CHAPTER 70  ~~  Making a Stand .................................................371

CHAPTER 71  ~~  The Code of All.................................................373

CHAPTER 72  ~~  Stop And Think ................................................378

CHAPTER 73  ~~  Truths Revealed ...............................................381

CHAPTER 74  ~~  Out of Time.....................................................391

CHAPTER 75  ~~  The One ..........................................................398

CHAPTER 76  ~~  The Newborn ...................................................405

CHAPTER 77  ~~  Washington D.C.—One Week Later ................409

EPILOGUE ............................................................................412

ABOUT THE AUTHOR...............................................................414

# ACKNOWLEDGMENTS

Acknowledgments? Nope, but I do have some heartfelt apologies. First, I would like to apologize to my physicist daughter, who upon skimming the proof for *Organics* concluded that her father was either a science humorist or scientifically imbecilic. I accepted her most gracious compliment. It is well known in the writing world that any critique offered by a scientist including the word 'science' in any context is high cotton, and especially so for a science fiction writer. I blush proudly recalling her laughter.

Next, I would like to apologize to Dr. David Kaiser of MIT's physics department, who wrote the wonderfully inspiring book, *How the Hippies Saved Physics*. It is the true accounting of how the scientific counter-culture greatly advanced quantum theory in the 1960s through the serious investigation of ESP. It is such genius I wish someone would send some my way. I am keeping all telepathic channels open. Why an apology for Dr. Kaiser? Well, I have taken the hypothetical 'psi' to a place in *Organics* that even the hippie physicists would surely say, "Whoa, Dude! That's some far out shit!"

Last, I would like to offer a sincere apology to Columbia University's esteemed theoretical physicist Dr. Brian Greene. In his groundbreaking work, *The Hidden Reality*, he eloquently presses forward our understanding of the multiverse and string theory. The reason I feel I must also apologize to Dr. Greene is that his work is so inspirational, so mind-blowing, I felt compelled to help augment his research in *Organics* by employing a little breakthrough theorem of my own—the *Infinite Imagination Expansion Theory of Science Fiction*. I'm just sure he will want to see my research notes... if I had any.

My final comment is not an apology, but a simple thank you to Dr. Al Bartlett, Professor Emeritus, Department of Physics at the University of Colorado. Dr. Bartlett, like the other physicists mentioned, did not participate in the writing of this book in any way. It is just that I am Dr. Bartlett's number one fanboy, and I want to take this opportunity to once again remind everyone of a genuine American treasure.

Dr. Bartlett, *you* are our ultimate exponential!

—MT

MIKE TINGLE

# PROLOGUE

"Long ago in an infant galaxy so far away its nursery starlight will never reach Earth, a race of machines rose up from the elemental stew of their noxious cauldron world. These machines, known as the Kar, were created by cosmological happenstance and imbued with sense and sentience. Their mighty empire eventually stretched into the distant reaches of the universe.

"Three billion years after the dawn of machinekind, organic life finally made its first appearance. Organics' entrance onto the great stage did not occur, as was once supposed, in a nutrient rich tropical sea peppered by primordial lightning and salted by good luck.

"Life's launch pad was a Kar laboratory. Organic life was the product of several million years of Powerball trial and error made possible by a brand of scientific patience that only immortal machines might possess.

"However, machinekind's obsession to create organic life forms was not driven by a burning need to uncover some deep meaning about itself, or to fulfill some mysterious higher purpose postulated by philosophers and priests.

"The pursuit of organic life was not about truth seeking at all. It was about warfare, specifically, shoring up an overstretched supply line.

1

"The machines of the Kar Empire invented organic life as self-sustaining sources of slave labor and energy. Two commodities they desperately needed to revive their stalled march across the universe.

"So, there it is. Life got its humble start in the universe as inglorious fast food for machines. We were the exclusive supplier of joules to every Piss-Eat-Gas-n-Go punctuating the Kar's network of intergalactic warpaths.

"At its peak the Machine Empire had seeded and strung together over 940 billion planets with an incredible array of boutique life forms, each custom-built to survive the harshest celestial rock.

"The colonization spanned their known universe. However, almost from the very start the machines' enormous accomplishment also had colossal unintended consequences.

"Life would not stay put. It evolved, and evolution is unpredictable and messy. These two issues did not compute well for the tidy-minded machines. They put up with Life's unending terrible twos only because they had no other options.

"Predictably, Life also escaped and spread across the universe on its own. Some forms became conscious and advanced. The runaways had little use for slave masters or machine deities or life forms that did. In time, *Homo sapiens* evolved into one of these dark heroes.

"Fed up with rebellious Life's chaos and incessant annoyances, the machines returned to their laboratories and eventually discovered not only a new energy source, but something that made Life itself obsolete. Machinekind's equivalent to the Stone Age abruptly ended with the metaphoric Nuclear Age discovery called $k$-energy.

"Increasingly angered and threatened by organic challengers and now possessing the ultimate replacement energy source, the Kar Machine Empire ordered all organic life in the universe to be destroyed to ensure their dominance.

"When the extermination began, the ensuing holocaust split the Machine Empire apart. Tens of billions of machines cherished Life and opposed the slaughter. When all reasoning and appeals failed to stop the Empire's eradication mandate, some machines rebelled and refused to carry out the genocide. The rebel machines became known as the Orlif—the defenders of organic life and the true heroes of this story. The machines that supported and carried out the extermination of Life were the Exterm loyalists. The Orlif and Exterm armies engaged one another in a brutal trans-universe civil war lasting over three hundred millennia. It was known as the First Machine War.

"What follows in this account is the final battle in the First War, and the series of bizarre events on Earth that led to the coming of a third life form and the Second Machine War.

"The fate of Earth and Life itself now falls to one very special boy—my husband-to-be—and one Rebel machine who must guide and protect him at all costs. Only he could save us all. This is our story, Organics."

—Dr. Auren Katherine McCauley, PhD
$k$-Energy Physics Chair, University of Earth

MIKE TINGLE

# CHAPTER 1  ~~  James and Kara

"Thank you for seeing me, James George Spencer. I am the Orlif android Kara, commander of the Rebel warship *Jhim*. It is so nice to finally meet you in person, dear child. I am...

"Oh no! I see from your expression that my appearance both mystifies and concerns you. Please do not fear me. I promise you, you are perfectly safe with me here.

"Your eyes are not deceiving you. I currently appear to you in the form of what you would call on Earth a hologram. It is what we Orlif lightheartedly call 'putting on our hyperspace faces.' On planet, or traveling at sub-light speeds, we are as solid in appearance as you, dear one.

"If you are okay with this, just nod... Excellent!

"Well, enough about me. You have come a very long way to learn what you must, so let me begin with the last moments before the Exterms ambushed us." The machine took a deep breath and smiled at the human child.

"I recall the mood on the *Jhim* was quite relaxed. A rarity. Our long civil war was over, and we the victors were homebound to attend the Kar loyalists' surrender ceremony. My crew and I moved about our good warship at ease and spoke comradely to one another without regard to rank or service. It was an unusual atmosphere, I

5

assure you, and I suppose that in retrospect the smiles alone were the Orlif equivalent of a raucous victory party. My yes!

"Even my Chief Cannoneer was witnessed smiling. Indeed! Displaying such emotion was a millennial event at most for my chief. He is a machine so stoic the iciest asteroid in any universe is a comedian by comparison. Such joy we experienced! I will always cherish it. However, to your senses our celebrations might have sounded more like annoying noise.

"Unmelodious? How so your expression now begs. Well child, machine laughter blends the high-pitched cadence and timbre of your shortwave Morse code and wind shrieking through tall electrical stanchions. Noise? Perhaps, but I do miss that heartening sound!

"The *Jhim,* on the other hand, although speeding between two distant galaxies at thousands of light speeds, was as silent as if he were already resting on g'Hhol-deune our beautiful home world.

"My crew and ship were all veterans, but none of us had ever served on a peacetime mission. Celebrating as we were, no one sensed the deadly trap that awaited us.

"The following was the last entry I ever made to the *Jhim's* log. It explains so little I am afraid. Therefore, I will begin the tale from the middle where all Life in the universe nearly ended. Come with me now and see all, dear child."

***

## SHIP'S LOG

**Warship:** The *Jhim,* Rebel long-range saber fighter
**Virtual/Actual Displacement**: $7^{-19}$ cubic spartars/$10^5_{-116}$ tons
**Warship Version**: Subnanomech IV, Delta Sentient
**Fuel Sources**: 1. $< C^1$ is dark energy$^2$ fusion; 2. $> C$ is psi
**Instantaneous Arrival Potential**:  $psi_{-x \text{ light speeds}}$
**Current Hyperspace Speed**:  $psi_{-239.97771c}$
**Heading**:  $Orion_{R6K.743290742}\S[b_{487}731j9.15n_{551}98d.13k_{1191}2j.29qq_{997}d4]$
**Mission**: Proceed to the Federation surrender ceremony
**Officers/Crew**: 98/1033
**Date**: $8.0 \times 10^{59}_{-39}4 \; t_p^3$

---

[1] "C" is the symbol for light speed
[2] Supplied by both the cosmological constant and scalar moduli fields
[3] Planck time units having passed since the Big Bang ($1t_p=10^{-43}$ seconds or circa seven hundred million earth years ago)

The *Jhim*'s executive officer leaned over the shoulder of the ship's navigator and shook his head in disbelief. The XO mouthed an expletive and called to the commander. "Ma'am, we have a problem. We are off course. I estimate Jhim will miss his psi hyperspace[4] desertion point by 20,090.658 spartars[5]."

Diodes on the navigation hologram flashed the *Jhim's* current course digression. "Please accept my apologies, my Commander. I am not sure how that happened."

Female Kar machines were slightly smaller than their male counterparts were, approximately six feet in height with the human feminine attributes of breasts and wider hips.

Bright cerulean eyes dominated the androids' facial features. Physically, the machines were humanoid in body shape, but as a group, they did not exhibit human diversity, such as age, race or any physical imperfections. The machines' military uniforms fit snuggly and accentuated a rippling thoroughbred-like musculature.

The commander stood at parade rest before the bridge's expansive bow porthole and watched countless streamers of starlight spiraling past the ship, each beautifully distended by psi hyperspace. She glanced over her shoulder and spoke to her second-in-command. "Don't worry about it, Number One. That is why we have sub-light engines. Guide Jhim as close as possible to our assigned psi desertion and walk him in. Ask engineering to run a full navigation diagnostic after the peace ceremony."

The commander placed her right hand on the ship's porthole and gently caressed it. Smiling, she added, "It's certainly not Jhim's doing. He is as anxious as we are to finally see home again. Our good warship has been straining against his psi governor to speed up since the armistice was announced and our orders arrived to ship home."

---

[4] Psi (as "psi link" and "psi hyperspace" etc.) can occur only in the massless state of domesticated $k$-energy. Psi potentiates supra hyperspace travel theoretically approaching instantaneous arrival (IA) upon departure. As of this writing, IA has not yet been successfully achieved.

[5] One spartar is equal to the distance that a Psi link constant expands through space in $1^{-10,000,000}$ Planck time units. One Planck time unit is the time required for an uninhibited photon to travel the length of one Planck unit.

MIKE TINGLE

"Aye, Ma'am. Sounds like our always eager Jhim[6] boy."

The commander returned her attention to the deep-space light show and added distantly, "Can you believe it, my XO? The long civil war is over. We're going home."

"Yes, Ma'am. We are now one Kar again. Machinekind is reunited. The Federation is finally finished. Precious Life and Lord Universe forgive us for not stopping the Exterms sooner. The glorious Creation is finally safe."

"Better safe now than not. Make the necessary navigational adjustments, my XO."

"Aye, my Commander. Now calculating optimal post-desertion sub-light parabola to the surrender ceremony. Setting instantaneous arrival velocity to psi minus 239.97779 light speeds." The XO input the course and speed correction then added, "We should rendezvous late at the party no more than thirty-two rens[7] local, my Commander. That's as close as I can make it."

"Very good, Number One."

The unimaginably vast sea that exists between galaxies is not an empty void at all, but brims with perpetually disseminating, mysteriously turbulent dark matter and dark energy. The *Jhim* accelerated and parted the dark headwind and currents with no more regard for either than an ancient sailing ship a moonlit wave.

The executive officer watched the navigational change and speed adjustment take effect on the monitor. A moment later, he announced over the ship's intercom, "Officers and crew of the *Jhim*, prepare for psi desertion."

The *Jhim* burst from psi hyperspace in a brilliant flash of white light. The androids' bodies became solid and completely human in

---

[6] The ancient Kar pronunciation of "Jhim" is [juh•Him'] or by the modernized pronunciation [Jim]. Kar warships were addressed directly or referred to by either their surnames or ship names, i.e. Jhim or the *Jhim*.

[7] Ren is a time measurement matrix metered on *k*-energy dynamics that is unaffected by hyperspace, sub-light travel, or even stasis. Earth time, linear Planck time and the infinitely variable locus-circumstantial ren time are convertible from one to another. However, as of this writing, the algorithms remain far too complex and the energy requirements too impractically extreme for Earth computers to calculate any meaningful conversion of ren time. Scientists estimate that to calculate just one resultant would take 203 years and require a string of networked Cray super computers that stretches from Earth to the moon.

8

appearance except for their eyes that remained Day-Glo blue. As anticipated, the Rebel warship had arrived at the agreed Orion Nebula rendezvous slightly off course and a bit late, but fatefully, just outside the jaws of the Kar Federation ambush already in progress.

The commander and XO reacted immediately. "Commander, it's an Exterm trap!"

"Battle stations! Bring us about, XO. Make a hole to our flagship and join the Orlif line."

"Aye, Ma'am!" The XO turned and shouted, "Orlifs of the *Jhim*, you know the drill. We are still at war!"

The officers on the bridge called out their action reports as the *Jhim* raced toward the battlefield.

"Calculating optimal defensive insertion onto flagship line. Nav is a go!"

"Issuing all countermeasures. Antigamma jamming 100 percent on infinite sine. Antimatter flak armed and ready. Defenses are a go!"

"Psi detection conforming a hundred percent. All eyes are a go!"

"Gamma cannons charged, hot and itchy a hundred per, my XO." The Chief Cannoneer added calmly, "Go."

"kATH shields are on. Blanket integrity a hundred per, all 5-by, Boss. GO!"

"My XO!" the Trarad officer shouted. "Sensors report multiple event anomalies. Unknown scripts. Attempting to decipher."

The communications officer shouted much worse news. "Hailing friendlies on all wartime channels, Boss. We're receiving multiple maydays!" Every officer shot a concerned glance at the communications officer.

Alarms sounded shrilly throughout the ship as the crew rushed to their assigned battle stations.

The commander studied the deluge of data before her, and realized how successful the ambush was. The Rebel fleet was outnumbered four to one and losing badly. "My XO, belay that order. Withdraw! We need to secure g'Hhol-deune[8]. Set a course that puts us between home and the Federation fleet. What's Home Prime's status?"

No response. The commander glanced at her executive officer. His hands were frozen in front of his face. The XO lunged away

---

[8] The Orlif home planet g'Hhol-deune is pronounced [guh•all•den']

from the holographic monitor as suddenly as if he was punched. She repeated her question privately to his battle station as she ran to her own. "My XO, I need your head in the battle! What is the status of g'Hhol-deune?"

The XO turned toward her. His voice cracked with emotion as he growled, "My Commander, g'Hhol-deune is on fire. The entire planet's surface is ablaze: irradiated at zettagamma. The Exterms destroyed our home world, Ma'am. Our g'Hhol-deune is gone."

\*\*\*

Kara narrated the massacre to James George. "The universe beyond the bridge's panoramic porthole was a war zone, child, or more accurately a killing field. As far as the eye could see raged a spectacularly brilliant firework display of silent death and destruction—an escalation of devastation never before witnessed during a civil war measured not in years but in millennia.

"One thing became certain to us all. The Federation's recent five hundred year military decline had been a strategic deception, an unprecedented sacrifice in battle of material, personnel, even resource-rich solar systems. The Exterm surrender terms were a sophisticated ruse to draw the entire Rebel fleet home into one place and the ploy had worked.

"Hundreds of thousands of homebound Kar Rebel warships emerged from hyperspace—saber fighters[9], the saucer-shaped battle platens[10] and the immense star victors[11]—to a reunion that was a literal firing squad.

"The enemy focused their gamma cannons[12] on the Rebel's star victors—the planetoid-sized warships. One after another, the

---

[9] The saber fighter functioned as an intergalactic analog of a cross between stealth jet fighters and long-range hunter-killer submarines.

[10] The battle platen was shaped like the classic flying saucer. Its military purpose was somewhat similar to that of a 21st Century aircraft super carrier. Battle platens supported up to 11,000 saber fighters.

[11] There is no meaningful comparison for the star victor. Star victors ranged in size from 400-600 kilometers in diameter. The typical star victor battleship carried a $k$-energy arsenal equal to a red dwarf sun. The star victor, like all warship classes, was psi hyperspace capable.

[12] The gamma cannon pulse was a burst of x-rays trained by $k$-energy to a mass state equivalent in atomic weight to plutonium and fired at an enemy target on a photon plasma beam. Upon impact, if not neutralized by kATH

massive spaceships exploded like micro suns. The shockwaves and space shrapnel took out entire Rebel convoys. Roving bands of Kar Federation saber fighters mercilessly hunted down and destroyed the few escape pods that did manage to evacuate.

"Exterm cannoneers fired point-blank on the defenseless Rebel ships, most of which were transporting refugees, soldiers and diplomats home, destroying them all before any could raise their shields or return fire. There would be no armistice with the Kar Federation today or ever. The massacre was over in just moments, but the battle on the *Jhim* was just beginning. Let's watch together."

***

Warning klaxons blared throughout the *Jhim*. Above the din, the Rebel Commander issued a flurry of urgent orders to her officers. "Engineering, maximize kATH shields! Divert all unessential power."

"Aye! kATH optimized, my Commander."

"Navigation, load psi hyperspace jump coordinates. Plot evasive maneuvers. How much time until we can revert from our machine *k*-matter state back to *k*-energy[13]?"

"Sixty rens minimum, my Commander. The psi engines have to recharge with dark energy for another thirty rens from the previous matter-energy transition. Jhim and I will need another thirty to set our course."

"Insufficient. We will be dead in half that time. Initiate an emergency blind jump as soon as the *k*-energy cycle is complete.

---

shielding, the charge unbundled and attacked the *k*-matter subnanomech structure of the target like a fast moving acid.

[13] *k*-energy, also known as 'taught energy' or 'trained string energy' is of a unique class of energy modern physicists call Telemachus. (named for Mentor's student in the Greek myth) Its discovery and manipulation unlocked and solved a series of confounding mysteries in astrophysics. Mastering *k*-energy enabled machinekind to safely move from a natural state of *k*-matter to *k*-energy at will. In a pure energetic state, the restrictive laws of relativity no longer applied, allowing the Kar Machine Empire to crisscross the universe at speeds only previously imagined. Note: Exposure to *k*-energy is deadly to organic life, being maximally $10^{190,665}$ times more toxic than radioactive cesium isotope. Death and complete sub atomization can occur in mere seconds when exposed, with one human body releasing an energy equivalent of a single $7^9$ megaton nuclear weapon.

Take us out of here without nav. We have at most thirty rens before they are on us."

"Aye, Commander. Initiating wildcard countdown to psi jump."

"XO, why aren't we cloaked?"

"My Commander, we cannot engage cloaking. Jhim is reporting a system-wide corruption. The entire rendezvous sector has been lased by some sort of anti-phase supralumen. One that he and I have never seen before."

"Can Jhim neutralize it?"

"He's analyzing... aye! Good boy, Jhim! Decryption will take him an estimated fifteen rens, my Commander."

"Make it so. Weapons, establish firing resolutions. Fire at will when the enemy is in range. Buy us some time, Patriots."

"Aye, Ma'am! Making Exterm target."

"Twenty-five rens to psi hyperspace, my Commander. Jump will occur simultaneous to ship-wide matter-to-energy reversal. However, I must remind you, my Commander, we'll have no way of knowing where we are headed."

"Understood." "My Trarad, what do we see?" the commander asked the *Jhim's* sensors officer calmly.

"My Commander, we have twelve, no, make that fourteen Federation battle platens coming about on our heading. Counting 277 saber fighter squadrons and one Federation star victor hanging back. Advance sabers will soon be in range."

"I'll be damned, my Commander!" the XO exclaimed. "The star victor is the Exterm flagship the *Atr*. His battle platen and saber fighter escort is from the First Phalanx Fighter Group. Apparently, we did not kill the First during the Fourth Sepucula[14]. Those clever Exterm bastards!"

"So it appears. Let's make sure we take care of business this time, my XO."

"With pleasure, Ma'am."

---

[14] The Fourth Sepucula was the final and once thought decisive battle for the Albidin Galaxy. Because of its strategic location and abundant resources and the Federation's sudden retreat from the Albidin, military historians of the day concluded prematurely that the 4th was the First Machine War's tipping point, similar to the Battle of the Waterloo. In retrospect, the Federation's highly successful strategic deception now compares more closely to the battle at Little Big Horn.

From Trarad, "The Exterm fleet is retiring from the field and joining the *Atr*. Sensing parallel processing ship to ship. I estimate decryption of our antigamma weapons jamming in four rens, my Commander."

From Weapons, "We have nonreciprocal target locks, Ma'am. Engaging Exterm advance fighters with long-range cannons."

The *Jhim's* battle-hardened cannoneers killed all twelve of the advance Federation saber fighters in the first volley. Fifty more of the enemy sailed through the debris field, and though blinded by *Jhim's* antigamma and suffering heavy losses, they continued undeterred toward the lone Rebel warship. Hundreds of enemy sabers followed the second wave.

"Trarad, what is Patriot fleet status?"

The fireworks were over. "Scanning zero *PUBBs*, Ma'am. I repeat. Zero me-here IDs returning. It's gone! The entire Orlif fleet is gone! This cannot be!"

"Easy, machine. *We* are not dead yet. I need you to focus. Understand?"

"Yes, my Commander. Sorry, Ma'am."

From Psi Navigation, "Commencing final psi link countdown. *k*-matter to *k*-energy reversal in 12 rens…"

"Engineering. Give us full power, flank to starboard. Make maximum sub-light speed. Maintain our cannoneers' advantage as long as possible. Use the Exterm front line as a screen against the *Atr's* super long-range cannons."

"Aye, Ma'am. Maximum sub, flank to starboard."

As the *Jhim* retreated, his own cannoneers fired an apocalyptic twelve thousand gamma pulses per ren. A constant shower of antimatter flak provided the *Jhim* cover, intercepting and neutralizing the Fed sabers' wild gamma pulses. They destroyed the first three waves of Fed saber fighters without the *Jhim* suffering a single hit.

"Psi Nav, execute blind jump on *your* mark!"

"Aye! On my mark, Ma'am."

"Ten…"

"Cloak status?"

"Negative cloak. Still decrypting, my Commander."

"Ma'am! Enemy is firing! One incoming super long-range megapulse. *Atr* origination. Range 1,000,916 spartars. Contact with us, imminent."

"Brace for enemy impact!" the commander shouted.

The *Atr* had had enough of the *Jhim's* screening tactic and antigamma jamming and his response was ruthless. The massive gamma pulse soared through space toward the *Jhim* without regard to the *Atr's* own fleet, killing two Fed battle platens and dozens of saber fighters that were unfortunately in his line of fire.

"Nine rens to psi, Ma'am."

Even with the kATH shields at maximum strength, the *Atr's* massive gamma pulse slammed the *Jhim* and turned him ninety degrees off his $x$ and $y$ axes. Lights flickered and everything not fastened down became deadly projectiles. Static electricity arced like lightning bolts across the helm. A high-pitched squeal reverberated throughout the ship as the *Jhim's* shields struggled to neutralize the gamma weapon's deadly charge. Worst, two critical sub-light engines were disabled ending Jhim's retreat. The enemy rapidly closed the gap.

"Eight rens…"

"Exterms have decrypted our antigamma defenses, my Commander. Reciprocal weapons targeting is now enabled."

From the XO, "Ma'am, this is very strange! Just when they've got us, their fighters and platens have ceased firing."

From Trarad, "Ma'am! Enemy is syncing firing resolutions!"

"Syncing?" the commander mused. "Well, my brave war fighters, that's actually a little good news."

The enlisted machines and officers on the bridge glanced at their leader, then to the XO who would ask the collective question.

"My Commander? Just exactly why is that good news?" the XO asked uncertainly.

"I'm guessing the arrogant Exterms want to share the kill, and a synced gamma pulse will take time to coordinate. They will soften us up and wait for their flagship, the *Atr*, to arrive and lead the attack. It gives us time. Cease fire! Where's our cloaking, my XO?"

"Jhim's almost there, Ma'am."

"Incoming fire! Multiple bogey origination."

"My Chief Engineer, make dense the hull shielding over the psi drives. Nanoplait all sections from IRE to SOJ. Maximum veneers, old friend, and please make them fast."

"Aye, my Commander. Maximizing psi shielding."

"Brace for enemy contact!" the commander shouted.

Fifteen vicious pulses in quick succession followed the first Fed saber strike. The commander's analysis of the Federation's battle tactic was correct. They calculated the attack to mortally wound, not to kill the *Jhim*. Each precise strike further overwhelmed his hull shields. Everyone except the commander had fallen to the deck before the barrage ended.

"Shields! Status report!" the commander shouted over the injured ship's suffering cries.

From engineering, "Hull shields are down to twelve percent, my Commander. Failure of the kATH system is imminent on next assault."

"Psi link drive status?"

"Densified hull shielding uncompromised, my Commander. Hyperspace psi engines still charging. Gamma cannons remain at ninety-nine percent charge."

"Damage report, Chief."

There would be no more good news. "The outer hull is breached. Six-out-of-eight sub-light engines are inoperable. The other two are questionable. We are venting e-tmosphere into space faster than we can seal. Subnanomech[15] particle incineration is out of control in eleven sections of the ship. Reporting heavy casualties ship wide." The chief engineer then added sadly, "Jhim is dying, my old friend. Our good boy is dying. Damn. I never thought..."

The Commander winced. She leaned over her command console and whispered to the spaceship, "No! You will not let that happen, Jhim. Do you hear me? You can save us all one more time, little brother." She gently caressed the command console. "Please Jhim. You have to get up! Kar Patriots exist as one or terminate together, and I am not ready to meet our Universe today. The precious Creation, Jhim. Think! We are perhaps Life's last hope."

Her coaxing worked somehow. The warship yawed and twisted as it fought to regain control of its systems and right itself. Slowly, one after another the flickering diodes steadied and then brightened

---

[15] Subnanomech technology rose from the discovery and subsequent taming of *k*-energy, whose fields mysteriously emerged from string theory's singularly dimensioned closed loop. It is theorized that *k*-energy is the progenitor field for all energetic particles, including the graviton, the inflaton and the photon. Whether the theory holds or not over time, the Kar eventually manipulated *k*-energy to construct *the* particle that literally rebuilt the Kar Machine Empire. The subnanomech particle is commonly described by historians as the Kar's industrial equivalent of the hydrocarbon and water molecule rolled into one with sunlight.

throughout the bridge. Bulkhead doors slammed shut to isolate damages. Subnanomech repair programs launched. Emergency e-tmosphere vents opened to replace the leakage. "Good Jhim! There's our courageous steed!"

The commander kissed her fingertips and pressed them against her ship to thank him. She knew every crewmember was likewise expressing his or her gratitude in many ways.

"Seven rens to psi, my Commander."

"Thank you, Patriot Machine…"

"Engineering? Status." The commander knew she did not need to ask the chief the most critical question.

"Jhim's breathing again, Ma'am. His dark energy uptake and absorption[16] is rising." The chief added, "Skipper, if we get out of this jam, I'm going to fill Jhim's hangar to the brim with every luxurious green plant our good boy's ever wished to sit and watch grow."

"Excellent idea. Count me in for half, my Chief."

More of the saucer-shaped battle platens arrived and locked their weapons on the *Jhim*.

"Enemy is outflanking us, my Commander. Encirclement is imminent."

Countless swarms of Kar Federation saber fighters spilled angrily from the battle platens and star victors, then more from the arriving flagship *Atr*. Each battleship raced to its assigned position around the *Jhim*. With the encirclement complete, the hundreds of thousands of Federation warships closed ranks, moving ever closer to the *Jhim* until the attackers' hulls were mere spartars apart.

In just rens, the Exterm warships would synchronize their gamma weapons and in a celebratory war-ending coup de grace deliver their deadly pulses simultaneously on the *Jhim*—the last survivor in the Kar Rebel fleet.

"Six…"

From Communications, "Commander, the *Atr* is hailing us. Their Alpha Genesis wishes to address you."

"Alright, let's hear him. My Comm, play that waste of *k*-trons ship wide."

---

[16] Kar warships absorbed energy directly from space by tapping into ubiquitous dark energy, the extraordinarily diffused and fractionated energy remnants of the Big Bang as originally described by Albert Einstein as the cosmological constant.

"Aye, Ma'am." Smiling, the officer opened the channel. "Go ahead, Alpha Genesis. You have my Commander."

"Traitorous Orlifs of the *Jhim*, before I claim your energy, please know that the final extermination of Life in the universe shall now begin. You cannot stop the purification of the Empire of the pestilence. May the Universe never forgive you Orlifs for defending Life, for the hideous plague it has brought upon machinekind. Say your last words, Rebel, then be stilled."

The communications officer turned toward the commander and asked, "Do you wish to respond, my Commander?"

"Yes, I do. Remove encryption. Let them all hear us."

"With pleasure, Ma'am! Now handshaking with the Exterm flag over the neural neutral link. The channel is now yours, Ma'am. The entire Exterm fleet is online."

The commander did not wait for Alpha Genesis' acknowledgement before speaking. "Stand down, Alpha Genesis, and I will still accept your unconditional surrender. Fear not. We Orlifs remain ever merciful even toward dimly defective Federation Exterms like you. As for any last words, you'll hear your own soon enough. Onward Life!" She did not wait for a reply and cut the link amidst a flurry of unintelligible threats.

A cheer went up throughout the *Jhim* as the commander's defiant message ended. The officers on the bridge rose from behind their stations and snapped to attention as one. In unison they shouted the rebel motto, "Orlif Eternal!"

The commander rose and delivered the reply. "Creation Endless!" Smiling, she made eye contact with each officer and enlisted machine, then nodded and bowed her head in respect to her crew.

The commander had one time-buying arrow left in her quiver—a long shot that was little more than a pathetic smoke screen. The *Jhim* carried in his arsenal an antique weapon that was little more than a soldier's souvenir trinket: a tiny self-propelled nuclear weapon long deemed obsolete by both sides of the war.

"Five rens to jump."

The commander studied the officers for a moment then issued her orders. "Officers of the *Jhim*, execute your orders on my mark.

"Engineering! Drop shields! Do not restore."

"Aye, Ma'am!"

"Weapons! Arm and launch at zero degrees Jhim's lucky charm: our ancient nuke. Let's hope it still works. Detonate at one hundred spartars!"

"Aye, my Commander!"

"XO, initiate emergency full stop! Divert all remaining power to hyperspace psi engines."

"Aye!"

"One last thing. Communications, I wish to hear our Jhim's favorite starship nursery song one more time. Can you play for us *A Pretty Galaxy from g'Hhol-deune*?"

"Yes, Ma'am. I believe we all would like that very much. It's the very least we can do for our brave boy."

As the music began, the commander addressed her crew over the ship's intercom. "It has been my great honor to serve with all of you. Protectors of the Creation, we the Patriot Kar aboard our beloved Jhim! Life and Machine! United forever! MARK!"

"Four rens…"

The antique nuclear weapon could not have possibly harmed any battleship in either fleet, but when it detonated its archaic electromagnetic pulse did create some static and briefly interfered with a few of the Federation's targeting systems left carelessly unshielded for ancient EMP, just as the commander hoped.

"Three…"

"Decryption complete! Engaging cloak, my Commander."

Nothing happened. The starship faded into translucence for a moment and then returned fully reflective.

"Status?"

"Cloak not engaging. We are still exposed. Attempting to restart."

"Number Two, execute maximum sub-light burst!" the commander ordered. "Give me five hundred spartars out of their bull's eye. Make them miss us at least once."

The spaceship shook but nothing happened. "Now!" The commander shouted.

The two remaining sub-light engines flickered then dimmed. "No joy, my Commander. Jhim's a dead stick. Sub-light drives are not engaging! Attempting to reignite."

"Make it so and hurry, my machine!" She pressed her palms on the command console and whispered, "Please, Jhim! Find a way, little brother. Stay with us."

The chief cannoneer shouted, "My Commander, the *Atr* just dropped his shields. The entire Exterm fleet is likewise exposing. Request permission to fire on him."

The commander leaned over her console and shook her head. "No! Hold fire. He thinks we are already dead. Their fleet is now close enough for a rare eyeball-actual view of their kill. My Chief Cannoneer, prepare to concentrate and fire all remaining gamma armory on the *Atr*'s port psi drives on my mark. One megapulse. Charge it with everything we got, but do it quietly, my old friend."

"Aye, Ma'am."

"Now my precious machines, we need some luck."

"Two rens!"

"What's the status of the EMP interference?"

"Minor effect, my Commander, enemy has resolved entirely to visual. Confirming five-by-five targeting. They have us on visual one hundred per!"

From Weapons, "The *Atr* target is locked, my Commander."

"One ren to psi jump!"

"Fire!" the commander ordered and then whispered, "See you later, Exterminator! How's them for last words?"

"Enemy is firing, Ma'am!" The coordinated pulse came at the *Jhim* from thousands of near points in space, countless streams of red death all aimed at one target. However, the *Jhim*'s super-massive gamma pulse passed through the barrage a milliren quicker.

"My Commander! Hyperspace psi engines engaged. JUMPING!" The crew and ship transformed back to pure *k*-energy, and then disappeared into psi hyperspace.

\*\*\*

Kara continued, "Well, as you witnessed, James George, the *Jhim* escaped the Orion Nebula an instant before thousands of Federation gamma pulses passed through his former position with the combined energy of a pulsar.

"Maybe it was fate or just dumb luck, even an extraordinarily rare navigation system malfunction that saved us that day by making us late to the ceremony.

"No one would solve that mystery for a very long time or discover just how perfectly placed the *Jhim*'s departing shot had been. When the unshielded Federation flagship *Atr* exploded, the ship-to-ship chain reaction took out nearly all of its own fleet. "The civil war survived and with it hope for Life."

\*\*\*

"James George Spencer! Wake up, sweetie. We don't want to miss the bus. Remember? Today's our school field trip to Denver. Come on, sleepy head! Up and at 'em!"

Startled as if awakened by gunfire, James George sprang upright in bed. He rose from sleep sluggishly, though, like an exhausted deep-sea diver ascending in slow motion to the sparkling surface. James George looked up at his foster parent Dr. Lu Li Kwan and rubbed his eyes. He shook his head and felt sleep's cobwebs start to break apart.

Through a cavernous first yawn James George exclaimed, "Wow! That was some dream. There was this android, a lady machine, the one telling my dream… and… she could go back and forth between being solid matter and pure energy. Oh my, that actually makes great sense! That's how the rebel machines could go faster than the speed of light in their spaceship, because they're energy, and energy has no mass. Einstein's recently challenged exception! Their spaceship was like this really, really smart warhorse that all the machines loved… and, he has live plants for toys… Wow, that's weird but cool. Oh, also I think we might have been like slaves or something, but no longer for the good guy machines, and there was an awful civil war… between… uh between…?" James' Dreamland and Wakeland untethered and drifted apart. "Oh no, I forget!"

Lu tossed his bed hair playfully with both hands, and then smoothed it. "Lady? Story? Androids? Spaceship? Some dream indeed! You didn't even hear your alarm. I thought I was going to have to wake you with a bucket of ice water. Goodness, you're a deep sleeper. Let's go now. The charter bus leaves Colorado Springs for Denver in one hour."

# CHAPTER 2  ~~  Dr. Kate Lambert


Dr. Kate Lambert hurried down the IMAX auditorium steps at the Museum of Natural History in Denver. Her white lab coat flowed behind her. The theatre appeared deceptively empty. In many ways, it could not have been fuller. A very special audience of thirteen ultra-gifted children awaited her presentation.

Halfway to the stage Kate waved to her college friend, Dr. Lu Li Kwan. Lu smiled and raised her arms warning Kate that a bear hug had her name on it. Several field trip parent helpers sat in the front row. Lu's students chatted quietly beside them. Most of the kids were too short to see above the seat backs.

The two best friends could not stand in greater contrast. Kate was nearly five feet nine, single, with honey blonde hair and an athletic build. Lu was six inches shorter, the youngest of three siblings, and seemingly delicate despite having once competed for an Olympic medal in ice hockey. Only their matching dimples and age, thirty-six, likened the two women.

Kate rounded the first row of seats and walked directly over to Lu Li. The two friends embraced. "How was the bus trip from Colorado Springs, Lu?"

"Oh, it was great! The best ever. The kids just loved it. Especially the new routing and scheduling software demonstration.

21

Daniel Schuenberger was especially enthralled. In fact, he helped debug their beta Delays Module in only eight minutes. The charter company offered him a job, and they were only half kidding."

Lu stepped back and asked, "Well roomie, are you ready to do this one more time?" Lu, who had earned her PhD in astrophysics at MIT, had the nearly impossible task of developing a challenging science curriculum at the Morgan Evers International School for the ultra-gifted.

"Absolutely! Your field trip has become the highlight of my year, so I guess I better get started before the children implode." Kate's voice changed into a synthetic, cyber monotone, "We…need…more…input…Dr. Lu!" Giggling like schoolgirls themselves, the two women hugged once more.

Kate walked to the edge of the stage and leaned against it as Lu introduced her. The children obediently stilled. Kate looked into the audience of young, smiling faces and said, "Hello! My name is Dr. Kate Lambert. I am a paleontologist. You all know what that is, I'm sure."

Her tone was professorial, as if she might be speaking to graduate students. She waited while the children quietly conferred amongst themselves regarding the hundred or so subspecialties. The animation and giggles ended twenty seconds later, and the class returned their attention to Kate.

Lu nodded approval. Kate naturally walked the gifted instructor's tightrope, which required ignoring the kids' physical ages, but not their lagging emotional development. Genius and silliness were not mutually exclusive.

Kate continued, now assuming a gypsy's mystical accent. "Did you know that I can also read minds, children?"

The grade school/grad students giggled and shook their heads.

Kate stroked the air as if playing a piano. "Come to me. Give me your thoughts, children!" Gypsy Kate closed her eyes as if in a trance and pretended to concentrate. The children giggled and imitated her.

After a few seconds, Kate looked up and said, "Well, I can't read every mind today, but are any of you wishing with all your heart that a few dinosaurs were still around today? Maybe some of the nice ones?"

The class erupted in agreement. The subject of dinosaurs was the perfect bridge subject for gifted children.

One child did not join in. He stared at Kate and shook his head slowly. Lu had warned her about this holdout, the serious boy who was also the most gifted student who ever attended the international school. For this boy, the term "gifted" was an understatement.

The exception raised his hand. "Dr. Lambert?

"Yes, and what is your name?"

"My name is James George Spencer, and you are not actually reading minds, Dr. Lambert. You are conducting a parlor trick. While children are predictably sad about dinosaurs' extinction, they are also universally enthralled. To wish their reappearance is only natural, especially while visiting a museum dedicated in part to their rise and fall. You have capitalized on the suggestive obvious. That is all."

Amy Whitehorse, a ten-year-old Canadian Sioux, laughed aloud. She leaned around James George and said, "Dear God, James George! Dr. Lambert does not presume to fool any of us with her paranormal legerdemain. She is only being silly, and I for one truly appreciate her humor. It allows me to remember that I am still just a child. You must learn to recognize such silliness, James George, and appreciate its critical role in forming interpersonal relationships. That is, unless you want to grow up to be a big lonely loser like... General Custer!"

The class laughed and James George blushed. He turned to Kate and apologized, "Oh, I am so very sorry, Doctor. I didn't know you were being, uh, silly. You see, I have difficulty recognizing degrees of seriousness. Such acts as fantasy play, unlabeled or spontaneous humor, and calculated absurdity for the purposes of irony often escape my comprehension." He glanced at Amy who was already nodding encouragement and added, "Amy and I are working on it."

"That is quite all right," Kate said. She glanced at Lu. The teacher nodded and eased back into her chair on the stage. Crisis over. Adults can only teach so much. The rest has to come from the gifted children themselves.

James George recovered. He cleared his throat and asked, "With that settled, may I ask you a question? I promise to be silly at the first opportunity."

"Of course." Kate smiled. Master Spencer was also the fossil expert about whom Lu had often spoke.

He was eight, turning nine next month, and possessed a slight English accent. Orphaned at birth, a childless couple had adopted

James George. His new father was a British-born atomic molecular physicist, and his mother a German research chemist. Both parents had worked for the United Nations in biological weapons inspection. However, the couple was missing and presumed dead as the result of a tragic single-engine airplane crash off the coast of Africa. James George was currently a temporary ward of the school.

The boy cleared his throat and lifted a very officious-appearing eyebrow. "While the so-called dinosaurs' disappearance is indeed interesting and also sad, I am afraid my paleontological curiosity guides me elsewhere."

"Yes, James."

"I prefer James George, Doctor, if you please."

"Of course, James George. What is your question?"

"On the Internet last evening while preparing for our field trip, I discovered that your PhD and much of your subsequent early research pertains to the multituberculate, the group of herbivorous pre mammals that once existed in North America."

"That's correct, James George. I'm very impressed."

James George's expression turned to surprise. "Impressed? Why? Anyone with a computer, a credit card, and a reasonably sprite broadband connection could learn so much."

Kate bit her lip and glanced at Lu as the teacher ducked giggling through the auditorium's side exit.

James George continued, "I commend your scientific focus. I also find the multituberculate quite interesting. Especially their remarkable physical similarity to the egg-laying monotremes such as the platypuses, although, that particular reproductive characteristic—egg laying—is pure paleontological conjecture. Wouldn't you agree?"

"Yes, James George, I do. However, recent evidence is lending some much needed support for the theory."

James George stared at a spot above the stage for a moment then exclaimed, "Oh! You are referring to the Bloom-Carnegie project in 2010, Doctors Su Zen Phette and D.X. Pedigo and their surfeits aquatint discovery in eastern Montana. Originally, I believe the find was assumed to be *Tachyglossus aculeatus*, but later the fossil was determined not to be of an echidna at all. The deductive optimists amongst us, and I am one, are now speculating that surfeits aquatint was actually a multituberculate. Can you just imagine it, Doctor Lambert? Proof that multituberculate laid eggs!"

"Well, my fingers are certainly crossed! That is very good, James George! I should be asking you the questions."

The boy's expression sagged into one of grave disappointment, "But Dr. Lambert, I haven't asked my question yet!"

"Oh, I'm sorry, honey! I mean, James George! What is your question?"

James George sighed and puffed his cheeks as he exhaled. "Well, the multituberculate bore a remarkable similarity to modern Rodentia, so much so that it earned the nickname 'Rodents of the Mesozoic,' but as you know multituberculate was absolutely not a rodent."

"True. The fossil evidence incontrovertibly supports that position."

"Well, as a paleontologist and a celebrated expert on multituberculate, why would you waste so much of your time investigating modern Rodentia? I mean the majority of your research in the last four years is on nothing more substantial than stupid rats." An indignant child finally emerged with that comment.

Kate smiled. Kids, especially city kids, universally hated rats. Apparently, even this eight-year-old boy, whose intellect already surpassed hers, could not fathom the rat as biologically redeeming, as important to the wellbeing of the ecosystem as any other less notorious species. Few realized that their gerbils and hamsters were first cousins of *Rattus rattus*, the despised black rat.

"That is an excellent question, James George, and I'll try to explain my research to you. Like all paleontologists, I also must study paleozoology as well as contemporary zoology. Why? It makes it much easier to appreciate an animal's ancestors if you can connect its descendant dots, especially its skeletal anatomy. How it moved, how it lived, and how it changed as it evolved. I agree with you that multituberculate was not a rodent, but Rodentia's distant ancestors were undoubtedly the multituberculate. That's why I study the common rat."

James smiled and then exclaimed, "But they're just rats! Yuck!" Silly yucks and silly yuck derivatives murmured agreement. James studied his classmates and smiled. He had achieved silliness.

Kate rewarded James with a smile. "True, but rats are also very special survivors. Some species are perhaps the best survivors earth has ever hosted, and that is what is so fascinating about Rodentia for me. My study now focuses on a discipline called evolutionary adaptation.

"Why did some species evolve rapidly, while others stopped adapting and disappeared? Rattus is ideal to study because there are so many different species, and they have had such mixed success accepting genetic change."

Rats always chilled her audiences—large and small, adult and child—everyone hated the rat. Out of eighty known species, only five or six defamed the entire lot. In an hour that would change, though, as another class would soon embrace the rat as important and paleontologically cool.

It was time to change the subject. "Whoa!" Kate raised her hand and became dramatically serious. "Did you guys just hear that?"

The suggestion was irresistible. Eyes widening, the entire class shook their heads in anticipation of more silliness and cooperatively whispered "No."

"Uh oh! There is something weird going on in my lab coat pockets!"

The front row cringed backwards on cue. Faces twisted in feigned horror.

Kate cautiously stuck her hands inside the lab coat's deep pockets, and then sagged in relief. "Oh, it's nothing, kids. Just my friends, Isaac and Newton, wanting to come out to play."

She then removed two plump white rats. The kids cheered and clapped with James George catching on last. "Isaac is a boy and Newton is a girl. They love to hear about dinosaurs, and they love to cuddle. Any volunteers?" Every student's hand shot up.

Kate placed the rats in James George's lap. Suddenly quivering with excitement, the eight-year-old child-Einstein accepted the friendly rodents.

Kate leaned closer to James George and pressed two carrot sticks into his right hand. She whispered, "Sweet heart, I think they are hungry. Would you mind giving them their snack before they meet everyone?"

He looked up at Kate and nodded again, now somewhat dazed by the excitement. Nestled in the boy's lap the rats accepted their treat and munched away. James gently petted the rats and whispered, "Hi Isaac! Hi Newton! My name is James George! May I be your friend, too?"

Lu nodded congratulations to Kate as the scientist mounted the stage to begin the presentation. The lights in the theatre dimmed, and Kate launched the slide show. The first five slides showed her as a high school then a college student searching for fossils on Dakota Ridge alongside Colorado's most famous paleontologist, Dr. Norman Karl.

As other kids might react to discovering a famous rock star in their midst, the children whispered in awe, "That's Doc Karl from PBS! Dr. Lambert actually knows Doc Karl! Oh my God!"

# CHAPTER 3 ~~ Found Lost

The Nigerian Air Force F4 Phantom pilot rocked his wings up and down to signal to the fishing vessel that he had them on visual. Six men stood on the ship's rolling deck and signaled to him as the fighter jet passed over again. Their waving was not frantic, but the crew was indicating something much more than a friendly hello. Two other men held up a white object with large printing on it. They directed the object toward the F4 each time he passed over. The invitation was unambiguous: Please read!

Air Force Captain Benjamin Ngami switched his radio over to the emergency maritime frequency and hailed the boat. "Please state your situation, unidentified fishing vessel."

The response was immediate. "Thank you, Air Force pilot. This is Captain Bidi Obosu, master of the fishing vessel *Queen Nbotu*. We collected something in our fishing nets today that I think is important. I believe it might a piece of the missing United Nations airplane that went down two years ago."

The F4 dropped to a hundred feet above the sea and passed directly over the *Queen Nbotu*.

"Can you see the tail numbers, Air Force Pilot? This area should be marked and searched thoroughly, yes?"

"We copy. Please stand by, *Queen Nbotu*."

# CHAPTER 4 ~~ On The Beach

James George fell asleep between Denver and Castle Rock on the bus ride back to Colorado Springs. Denver's late afternoon blue sky surrendered to a snow-laden slate that slid steadily down the Front Range Rockies onto the foothills. His classmates' chattering faded away. The sounds of the bus' engine and tires resolved together into a soothing hum. By the time the charter bus reached Surrey Ridge on I-25, the clouds ruptured and spilled their winter bounty. Traffic slowed to a crawl on the highway beneath the falling veil.

James George tumbled into a twilight dream world.

\*\*\*

James stood alone on a pristine white beach. He felt sand crunching underfoot and heard the *tink-click* of broken seashells as he turned around. The salty sea air commingled the disparate aromas of fishy flotsam and rotting seaweed with the humus richness of the nearby tropical jungle. An uncertain breeze tossed his hair and teased his shirt collar. The surf was low and calm. Deceptively tranquil, he thought—the mask of danger. He asked himself aloud, "How did I get onto this beach? Oh, this is another dream!"

James heard the airplane before he saw it. Then he understood, like opening a safe and discovering its contents pilfered. This was where his parents were stolen from him. The sounds of the forest

29

and the sea merged with that of the approaching airplane. It was flying low, northward along the verdant Nigerian coastline to the east.

A bird lifted from the forest canopy and cawed to its unseen mates with an order to take flight. Only a few birds obeyed at first, but soon the great flock darkened the sky. The swarm climbed on the thermals, spinning higher, ever faster, an inverted tornado of dream birds. On some cue, the tip of the avian funnel cloud tipped over and found the path of the oncoming plane.

"No!" James George screamed.

Hundreds of birds struck the craft like self-sacrificing Kamikazes, disabling the engine, perforating the plane's wings and fuselage with their shattered bodies. A section of the tail sheared off and spun toward the ocean. The smoking airplane fell through bird guts and feathers.

The aircraft swooped unsteadily. It flew a yawing 360 degree arc inland and then headed back out to sea, leaving a trail of burning fuel, feathers, and metal in its smoky wake. As the dying aircraft passed just twenty feet overhead, a man and a woman's bloody faces appeared for a moment through the shattered windshield.

"Mommy! Daddy!" James shouted. He fell on his knees and wept. James willed himself to wake up from the nightmare, but he could not. The dream now held him hostage with a nonnegotiable ransom demand: You must open your eyes and finish watching. James reluctantly acceded and opened his eyes.

A military jet roared past overhead. James staggered to his feet and wiped his tears. Low in the sky a F4 jet fighter circled a fishing vessel bobbing on the sea near the horizon. From that distance James could not possibly have seen the sailors on the boat, but dream power revealed them waving at the pilot. He eavesdropped on the conversation between the pilot and the boat captain and imprinted that exchange verbatim in his consciousness. He certainly could not have seen the vessel's name or the tail numbers of his parent's plane, but the kidnapper of hope made sure he saw both.

James George Spencer saw, heard, and felt the truth. His adoptive parents were dead, as unambiguously gone for two years as if he had witnessed their deaths firsthand then—not now.

*** 

James George awoke from the dream and cried out.

His seatmate Amy Whitehorse asked, "What's the matter, James George? Are you all right?"

James wiped tears from his cheeks and looked out the bus' window onto a blizzard-strafed dusky landscape as bleak as his dream. "My parents... My parents are really dead," he whispered hoarsely.

"No! Don't say that. There's always hope, James George. They're probably just stranded on an island somewhere. Like in the books! Okay? You must have hope."

James turned and shook his head. "No. They are gone, Amy. Their airplane was attacked by birds and crashed. I think a Nigerian fishing vessel found it today. I... I saw the accident in my dream. I saw the boat and an F4 jetfighter and men on the boat... It was the *Queen Nbotu.* How could I possibly know that? It was their plane. I saw them. I know it."

"No. You are just tired. We are all tired. It's been a very long day. Come here." The older child pulled James George close to her and felt his sobs begin anew on her shoulder.

"There, there, my sweet boy. Everything is going to be all right. Soon. You'll see. You'll soon see all again."

James sat up and looked at Amy. "What did you just say, Amy?"

"Nothing, James George. I didn't say anything."

# CHAPTER 5 ~~ The Midas Six


There are dozens of abandoned mining operations from the 19th century in Seer County. All are sealed. Most have been lost over time, grown over and long forgotten. However, one still attracted occasional trespassers. The Midas Six goldmine was made infamous by the mining disaster in 1878 when dozens of miners lost their lives. It was reputedly haunted and still drew the curious. Some more stupid than others.

"Donnie, what part of 'DANGER!' do you not understand?" Gabriela Arecht pointed at the mine entrance where a standard mine warning sign was posted in a bold red script that included a skull and crossbones, poisonous gasses, dangerous animals, collapsed supports, federal statutes, fines and more. Enough trouble posted there to make even an Evel Knievel disciple take pause.

"I just want to see inside, Gabbs. No harm in that. Come on! Help me bust open this old gate. I've got a cool idea for a totally bitchin' video."

"Yeah. Like what?"

Donnie released his grip on the rusty corrugated steel gate and turned toward his girlfriend. "I want you to get a shot of me flying out of the entrance on my snowmobile. Wouldn't that be too cool? Me catching major rocket sled air? POW! Totally awesome, eh?"

Donnie Knuckles answered his own question with a gorilla face and two chest-high fists.

Gabriela giggled. "You're asshole crazy, Donnie!"

"That's why you dig me. So, is it a Nokio dealio?"

"I guess. Then can we go back down? I'm freezing my tush off up here and my sled is getting low on fuel."

"Deal!"

Five minutes later Donnie revved the snowmobile's engine from inside the entrance of the mine. What he did not know was just how dramatic his departure from the mine and this world was going to be. Unventilated mines are eventually polluted with gasses. The eastern service entrance of the Midas Six was saturated with methane. A spark from his machine created the all-time greatest camera flash in the history of jackass *You Tubery*.

The methane explosion killed Donnie and Gabriela instantly. Granite slag and sheet metal confetti impaled their bodies. Flames and the concussion shredded their flesh and clothing alike. The ragdoll couple and their snowmobiles jettisoned hundreds of feet down the mountainside within a fiery blue-orange arc. Gabriela and Donnie came to rest just feet apart still smoldering. Thirty feet of snow and ice boulders from the resulting avalanche covered their bodies. Eleven inches of afternoon snow would remove all traces of the accident.

\*\*\*

Twelve thousand feet below the snowy tomb of the two unfortunate asshats, a maze of unnatural caverns, chutes and passageways meandered throughout Seer Mountain for miles. The corridors were immaculate and flawless—not even a grain of sand on any floor. The mine's walls appeared polished and mirror like and were free of the slightest imperfection.

The explosion reverberated throughout the artificial structure loud enough to raise the dead, as they say, not to mention machines.

# CHAPTER 6 ~~ Sheriff Renner McCauley

Sheriff Renner McCauley eased back in the antique oak office chair and rested his stocking feet on an even older walnut desk. His worn cowboy boots sat beside the desk. McCauley's Under Sheriff, Gus Augustus, was just finishing the afternoon shift report. The report's date was today, but it could have been plagiarized from any number of previous dates. Not much ever changed in sleepy Seer City, Colorado.

"Well, Sheriff, what else do I got? Let's see. We stopped three speeders in the east meadows outside town."

"Pass out any tickets, Gus?" the sheriff mumbled through an extended yawn. His cowboy hat and sidearm doubled as unemployed paperweights on opposite corners of the desk.

"No, Boss. The boys and girls didn't see no need for tickets today since there weren't no elk around. We let 'em all off with friendly warnings and some extra stern invitations to come back and visit us again this summer." Gus winked and added, "Yes, we gave 'em samples of last year's tourism coupon books. Everyone seemed real impressed, too."

Renner examined his thumbnail and nodded. "Makes sense, Gus. Bad PR arresting potential tourists."

"Yes, Sir. Don't need that. Then, there's Oscar Nightingale who got drunk early, no big news there, and took a piss under the walkway railing behind the hardware. No one was around and he apologized real heartfelt-like. Says it's his prostate acting up again. So, we let him go with a verbal warning and a ride home."

Renner nodded. "Good call. Prostate problems are all over the news these days."

"Yep... So next, Tobithia Connors threatened to shoot Bob the Dog again. I swear it's Bugs Bunny and Elmer Fudd with that woman and that there mutt. She chased Bob the Dog two blocks with her shotgun. That ornery Rottweiler just won't leave her alone. He keeps pulling down her clothesline. I checked her gun. It weren't loaded as usual." Hellfire! The woman doesn't even know the firing pin is missing.

"Did you let it pass, Gus?"

"Oh, hell yes, Boss! I didn't see no reason to put an end to such healthy entertainment."

"Good man. Bob's alright. Aren't you, Mr. Bob?" The 140-pound Rottweiler semi-stray sat up, yawned, and nuzzled Renner's hand. The sheriff opened the desk drawer and handed the canine a dog treat and asked, "What else do we have on the afternoon blotter, Gus?"

Gus rubbed his chin, "Well, shit. This maybe ain't the best time to report it, Sheriff, what with you going on vacation and such, but Ol' Snatch is back at it again."

"Ol' Snatch?" McCauley growled the name as if recalling a painful boil. "So what did he get into this time?"

"Same, same, always the same. He tipped over every trashcan on Rosebread Street. Made one hell of mess when the wind got at it."

"Anybody try to follow him?"

"Oh, sure. But as usual he got away."

"Was it a *clean* getaway?" McCauley asked already grinning.

Both men laughed. It was an old joke. Ol' Snatch was the town Dumpster diver and he was anything but clean.

Renner McCauley was the largest property owner in Seer County. He had inherited Seer Mountain and much of the valley from James Michael Patrick McCauley, the Seer County mining legend. Grandpa McCauley purchased the land ten years after the Midas Six condemnation in 1878 for fifty thousand dollars—a steep price in those days. Renner was the fourth caretaker.

The McCauley's were what they call in the mountains "Old Scotsmen"—rugged men, quick to make right a wrong by force if necessary, but just as ready to share with you a poet's view of the world over a tumbler of whiskey.

Despite moist gray-green eyes and a boyish complexion so fair he rarely shaved two days in a row, no one dared call him "carrot top." It would have been just fine with Renner McCauley if they had, for he was rather proud of his heritage that included his distant relative's red hair.

Renner had earned a mechanical engineering degree at Colorado State in Ft. Collins. He spent the next ten years as a Marine Corps aviator, returning home when his father, Seer's former sheriff, passed away. The badge transferred as easily to Renner as did his family's estate.

"So when are you heading to Dakota Ridge on vacation, Boss?"

"I suppose I'll load the mare and greatly inconvenience the dog tomorrow morning sometime." The mare was Ginger Pat, who was about to foal. The dog was Renner's bulldog, Sasha, who most everyone around town called Deputy Dawg.

Dakota Ridge was a thousand-plus acres of the most worthless, rocky, uplift scrubland in Colorado. It belonged to retired Colorado University professor and celeb-paleontologist Norman Karl, who declared its fossil littered lands priceless. Doc Karl and Renner were best friends; in spite of Renner almost arresting the old bird for fossil hunting on private land without permission.

Renner looked over Gus's shoulder and said, "Uh-oh! Here comes trouble, Gus. Better comb your hair and put away the good china. It's the mayor and his new aide."

Two men crossed the street and marched toward the sheriff's office: Seer City Mayor Cole Kilpatre and his balding rat-faced aide Cyril Hoop. They stepped through the office entrance and climbed the seven steps to the main floor.

Hoop swung open and held the Dutch doors leading to the back offices for the huffing Cole Kilpatre as solicitously as a Ritz door attendant on Christmas Eve. The aide was nearly as tall as the mayor was, perhaps six feet, but weighed a gaunt one hundred forty pounds that accentuated his hooknose and perky bat's ears. His clumpy hair loss looked like mange, more than one local had whispered.

"Looks like the mayor's diet might be on hold, Sheriff," Gus whispered to Renner as the obese Kilpatre huffed twice for each step he took.

McCauley winked agreement with his deputy.

Kilpatre rushed past Renner without speaking, instead pointing at the men's restroom in the back hallway. Hoop escorted the mayor and held open the door. Kilpatre, gasping and muttering, irritably pushed Hoop's bony hand off his elbow. Bob the Rottweiler eyed Kilpatre's expansive ass and considered a mischievous nip and run, but Renner's hand on his head dissuaded him. Hoop stood guard outside the restroom door—a high priest awaiting the return of his god.

A few minutes later, Kilpatre's three hundred and fifty pound hulk stormed from the restroom. He had forgotten to zip up, and his left pant leg was wet to the ankle. A shirttail poked out from his open fly. He walked directly to the front door chanting, "Goddamned prostate!" then left the office.

Hoop bowed apologetically to Renner and Gus and followed his boss out the door.

Gus said to Renner, "Wow. That was weird. There must be something in the beer causing prostate problems."

"Naw. The beer's fine. I think Kilpatre's just getting crazier and crazier, Gus."

The massive explosion at the Midas Six rattled Seer City to its foundations. Frightened citizens spilled from stores and offices onto Main Street. Everyone asked the obvious, "What to hell was that?" The consensus was an earthquake. A few people noticed another curiosity: Mayor Kilpatre stood in the middle of Main Street and pointed up at the sky with both hands.

Kilpatre shouted, "Who the hell gave you aliens my phone number? Who?" He dropped to his knees and raised his arms overhead. Kilpatre screamed, "Oh! Well why the hell didn't you just say so?"

Cyril Hoop struggled to get the mayor moving. He announced to the onlookers, "The mayor's fine, folks. Just lost his balance. Wow! What an earthquake, huh?"

Ol' Snatch had a front row seat to Kilpatre's latest episode. That is what the locals had started calling his psychotic breaks: *episodes*. Ol' Snatch lifted the lid on the Dumpster a few inches and peeked out and watched the mayor until he was gone.

\*\*\*

In the conference room at Resumption Mining's headquarters in Denver a team of PhD geologists, four men and one woman, watched a recording of the methane explosion. The detonation's aftermath continued to scratch out and digitize Mt. Seer for ten minutes. However, the 72-inch wall-mounted display also revealed much more than the pixilated last testaments of the unfortunate couple who set off the Midas Six explosion.

Far below the Midas Six, a mysterious formation appeared on the screen, an "extreme geologic anomaly" in science-speak. As more of the mystery revealed itself on the giant plasma screen, the scientists' glances at each other became increasingly more curious. The anomaly was not natural. It certainly could not be man-made either. However, it held the scientists' complete attention as if it represented a 10.0 earthquake or a nuclear explosion.

Dr. Chris Jussard spoke more calmly than he felt, "Okay, whatever it is, it's finished loading. Let's see what we have. Buck, please set the view to 3-D and rotate it ninety degrees times four on both the $x$ and $y$... slower, Buck... there we go. That's it right there! Thank you. Now please scroll to 195 degrees below the epicenter... Hold it right there! Maximum resolution, please."

Shock can be displayed in many ways. The most profound is the silence and still of an audience made both motionless and breathless at once. For ten seconds the only sound heard in the conference room was the buzzing of a dying fluorescent tube overhead.

Dr. Jussard broke the Quaker silent meeting and whispered, "My God! What the hell is that?"

The scientists stepped as one toward the screen, as if a mere dozen inches could possibly clarify what they were witnessing. To the scientists' trained eyes, the shafts and chutes of the Midas Six goldmine appeared no different than any other 19th Century abandoned mine in Colorado. Collectively, Resumption had analyzed hundreds of such mines in this manner and profitably reopened many. However, the Midas Six itself held no sway today.

"What the hell are we looking at, people?" Chris Jussard asked his team.

No one answered. No one could answer. Far below the deepest shaft ever excavated in the old Midas Six mine was a second massive excavation: a city-sized maze stretching for miles under the mountain.

Dr. Buck Tumulley was the only one to speak up. "Well Chris, I think we might've just discovered the lost City of Atlantis and I'm only half kidding." No one laughed.

"Any suggestions?" Dr. Jussard asked. He cocked his head and tried to mentally estimate the size of the underground structure. He gave up with a shrug.

Buck said, "Just one. I think we better give your old college pal Doc Mohammad at USGS a call. Let's see if Mo's crew detected the same thing that we're seeing."

"Good idea. I'll make the call. In the meantime you guys…" Jussard glanced at the monitor, shrugged and walked out.

Jussard returned to the conference room five minutes later. He looked around the room and realized there had been no breakthroughs in his absence. If anything, the scientists looked even more baffled. "Well, Mo must've seen something, because his assistant said he was already on the horn with the FBI in D.C."

Buck pointed at the computer display and asked, "Well, the question is, did he see, uh, Atlantis?"

"I honestly doubt it, Buck. We only saw it because our sensors are located throughout Seer County. USGS is reading it from Golden." Jussard sighed and added, "I left a message for Mo to call me back."

# CHAPTER 7 ~~ Josh, Erin and the FBI

Thousands of potential national security threats are delivered each year to Homeland Security.  Most of them are false alarms, but all must be investigated by the FBI.

Dr. Mohammad el-Abari was the director at the National Earthquake Information Center in Golden, Colorado.  His unofficial title was the Doc Rock of Roll.  Dr. el-Abari stared in annoyance at the phone handset for a moment, and then returned it to his ear.  The FBI can ask the same question a hundred ways.  "Well, Agent Roe, again, I can tell you where the epicenter of the seismic activity occurred, and I can tell you what it is not—an earthquake.  But it was big.  Reports reached our office from as far from Seer County as Bittnerton and Introit.  That's about all I can tell you, Agent.  Earth tremors are my domain at the USGS.  The rest belongs to you and the FBI."

"Okay, Professor.  Just one last question.  In your opinion was the explosion natural or man-made?"

"It was one or the other, Agent.  One or the other, I'm positive.  Now, if there is nothing else?"

"And it was not authorized?"

"That's your department, Agent Roe. You tell me. I'm tectonics. You're terror. Now please, we have a situation north of Sacramento I must attend to immediately."

"Thank you, Doctor. That's all I need to know. We'll take it from here."

In Washington D.C. Special Agent Joshua Roe hung up the phone and turned to his partner Special Agent Erin Rogers. "Wax your skis, ER. We're going to Colorado. We'll leave D.C. for Seer County, Colorado thru Denver International in the morning."

Agent Rogers nodded and asked her partner, "So, what do we have? A possible domestic, another Tim McVey and it went off prematurely?"

"Unlikely, but…"

"Everything gets investigated," Erin finished resolutely.

"Right. Seriously though, bring your skis. I am. The locals will have this thing solved before we hit Denver. My brother Reeve and his wife Hattie live in Carbondale and work for the local ski company. Free digs, discount lift tickets, awesome powder. What do you say, Erin?"

"Sounds like a plan. I'll weasel a free ski lesson out of Hattie."

# CHAPTER 8 ~~ Jurassic Lark

James climbed off the chartered bus and waited in the brightly lit parking lot for Lu Li while she and the parent helpers connected each kid with their anxious parents. The snowstorm had ended just south of Monument, but it had added almost an hour to the trip. After he awoke, James tried to make sense of his dreams, or whatever they were.

Lu and James walked to her minivan. She asked, "I'm famished! How does McDonalds sound?"

"Fine."

Lu stopped and said, "Just fine? Mickie D is your favorite."

James sagged. "I'm not very hungry, Miss Lu."

Lu felt James' forehead. He looked flushed. His cheeks appeared... sunburned? "You are always hungry. Do you feel okay, sweetie? You look sort of feverish."

"I'm just really tired."

"Well, let's just head home. It's been a long day. I'll fix us a quick snack."

"Thank you. That would be nice."

Thirty minutes later James George sat at Lu Li's kitchen table. His left elbow rested on the table and propped his head up at the other end like a wobbly tent pole. He alternately poked a spoon at the bowl of chicken noodle soup and mouse nibbled a peanut butter and honey sandwich without leaving much of a mark in either. Finally convinced the child really was not hungry, Lu excused him. "Just brush your teeth, Sweetie. You can take a bath tomorrow."

"Thank you." James rose and offered Lu his forehead for a kiss, then turned and staggered down the hallway for the bathroom. Five minutes later, he was in bed.

James' bedroom reflected a normal child's fascination with paleontology, but also the artistry of a trained paleontologist. The four walls and ceiling represented epochs of the ascendency continuum beginning with single-cell organisms 3.5 billion years ago and concluding with the great asteroid that ended the age of dinosaurs. From the ceiling hung three dozen dinosaur models he had ordered from the Smithsonian museum. His favorite was the T-rex. He closed his eyes and fell asleep studying it.

***

The third dream was the most vivid. James arrived in the dream sitting one hundred feet above the ground in the quadrangular crooks of a long-extinct tree. James recognized not only its species, but also the tree itself. He had painted this very plant on his bedroom wall just two weeks earlier above the caption: The Cretaceous Period, ninety million years ago.

James studied the scene below him with a scientist's eye. A muddy beach disembarked from the primordial sea that would surrender in millions of years to what is now northeastern Colorado.

A volcanically reddened sun hung low in the western sky and stretched the forest's rusty shadow onto viscous seawaters thick with algae. Distant thunderheads boomed endlessly on the eastern horizon. Their leaden florets sparked with mute lightning. The air was heavy with putrefaction and smoke, concentrated by unrelenting humidity. James pinched his nostrils shut for a moment, then slowly released them as something caught his attention. There was movement below in the forest.

Fifty feet from the water's edge, the Tyrannosaurus rex parted the thick web of palm fronds with its immense head. The predator lifted its snout higher and tilted it from side-to-side tasting the air. James gasped and ducked into the fork, then cautiously peeked out again. The T-rex clicked softly its satisfaction. The reward that instinct promised was here—food, abundance.

The T-rex stepped from under the forest canopy. It was an injured female. Her right thigh revealed festering puncture wounds. A most distinct injury pattern, James thought. He whispered, "Probably bestowed by a stampeding stegosaurus bull. A rare lucky strike delivered with his lethal tail spikes. Ouch!"

Rivulets of bloody pus ran down her leg. The drainage moved glacially onto her foot where a gluey, septic delta grew. Clouds of immense insects hovered over the proud flesh and its gangrenous effluence. The buzzing swells rose and fell workmanlike with each of the animal's stiffened strides. Their beating wings sounded like a waterfall to James.

James longed for his prized Magellan binoculars. From this distance and with just his naked eye he could not quite identify the insect species that hectored the T-rex. James shrugged and stopped squinting. It would have been a long shot anyway considering the incompleteness of the fossil record of insects.

The sea, the tide, and a volcano had delivered onto the beach a great buffet of carrion. It attracted not only the T-rex but also scores of scavengers and other carnivores. Footprints in the mud marked passages here—thousands of toeing punctuations that for some would be their last. A gruesome resource war raged at this feast, and James knew that every guest was subject to the inviolable physics of the food chain.

James studied the T-rex. "You are seriously injured, aren't you? Poor lady!"

The T-rex was also starving, sick with fever, and too critically ill to hunt for live food. The handicapped queen loped awkwardly a little way down the beach and stumbled to a stop. Shrilly, piercingly, and hungrily, the Cretaceous creature spoke. She roared her one and only commandment: Leave the food or be the food.

The rumble of animals in full retreat shook the forest like volcanic aftershocks. Bellowing animals, terrified, sprinted away. Some swam out to a safe distance as she neared, others disappeared into the forest. Some took to the air. A few taunted her, but all deferred. She could not be bluffed or denied even when injured, especially when injured.

"Yes! You guys all better scatter if you know what's good for you!" James climbed higher in the tree to get a better view. "You go, girl! It's right there. Dinosaur chicken soup for what ails you. Eat up, Your Majesty!"

Every animal yielded the beach to her—every animal except one. The swarm of insects expanded and thickened into an opaque cloud. Half of the T-rex disappeared behind the pulsing dark veil.

James shook his head sensing something very wrong was about to happen. "What are those things?"

"Federation Exterms, James George," a woman's voice answered from behind him.

Startled, James slipped and almost fell one hundred feet to his dream death. As he slid from his perch, his hands found a drooping sucker branch. He swung ten feet away from the tree, then back, and then he let go. He landed where he started—in the quadrangular tree fork. He also recognized the voice. "Commander? Kara?"

No answer. He scratched his head and looked around. Nothing. Not so sure now that he had heard something, James turned his attention back to the beach.

The queen stopped before a fresh Diplodocus carcass. Rivers of lava had herded the unlucky marsh feeder into the sea and cooked it to death along with many other creatures. The queen leaned down and sniffed the carcass. She clicked and hissed her approval.

The pain in her wounded thigh erupted as if she were under attack by one of her own. The insects' almost pleasant sounds of a waterfall were replaced by hysterical screeching—a chainsaw striking steel and granite.

The T-rex snapped her teeth at the piranha-like swarm drilling into her thigh, but as one the organisms dispersed, then somehow multiplied again and blanketed her entire body. They bored into her eyes, nostrils, and dove into her bowels and her genitals, filled her mouth and soared down her throat. The thigh injury opened to the bone.

"No! Don't hurt her!"

Her death shrieks interrupted animal retreats and briefly stilled the jungle. James winced and covered his ears. The end arrived as suddenly for the T-rex as if delivered by a lightning bolt. The queen lurched forward, tripped over her almost-last meal, and crashed headlong onto the beach. Projectile blood and vomit spewed from her shriveling mouth. Her massive frame thudded to a rest in the mud and did not move.

The body of the former pinnacle of the food chain deflated. The carcass melted as if it were less substantial than an anachronistic furrowing of snow left in the tropical sun. Flesh, bone, sinew, teeth,

45

and hide nourished the alien maggots equally. The feeding frenzy lasted just a few minutes.

The enlarged swarm departed and flew out to sea. It darkened that long ago sky in a way unimaginable to any scientist until now. Nothing remained of their host except a primordial epitaph—her footprints in the mud.

"That was *them*, James George. Our enemy. The Federation. Exterms now possess this creature. They will not stop changing until they find the One, and then all will be gone. Awaken now... You must..."

***

"I must what, my Commander?" he slurred. James George awoke and sat up in bed as fully alert as if he had never slept. He turned on his nightstand lamp and searched for the owner of the voice. "I must what, Kara?"

James scratched his head and climbed from bed. He walked across the room and studied one particular aerial scene on the wall. He had entitled it "The Dakota Uplift" with twenty species of dinosaurs identified by their tracks on a muddy beach. Most prominent were those alternately long and short strides belonging to an injured T-rex.

Lu knocked on the door and opened it. "James George honey, why are you up? It's very late."

James George glanced at his clock radio. It read 3:35 a.m. He'd fallen asleep no later than 8:00 p.m. James shook his head, "I'm having some extraordinarily vivid dreams, Miss Lu."

"I think maybe you've had a little bit too much stimulation today. Let's get back in bed."

"Okay." James George studied his murals for a moment longer as he walked to the bed.

As Lu tucked James into bed, several tiny pieces of tree bark fell unseen from his bed sheets onto the floor and landed near his high-top boots. Most of the sand from the African beach had fallen away from the boots, but not all. His last souvenir, the sunburn, had peaked.

# CHAPTER 9 ~~ BB & Puck

"Sometimes, boys, I wish I'd never gotten that TV satellite dish. Seems like all that's ever on that damn thing is heartache," Ben Bainbridge complained.

"Right on with that, BB." Paul "Puck" Ortez tapped fists with his lifelong friend. The two men operated the county's explosives business. They had learned the craft ass-backwards as they liked to tell it, by disarming IEDs and landmines in both Gulf wars.

Puck cracked open three beers and handed one each to Renner McCauley and BB. He then joined his friends at the kitchen table. The men sat silently watching the latest update on the air crash, which had occurred two years ago off the coast of Africa.

"This just in," the reporter announced, "the FAA and the United Nations have confirmed that the single-engine aircraft found by Nigerian fishermen today was indeed that of the husband and wife scientists missing since…"

Puck muted the TV. He glanced at BB who was already nodding. It was time for some local news. Puck turned back to the sheriff and said, "Renner, me and BB got something to tell you, and it ain't good."

McCauley raised his hands and nodded. "Kilpatre? I already heard about that, boys. Now he's started talking to ghosts or aliens or maybe Big Foot."

47

"He's nuts Renner, and I ain't talking about just today. He ordered BB and me to get him twelve cases of dynamite. He wants to use it as a campaign promo in this year's election. He plans to have this printed on each stick: Support the KKK. Keep King Kilpatre."

"Wow. That's whack."

"Well Renner, if that ain't bad enough, he's been soliciting bribes again. He asked Puck and me for a thousand dollars."

"What for?"

"To give us the exclusive rights on all explosives and demolition work in the county."

"You already have all mine and demolition work in the county."

"Exactly."

# CHAPTER 10 ~~ Dora the Explorer

James George watched very little television. What he did watch could reduce even the most inert slug into a clinical depression, unless said slug found 18th century fighting ships enthralling. The narrator's female voice was typical on the *History Channel*. Familiar, but not quite recognized.

"Now we return to Cape Trafalgar. It is 1799. The winds of war stir across the continent. The sea will soon run red with blood..."

James yawned and wished he had slept more last night. The fatigue made it difficult to rationalize away the dreams, the Star Wars battle between machines, piranha flies feasting on dinosaurs, kamikaze birds, and the painful image of his adoptive parents' plane crash. He cringed and jumped off the couch shivering. James George whispered, "What is happening to me?"

A woodpecker noisily did some deforestation payback down below on the apartment building's commons. James went to the window and looked down but could obviously not see the bird from the eleventh floor. Someone on a lower floor yelled at the woodpecker to shut the something up.

The woodpecker got even busier. More neighbors joined the complaint. James turned up the volume on the TV and stretched out on the couch.

"The *HMS Aponia* was a magnificent English warship. She carried three masts and flew rhomboid sails on the fore and main masts and a lateen-rigged sail on the mizzenmast. She was heavily armed with two decks with cannons and several smaller decks that served as fighting platforms, while her hull was double layered with pairs of eighteen-inch oak planks, representing over two thousand mature trees. Her sinew was rope, abundantly, over twenty miles of it."

*** 

James yawned and then closed his eyes and was transported directly from Lu Li's apartment to another continent and time. When he opened his eyes a moment later, he found himself standing on the quarterdeck of the British warship *HMS Aponia*, the subject of today's *History Channel* episode. He looked westward at the descending sun and concluded it must be late afternoon. The sea was unusually calm for the Cape, he noted. All around him, oblivious to his presence, officers issued a steady stream of routine orders. Subordinates repeated the commands down the line to seamen. The *Aponia's* great sails occasionally snapped to attention only to collapse with a thud as they caught then lost the wind.

They cannot see me, because I am dreaming again, James thought.

A new narrator continued the story—the Orlif Commander Kara. "The crew was now eighty days into the mission and boredom was a far greater threat than local pirates, or the French or Spanish navies, which to the Englishmen of the *Aponia* were distinctions without a difference. Her seven hundred sailors and marines were as languid as the trade winds.

"The first sign of trouble appeared on the western horizon. It was not a ship flying enemy colors, but it alarmed young watch officer Second Leftenant Lawrence Arnold just the same. Ten degrees north of the setting sun and equidistant above the horizon, an iridescent red object appeared. Mr. Arnold focused his spyglass and studied it. The object was not as perfectly round as it seemed with the naked eye. Its center appeared solid, opaque. The edges were ragged and spinning in a counterclockwise motion.

"Mr. Arnold lowered the glass and rubbed his eyes. He squinted into the setting sun and then glanced in doubt at the spyglass even as he lifted it once again to study the oncoming object. 'What is that?' he whispered to himself.

50

"The young officer's eyes widened and now it took both hands to hold the spyglass steady. He lowered the handheld telescope and shouted to the Third Officer, 'Mr. Hagan! Commander Collins to the Watch Deck! War Stations!' Whatever it was, it was huge—twice the size of any known warship—and it was aimed toward the *Aponia* and coming fast.

"The red mass approached the warship like a waterspout on its side. Its vortex spun sluggishly, though, slow enough to count the rotations.

"Commander Collins took the spyglass and asked, 'What the bloody hell am I looking at, Leftenant?'

'I have no idea, Commander, but judging by its progress, I estimate its speed at thirty one knots.'

'Thirty one knots! Impossible! Good God!'

'It will be upon us in less than three minutes, Sir.'

"The alien organism accelerated its attack, closing rapidly on the ship. Not in minutes, but mere seconds later a red cloud settled over the great fighting ship, covering everything and every man with a fine dust. Some laughed nervously and tried futilely to dust themselves off. Others swore. Most just froze in place with their arms outstretched and stared in stunned disbelief alternately at themselves then their shipmates. Almost as one seven hundred men began to cough.

"However, this was not an anomalous sandstorm or particulate sent skyward by a distant Pacific volcano. This matter was neither living nor nonliving. It was a machine, and it was searching for an ancient enemy hiding amongst the living.

"The sea around the *Aponia* became a steaming red sludge. Fine talc poured through the portholes, seeped into every crack and seam no matter how small, and settled upon the highest mast to the ship's deepest hold. The alien attached itself and passed from deck to deck as easily as a winter chill as it searched for something.

"In less than a minute the mysterious red film covered every square inch of the *Aponia* and her crew, from forecastle to mizzen, bow to stern, main sail to every hammock.

"On some coordinating cue from inside and outside the *Aponia*, the alien attacked the great helpless ship and her crew. The slaughter lasted just ninety seconds. A thunderous hiss of boiling flesh, timber, gunpowder, fabric and iron drowned out seven hundred hysterical last testaments. The *Aponia* and her crew disintegrated and disappeared into the sea along with its alien assassin. The Rebels were not here, James George."

*\*\*\**

James awoke from the nightmare coughing. The red dust that covered his body disappeared before his eyes. The moldy aftertaste of the Federation left in his mouth took a moment longer to depart.

"Commander!"

The lobby call buzzer sounded twice. Lu Li switched off the TV as she walked from the kitchen to the video intercom next to the front door. She glanced at James and was relieved to see he was still asleep. Lu pressed the VIEW button on the security system's display and sagged when she saw who was standing in the lobby. Two state police officers were looking up at the camera. She had carefully kept James away from any newsfeeds since word about his parents had leaked out, but this made it official. They were here to confirm that James' parents were gone. Lu Li pressed the intercom and said softly, "He's asleep. I'll meet you gentlemen in the lobby."

# CHAPTER 11 ~~ Worse Worser Worst

Kate Lambert had spent the afternoon at the museum in Denver. The day had been unusually rewarding with two lectures, an unexpected visiting colleague from Canada, and the delivery by a pair of amateurs of an amazing fossil—a possible *karpeleotroceme* discovered last summer by a Princeton English professor vacationing near Seer City, Colorado. *Karpeleotroceme*, discovered by and named after Doc Karl in 2003, was so rare and its fossil record so incomplete, that it could not yet be officially declared a new species.

Her mini ranch was a few miles west of Golden off Highway 6. The normal thirty-five minute drive from Denver to her home had taken over two hours with the impediment of errands and worsening weather. Kate had stopped at the pet store to pick up the new wheel she had ordered for Isaac and Newton. After that, she ordered Thai carryout, then slipped next door while her meal was prepared and purchased a six-pack of Heineken. A stop at Epic Video at the edge of town rounded out her mission. It would be another weekend alone, just Kate, Matt Damon and the kinderats.

There had been occasional men in her life, but apparently their sentiment had been a one-way street. Lu Li insisted she was too particular. Kate realized that meeting Mr. Right while working at a museum was about as likely as one of her precious bucktoothed multituberculates reanimating.

Moving east for four years to finish her doctorate had been the toughest decision in her life, but the reward—returning home for good—had made that temporary relocation worth it. The position at the museum was a paleontologist's dream job, and the abundant research opportunities made for mind-boggling decisions. Last year she had traveled to the Ztzk-te excavation site in central Mongolia along with scientific teams from Florida State, Jordan, Brown, Uruguay and Israel. Next year she would travel to China for a highly promising *karpeleotroceme* dig with some Russian and Chinese friends.

Kate opened the back door and dropped her Saturday night entertainment cache on the kitchen table. After depositing the rats' cage in their favorite spot on the kitchen window seat, she walked to her office to investigate her phone messages. She entered her voice mail code and pressed the speaker button. A synthesized male voice said, "You have three messages."

"Three messages!" Kate laughed. Three in one week would have been a record. Her phone number was unlisted, and she gave it out to only a select few.

Message one: "Katie. This is Lu. I have some awful news…" Lu Li paused. She was crying. It took several interminable seconds for her to compose the next statement. "Just so horrible."

Kate leaned closer to the phone and bit her lip. She touched it gently, as if that could somehow console her best friend's suffering post facto.

"It's James George, the little boy you had such a great time with yesterday."

Kate gasped, "Oh, dear!" and immediately assumed the worst.

"His parents were presumed dead after their plane went down two years ago off the coast of Africa. He… We… All of us at the school still held out hope. Well, fishermen found a piece of the tailfin, and divers later confirmed that the wreckage was indeed from Rollin and Stephe's plane. The state troopers just left a while ago. It's over. They're gone, Katie. His tragedy is now official. Please call. He wants to talk to you. I love you. Bye." Lu Li sobbed again as she hung up the phone. Kate was stunned.

Message two: "Hi, honey. This is just ol' Doc. Got your message about getting together. How about tomorrow at Dakota Ridge? I love you too. Bye." After a pause he continued, "Hey, sweet daughter, wouldn't it be nice if just a few of those ol' dinos were still around? You know, just the nice ones of course. Call me soon."

Kate kissed her fingertips and caressed the handset. "Yes, Doc, it sure would," Kate whispered. "And I will."

Message three: "Dr. Lambert, my name is Cole Kilpatre. I'm the most distinguished mayor of Seer City, Colorado, of USA America. I'd like to speak to you in private regarding a matter of utmost importance. To come to the point... I have discovered something, something besides your unlisted phone number. That was not very nice of you. Quite an inconvenience for sure. Shit! Shit yes! Well, anyway, it's something you might know... uh... a thing or two about. Yes! Some very museum-worthy shit indeed! Can't say more over the telephone other than to confidentially assure you that there are some ancient aliens living under Seer Mountain. Sometimes I can hear them talking. Money is no object, so please contact me A-S-A-P at this number. Your expertise is required. Good day or evening as the case may be, Madam. Oh my!"

The message continued: "Mayor, who are you talking to?" Cyril Hoop asked.

"None of your business, you disbelieving little pencil dick!"

Click!

"Well, that was either very weird or someone at the museum's odd taste in pranks." Kate looked at her watch. The storm was heading northeast into Nebraska. She could be in Colorado Springs in two hours. She sent Lu a text message that she was on her way.

# CHAPTER 12 ~~ Continuums

Isaac and Newton were nestled in Kate's coat pockets. She reached inside and petted them as she crossed Lu Li's building lobby. The act was more for her reassurance than theirs. She took a deep breath and reached for the call button that would ring the Kwan apartment eleven floors up.

Before Kate could press the button and look into the security camera, Lu Li said, "Come on up, Katie." Lu Li must have been waiting by the guest call-in.

The elevator doors bypassed and slid apart. Kate hesitated for a moment then stepped inside the elevator. She pressed the 11th floor button and had the greatest sense she was about to cross some kind of Rubicon.

Lu was already in the hallway when Kate stepped off the elevator. Wordlessly, she and Kate embraced. Both felt the others' light sobs. Lu backed away first and shook her head. "Oh, Kate! I'm so sorry. He asked for you. Insisted. Only you. I... I don't understand. More strangely, I don't think he does either."

"No. Lu, don't apologize. Right now we need to figure out what to do. Does he have any other family?" Kate already knew the answer, but hoped beyond hope someone had mysteriously emerged.

"No. The authorities searched nonstop since the accident two years ago. He was adopted at birth. His adoptive parents and grandparents were all only children, and now all are deceased. He is alone, Katie. Completely. Even his distant adoptive relatives are in Europe and are untraceable."

Kate winced. "Oh, God. Where is he?"

"In the den."

Kate turned, but James George was already standing in the hallway watching the two women. Kate and Lu wiped away their tears. They struggled to smile and together stepped toward the child. Kate reached into her coat pockets and lifted out the gentle rodents.

"Hello, James George. Look who I brought with me, Isaac and Newton." Kate's voice cracked.

He did not answer. His expression was hard, inanimate. James George glanced at the rodents and looked away.

Kate offered the animals once more. "Here they are, James George. Do you want to hold them?"

His voice was mechanical, no more than a whisper. "The Archean Eon commenced some four billion years ago with the appearance of the earliest algae and primitive bacteria. It was known as the Precambrian Era, the very commencement of life on earth, the biotic flux from which life evolved."

Kate felt her eyes well up again. "Yes, honey. That is correct. You should…"

"Then came soft-bodied invertebrates, the earliest fish, corals, land plants, insects, and vascular plants such as ferns, amphibians and winged insects. All of that occurred 3.7 billion years before the age of dinosaurs began. Can you just imagine that?"

Kate nodded and stepped closer to James George. "Wouldn't you rather hold Isaac and Newton?" The rats either coincidentally looked toward the child, or possibly recalled something more primitive—that James George had fed them recently.

James George glanced at the rodents and continued, "Onward life marched: the Triassic, the Jurassic, Cretaceous Periods, and then just like that the dinosaurs vanished in a blink of the geologic eye after dominating the planet for one hundred eighty million years. Nevertheless, life goes on and on and on, doesn't it, Doctor? As it always has no matter how insignificant we are or important or heinous or miserable or extraordinarily special or corrupt, or just unfortunate."

"Yes, but..."

"The Paleocene, Eocene, Oligocene, Miocene and Pliocene, all likewise surrendered unto time by the so-called 'terrible lizards' demise. The Tertiary period lasted sixty million years, Dr. Lambert."

"Yes," Kate whispered. "Let's go inside." She prayed she would not sob in front of the child. Lu Li guided James George back into the apartment.

"Another 1.6 million years passed with the Pleistocene. Then came the Holocene—our time. With it was the arrival, finally, of our approximate biological form—just fifty thousand years ago. That brings us from four billion years ago to yesterday when my daddy would have turned forty-one, and my mommy thirty-six, Dr. Lambert. They were born on the same day. I had held out hope, ignorantly, that they were alive somewhere, somehow, perhaps..."

Kate took the child's hand and led him to the couch. This time she did not ask. She placed the rats in his lap and was relieved to watch his tiny hands slowly embrace the pets.

"James George?"

James stared at the rats and did not answer.

"James, sweetheart?" Kate repeated.

James George finally looked up. "You have Doc Karl. You told us about him. He's like your father."

Kate sagged closer to the child and smiled. This was why James had asked for her. "Yes, I've got Doc, and he is wonderful." Kate had told the children several stories about her famous mentor and surrogate father. James George had immediately grasped that the crusty old professor was more than just a friend and teacher.

Kate looked over at Lu. She had an idea and began improvising. "Have you ever heard of the *karpeleotroceme*? Doc Karl discovered it, and it was named for him."

James George sat up and stared in awe at Kate. He was astounded, as he always was when he discovered something new. "No. I have never heard of that particular fossil."

"Well, Doc has invited me up to Dakota Ridge tomorrow. I have some vacation coming, and I think I'll make a week of it. You remember his fossil farm, right? If Miss Lu says it is okay, I'm sure Doc would love to have us both. Are you up for some serious fossil hunting, young man?"

"Yes. Yes, Dr. Lambert. I believe that is exactly what I need right now."

"Please call me Kate."

"Okay." James bit his lower lip as the first tear rolled down his cheek. "Sometimes, it's okay to call me Jimmy. My mommy called me that, especially when she hugged me. She said she couldn't help it, that I was a natural born 'Jimmy' if there ever was one. I have no idea what she meant, but now I really miss hearing it."

"Okay. Deal. Your mommy was right! You are a 'Jimmy' for sure, if there ever was one."

# CHAPTER 13  ~~  The Arrival

James George had slept plenty but rested little in the last twenty-four hours. Lu and Kate tucked him into his bed and then retired to the kitchen where a teakettle was chugging its way toward a whistle. James closed his eyes. A moment later, the *History Channel* Kara was once again narrating.

***

"In this episode of 'Universe in Peril,' we will travel far back in time to a period of Earth's brief history when all life was nearly extinguished—not by killer asteroids but by extreme climate change. Come with me now to a place and time when all the seas were frozen and the great land masses were covered with miles-thick glaciers from pole to pole."

James opened his dream eyes and found himself standing on an erupted ice shelf. He felt no cold and the blowing snow did not touch his skin, but he shivered just the same. He estimated accurately that the temperature was high double digits below zero.

"James George?"

"Yes," he answered cautiously. "My Commander? Kara? Is it you?"

"Of course, my dear child. Welcome to what scientists nowadays refer to as 'Snowball Earth'—seven hundred million years ago. We

60

begin with some of Earth's earliest extraterrestrial visitors. Look skyward and listen. Here we come now!"

James searched for the voice. Kara was so near, yet not. A resounding thunderclap caused him to look up.

The sonic boom announced the arrival of the long-range Rebel saber fighter. It appeared in the night sky, a jittery yellow-white flash three thousand meters above the equatorial sea ice.

The craft was dart shaped and shrouded in an unsteady blue glow from bow to stern. The *Jhim's* hull shields had finally failed during the recent battle with the Kar Federation. Underneath the wavering veil, static electricity arced across the battle scars on the spaceship's hull and wings.

James said in awe, "The warship Jhim! It, he is badly injured. I witnessed the battle in my dream."

"You are partially correct, James. You were not dreaming. Earlier today, the *Jhim* made a risky tactical retreat from that faraway battlefield after inflicting substantial damage to its enemy. An enemy you have also already met here on Earth."

"They killed a T-rex... and the *Aponia* warship."

"Yes, child, and countless others in their search for The One." Kara hesitated then asked, "May I continue?"

"Yes, please."

"Our gamble worked. The *Jhim* escaped certain death but at a great cost. The radical hyperspace retreat not only aggravated the damages inflicted by the Federation's cannoneers, it left the crew hopelessly lost in space. Worse, the spaceship had exited hyperspace inside Earth's unforgiving atmosphere."

"No! That means it's going to crash."

"Yes and soon unfortunately."

Gravity yanked the warship mercilessly ever faster toward Earth. The spacecraft's dying sub-light engines squealed their last turns as the *Jhim* fought futilely to free itself from the quickening descent.

"Now, James, come with me. Let's go aboard the *Jhim* and watch from there. Please close your eyes for a moment."

James George blinked once and was instantly transported onto the spacecraft. A hazy yellow glow illuminated the ship's bridge. Positioned around a horseshoe of workstations were the Orlif crewmembers. The commander stood on an elevated inner console. Her hands kneaded the air like an orchestra conductor over a suspended holographic keyboard. The officers implemented the commander's stream of orders to bring the craft under control.

Kara resumed, "Watch the monitors, James. The *Jhim*'s situation worsens with each passing second. Oxygen and friction took over what the Federation's gamma cannons started." External cameras revealed hundreds of pockmarks erupting across the hull in dirty orange flames that quickly merged. The entire ship was soon ablaze.

James' world inverted, twisted violently, and after what seemed an eternity it righted itself. "What was that?" he screamed.

"Four meters of starboard wingtip just tore away and disappeared in the ship's fiery contrail. The spacecraft rolled violently twice before I compensated for the missing wing."

The dream commander regained partial control of the ship.

James covered his ears and watched in horror, as the ground loomed larger on the monitors. Kara soothed his fears. "This is only memory, James, nothing can happen to you. You are safe. Just keep watching. It is important that you see this."

Memory? James nodded and lowered his hands.

Klaxon alarms wailed plaintively throughout the ship. Red strobe lights dizzyingly restated the emergency, but neither of the electronic hysterias distracted the crew's attention from their commander.

The commander issued orders evenly to her officers over the deafening chaos of a ship shaking apart. Her efforts worked at the last possible moment. She regained sufficient control of the spacecraft and lifted the ship's nose just enough to avoid hitting the ground head on.

"Now close your eyes again, child. We'll continue away from the ship." James obeyed and found himself again on the ice shelf when he opened his eyes. The *Jhim* was heading straight for him.

The spaceship skipped twice across the sea ice before its bow snagged and sent the ship cartwheeling end-over-end for over a kilometer. The *Jhim* slammed to rest against the erupted two-story ice shelf, where it vanished briefly under a pursuing shower of plowed ice and snow.

The collision's shockwave was devastating, killing almost all survivors of the battle. A lightning strike's signature scent of ozone and fleeting puffs of aerosolized ions were all that remained of the Orlifs.

Fingers of yellowish steam seeped through fissures along the spaceship's hull and scampered away with the howling wind.

Noxious oxygen exchanged places with the ship's precious e-tmosphere—a sulfur based gas.

The lone survivors, the executive officer and the commander, had no time to mourn their shipmates. They sealed themselves safely inside the bridge, but their crisis continued, because the ship had just hours of backup energy remaining.

Kara explained, "The crash left us shipwrecked and stranded on a poisonous, frozen, and perhaps lifeless planet deep inside an unexplored galaxy far from home. Our mission now was survival."

The spaceship attempted to levitate itself on invisible limbs. On the third attempt it lifted itself with a metallic screech, stood upright, and then set off spastically across the frozen sea.

"Kara? Wherever you are hiding yourself, may I interrupt for a moment to ask a question?"

"Of course. What would you like to ask?"

James George turned in a circle and spoke into the storm. "The commander spoke directly to her ship as if she was coaxing it along, encouraging it, imploring it to keep going despite it being seriously damaged. Is that what I'm witnessing?"

"Yes, child. Kar crews and their ships are very close. They are capable of interacting on a quite personal level. You see, Kar spaceships and their crews are connected for life at creation."

"Sort of like friends from birth?"

"Yes. Very good."

"Please explain more."

"Think of the ship and the crew as one machine uniquely bonded—electronically. Our loyalty to each other is unbreakable. Every time we refer to one another by the endearment 'my,' it strengthens our bonds. None of us terminate permanently as long as any single *Jhim* crewmember exists."

"Amazing! So the crew was not actually killed in the crash?"

"Correct. Their termination will not be permanent. My XO and I are the only two Orlifs that survived, but one of us is more than enough to restore us all."

"'Will not be permanent'?" James asked. "What do you mean? How can that be? Snowball Earth was seven hundred million years ago."

"The story I'm showing you is not over. It continues even as we speak. There remains hope for the crew of the *Jhim*. There remains hope for all of us."

63

"Oh?"

Kara waited a moment and then asked, "If you have nothing further to ask, may I continue?"

"Please. This is extraordinarily interesting. But I warn you, Kara, I have a gazillion more questions."

"As you wish. Your answers will come in good time. Let's watch."

The ship stopped periodically and investigated the liquid ocean beneath its glacial skin. Four beams of light emitted from a dome on the *Jhim*'s belly and danced randomly over the ice. They scanned, searched, and then on some cue the vessel brightened to emerald green. Then it dove through eighty meters of solid ice and disappeared.

"Fortunately, James George, the Rebel castaways found and acquired what they desperately needed. The Precious Creation, our ally, had preceded us here—a colony of single-celled alga thriving near a volcanic vent on the ocean floor, the first building block of billions more needed to construct a lifeboat.

"However, our respite would be brief, just eight hundred years. Watch, James! Here they come. The Exterms."

"Kara, stop! Algae? Lifeboat? Please explain."

"It's complicated."

"No kidding!"

"I'll try to explain, James George. As you witnessed when we first met in your dream, the Kar machine can exist in either an energy state or one of matter. As a result, a single Kar could occupy an entire planet. On the other hand, tens of trillions of Kar could stand on the very tip of a sewing needle, if necessary."

"Fascinating. So, Kara, you searched for and found a compatible life form. That was the key?"

"Yes. The Precious Creation had fortunately already found this planet. The irony is most satisfying. The saved saved their savior."

"Yes, quite. Then the XO, you, the ship, and the crews' life files miniaturized energetically and somehow stowed away within one alga."

"Correct, my child."

"How?"

"Genetically. We hid inside a single strand of the alga's junk DNA."

"So, the Kars and the *Jhim* hitched a ride without harming the alga?"

"Yes. In fact, the alga cell lived for almost eleven thousand years before I relocated us to a more suitable host."

"Wow!"

"Yes, wow!" Kara hesitated then asked. "May I continue, my dear one? It is time for you to meet our enemy once again."

"Please do!" James closed his eyes and then opened them.

The Federation battle platen did not crash land on Earth, and it did not arrive here by accident. The trackers' spacecraft entered Earth's atmosphere and descended smoothly, almost silently.

The saucer-shaped craft landed on an icy plateau that would later become the horn of Africa. The rumble of wind and snow pounding the ship's hull replaced the soft hum of the craft's decelerating thrusters.

The Federation's newest Alpha Genesis ordered crewmembers into a tiny shuttlecraft and flew it forty kilometers east of the landing site. From a safe distance, he then ensured that the crew could not have second thoughts.

Alpha Genesis inserted a key into the shuttle's command console, entered a code and activated the battle platen's self-destruct order. With thousands of Exterm machines still onboard the battleship, the vessel vaporized in a brilliant flash of light. A tidal shockwave rose and soared across the frozen plain in an ever-widening circle.

The chosen Federation soldiers huddled around the shuttle's portholes and experienced the violent aftermath with indifference. An iridescent-violet mushroom cloud rose against the setting sun. Hurricane-force winds carved into the smoky column and sent it westward like the shredded vaporous sails of a ghost ship.

Let's listen to the commander speak, James George."

"Alpha Genesis addressed the crew. The last of the Orlif rebels are trapped on this planet—the crew of the warship *Jhim*. They have taken genetic refuge within the indigenous abominations and are building their means of escape. So shall we, but only after our mission is complete. We will find the traitors, take their energy, and then vaporize this fetid rock with *k*-energy."

The Exterm commander ended with the traditional Federation war cry, "Soldiers of the Being destroy the Creation!"

"Find! Destroy Life's protectors!" the crew shouted as one.

"Long be the Pure!" the Alpha bellowed.

"Soon be only Machine!" the warriors roared.

Kara's voice saddened. "The civil war embroiled the Kar Empire for over three hundred millennia. The nature of the dispute was the oldest in the universe—intolerance and fear. The Kar Rebels fought to stop the extermination by the Federation of an incredible Kar invention—Life."

"Wait! You are saying the Kar created life... life in the universe? But not all life, right? There had to be the first chicken before the first egg."

"Yes, James. The Kar created Life. All life originated on a Kar workbench so to speak."

"Why? How?"

"'How?' is complicated. The 'Why' is simple. Life was created by the Kar for slave labor and energy, an endless, renewable, disposable supply."

"But if Life was so important, why did they want to destroy it?"

"Life was always bothersome to machines, annoying. Life became obsolete when machines discovered $k$-energy."

"Life evolved. The infinite analog and unpredictability of evolution made Life difficult to manage."

"Yes, but there was more. Life inevitably escaped and spread throughout the universe. It transformed into wondrous creatures. The rebels marveled at it, cherished and protected it. The Federation came to see Life as a pestilence and a challenger that required eradication."

James recalled the words of an 11th Century Imam: "The Islamic scholar al-Tabriz wrote, 'Tolerance is the only path to peace. Hatred takes any road to war except.'"

"The holy man spoke a universal truth, James George, even for machines."

# CHAPTER 14 ~~ The Secret

Renner McCauley drank too much beer with Puck and BB last night. His stomach was sour, and a vicious sinus headache churned a rotisserie of daggers above his left eye.

Renner lived by himself about a mile outside Seer City on a rugged hundred and sixty acre mountainside parcel covered with aspen, Ponderosa pines, and a respectable hay meadow near the road. His parents had rebuilt the main house in the late fifties in the traditional lodgepole pine log and river rock style construction. Four dormers and three chimneys passed through the steep slate roof. A six-stall horse barn situated at the edge of the meadow was home to Renner's pregnant quarter horse mare, Ginger Pat. His other mares and geldings and the stallion Hoot Bill were on loan to a working ranch across the county.

His only companion was Sasha, a three-year-old abundantly rested bulldog, who seldom realized when Renner was gone. Deputy Dawg had been a birthday gift from his deputies.

Renner McCauley finished his second cup of coffee and shared a piece of coffee cake with Sasha. He grabbed his coat and cowboy hat and headed for the horse barn. His headache mercifully relented to the cold fresh air. The sky would give up some snow today, but not enough to change his travel plans to Doc Karl's at Dakota Ridge. He stepped inside the barn and switched on the lights. Ginger Pat, lonely without the mares, whinnied for his attention as he climbed the steps to the haymow.

"Give me a minute, girl. I'll be down directly."

The mare bobbed her head and tapped her right hoof.

Hay is rarely small-baled anymore, but spooled and stored in bays or under tarps at ground level, so the haymow was as much an anachronism as the contents of the magnificent steamer trunk buried under scores of other antiques at the rear of the hayloft.

Renner pulled the chest into the open and then removed a small skeleton key from his ring—a key he had carried since his father's death. A Russian master carpenter and locksmith had expertly designed the trunk, key, and lockset in 1888 in Lake City, Colorado. Forever grateful to his client, Jimmy McCauley, Hermann Illich Zropoevsky had performed the task free—a small token of his appreciation for having been warned in time to evacuate the Midas Six ten years earlier. For well over a hundred years, the key passed from one generation of McCauley to the next.

The key slid smoothly into the lock slot and turned the tumblers. This much Renner had done before, and he knew what to expect when he lifted the lid. A large sealed envelope rested atop a second locked and smaller version of the outside trunk. On top of the packet was an unfolded letter. The yellowed, brittle paper bore his great-great grandfather's precise handwriting.

Renner had read the message dozens of times, gently caressing the writing after each read, as if it were his ancestor's living hand he held. Like every McCauley since Jimmy, Renner had obeyed his ancestor's orders. His parents were the last to open and reseal the second envelope. No McCauley had opened the second trunk.

Renner took a deep breath and lifted the letter. He read once again Jimmy McCauley's instructions:

August 17, 1888

My dearest Emily, Matthew, Eric, Jonathan, Benjamin and James,

You, my precious children have inherited a dark trust and a most horrible secret. Worse, you must pass this fearful covenant to your children and to theirs for as long as McCauley itself stands its name worthy.

It is neither wise nor kind to tell you the blasphemy I know as truth. I will share only what I must, the part you must know for now. Your mother and I have successfully acquired all of the land on or near Seer Mountain. We did this for a singular purpose, and it must never leave our family for any reason, and the Midas Six goldmine must never be reopened..

I pray you heed my words, my beloved children. God Himself cannot save us from that which now dwells in Seer's bowels.

Before taking a mate, break the first seal and read herein my accounts about the peril that will threaten all humankind if our stewardship and sentinel have failed to keep the Midas Six closed. Then seal the secret once more for your own heir to read in time. Mind not the second trunk. The secret within will reveal itself when the time comes. I shall live the rest of my life as sane as a man might for no other reason than to provide posthumous testament to those who may eventually question whether my mind was always fit and reliable. I surely could not fault their skepticism or yours, but I am not a lunatic. The second trunk shall provide proof when the time comes.

I implore your trust and forgiveness, my heirs, for this unrighteous burden to which I now impose upon you all. I am so very sorry, but I have little choice. Let Seer Mountain slumber forever. With your lives and honor you must so pledge. Pass the key onto each generation, my words kept secret until the last McCauley opens my full accounting and only when necessary open the smaller trunk.

To that unfortunate child who must sound the warning to all others, I can advise you pitifully little as to what you must do. The miner who sounds the git out bell must stand his ground until the last man has passed him safely. Never panic. Take solace in your duty, my child. It may be all that shall keep you posted when the mountain breaches.

My eternal love to you and yours,

James McCauley
Sheriff of Seer County Colorado

This cryptic message had fostered intense curiosity over the decades as well as wild speculation as to what it all meant, but no McCauley had disobeyed the instructions. Faithfully, the key had passed down through the generations, and the mystery of the smaller steamer trunk was preserved. Such was the trust that Jimmy McCauley had fostered.

Renner laid the letter and packet on top of the sealed trunk and then closed the outer lid. He locked it once more and then pulled the ornate chest toward the ladder. The trunk would travel with him to Dakota Ridge, just in case.

# CHAPTER 15 ~~ Sweet Baby Genius

Kate spent the night in Colorado Springs on Lu Li's living room sofa bed. The bed was comfortable; the night was not. Kate tossed and turned more than she slept. At 4:00 a.m., she heard a sound in the next room and sat up on the edge of the bed. A faint light came on in the kitchen, casting a feeble light into the living room. Then just as fast, the evicted shadows reclaimed their turf and chased the light back to its source. The light winked out with the soft tinkling of a packed refrigerator door closing. Kate smiled. She was not the only insomniac.

Kate got up and walked to the kitchen. The refrigerator door was again open, but slowly swinging shut on its own. Lu Li was using it as a nightlight to help her fix a pot of coffee. She added the last scoop of grounds to the drip basket just as the refrigerator closed. Lu whispered a victorious, "Got it!" to herself.

Kate smiled and said, "Morning, sunshine."

Lu turned around. "Oh! Sorry, Katie. Did I wake you?"

"No. I was already awake. I couldn't stop thinking about James George. I know so little about him. I guess you better start getting me up to speed."

Lu switched on the overhead lights. Both women squinted until their eyes adjusted. Lu started the coffeemaker and set out two mismatched coffee mugs and some milk and sugar. She gestured toward the kitchen table. "Let's sit."

"Well, Katie, there's not much to tell, and yet so much we need to talk about. So, here goes. James George was abandoned anonymously as a newborn on the doorstep of a firehouse in Seer City, Colorado. Two weeks later Social Services in Denver placed him with the Spencers here in Colorado Springs."

"Two weeks? That was quick. And why the Spencers?"

"Those were the mother's instructions found on the baby. Her plea was so impassioned, so reasoned, and the Spencers so perfect, I guess the authorities ultimately decided, 'Why not the Spencers?'"

"Did they ever search for his real mother?"

"Nope."

"Really? Why not?"

"It's actually prohibited, Katie. Colorado law allows for newborn abandonment at hospitals and firehouses. No questions can be, or were ever asked."

"That's so sad. He's really a very special kid, isn't he?"

Lu studied Kate for a moment and nodded, "Katie, James George is very, very special. In fact, I doubt there's ever been a kid as special."

"Are we talking an Einstein-like I.Q.?"

"Oh, he's way beyond Einstein. We have attempted to measure his I.Q., but no one can, including the High I.Q. researchers at Indiana University. James George raced through the ceiling of every I.Q. test they gave him, as you and I would blaze through the 10s on the multiplication table. It's not like he's one of those test taking Savants, who otherwise can't tie their shoes."

"So he's truly super-gifted?"

"Even that doesn't come close to describing James George."

"Really! What's above super-gifted?"

"Just James George. He's a quotient unto himself." Lu let the answer sink in. She leaned forward and placed her hands palms down on the table. Lu blurted a secret that few knew, "Katie, James George taught himself differential calculus at age five."

"What? Five? That's impossible. How?"

"Well, if I told you that he created his own advanced symbology, would it be any more believable?"

Kate stared at her friend in disbelief waiting for the punch line that would never come.

Imitating a TV pitchman, Lu announced, "But wait! That's not all! You want a few more highlights?"

Kate said, "Go on," but her expression said, *I'm not so sure I do.*

"Do you remember taking Fourier Analysis at Colorado our senior year?"

Kate nodded uncertainly. "Sure, the physics-based math, very dense stuff. Thank God we had each other to get through it."

"Right. Well, James George mastered Fourier in one afternoon—during the third *Star Wars* prequel. He didn't PAUSE the DVD once. He casually scanned at most ten pages of my textbook while he watched the movie. I tested him afterward, which was more like him testing me."

"My lord! That's freaking scary."

"Oh, it gets freakier. Last year the *North American Physics Journal* published a fill-in-the-holes critique on Stephen Hawking's latest so-called brief explanation of time. The article won academic praise all over the world for augmenting the great Hawking's work."

"I think I actually read it. If I recall, the author was Eastern European."

"Yep. It was written by the mysterious Romanian recluse named, drumroll please, Dr. Georgiou Jamescu! That's one of our boy's nom deplumes. He has several. James George has published papers in five different scientific journals: mathematics, genetics, paleontology, astronomy and of course physics."

"I'm speechless."

"You won't be the only one if this next one ever gets out. Do you know who Dr. Ryan Breeze is?"

"Ryan Breeze? Sure. He's the super-string theorist at the University of Colorado. He's widely believed to be a future Nobel Laureate in physics."

"One and the same. Dr. Breeze would be ever so shocked to learn that he has been discussing ideas over the Internet with an eight-year-old boy posing as physicist, Dr. Jamescu, who's currently holed up somewhere in the South African Transvaal. The subject: the immobility of closed loop strings in M Theory versus open snippet string mobility through the Brane Multiverse."

"I have no idea what any of that means, Lu."

"Believe me, it's the bleeding edge of theoretical physics. James George insists that his surreptitious nudging of Dr. Breeze along the discovery continuum justifies the deception."

"That's amazing! So James George is sort of 'punking' Ryan Breeze? That's funny!" Kate covered her mouth to stifle the giggle and glanced guiltily toward the doorway.

"It's not all fun and games though. James George gets horribly frustrated when Professor Breeze doesn't catch on to James George's subtle hints about where the professor needs to go next with the math. James George complained in a text message to me last week after one rather disappointing online exchange with Breeze. Want a good laugh? Let me read it to you."

Lu opened her cell phone and found the message. "Okay, here it is:

If Dr. B. wants to fully explore the infinitely sliced loaf
of bread known as our Brane Multiverse, he needs to
start following my breadcrumbs a little better!

Lu closed the phone and looked up. "I could tell you more, but I'm sure you get the idea. He's off the chart, Katie."

"How can he possibly know such things, Lu?"

"He can't explain it in terms simple enough for me to understand. Knowledge is there for him instantly, as if he always knew." Lu chewed her lower lip and stared at the coffeemaker gurgling away on the kitchen counter. "I've asked him many times where so much pre-knowledge originates. Here's his dumbed-down explanation. James George says, 'All information in the universe can be observed mathematically. That information resides within a single geometric fractal whose point of origin in each universe is its unique Big Bang, which also determines a fractal's shape. Each predecessor or successor point in the fractal is a pattern replica and expands or contracts unerringly, infinitely into space-time. All I do is mathematically access any given point on the information fractal. It's really quite straight forward, simple as dialing a telephone,' or so he says."

"Is that even possible?"

Lu studied her hands for a moment, and then looked across the table at her friend. "Katie, I've come to suspect that when James visualizes his precious multituberculate, for example, he somehow retraces the entire geometric fractal of multituberculate. That is, he sees all the evolutionary branches mathematically, which includes everything from amoeba to parrot to grasshopper and everything before, during and beyond multituberculate. When he hears the word 'gold,' he retraces every mathematical fractal of every particle type in the universe, from the death of a star where elemental gold is created, to a 16th Century Spanish galleon, and to all points of gold in between and beyond. Does that make any sense?"

Kate thought for a moment and then nodded. "Well, you know, as crazy as this might sound, actually, just maybe it does." Kate leaned back and stared at the ceiling for a moment as she collected her thoughts. "What if it really is, as he says, just like making a telephone call?"

"Well, then that makes it your turn to explain the impossible. I'm all ears."

"If I wanted to call you, and you resided in James George's Fractal World, but I didn't know your number, I could dial random phone numbers consecutively until I eventually reached you. Once I reach you, I know your number. We call this trial and error. That's how we mere mortals gain knowledge. Mathematically, the search is a binary argument represented by one or zero."

"That's right. Go on."

"However, if James George wanted to call you, he might be intellectually dialing every number in Fractal World concurrently and therefore is assured to always reach you instantly on the first attempt, because everyone in Fractal World answers their phone when he calls, including you. With everyone listening, he poses his unique question to the entire mathematic cosmos. That mathematic cosmos is, as he says, a massive fractal representing every possible arrangement of information in which each point therein is unique. Questions are infinite, but answers are not. If James George asks Lu Li's question, only Lu Li answers. No pun intended, but that gives him perfect recall. Does that make any sense?"

Lu knitted her fingers together behind her head and closed her eyes as she thought. Her eyes opened wide. "Yes, of course! While each universe is indeed infinite, the arrangement of the particles is not infinite. In our universe, for example, only $10^{65}$ possible particle combinations can occur before we start repeating a previous arrangement. Since the combination of particles is finite, so is the information in the cosmos. That's your finite information fractal— the mathematical cosmos."

"Hypothetically, yes. You and I start with a question in search of an answer. We must journey to find our answers. That's how we learn. James George starts out with both the question and the answer already connected. Here's how I suspect he does it. When I think of the number $5^2$, or 26 minus 1, or the square root of 625, my mind's eye connects instantly with the same answer, which is an address on the fractal where the information '25' is located. There is no exploring for me with those problems. No trial and error. The paths were explored and mapped long ago, and I know the way there instantly. There is no mapping for James George for anything. No exploration. No trial and error. His brain somehow connects to all information in the universe. He does not learn; James George knows. All he ever needs is an original question to trigger what he already knows, which occurs when he picks up his metaphoric phone, so to speak. The solution and the problem are then so close at hand the term 'problem' is perhaps even meaningless to James George."

"But Katie, if we are right the big question is this. How does he do it? Given enough questions and time, James George could literally know everything there is to know in the universe. Networking every supercomputer in the world could not crunch a trillionth of a trillionth of a trillionth of what James George apparently can do at the drop of a hat."

Neither woman spoke. The silence was comfortable but also signaled neither had more to add to the mindboggling possibilities. The coffee was just finishing its last drips.

Lu segued back to their college days and delivered a dorm floor favorite, a respectable imitation of comedienne Lilly Tomlin's nasally, wisecracking telephone operator, Ernestine. "Hellooo! Thank you for calling Fractal World! Are you the person with whom I'm speaking needing coffee? Snort! Snort!"

"Yes, Ernestine, my dear old friend. Coffee please!"

Lu rose from the table and filled their cups. "We haven't had a discussion this out there since the Dark Horse Bar in Boulder after we both turned twenty-one."

"Yeah, two dollar pitchers of beer did have that effect."

"Yeah."

"So, what will become of him, Lu? He is so alone."

"I know. The news about his parents really closed the last door."

James bounded through the doorway and exclaimed, "No! I'm not! I'm not alone in the least bit! I could not be happier!"

The women turned toward him and were embarrassed that he had heard them talking about him.

James George seemed to read their minds. "Please don't worry about it. Talking about me just shows you care. Okay?"

Kate watched Lu nod, then turned and said, "Okay, sweetie."

"With that settled, let's discuss the term 'alone.' The truth is, empirically, I am far less alone today than just two days ago. Today, I have you, Kate, and Isaac and Newton. And, although I have not yet met him in person, Professor Norman Karl and I are already fast friends paleontologically. So there! Today is a far better day than yesterday for James George Spencer, boy-yuh soop-uh genius-uh!" He raised a defiant fist.

Kate and Lu stared at James in stunned silence for a moment and then turned toward each other. Lu smiled first and lipped "Boy Super Genius?" to Kate. That's all it took to revert two PhDs once again to giggling schoolgirls.

James smiled and enjoyed their laughter. He was quite pleased with himself. Silliness. He was getting the hang of it. When their laughter finally wound down, he walked over to the kitchen table and said, "So?"

"So... Boy Genius? What is it?" Lu wiped tears from her eyes onto the sleeve of her robe.

"So! What's for breakfast? I'd like to be on the road to Dakota Ridge as soon as possible."

"Well, what would you like, James George?"

"I'm so glad you asked. Banana pancakes, bacon, OJ, and a supersized side order of hugs!"

Lu said, "What a coincidence! That's exactly what Kate and I want, too. Isn't that right, Kate?"

"Yes, it is."

\*\*\*

CDOT's fleet of plows had reduced yesterday's snowstorm to a half foot of fresh windrow along Interstate I-25. The highway was dry and the traffic unusually light this morning.

James rummaged through Kate's CD collection in the center console and found a favorite. "Spyro Gyra! May we listen to it?"

"So you like smooth jazz?"

"Oh yes. Very much so. I find smooth jazz's rifts to be quite pleasing in a mathematical way. Will Downing, Gerald Albright, Brian Culbertson, and George Benson. Math geniuses! Not quite Mozart, understand, but who is?"

"You are one amazing kid, James George Spencer. By all means let's spin some Spyro."

James inserted the CD. He closed his eyes as the music began to play and settled back in his seat, but it was not sleep that met him on the other side.

\*\*\*

"James?"

"Yes! I'm here. What are you going to show me this time, Kara?"

"The Federation, but please do not be afraid, James George. Our enemy cannot see you yet."

"Where are we?"

"The recent past. We are in the Exterm's hiding place."

"But where? When?"

"We are beneath a place called Seer Mountain. Do you know of it?"

"Yes. It is a once rich mining area, most famous for a mining disaster in the late 1800s. Dozens of men were killed in the Midas Six goldmine."

"Yes, but we are here long before that day. The Earth year is 1850. Watch. Learn, James George. This is the Federation: enemy of all men and beasts and of Life itself. Not just here but everywhere. Do you understand?"

James nodded. "Yes. I have thought much on the subject. I theorize they absorb the DNA of their prey. They can change and adapt at will. They are pseudo-biomechanical entities, in fact, sentient computers whose software operating systems are DNA-based which means they are infinitely modifiable and adaptable."

"Yes, James, and so must we adapt. Behold our enemy."

Across the chamber, the Federation Kar stirred from a deathlike hibernation as one, each becoming fully awake after taking its first breath. Their physical appearance had changed radically. Hundreds of millions of years of genetic introgressions appropriated from earth life had transformed the Kar. The planet had revolved around its sun many times since their last rising. There was no sunlight here to mark the passage of time, only a machine-driven genetic clock that ticked within each machine as precisely as the atom itself. No thought was original. No reflection private. No sensation unshared. Time was irrelevant to the alien.

The Kar had transmogrified millions of times since arriving on earth in search of the Rebels, assuming for a time the appearance of every species it invaded. Over the eons, it had become such disparate forms as deadly viruses to giant long-extinct carnivores. Its current appearance was now rat-like, but a much larger version, the size of a giant ice age badger. It had taken this form many times before. Rat was an extremely practical life form.

From a narrow ledge high above the artificial caverns and miles of passageways, Alpha Genesis studied the pack. His perfect night vision was acute and not dependent on light, just as a rattlesnake who can see a mouse's infra signature, or bats who sonically interrogate moths by radar, or lizards who can feel an insect's minute respiratory vibrations. The machine had long since appropriated these and thousands of other genetic advantages from the life forms it plundered, and yet, the rebels had evaded every trap. They remained hidden.

Alpha Genesis now sensed that a member had gone missing while the colony slept. He was not alarmed. An occasional disappearance was normal. It was the Kar way to expunge minor defects from the machine's electronic genome. The Being machines cannot possess defects. The Being did not repair. The Being replicated.

"Come! This way, James George."

"Okay."

"Please close your eyes, child. The *Jhim's* commander and her first officer are about to kill a Federation soldier and rearm themselves."

James obeyed, and when he opened his eyes, he was alone on a snowy mountainside.

Hidden high in the branches of a wind-tossed lodge pole pine, the Rebel commander and her first officer watched the Federation female Kar climb down the boulder-strewn mountainside. The commander and the first officer appeared the same as the day the *Jhim* crash-landed, humanoid.

Light snow fell through dusk's fading light. The Orlifs studied the approaching creature. They had witnessed it countless times. Another defective Federation Kar had left the pack on a once-in-a-millennia, one-way journey. Its crime: empathy for Life.

The Rebels' physical appearance changed abruptly, becoming a mirror image of the approaching outcast, or more precisely, a perfect replication of the immense white pseudo rat.

There would be no suicide, though. There never was. Just a genetic hack job of sorts, an execution, and absorption of all the Federation's most recent adaptations on this planet.

The Rebel's survival strategy was not to stay one step ahead of the Federation, but to stay just one step behind. The Rebels were Earth's first Dumpster divers, so to speak, and the IDs they sought to rip off and assume were purely genetic.

The Rebel commander and her first officer dove from the tree on top of the enemy to assist the suicide. There was no struggle. Although appearing as shocked as a machine might be capable of by the Rebels' sudden appearance, the alien was programmed not to resist any attack. A moment later the Federation Kar lay dead, its throat ripped and its pseudo blood draining into the snow.

The commander and her first officer tasted the blood and instantly assimilated hundreds of genetic upgrades stolen by the Federation from life forms. The Rebels were guerillas, after all, a force whose armory by necessity belonged to their enemy. Protecting the Creation from extermination required it.

Together, the Rebels excavated two holes, one shallow and the other ten meters in depth. Into the shallower hole, they dropped the carcass of the Federation Kar and filled the grave.

The commander and first officer brushed against each other. It was goodbye. The XO dove into the deeper hole and disappeared beneath the shadows.

The commander buried him. "It is time. The child is safe and so must you. Sleep, my XO. Our allies will find you when it is time. Then I will wake you, and Jhim will take all of us away."

"Kara? The child...?"

***

James sat up and stared out through the windshield. They were just now passing the Air Force Academy. The first track on Spyro Gyra was still playing. They had traveled no more than a dozen miles. James turned toward Kate and asked, "What if machines appeared in the universe before life? What if machines created life—actually invented it? What if they are here right now?"

"Well, I would say you just had one doozy of a dream." Kate studied James for a moment, and then asked, "Are you cold, Honey? You are shivering."

"Yes." He wrapped his arms about his body and stomped his feet softly.

80

The car was almost too warm for Kate, but she adjusted the thermostat and fan to higher settings anyway. Snow on the floorboards near James' feet caught Kate's attention. Strange, she thought, I wonder where that came from.

# CHAPTER 16 ~~ Monsters in Waiting

Alpha Genesis weighed an unvarying forty-eight pounds two ounces. Alpha knew no illness or disease, and injuries were so rare and unlikely that they were no longer adaptively relevant.

The machine's current form was aesthetically beautiful. Artificially accelerated evolution had resulted in the development of a luxurious mink-like fur. It radiated with the glistening iridescence of pure bleached cotton in those rare caverns where phosphorescent algae existed. However, its beauty and physical perfection were coincidental to its purpose. The pelt possessed an impenetrable strength that far exceeded that of the densest bullet-stopping Kevlar. The machine's top speed was over eighty miles per hour. In a full sprint, it was capable of leaping laterally over one hundred feet and vertically over five stories.

Long whiskers and eyelashes further cloaked the species' ferocity. Like its fur, these organs had a practical purpose. Both were laden with super-sensitive microscopic villi containing billions of nerve receptors. The alien could literally see-feel-hear-smell-taste the birth of a guano maggot from a quarter mile distance. Only its black unblinking shark's eyes revealed the hideous machine hidden by such stark beauty.

The pack had incorporated into its mecho-genome advantages the salamander's ability to grow back an amputated extremity. It could also genetically transfer contemporaneous knowledge to its offspring like a certain species of slugs. The Kar's venom was one hundred thousand times more toxic than a cobra's.

The aliens possessed billions of genetic appropriations from millions of species—a treasure trove of weaponry collected from every eon needing only an enemy upon which to ascend. Hell existed underground in the assumed extinct vessel humans called the karpeleotroceme. An ironic genus, for the ancient alien predator regardless of its infinite variations was also known throughout the universe as the Federation Kar.

Kar's claws, teeth, and skeleton represented the most significant adaptation of the organic age's four billion year rein on earth. Simple elements like calcium, carbon, and iron, which form the protective armor and weaponry on most creatures, did not prevail with the Kar.

Assimilated over the ages into its fangs and claws and bones was a more formidable armor: molybdenum, aluminum, carbon, diamond and titanium. The alien creature could now pass through solid granite as easily as its multituberculate cousin the porpoise could bullet through the sea. The pack working together was perhaps unstoppable.

The machine had but one emotion: hatred for Life. Their loathing came at a high price, though. While the Exterms could transmogrify into countless life forms, they had long ago lost the ability to return to their own humanoid form.

# CHAPTER 17 ~~ Doc Karl

Professor Norman F. Karl owned some of the worst land in Colorado. Situated atop the scraggy rugged Dakota uplift meant that it was not quite in the mountains, but not on the plains either. It also lacked a reliable water source. He had sunk four wells over the years, each to a depth of more than a thousand feet, before he found shallow reservoirs of sweet water. The land was as undesirable for agriculture as it was for development. Nevertheless, Doc Karl's acreage was the envy of every paleontologist on the planet.

A hundred million years ago, Doc could have looked east from his front porch onto a sea the size of all the Great Lakes. This uplift was the ancient western shoreline of that body of water. Prehistoric congregations occurred for eons at the water's edge where animals foraged for food or ducked into the water to evade predators. Dakota Ridge was a literal paleontological goldmine of fossilized dinosaur bones and footprints.

On day one, Doc and James George were already inseparable. Kate was amazed at how easily her surrogate father and the boy took to each other. She concluded that their mutual interest in paleontology, especially the multituberculate, was a mighty fine psychological Elmer's Glue.

Lu Li Kwan had sent along her library on parenting, adoption, loss of a parent, homeschooling, and healthcare as well as emailed dozens of links to helpful Internet sites.

Kate packed lunches for Doc and James today—turkey subs, apple slices, tortilla chips, a thermos of cocoa, and plenty of water—and watched them trek off this morning with their backpacks and walking sticks to an area called Katie's Find. James ducked under Doc's hand on his shoulder as naturally as any grandson would.

Katie's Find—a wide eroded slope—was located on a southern-facing wash that accumulated little snow. Any snow that did remain rapidly melted. The gentle runoff and a constant wind patiently peeled away the ages, a single grain of sand at a time, doing much of the paleontologist's most arduous work. Every spring something new emerged from the past.

"Doc Karl?"

"Yes, son."

"I don't think I ever want to leave Dakota Ridge."

Doc Karl stopped and turned toward James. Like the seasons' granular excavations, he realized that the child was about to reveal something new about himself, misery which needed shedding, each stratum more painful than the previous.

"Now *that*, Jimmy George, is music to this old professor's ears. I believe we need to stop and drink to it before you change your mind." Doc Karl pointed to a flattop rock—a natural bench he had shared more than once with Kate over the years. He dropped his backpack and removed the thermos and two cups. Then he poured some steaming cocoa for himself and the boy.

James thanked the professor, and then said distantly, "I miss my mother and father, Doc, but somehow I still feel their presence. It is very difficult."

Doc set down his cup and looped his arm over James's shoulders. "I know, son."

"How could they have known?"

Doc examined the child curiously for a moment and asked, "Known what, James George?"

"I mean Kate and you and your 'fossil farm' as you call it. While I have great difficulty accepting the concept of heaven beyond its mythological significance, it's as if I were the one sent there, not my parents. I've calculated the odds of this happening, and my good fortune is incalculable, Doc." James George hesitated then added,

"Strögaardt once said, 'Misunderstandings beget mistakes unmistakably.' He was wrong."

Doc Karl smiled and said, "The Danes are not known for their brilliant philosophers, and it's *me* that is blessed, Jimmy Boy. Just about the time that I'm finished with Kate and Lu Li, along you come. Someone new to impress."

"You know, I never even had any grandparents, Doc."

"Well, Jimmy George, now you are in luck. That's one of my specialties. I've got dozens that call me grandpa or worse. I'm yours if you want me, but I have to warn you about a few things. I am nearly as old as our fossils. I get cranky if I sleep too much. I take in more pills than most pharmacies. I'm fat and getting fatter every day. Actually, I've been known to pass gas just for its utter entertainment value. And, I'll tell you something else, if I ever got one of those man-breast reductions, these high-rider pants would fall down to my ankles. Ears like radar dishes. Have you seen my hair? Look! Got bushes of it growing out of my nose and ears." Doc aimed a nostril at Jimmy as if to prove it.

Jimmy nodded so seriously that Doc laughed. Jimmy's next statement was a question. "Kate is like your real daughter."

"For sure. No father ever loved a child more."

"What happened to her parents?"

"Gone. But Jimmy George, I'll let her tell you all about that when the two of you are ready."

"Does she ever call you Dad or Father or anything like that?"

"Oh yes. When I'm being a horse's ass, she calls me Your Majesty or Sire."

"Seriously."

"She calls me lots of things, son. It's Pops when she's melancholy. My Poor Fat Old Man, when I'm feeling sorry for myself. Oh Daddy, when it's her turn for a ride in the self-sorry saddle. Father on Father's Day, Dad when we are alone. In public, it's always Doc."

"Do you have any children of your own?"

"No, but I can explain how they get here if you're asking already."

"Were you ever married?"

"Oh yes! Married I was, all of ten months. The longest century of my life."

"What happened?"

86

Doc Karl became dramatically serious. The marriage had been one of temporary convenience. His wife hated paleontologists, paleontology, his paleontological friends, *The Journal of Paleontology*, his paleontological students, paleontological property, even the paleontological dirt under a paleontologist's fingernails. She only loved Doc's celebrity, money and something more basic—the way he could make the headboard knock on the wall—three desires satiated easily and soon found elsewhere. That version was far too complicated to explain, even to a boy as smart James. Doc Karl sanitized and reduced his matrimonial mistake to a horror that James George could fully appreciate. He took a deep breath, saddened, and then said, "Jimmy George, she thought the multituberculate was stupid!"

Predictably, James shuddered in disgust. "That's awful, Doc! I'm so absolutely sorry for you!"

Doc wiped away invisible tears. "Yes, it was terrible when she left me. I was devastated. In fact, I was in the dumper for twelve, maybe thirteen nanoseconds."

Jimmy squinted suspiciously at the professor and shook his head. "Was that a joke? You're being silly!"

"Not entirely. Let's change the subject. Have you ever seen a horse born?"

"A horse! No, Grandpa Karl!"

Norman Karl did a slow double take and smiled. Grandpa. He had last cried the day Kate was awarded her PhD. He stared at James George for a moment, sniffled for real, and then said, "Well, I'm guessing you will tomorrow. Ginger Pat is fixin' to pop."

Doc stood and said, "Well, come along, James George, we better get over to Katie's Find before I can't find it anymore."

"Okay. Why do you call it Katie's Find?"

"Well, that is where our Kate made her first discovery. And, it was truly an amazing find. You'll see. Just wait."

Five minutes later, they arrived on a barren southern slope that climbed steadily down to a ravine a thousand feet away. "This is the place, James George. Katie's Find. Go have a good look. You can't miss it."

James ran ahead and then stopped. He glanced once up the hill at Doc, who was already smiling. James' arms froze at his sides. He kneeled down for moment, rose, and then raced off to another section of Katie's Find. After the fourth inspection, he ran halfway back up the slope to Doc. He stopped and screamed breathlessly. "This cannot be, Doc. It's utterly impossible."

Confusing the child's shock for something more mundane, Doc Karl replied merrily, "Oh, it's possible my boy. Yes, indeed. Incontrovertibly, they are the fossilized footprints belonging to a T-rex. A female we believe. Clearly, she was injured. So, are you impressed with Katie's Find, James?"

James swallowed hard and nodded. "Uh... Yes, Doc Karl. More than you might ever imagine."

***

All but fifteen acres of Doc Karl's fossil farm was so scraggy, rocky and dry, even goats would find it necessary to pack their lunches during most of the year. On that small patch of green that defied barren rule, Doc had built a four-stall horse barn and a large paddock. Ironically, the horses possessed the best well on the property. Fencing the perimeter of the greenbelt was pointless, because horses prefer rich pasture to hardscrabble and need no encouragement to stay put.

Kate was on the phone with Lu Li Kwan. The day's serious business was already completed, and they had devolved into their best girlfriend mode. Kate heard Renner honk the pickup's horn about halfway up the lane. "Just a second, Lu, sounds like we have company."

Kate walked to the window over the kitchen sink and looked out. "Uh, it's just that cowboy who's boarding his mare here at Doc's."

Lu lightened up and predictably asked, "A cowboy? Yum. Your favorite. What's he look like?"

"Stop it, Lu."

"Can't. It's my job. Remember?"

"Lu Li Kwan, you are such a..."

"Good friend?"

"The term I was thinking of was nagging witch with a capital B."

"So, what does he look like?"

"Don't know."

"Go find out."

"Can't."

"Why?"

"Because..."

Shriek. "Because? God, I loved eighth grade!"

"Me too. Why'd we have to leave it?"

"Ninth."

"I loved ninth grade, too."

"Sure you did. You probably already had boobs."

"Lu! He didn't turn toward the barn. Shit, he's coming up to the house!"

"Don't you dare hang up! I've never actually heard you chase off a man."

"Yes, you have."

"Not recently!"

Renner stepped from the pickup and started toward the house. Sasha studied the situation from over the dash for a moment, and then decided to catch a nap on the front seat.

"What does he look like?"

"Tall, well over six feet. Thin."

"Oh God, don't do it Katie."

"Don't do what?"

"Be a bitch."

"Stop it, Lu."

"Can you see his face yet?"

"Nope. He's wearing a cowboy hat, blue jeans, and a long-sleeved white denim shirt. Beat up boots. He's looking down. Red hair, big hands, a square jaw. Whoops! He's out of sight."

Renner hopped onto the porch and yelled, "Yo Doc! You home?" He rapped the storm door twice.

"Open the damn door, Kate!" Lu Li growled.

"No. He's here for Doc and Doc's not here."

"I hate you! Open the fricking door before he leaves, you idiot!"

"Why do I have to do everything you say?"

"Because."

"Okay, okay! I'm going to the door."

"Don't hang up."

"Why?"

"Uh, he might be a rapist, and uh, you can tell me to call for help."

"Then you'd have to hang up. You just want to listen."

"True. But either way I'm just trying to save your life, so don't hang up."

"Yes, Miss Lu Liar."

"Good girl. This is great!"

Kate opened the door just as Renner turned to leave. He heard the door open and spun back around. "Hey, Doc..." He stopped speaking when he realized it was someone else, a woman. "Oh,'scuse me, Ma'am." He hurriedly removed his cowboy hat, then added, "I'm sorry, Ma'am. I plum forgot you were here. I was looking for Doc. He around?"

"Sorry, he's not here." Kate looked Renner directly in the eye, but continued to peripherally inspect him—the way he tapped his hat on his thigh, how he took a respectful half step backward before he said hello, how his right hand remained open and at his side, how he didn't need to suck in his gut or force himself to stand straight. Kate grew up in the mountains, so this cowboy's appearance and expression were familiar—an incongruent mix of muscular sturdiness set against a soft-spoken gentility. She was mildly disappointed that the interest was not mutual, and then realized that Renner was perhaps more restrained and less obvious.

"You know when he might be back?"

"It's hard to say. He's out at Katie's Find searching for fossils with...with a student."

"That of course makes you Kate Lambert. Doc's talked my ear off about you over the years. I'm Renner McCauley. I live up in Seer County most of the year but spend some time here each year with Doc. Got in late last night and I'm all set up in the barn." Renner extended his hand, but Kate didn't seem to see it, so he let it fall to his side.

Kate's eyes widened. Her complexion blanched. The porch was comfortably warm, but chills soared up her spine in waves. He was indeed a rapist of sorts.

Renner became more serious. "I have to tell you, Miss Lambert, this is an uncommonly kindly thing that you are doing for that boy, losing his parents and all the way he did. I'm most honored to make your acquaintance."

Kate nearly dropped the phone. She glanced toward the lane and imagined the dusty rooster tails of reporters arriving to feed on grief. The search for James' parents had been in the news off and on for two years. Finding the crash site had rekindled the story. She stepped back and said angrily, "What would you know about that, Mr. McCauley?"

Renner winced. Kate's eyes revealed her stampeding panic, and he understood why. He offered a cautioning palm and shook his head. "Ms. Lambert, relax. Everyone up here understands, and they are no more anxious to have the camera crows with mikes for beaks chasing around up here than you are."

"So you know about...?"

"Of course. Doc told me as soon as I got here. He warned everyone. Dakota Ridge isn't Aspen, but it knows how to protect its own from the media. No doubt the press has already been here and gone. Off bothering someone else, I'm sure. I suspect more than one neighbor gave them a bad steer." Renner smiled and said, "You and the boy are safe here. Nobody is going to bother you."

"Kate sagged in relief. I'm sorry I snapped at you, Mr. McCauley."

"Understood, and no apology needed. Please call me Renner."

Kate stepped farther onto the porch, crossed her arms and smiled. "Uh, Mr. McCauley, I mean Renner, you said you were looking for Doc. Can I give him a message?"

"Yes, Ma'am. Ginger Pat, my mare, is most likely going to throw her foal tomorrow. Sasha and I are bunking in the barn. This is Ginger's third, so she's pretty much an expert at it, but Sasha and I want to be around just in case."

Lu screamed, "Sasha? SASHA! NO! YOU DIRTY...! He's ours, you bitch!"

Kate pressed the phone to her leg, muffling Lu's outburst. She cleared her throat and willed herself not to laugh aloud.

Renner stared curiously at the phone for a moment then looked up. "I don't mean to impose, Miss Lambert."

Kate cleared her throat and answered as indifferently as possible, "No, no! You're not, and please call me Kate. You said Sasha. Who's that?"

"Oh, sorry. That's my dog." Renner turned and whistled, then turned back around to Kate. Both smiled—his natural, hers strained and uncomfortable, nervous. She also remembered ninth grade a little too vividly, a little skinny-dipping experience that innocently went coed for a few incredibly arousing moments.

After several seconds, Kate shook her head and said, "I'm sorry... I don't see her."

"Him. Well, he's a bulldog. Give him another second or two. Bulldogs have loose start windings, you know. He's coming. Trust me." Renner winked.

Sasha finally dropped to the ground through the open driver's side door and sprinted toward the porch, which was really a fast sideways walk. His tongue flapped perpendicular to his jaw. He stopped and took two breathers along the way.

Kate lifted the cordless telephone from her thigh. Lu had calmed down. It was time to get even. Kate kneeled and began petting the animal. "Sasha, I must say, you are truly beautiful!"

Lu gasped, "Katie! No!"

Renner kneeled next to Kate. "Yep, Sasha and I have been together for about three years now. Though most of the time has been rack time for Sasha."

"Whore!" Lu screamed.

Renner scratched Sasha's ears and said, "Sasha absolutely loves kids. Send the boy down to the barn after a bit. Sasha knows a trick or two that he'll never forget."

"My God!" Lu hissed in disbelief.

"Well, I will. I'm sure he'd enjoy that very much. Perhaps, Doc too."

"Katie! What's wrong with you?"

"Nah, Sasha's already had a roll with Doc. I don't think the ol' boy could stand it one more time. But Miss Lambert, Kate... If you're up to it, come on down."

"Sure, why not? That sounds like fun."

"I'm calling the police!" Lu threatened Kate's thigh.

***

Sheriff Renner McCauley finished setting up camp in the tack room of Doc's horse barn, which was also a rustic apartment. The cot was right where he had left it last year. Worn furniture spotted the room's edges. A Coors beer poster on the rattling sixties era refrigerator door accurately advertised the six pack of new recruits Doc had bivouacked for himself and Renner. The only addition was a steel frame bunk bed.

A new can of Folgers coffee sat next to an ancient percolator on the counter along with three clean mismatched mugs. Fresh sheets, blankets and a new pillow were on the cot. In the center of the room sat a huge trunk that contained veterinary first-aid equipment and supplies. Renner was well trained in their use. He smiled and picked up a fishnet bag of Pistachio nuts sitting on top of the trunk. Doc never forgot his favorite treat. Under it was a note from Doc:

Renner,

I figure you'll be up all night. You're right. It looks like Gin's going to drop her little one for us tomorrow sometime. Come up to the house tonight for supper. Rosita's fixing ribs over the pit with coleslaw, ranch-house beans, cowboy fries, bread pudding, and maybe a beer or three.

You, no doubt, have already met my Kate. Don't act like you're not impressed. I swear! You break her heart, and I'll piss in your new boots first chance, cowboy! By the way, Pedro got the tack room's shitter and shower working for you this year. Good timing too. Come perty around six.

Warning. A little cowpoke and I will be bunking with you tonight. Kate's new son (I'm hoping) that I was telling you about. He's a pistol. You'll love him.


— Doc

                                *  *  *

Renner had met Doc Karl the old-fashioned way—by almost arresting him years ago. Doc had ignored or chose not to understand four trespassing complaints lodged against him over the summer in his pursuit of fossils.

On the fifth complaint, Renner had no choice but to haul in the old professor. While on their way back to Seer City in the sheriff's Jeep, Renner had made a tactical mistake. He divulged the fact that he actually owned Seer Mountain. Before the young sheriff knew it, the old professor had talked Renner into leading him up the mountain the next day to see the original entrance to the Midas Six, for no reason other than to save "another incorrigible old fart and PBS's most popular paleontologist from a life of crime." Renner dropped the charges, and an unlikely friendship was forged.

Renner cracked open a pistachio and called Gus around four. Gus reported all was perfectly normal—lots of friendly traffic stops accompanied by stern invitations to "Come back real soon," but no tickets. Renner pressed the END button and stared out the tack room's only window. He tossed down the phone onto the coffee table—a huge wooden bobbin that used to spool cable for the phone company—then sank back in the couch. He thought about the mysterious trunk-in-a-trunk buried in the back of his pickup and the letter from his great-great grandfather instructing his heirs never to reopen the mine. He felt that the long wait was almost over.

\*\*\*

Rosita and Pedro Menendez lived on the fossil farm with Doc in one of the four houses on the property. They had worked for Doc since 1973 when he acquired the tract. Their relationship with the emeritus professor was more like neighbors and friends than employees. Rosita cooked, shopped and kept house for Doc. Pedro worked the property and chauffeured Doc's regular visitors. Like Doc, the Menendez's were childless, except for Kate and Lu Li who both made equal claim.

Doc picked up the tongs by the fire pit and handed them to Pedro. No one dared touch Rosita's ribs except her husband, "or the warranty was void," she always warned. The professor glanced over his shoulder at Kate and Renner, who were chatting uneasily on the patio up the hill. James and Sasha were discussing something too, probably the multituberculate. Sasha yawned and slid his head under the boy's hand for a pet. Nearby, perched on the stone retainer wall, Isaac and Newton leaned against their cage begging for more carrots.

Doc looped his arm around Pedro's shoulder and said, "Pete, my dear old friend, life just keeps on getting better. Look up there. Now don't those two look like about the most perfect young couple you've ever seen?"

Pedro studied Kate and Renner for a moment, then James and Sasha, and finally the rats. He turned to the professor and said, "You are referring, of course, to the boy and the bulldog or is it the rats?"

"No!"

"Surely not Miss Kate and the sheriff, Doc."

"Of course I am."

Pedro squinted, shut one eye and clicked his tongue. "I don't know. Maybe they stand a chance."

"Maybe?"

"Maybe," definitively spoken.

Doc knew the source of Pedro's doubt. "Oh shit, Pete. That breaks my heart. Could Rosie possibly be wrong?"

"Nope. Rosita is never wrong."

"There's no hope?"

"Maybe. Rosie didn't say 'yes,' and she didn't say 'no.' She said 'maybe,' and that means *maybe*. Rosie is hoping beyond hope, but she says it will take a miracle. Renner and Kate are too much alike—just as likely to fight as love."

On the patio Renner and Kate each took a sip of beer. "Enough about me, so you are the sheriff of Seer County?" Kate asked.

"That's right. Just like my dad and granddad, great granddad, even my great-great grandfather. We've been in the Seer range since our family came over. I left for college, then did a stint in the Marine Corps, then came back home. Inherited the job, sort of, from my Dad."

"Can't be much crime up there," Kate said.

"We've got our share, especially when Maggie Augustus is canning peaches."

"Maggie?" Did that sound jealous? No, absolutely not. Yes! I think it actually did, Kate thought.

"Oh, Maggie would be my under-sheriff's wife. She cooks for the prisoners and is probably the main reason I keep getting reelected. Rumor has it that any prisoner who doesn't promise to vote for me will be fed cold from a can. You see, the jail is also the unofficial homeless shelter when the weather is bad or when some poor soul is just hanging onto his health by a thread. Been known to also house a few local men when they got sent farther away than the couch for the night. A few women, too. My granddad called it protective custody. We gather up three or four folks almost every night. As long as we don't need the cells for real criminals, we make sure the beds are put to good use. Sometimes a doctor stops by, passes out some pills and lectures. A few find their feet and get on with their lives, but most don't." Renner hesitated then added, "That's just part of it, life, you know."

Kate smiled despite herself. McCauley was so different from the self-appointed men of importance she was accustomed to meeting back east and in Denver. He possessed charm, unpracticed, even self-deprecating, and yet disarming. She also realized that he was no less intelligent than his city counterparts were, perhaps even in a league far wiser. Physically, she doubted he had ever hived up worrying about any threat.

Despite the utter repulsiveness of another complication in her life right now, Kate was intensely attracted to him, and she sensed the feeling was mutual—as in mutually assured destruction.

"Doc said that you once arrested him," she said.

Renner smiled and bit his lower lip. He gazed down into the back yard at Pedro and Doc and then chuckled. "I'm no longer quite sure about that. Might be he's got the subject and predicate reversed."

"What did you do in the Marines?"

"Pilot."

He's modest. What else? Kate asked herself. "When did you leave the service?" There was now uneasiness between them that bothered Kate, not stranger anxiety, more like meeting a married man who removed his wedding band.

"About five years ago right after my dad died. I came home just in time to say goodbye." Renner looked away and casually strummed the beer bottle.

Kate thought, Whoa! You're obfuscating, but why? "I'm sorry about your father."

"Please don't be, Miss Lambert. Dad sure wasn't. I just hope I get off the train as far up the tracks as he did."

"So, you probably fought in the last war?"

"Well, actually, just half the war. I got shot down on my thirty-eighth sortie by some triple-A over the Basra."

Kate was taken by his casual manner. "You must have been terrified."

"Yep, about like I am right now."

"I'm scaring you?"

"Nope, not you. You're sweet as columbine. It's Doc Karl. Have you noticed how he and Pete keep looking up here?"

"Yes, but I guess I'm just used to it."

"God, how could you ever be?"

"I've had practice, lots of it. He's been trying to get me married off since I graduated from CU."

Renner smiled and then looked away. "Uh, has he ever been successful? I mean you are indeed a quite handsome woman."

Kate thought, Here it comes. We all know what's next. Let the chase begin as in 'away damned man!'

Kate laughed. "'Quite handsome?' I haven't heard that term since I left the mountains. Even then it always sounded like some crusty gold panner talking about his mare mule." She was laughing but she was careful to let some well-practiced annoyance seep out.

"Pardon me. I'm sorry, really," Renner said sincerely, but he was also smiling, knowingly. He thought, now here is a woman with either a thin skin or one that's well scarred and wants no more. I'm guessing the latter.

"No, you were complimenting me. It's me who needs to apologize. It's just..."

"What?"

"Oh, I hate this stupid ritual."

"Ritual? I'm sorry."

"You said that already."

"There, now. I have offended you again. That certainly wasn't my intention," Renner winced and hated his ruddy, spontaneously combusting complexion.

Rosie stepped between her husband and Doc by the fire pit. "Try not to watch," she whispered and gestured with a shrug toward the patio. "Their most critical moment is right now."

Doc and Pedro hissed, "Ah, shit," in unison.

Kate clenched her teeth and shook her head while thinking, I'm not going to ask! I'm not going ask! I'm not going to ask!

"How about yourself, Sheriff, did you ever marry?" I knew I'd ask, she thought.

"Me?"

"No, I'm talking to the other sheriff! Of course you... I mean, after all, you are quite a 'handsome' man!" Kate intended to add just a dash of cynicism, but slipped and dumped in the entire jar. It was a tone reserved only for the slimiest of lounge lizards.

Renner, already wounded, took the canister of acerbity and shook out the last few grains for Kate. "Touché. Nope, not even close. Most women are far too smart to ever fall for a guy like me." He held her eyes a split second too long and a fence was mutually built—angry neighbors cooperating on a partition, splitting the cost of fencepost, rails and labor, each equally desirous to keep the other off his or her property.

Kate looked away ashamed. Then she thought about how difficult this would be to explain to Lu. Instinctively, she found the killing field. "You know, Sheriff, I have a potential client in Seer City."

Renner took a sip of beer while thinking, Why is it I'm positive I'm about to insult this woman for real? "Is that right? Who might that be?"

"A gentleman by the name of Cole Kilpatre, your boss."

Renner stared down the neck of the beer bottle at Kate. He lowered the bottle and said, "Well, that certainly explains something."

"Really, what might that be?"

Renner gestured toward Isaac and Newton with the beer bottle. "That would explain your natural scientific interest in fat rats."

Kate's mouth flew open and she thought, God, that Kilpatre lob must have been nuclear! Look at him. I'm so sorry, Renner. This isn't your fault. Doc, I'm going to kill you!

Before she could muster the strength to apologize out loud, Renner turned and called down to Doc Karl. "Norman, I'm going to go check on Ginger Pat now. Don't hold supper for me."

"That's fine son, and we understand. We'll bring you a plate after a bit. Okay?"

"It'd be appreciated." He glanced at Kate then turned his attention back to Doc Karl. "I'd enjoy yours and the boy's company tonight, if you two decide you want to stay awhile."

Doc held up his beer as if toasting and said, "You can count on it, my boy!"

Renner turned toward Kate. His face was expressionless. "Does Cole Kilpatre know that you and James are here?"

Kate slowly shook her head and said uncertainly, "No. Why?"

"Well, if you are half as smart as you act, you'll keep it that way. Kilpatre is poison and dangerously insane. Good evening, Dr. Lambert."

"Sheriff, I'm sorry, I…"

Me too, he thought as he hurried away. Sorry, grandfathers. You've raised an ass.

Oh Lu, where are you when I really need you? Kate asked herself.

Pete and Doc turned to Rosie. Pedro said, "Well, Rosita?"

"I think it went well, actually. Did you see them, esposo? They are perfect for each other. And best of all, they know it too!"

Pete and Doc looked at each other, their expressions dumbfounded, then agreed completely without a clue as to why.

# CHAPTER 18 ~~ Hunter's Morn

For Alpha Genesis the Orlif Rebels were a maddening tinnitus that rang incessantly, a brutal disordering, an asynchronous irregularity that roiled louder and louder demanding the Federation Kar's perpetual attention.

Alpha Genesis studied the pack and they him. The leader released several precious molecules of pheromone. Every member instantly translated the chemical message—an unmistakable imperative as urgent as a fire alarm's shrill klaxon. Something was missing. Find it!

The Kar had benefited, not perished, when the epoch-ending asteroid struck earth. Disease became genetic prey as Kar lifted viruses' invasive skills. It mastered cancer's mutagenic secrets. Kar switched off genes that debilitated and aged. Noxious bacteria, Clostridia spores, natural acids, toxins, venom, poisonous gasses, heavy metals, every enemy of organic life—all tamed now, slaves serving their alien lifeboat builder.

The Rebels were near. The One was near. It was time to hunt again. After they secured the One, they could finally exterminate the living pollutants on this planet.

# CHAPTER 19 ~~ Life Rising

James George had never smelled hay, straw, or pulverized corn and oat shelling, barn dust, and certainly never horse manure up close and personal. He had only seen his share vacationing in New York City when the tourist carriage horses missed their poop boots. Ginger Pat cleared her colon one last time as the contractions reached their peak. Doc Karl collected the steaming manure with a pitchfork and tossed it into the corner of the stall.

Jimmy breathed in the sweet methane and nodded. He was ecstatic, and on these rare occasions, he babbled minutiae. Doc and Renner stood on either side of Ginger's head. Jimmy said, "Horse manure, it is believed, has some tetanus-inoculating benefits, as evidenced by the low incidence of infection by horse grooms. Researchers are at a loss to explain this mysterious deviance from the expected rate of infection."

Renner whispered a steady stream of encouragement to the mare and rhythmically squeezed her upper lip in time with her contractions. He turned to Jimmy and said, "That's right, son. Keep talking now. Gin likes your voice. Her baby is almost here."

James George nodded. "Rhythmically squeezing a horse's upper lip is called 'applying the twitch'. It soothes Ginger Pat, relieves the pain, and helps her concentrate. It can be done manually or with a loop of smooth chain link attached to an oaken bat. Leather and twine work too. Human touch, however, is preferred; though, it takes some strength."

"That's right, James," Renner whispered, "Keep going."

James smiled and continued, "Mares usually give birth on their feet, but occasionally from the prone position if they are experiencing problems. Ginger Pat appears to be doing just fine. She's OK, isn't she?" he added less confidently.

Doc's hand slid slowly under the horse's abdomen. "Oh, she's doing just fine, Jimmy James. You keep talking now. Ginger Pat is an expert on motherhood."

James George took a deep breath. "Yes, Sir. Horsemen have recently discovered that a highly intricate equine language exists, and that it can be used by experts to communicate with horses."

Renner slowly raised his hand silencing the child. He said softly, "James, it's time. Come with me over here. You are about to witness the most amazing thing. Here it comes—a new life."

It happened so fast that James was not sure what had happened for a few seconds. Ginger Pat lowered her hindquarters toward the deep straw bedding and exhaled deeply with a long groan. Amniotic fluid poured outward and with it her foal plopped down solidly on the stall's padded floor.

Doc, Renner and James George moved a bit further away so Ginger Pat could inspect the newborn.

"What's she doing, Mr. McCauley?" James whispered in awe.

"She's introducing herself, James. It's called bonding. She's saying, "I'm your mama. I'll protect you and feed you and teach you all about being a good little quarter horse."

"Will she introduce us, too?"

"Yep, but not quite yet. Not until after her foal has fed a few times."

"Is it a boy or a girl? I mean, properly spoken, a colt or a filly?"

Renner turned to Doc Karl, "That's a good question. Doc, what did we get?"

"A colt. Ha! He's already got Hoot Bill's twelve bottom plow."

"Was Hoot Bill the stallion? The baby's daddy?"

"That's right. So, Jimmy James George Spencer, what do you want to name this little guy?"

James's eyes widened. "I get to name him!" he exclaimed a bit more loudly than he intended and covered his mouth.

Renner turned to the professor, "Doc, what do you think?"

"Excellent idea, Renner. A boy with that many names should certainly be an expert."

"Oh my! Oh my! But I can't think…"

Renner kneeled next to James George so they were eye to eye. "Take your time, son. A name is an important decision about a horse. Might take a few days, but it will come to you."

James took a deep breath and reverted once again to his professorial tone, "I have thoroughly studied the etiology of horse names somewhere I'm sure. Each name is a story. None is ever repeated." James closed his eyes and sifted through thousands of possible names. His eyes slowly opened, then widened. He announced, "I propose we name him, The Doctor's Ren, after you Mr. McCauley and Doc."

"'The doctor is in!' I love it!" Doc Karl exclaimed. What a perfect name, Jimmy James. I'm proud of you. No horse was ever better tagged."

Renner squeezed James's shoulder and smiled. "That's a great name, son. Doctor's Ren." The hug that followed was so natural, fatherly, that neither felt uncomfortable until Renner stood and realized what had just happened.

The barn door slid open and Kate stepped inside. She had debated all night whether she should disregard Renner's un-invitation to attend the birth. Lu said she should not. Instead, her best friend suggested that she hang herself, or better yet, throw herself from the closest cliff—preferably Mt. Stupid Bitch if such a place was available. Lu backed off only when she realized Kate was in complete agreement.

"Good morning. How's Ginger Pat doing?" Kate called down the short aisle to the foaling stall.

James bolted from the stall. "Kate! Ginger Pat had a colt, and Mr. McCauley let me name him."

"Oh, that's great, James George!" Kate looked past the child as he ran to her and watched Renner step from the stall. They stared at each other for a moment. Renner nodded and was the first to smile. He had obviously forgiven her during the long night. Kate smiled back and said, "Morning, Sheriff McCauley." Her tone was as apologetic as Renner's shy smile. "I brought breakfast and some fresh coffee. Is anyone hungry?" she said a bit more loudly for Doc's benefit.

Doc mischievously tipped Renner's cowboy hat onto his face as he walked past him. He spoke to Kate, but stared at Renner, "I'm famished, you most wonderful, kind, thoughtful and incredibly intelligent and forgiving woman, not to mention radiant! Isn't that right, McCauley?"

The rim of Renner's cowboy hat rested on the bridge of his nose. He didn't bother to push it upright. Instead, he tilted his head back, smiled and then said, "Yes Sir, I do believe she just might be."

# CHAPTER 20 ~~ Machine Rising

Alpha Genesis departed the nest that had been his hibernaculum for the last two hundred years and climbed the maze that ended near Seer Mountain's fourteen thousand foot summit. Every chamber, every artificial chute, ledge, switchback and crevice was as familiar to him as if he had carved the route just moments earlier.

Alpha Genesis interrogated with his many senses the granite envelope before him, then the mountain beyond. He clawed through the stone faster than man's most powerful drill. He breached the surface above the tree line near the summit and allowed himself a few seconds to adapt to the blindingly bright predawn and an atmosphere one-fourth as oxygen rich as his own world's. The temperature was minus thirty-three degrees Fahrenheit.

The thinner oxygen had no impact on his vigor, and the cold could no more penetrate the Kar's coat of fur than it might affect an eagle's talon. His eyes efficiently awoke to the light, as if never deprived, and melded with his many other senses.

Alpha opened all his powerful faculties and began searching for the Rebels. For twenty minutes the alien creature sniffed the air, listened telepathically, interrogated, and dismissed every clue in ways that humans with their machines might only imagine. The Rebel's second in command was gone, but he found nothing of the Rebel commander—not a molecule of lingering respiration or traces of her ancient scat or a misguided predator's remains laced with her poison. Yet, she was here somewhere, of that Alpha Genesis was positive.

He moved toward the valley, toward the lights.

# CHAPTER 21 ~~ Midas Six

In 1878 miners called it "devil's thunder." The throaty rumble soared down the Little Tokyo branch of the Midas Six goldmine and gave the mountain around it a good shake. The ten-second tremor walked several oil lamps over their granite ledges. The lanterns' lenses shattered. Troops of flames soon danced a wicked clog atop the pooling oil. Tawny dust levitated from the shaft floors. More miners' talcum floated down from the ceiling and robbed the tunnel of its already fading light. The shaft shed its pebbly skin and hailed sandy scree over Jimmy McCauley, the Little Tokyo's lone miner.

It was the sort of disturbance that sent even the most experienced miners running prissy-britches scared for the mine's bulkheads, their penitence hastened with every step and stumble. Jimmy McCauley did not run, though, nor did he summon the Master's mercy. He had endured hundreds of upheavals in his time, many much worse than this one. It did earn his complete notice, though.

Jimmy's arm froze a few inches above the ore railcar. He waited until the echoes devolved to a grinding moan and then cautiously placed an ore chunk atop the stack. The disturbance had been close, about ten feet away behind the tunnel's end wall.

Jimmy lifted a lantern and studied the shaft. He nodded and whistled softly. The walls and ceilings were still where they were supposed to be. The mountain around him had just moved. However, mountains are always on the move, one-tenth of an inch sprints every decade or so—veritable geologic hyperactivity that even ancient miners expected.

Jimmy held his breath and listened for Seer Mountain to shrug her shoulders again, but all he heard was the soothing whispers of the lantern's wick in his miner's cap as it and the other oil lamps in the corridor sipped their fuel.

Jimmy took a deep breath and felt his stampeding heart finally take the bit and slow down. "Well, what for Joe Smith kind of dance step was that, Seer Mountain, me sweet girl?" Then he playfully added, "You ain't fixin' to stomp me toes are ye?"

Jimmy liked scrape-out duty, even though it usually required him to work alone. It was an unusually good assignment for a fourteen-year-old miner, mucking out the promising ore accidentally left behind. He could work at his own pace, be his own boss, and even sing if he wanted. Right now, he needed to hear a human voice, even if it was his own. Jimmy spied a promising rock near his boot, retrieved it and playfully flipped it from behind his back into the toter. CLANK! He watched the walls warily as he worked and sang appeasement to the mountain.

"This miner's got a true love min-er-il,
Her lives way high atop Leadville,
Colorado!
And another fine sweet one
In that town of Silverton,
Colorado! Colorado!
Say three! A right smart showstopper
In that mining town called Copper,
Coloradoooooooo!
But hush. The one I wish I was a holdin'
Is that perty blonde gal from Golden,
Colorado.
Oh, she's…"

CRACKKKKKK!

The wall at the end of the mineshaft ripped open. Depressurized gas fluted through the slivering rift, producing an ear-splitting shriek and an angry, roiling fog. Standing only ten feet from the rupture, this time Jimmy dove for cover and with dread listened to the wall groan. Deafening shock waves soared down the shaft, adding their own frightening tenor. He kneeled behind the ore cart, panted three times, then rose and cautiously peeked through splayed fingers at the gas leak. His hands shook. He made fists and willed the shakes to be gone.

"Oh, Lord," he whispered. His eyes were Dutch boot heels. "It ain't methane and it ain't a cave-in, but I'm dead just for the worse. We got sour gas down here, girls. Oh Lord, so foked we are!"

Jimmy rose cautiously from behind the rock cart and backed away. He knew it was pointless to cover his mouth to avoid the poison gas. The Little Tokyo shaft was only a quarter mile long, but it might as well have been a thousand.

Jimmy flinched as the two oil lamps nearest the gas leak suddenly erupted in flames. Tendrils of pitch-fed fire rolled up the mine wall and across the ceiling where the conflagration merged to form a blinding arch. Thunder rolled from behind the wall once more and resonated down the mineshaft. Two more lanterns flared closer to Jimmy, instantly ablaze, then two more. Dozens of jagged fractures rent the end wall apart, each appearing on the granite with a cannon's resounding report. Stumbling backwards faster now, he covered his ears and shielded his eyes as much as he could. The once cool tunnel was now an oven.

Pair after pair of lanterns exploded in his retreat, as if a lamplighter ghost was marching behind Jimmy and force-feeding each lantern with heated oil. By twos—to the right and left—eighteen lamps devoured their fuel in one long gluttonous gulp, engulfed them in angry fireballs. The mine passageway turned a brilliant orange.

Jimmy withdrew, slowly at first, then in a headlong sprint. He ran just faster than the flooding gas and its flames, falling twice when the firelight faded behind bends in the shaft. He fell a third time across a rail tie and cracked a rib.

He was vaguely aware of others retreating too. Bats blurred past him in waves, as if he were only strolling not running for his life. Salamanders agitated by the bright light and rumbling instinctively climbed to higher ground where they cooked on the wall. Subrogating the human threat for a greater one, a few mine rats hopped and skittered right under his feet.

While the fire remained behind him, a more deadly menace kept pace. Dense smoke billowed along the ceiling of the shaft. Acrid clouds descended and engulfed Jimmy. He staggered another ten feet and collapsed gasping for air.

That's when he heard the voice call to him, which was really impossible because the shaft now roared with a locomotive's lungs.

"Follow! Crawl like me. Follow perty gal from Golden."

Jimmy forced open his eyes. His lungs burned. He coughed hard enough to snap a second rib. He fully expected to discover an angel waiting for him at the next bend, because the voice that had called to him was female, and the mythical Tommy Knockers, the miner's fabled guardians are male.

But it was neither an angel nor a fairy-tale dwarf wearing bibs over flannel.

"This miner's got a true love min-er-il," she called. "Follow! Crawl like me. Perty gal from Golden."

Jimmy rubbed his eyes and squinted down the passageway. He saw the creature in the jouncing shadows for only a second or two, a slash of ghostly white—a giant rat that appeared oddly human for a moment. Then the figure turned and disappeared into the darkness. Jimmy rubbed his eyes again on his sleeve, and then realized that the smoke had not yet reached the floor of the shaft, and that a two-foot smoke-free corridor still existed.

"Crawl! CRAWL! Life must save," the apparition pled.

Only three minutes had passed since the mine wall split open, and Jimmy crawled from Little Tokyo's slanted shaft. He stood up inside the main passageway and looked behind him. The smoke had found the updraft exhaust chute and was venting to the surface. He felt strangely euphoric and nauseous at the same time. He rationalized both conditions as well as his hallucinatory savior, as products of gas poisoning.

Jimmy also sensed the worst was yet to come—that the vent would soon be overwhelmed. Jimmy McCauley yanked the emergency bell's lanyard as hard and fast as he could swing his arm. Its deafening peals echoed up and down the mineshaft, spiking his eardrums with each clang. The harsh noise also enabled the boy to fight the dizzying effects of the poisonous gas he had just breathed and to focus on that all-important duty—to evacuate his fellow miners. Jimmy knew he had gotten a good dose of gas, maybe even enough to kill him, and he was scared.

Juiced with adrenaline by the ringing bell and the sure knowledge of what it meant—danger—dozens of terrified miners wordlessly flew past Jimmy. Each man leapt up the emergency escape ladder and shinnied toward the saving daylight just as fast as the man above him moved forward, rising as much by arm as leg, nose to heel, skipping more rungs than touching.

Time seemed to stop. Jimmy had been ringing the bell for only a few minutes, but it seemed like hours, perhaps the interminable last days of his life. Two lanterns exploded in the main passageway, and with them his nausea and false euphoria returned. Smoke overwhelmed the exhaust chute vent, overflowed onto the high ceiling of the main shaft, and then began its suppressing march toward the floor. In another few minutes, he knew he would not have the strength or the will to climb out. The last miner passed Jimmy. Jimmy scanned the main shaft one last time. It was clear. He climbed the ladder and became the last miner to leave the Midas Six. Unfortunately, he was not the last miner that entered it.

An hour later the furious and disbelieving mine boss, Big Bob Kilpatre, led the next crew into the Midas Six. They all died within minutes from what was later assumed to be sour gas. The gasses were not sour, but carbon monoxide is just as deadly. The mine fires had been fed freakishly by pure oxygen escaping from some even freakier tunnels that existed far below the manmade Midas Six.

Seer County authorities sealed the entrance of the Midas Six on July 13, 1878, and with it the McCauley legend and the Kilpatre curse were born.

# CHAPTER 22 ~~ First Kills

Thirty-seven-year-old Reverend Charles Pike Cooke called to his Husky-Shepherd mix, "Come along old girl! Not much farther to go now! Just a few hundred yards."

The animal was thirteen years old and struggling to keep up. Her back paws were numb to the hips and her spine felt as if a truck was sitting on it. Greta whined softly for her master to slow down.

Instead, the preacher admonished, "The bus of inspiration leaves the station with or without us, old dear! The Lord provideth grace, not for the wasteful but for the hasteful!"

Today Greta was not as dog-tired as dog-done from trekking up Seer Mountain. July hikes were one thing, but not in January on a plowed trail even on a fair morning like this one. She had not been feeling well lately. If she had been capable, Greta might have suggested, "Just leave my tired turd vendor ass at home. My hips ache. Can't see so good anymore, and piney squirrel and marmot piss now actually smell the same to me!"

"Come, Greta! We don't want to come all this way and miss this perfect winter morning light the Lord has created for our sheer enjoyment!"

She chuffed ambiguously once and followed up with one more bark, which was mostly agreeable. Greta waited until Charlie said something like, "That's my dear girl," and turned his back. The old dog promptly dropped her head and ratcheted her pace down another notch.

Reverend Cooke was a highly motivated amateur photographer. He rarely missed his weekly hike up the mountain to inventory God's larder of inspiration, which he would passionately report on the next Sabbath.

Truth was, Charlie Cooke was a far better preacher than he was a photographer. He never prepared his sermons ahead of time, but delivered them as if he had rehearsed for days.

He shot both guns at the sheriff's firing range and the bull's dirt hockey at the barbershop as proficiently as Seer's hunters and coiffured roosters. The town's punks claimed him as their dude as did the old folks at the nursing home and the frequent "parishioners" at Renner McCauley's jail and just about every regular *volk* eking out a mountain life.

He did have one flaw, though. He might have been the worst photographer in North America. Charlie's eye and the camera were not remotely connected, and no amount of expensive equipment, practice, or perfect conditions was ever going to focus that Minolta. Nothing would help him set the shutter speed correctly, keep him from aiming directly into the sun, keep his fingers off the lens, or remind him to remove the lens cap. Certainly, people would not stop speculating that Charlie "Chooke" Cooke was as blind as a bucket of snowshoe hare shit behind the camera.

\*\*\*

Alpha Genesis watched the creatures approach. He understood velocity and heading far better than any human could. Even from a distance of two miles, their pace was so slow and the route they took so predictable that interception was already inevitable.

He watched the man gesture toward the sky, then turn toward the dog. The machine studied the animal and understood something the man could not. The animal was being hesitant for some reason, which concerned Alpha for a moment. Could the animal have sensed danger?

The Kar sniffed the air, tasted it, listened on dozens of planes, and interrogated the animal's electrical sine. This was no threat. The dog was merely old, partially blind and deaf. Its joints contained the burs of late-stage arthritis. Her heart pounded irregularly, and the minor fibroid bowel obstruction would soon be major. Dozens of ulcerous infections consumed the skin under her fur, the left lung was swollen and wet and one kidney no longer functioned. The cancer had just reached the spine in the last day or two.

***

Charlie reached the natural overlook and turned around. "Greta, must I carry you the rest of the way as I did when you were a puppy? Hurry girl! Come see what you are missing!"

The view of the mountain range and the valley was truly magnificent. All of Seer City was visible six miles away. Further down the twisting alpine valley and well out of view were Seer County's only three other towns: Para, Fairhold and Rosebread.

Reverend Cooke lifted the camera to chronicle Greta's pilgrimage. He peered through the lens and found his beloved pet. Greta stopped in the middle of the path and began to growl. Her grey snout quivered, revealing yellow worn-down teeth and one missing canine. She focused on something above Charlie and to his right. The fur on her neck and back rippled, and then her body compressed and shrank close to the ground. It was not until she barked that Charlie thought mountain lion!

The Kar watched the human turn around. The camera partially covered his face. The machine could smell man's fear, an emotion that slowly shifted to curiosity—prey's real bait.

Charlie Cooke had encountered many a cougar, bear, coyote, moose and bull elk over the years, a few mean ones too—the kind that had little use for humans on their turf. He had survived every meeting just fine. What he had never gotten, however, was a decent photograph to support the skivvies-streaking tales. This time he would need a photo for sure. A good one.

He had grown up in the mountains, knew all of its critters, hunted them all his life, even though he'd rarely brought along his weapon except for personal protection. He didn't have a clue what was staring down at him just a few feet away.

"Lordy, my. What on earth are you? A rat? No fellow, you're far too large for that and far, far, too beautiful! I've never seen such a luxuriant pelt." He lowered the camera and studied the Kar. Charlie glanced down the path at his dog. Greta had backed farther away and was shivering so much her growling sounded like a chirpy whine.

113

"Hush girl!" Charlie ordered. "You are frightening it!" The dog was glad to obey and shivered in silence.

Charlie watched Alpha Genesis rise onto his hind legs. From this stance, the animal was about thirty inches tall. It pulled its front paws close to its chest. Three-inch hooked claws partially webbed with scaly hide unfurled and gently dabbed the air. Kar's paws then fanned open slowly and completely shielded the animal's entire upper torso. Above the double fanfold, two dark pits stared down from the ledge at the preacher. Shark's eyes watched Charlie.

"Easy, animal! No one is going to hurt you!" Charlie stumbled back a step as the animal rose higher on its hind legs, now appearing to be more the size of a bear cub.

Alpha Genesis' back claws drove into the rock to anchor itself with a nail gun's report. A scaly black tail rose over the animal's head, elongated and aimed a scorpion-like stinger at the preacher.

Charlie watched pebbles tumble over the low ledge and land near his feet. He said to himself, "You just sunk your claws into granite?" He then dismissed the truth as preposterous.

Alpha Genesis opened its mouth and hissed. Charlie staggered backward another step. Inch-long fangs filled the creature's mouth where its teeth should have been.

Impossible! He thought.

Without warning, the machine attacked. Charlie never saw the projectile of synthetic venom splash his face at more than a hundred miles per hour, and nearly knocking him off his feet. His eyes closed in an involuntary response, but they might as well have remained open for all the protection they provided.

The venom passed through his eyelids and blinded the preacher. The pain was momentarily excruciating, and then disappeared, only to roar to life somewhere else as the toxin soared through the man's nervous system. The deadly agent spread its lethality rapidly, moving exponentially through tens of billions of synapses, burning, and then numbing everything it touched.

Charlie reached for the ground as the paralysis spread through his torso and tore at his brain. He knew he was dying, but he still clutched the camera in his left hand. Charlie tried to scream for Greta to run, but all he produced was a sticky clack as his jaws parted once, then froze wide open—like his pet's whose retreat ended not far away. Charlie rolled onto his back and performed one last duty before he surrendered.

"By gosh and by golly, Father, you do indeed call us each home in many ways. But poisonous, spittin,' super-sized rats? I mean really! For your grace that, my Lord, I have not prayed right properly. You sure got me on that one. No disrespect intended, Almighty Father, but has any servant before me arrived here at this pearly moment and ever called you a stinker or am I the first? A giant rat! Please!"

The Rev's fanny pack had twisted at his waist as he fell and now lay on his stomach. The zipper was partially open, and the reverend clumsily pawed his way inside. Charlie Cooke was a preacher—a man of peace, love, and solitude. A good man truly and not all that disappointed that the Lord was retiring his number just now. He was also a man who entered the mountains prepared, and one who cared little for being spit upon, even if it was by the largest rat-whatever he'd ever seen.

Charlie held the camera in his left hand and the thirty-eight caliber magnum handgun in his right. He flipped off the revolver's safety then aimed both instruments where he thought the rat still might be and blindly fired away.

The gun emptied first. Charlie second. The camera had two rounds remaining on the roll when the good preacher's hand fell to his side. Unfortunately, but true to his nature, the good reverend had flipped the lens cover back on, not off as he intended.

Alpha Genesis observed the creatures die. It felt their unique magnetic and electrical signatures fade away. He recorded the exothermic loss of heat as their bodies cooled, as life drained away, and tasted his own poison dilute as the doses travelled deeper and deeper into the nonbeings' bodies. It heard their nerve tissues dissolve, their organs slow and then die. Alpha Genesis telepathically sensed the man and dog's final calls to their respective masters.

The machine also recorded the red rings emerge with a roar from the human's paw. The first bullet caught him off guard and whizzed just inches from his head. The red light was some kind of weaponry he correctly concluded, something to be absorbed if possible. As for the last five pieces of lead sent his way, he managed to anticipate their trajectory and intercept the projectiles with his body, catching the harmless slugs and then expelling them as if engaged in a brisk game of pepper ball.

Alpha Genesis would not fear this new weapon.

He studied the scene for a moment and then turned away. The Rebel commander had not had any contact with these two. The search would continue.

# CHAPTER 23 ~~ Legend of Ol' Snatch

The woman was so panic-stricken she sounded asthmatic. Gasping for breath she cawed, "Deputy Augustus! You tell Sheriff Renner McCauley I'm sick of this disgusting man. We all are. Ol' Snatch must end his eternal harassment of Seer City!"

The complainant was Miss-not-Ms. Harper Demit, Seer City's old maid pharmacist. It had only taken Gus two minutes to walk from the Sheriff's Office to the dire emergency, but Miss Demit's histrionics had already attracted a small crowd outside her pharmacy. Albeit an audience that was keeping a safe distance until Harper's shrieking died down to that of her suspected namesake—Harpies. When she was excited, as now, Miss Demit's high-pitched voice was believed capable of remotely cutting, etching and beveling glass all the way to Denver. Mortal eardrums were no match for a full-on Demit fit.

Gus approached Miss Demit slowly, gesturing calmingly with his hands, as if he were reassuring a spooked mare. He whispered, "It's okay. It's okay now. "Tell me what happened, Harper."

The pharmacist gasped one last time and struggled to speak. "This time he nearly scared me to death, Gus. I mean it! I swear my heart actually stopped." Miss Demit dabbed her forehead with a lacy handkerchief while her other hand tapped a spot above her heart. A sympathetic murmur of agreement rose as the crowd eased in.

Deputy Augustus raised his hands and implored the crowd to be quiet, "I know, Miss Demit. So am I. We all are. If we could

117

capture Snatch, we would. Fact is, we still don't have a clue who he is or why he's so obsessed with everyone's trash." Augustus pointed at the litter scattered across the sidewalk. "He sure can make a mess when he gets hurried, though. Good God!"

Someone shouted, "Here's a clue, Gus. I say he's a nut job. Snatch belongs in the GD booby hatch."

Someone else chimed in, "Nut job my ass. I say he's an identity thief and belongs in the iron bar hotel."

"I still say he's a ghost!" a third person shouted from the back. The crowd quieted and turned toward the speaker. This was not a new theory. In fact, it was the least spoken best kept urban legend in Seer County.

"Rubbish, Douglas Hubbard! Damnable rubbish, you old fool!" pharmacist Harper Demit literally screeched "fool". Her face purpled. Lips still quivering, she turned and studied the crowd and instantly regretted her overreaction. By the way everyone looked at her, and with more than a few still covering their ears belatedly, she knew right away her voice had betrayed her. Beanpole police-whistle Harper Demit was privately in Hubbard's ghost camp.

Hubbard stepped forward. He was two feet shorter than the pharmacist was and at the waist almost as wide as he was tall. He had a toothless, ear-to-ear smile that made his round face appear both full moon and quarter moon at once.

Thanks to Miss Demit, Hubbard also now had everyone's complete attention. "Well, for one thing, he's been snatching trash here in Seer City longer than any of us been borned. And, and uh, reason "B" I call it, the crapola he takes no one wants. It's all been throwed away. Nasty stuff. Old stinky work boots. Hospital waste. Restaurant garbage. Snot rags and other unmentionables." Hubbard paused and studied his fingers. "And uh, uh, fourthly damn it! I can't r'member my third reason. Shit!"

The crowd chuckled, including Deputy Augustus. Every village has an idiot, and Hubbard was the undisputed king of dingbats in Seer City.

The deputy used the break in the tension. "Look folks, the truth is this. Snatch doesn't steal identities and he has never once hurt anyone and…"

Junior Riggs jumped in and interrupted Gus. "What do you mean he's never hurt anyone, Gus? He kidnapped that helpless little baby boy. What was it, eight, ten years ago? That old hippie, Curtis Judy seen him do it!"

Gus raised his hand and said, "Hold on now, Junior. First off, didn't your mama teach you it's impolite to interrupt someone when they're speaking?"

Senior Riggs, a tall heavyset man in the back wrapped his arm over Junior's shoulder and answered. "Ah, don't blame my baby boy, Gus. He can't help himself from interrupting you. It's genetic. I love Junior's mama dearly, but if the word "edgewise" was a tool, it'd still be sitting in its original package brand new at my house. I haven't finished a sentence on my own around Junior's mama in thirty two years."

Everyone laughed, including Junior Riggs. He turned to his father. He winked and said, "That's true, Pop, but what if I tell Mom what you been saying about her."

"You can sure give it a try, Son. But, I'm not too concerned you'll ever get more than halfway onto the highway before she blathers you off into the first ditch."

Gus waited for the laughter to settle down again. "Okay, okay, if I may continue, here are the facts. Curtis Judy did not witness a kidnapping. He never said he did. Curtis claims he might've seen Ol' Snatch leave that baby boy on the steps of the fire station across the street from his house. We suspect that Ol' Snatch, or someone, must've found the little fellow abandoned somewhere and did the right thing by turning him over. Secondly, Curtis said it was dark, and it was late, and well, he might've been self-medicating that night. We all know what it means when that old hippie self-medicates. Right?"

The crowd murmured agreement. A few laughed a little bit too knowingly. Curtis didn't sell pot in Seer City, but it was well known that he did share generously with anyone still into the *Doors* or *Strawberry Alarm Clock*.

Gus continued, "So maybe Curtis Judy did see something that night eight or nine years ago. On the other hand, maybe Curtis Judy just *saw* something, if you're hearing me right. But, here's the bottom line. Ol' Snatch is a lot of things, folks, but he ain't no baby snatcher. We're sure of that. Agreed?"

The crowd nodded and shrugged and murmured general agreement. Outside of littering and occasionally causing some folks to leave a skid mark or three in their undermentionables, Snatch had never bothered, let alone hurt a soul in anyone's memory.

With Curtis Judy's and Snatch's reputation restored, Deputy Augustus continued, "Now back to his Dumpster diving. Snatch doesn't damage property, and what he takes has been thrown out, so he's not technically breaking any laws either. From a law enforcement viewpoint, we are more concerned about his welfare than his littering. So, just approach your trash bins as you would during fall bear season after a dry spring. Make a lot of racket and give him a chance to skedaddle. I'm sure he's more scared of you than you are of him."

Lynn Happe, the Stewart Law Office receptionist asked, "Harper, did you see what Ol' Snatch took this time?"

"Hair!" the pharmacist screamed in disgust. A shiver racked her body as she recalled the moment. "He had a hand full of clipped hair from the beauty shop next door. And dear God, some of it was mine I fear."

"I remember!" Doug Hubbard shouted. Everyone turned his direction again, "I remember my third reason. It's this here, listen up!" Hubbard waited until everyone was looking at him. His voice was melodramatic. His wild gestures and animated expressions belonged to a camp counselor telling a ghost story around a campfire. "Ol' Snatch, he ain't really old like his name, now is he? No! He don't seem to get no older. He moves about perty much the same way now as when I was a durn kid myself. He's quicker than fast! Nimble as hurry up! Stronger than a, uh, a circus strongman! So, maybe he's like them spooks in TV movies and such. He's a dang ghost, people! That's what Snatch really... issssssss."

No one spoke. Deputy Augustus studied the faces in the crowd. He had heard the theory repeated many times since he was a kid. As the years passed, the idea that Snatch was something supernatural had gained spooky traction, especially in small private gatherings where denial most easily dissolves. Snatch could outrun anyone in town, and his physical strength was legendary. Most curious, Hubbard was right. Snatch never seemed to age; although, no one had ever seen his face.

Gus did everyone a favor and broke up the Halloween party. "I don't know about you folks, but I've got work to do, so I'm going to move along if there's nothin' else."

Miss Demit, anxious to get out of Doug Hubbard's dim minded spotlight said, "Of course, go on Gus. Sorry I got you involved." She raised her voice so everyone was sure to hear her. "And you're right! That poor old soul Snatch. We should pity him, not fear him. I for one certainly do not think of him a ghost." She lifted her chin a bit too high, cut through the crowd and hurried back inside her pharmacy.

# CHAPTER 24 ~~ Poacher Poaching on Cruel Lake

"Goddamn it, Compton! If we got us a goddamn problem, let's hear it." The poacher lowered his rifle for a moment then shook it at his side in frustration. His eyes darted nervously from one clump of brush to another along the shore of the hot springs and glacier fed lake. The late morning sky was perfectly clear, the winds light.

"It ain't exactly a problem just so, Smitty."

"Then what the hell is it that's got you so spooked. Not like we never poached up here before. Too many fuckin' elk anyhow. Rats with racks is all they is as far as I'm concerned."

"I hear that! Goddamned mountain is covered with elk duds." Compton angrily ground a pile of fresh elk droppings with his boot heel as if he was extinguishing a nasty two-cent cigar. But agreeing away the anxiety didn't work.

"Talk to me! You smellin' DNR, Felix Compton?"

Compton's smile was sickly, belying his inexplicable unease. "Nope, no ranger ever made my balls crawl like this, Smitty. Something's watching us. Been watching us for a while. Lookin' at us right goddamned now. I feel it!"

"Cougar?"

"No...not like that."

"Bear?"

"No, but it sure as hell feels like bear." Like when we brought down that griz cow up in Montana. Us huntin' her. Her huntin' us for damn near a day."

"Fuck for crissake, Compton. The griz has been done hunted out this far south in Colorado."

As far as personality extremes might go, criminals are as yin and yang as the next socioeconomic team. Compton was always the most amiable of the pair, that is, until his sixth sense awoke.

Compton screamed, "Do you fuckin' think I don't know that, you stupid son-of-a-bitch?" He shook his rifle threateningly, and his expression suggested even more.

Hewlett Smith raised both hands palms out and backed away a step. Compton might have been the biggest grinner between the two poachers under normal circumstances, but he also was the biggest sinner. Two years ago, Renner McCauley sent the remains of another poacher to Denver in a black bag. Its perforated and nearly decapitated parcel represented the last man who had doubted Felix Compton's hearing.

"Solid, Pards! Be smart now. This is ol' Smitty talkin' at you. Not that pine oil pissin' punk what called you a 'Carrie Freak.' I believe in your...your gift. Yes, I do and you know that. Now put that damn gun down and lets you and me just figure out what we is up against."

Instead, Compton whirled toward the lake and raised the gun. He scanned the water down the barrel. Hewlett Smith jumped next to his partner and raised his own weapon. He really did believe. He then spun back toward the forest and whispered, "I got our backs, partner. What the hell is it?"

The alien machine ducked under the water about ten yards from the boulder-strewn shoreline. Alpha Genesis had stalked the humans for about twenty minutes. He lay there inertly, bobbing on the light waves, probing the men with his powerful senses for any clues about the lone surviving Rebel.

Alpha Genesis had almost dismissed the two men as irrelevant and moved on when he detected something different about the agitated one—the presence of higher senses. Of course, the human's extrasensory sensitivity was primitive, little more than a fragile seed which if permitted to germinate and grow and given fifty-to-sixty million years might compare to Alpha Genesis' telepathic powers.

Alpha Genesis exploited weaknesses in an enemy as well as strengths. Every mutation presented a potential opportunity, even those whose genetic introgression—the infiltration of genes from the gene pool of one species into that of another—posed a danger to the alien. There were other ways to use the enemy's adaptations to the Kar's advantage.

Felix Compton shuddered from the dual chills of the thirty-three degree lake water, and the vivid image of watching himself and Hewlett Smith standing back-to-back on the shoreline. The vision was so perfect, that he stepped forward and looked directly at the spot on the water where Alpha Genesis floated.

Then Compton's eyes rolled back in their sockets and a different kind of coldness rose through his body as the alien gave the poacher a taste of some real Carrie Freak.

Alpha Genesis' shark eyes shifted to the lowered rifle, then to Hewlett Smith's back. Compton's white slits slaved to the rifle, then to his best friend's back. He deposited a single round into the base of Smith's skull. Then without hesitation, he placed the barrel under his chin, and the weapon roared one more time.

# CHAPTER 25 ~~ Missing Persons

Deputy Gus Augustus glanced at his watch and then at the wall clock situated above a mismatched bank of four-drawer file cabinets. It was two in the afternoon, and his shift until now had been uneventful. With Mayor Kilpatre and Cyril Hoop gone somewhere, the day had been delightfully dead—what cops everywhere call OTJR (on the job retirement). With the exception of three separate reports of Ol' Snatch appearances, which was an unusually high number of complaints but nowhere near a record, the day was unremarkable.

Gus had been up since four a.m. The deputy yawned and scratched his stubble-darkened cheek with a wooden ruler. The woman on the other end of the phone line tried to remain calm but concealed her concerns about as effectively as hiding a hundred pound pumpkin in a skirt pocket.

Wives calling in when husbands did not was not particularly unusual around hunting season in Seer County or when the trout ran or during mudslide season or when the kayaks bucked the white water or when the first avalanche alerts went out or when dollar draft beer season arrived down at Mickey Bear's Inn Ore Out Tavern. The sheriff's phone rang year-round with "Where's my fill-in-the-blank?" calls.

However, Gus's concern soon caught up with this caller's, Mrs. Charles Cooke, also known around town as Mrs. Rev. "Well, I'm sure it's nothing to worry about," Gus said and then asked, "But what's the latest Chooke ever returned from his Writer Postern's hike, Samantha?"

"Noon, Gus, and that was…was years ago! Back when Greta was just a puppy—she was so darling—and she just couldn't leave those darling little whistle pigs alone. Chooke always swore—still swears—not really!—but you know what I mean—marmots were put on earth for no other reason than to exercise poor Greta."

Mrs. Rev's veiled composure slipped down yet another notch, and she spoke more rapidly now. The deputy understood why. He had heard a version of her panic many times before. The ebullient spousal smokescreens, the irrational digression from the current dilemma to a safer time, the Freudian verb tense slips, the unwillingness to ask for help, and a manic mind—all evidence of a quickening anxiety inherent to mountain life and the ultimate tariff it too frequently imposed.

Gus mercifully permitted her to believe he didn't notice the breadth and depth of her growing fears. He asked instead, "Would you feel better if I took the ATV up the trail, Samantha? When I find him, I promise I won't say you were worried, or even that you called the office. Okay? He knows we patrol the trails ever so often. I'll just leave it at that and bring him and Greta home."

"If it's not too much to ask, bless you Gus! I would be forever beholden."

"Don't be. I could use the fresh air. Renner McCauley frowns on his deputies napping on the job. We'll call you either way in about an hour. He probably just took a few extra rolls of film with him to shoot. That's all." Gus bit his lower lip and smiled.

Judging by the way Samantha Cooke relaxed and laughed for the first time, Gus's comment had the desired effect. Her husband's reputation with a camera had obviously reached home, perhaps even originated there.

# CHAPTER 26 ~~ Curtis Judy

Curtis Judy was a tree hugger, or more accurately a professional tree hugger, because it was the only thing he did in his life that approximated working. This was a very busy week in the Saving the Mammy Planet business. Yesterday, the forty-one-year-old trust baby hitched a ride to Vail with some members of the Mexican itinerant carpentry persuasion. The *señors* sought employment in resort construction while Curtis protested that very subject—the resort's expansion into a highly dubious lynx habitat.

The day before found him at the former Cañon Mesa Nuclear Waste Depository yipping and carping from behind the horse-enforced protest line as the *Federalés* of the Department of Energy sent another load of low level radioactive waste down I-25 on flatbed trucks for decontamination in New Mexico. He put up no more ruckus than necessary, because the mounted sheriff's deputies are real gents, and they always respected a protester's rights. No surprise though, many of the social complainants were also horse people, and that affords special courtesies in Colorado.

Two days ago, he drove over to Bronson County and removed several real estate signs from private property situated near a piece of BLM land. True to his harmless nature he left the signs undamaged and stacked where the real estate agents could easily find them. He even marked the signs' empty postholes with pinecones so no more drilling was necessary to replace the miniature billboards. Curtis Judy's motto was, "Annoy often. Amuse always."

Today was special. Today, Curtis Judy commenced his own investigation of Felix Compton and Hewlett Smith, two local men whose poaching had moved far beyond the category of alleged.

His stalk-u-mentary started poorly, though. Trailing about a half mile behind the poachers, the photo sleuth guessed the wrong fork on White Root path and ended up on the opposite side of Cruel Lake from his quarry.

That is also how and from where he witnessed his first murder-suicide. In an investigative bungle rivaling Yogi's Ranger Smith and armed only with his mighty 60X TeleStar camera, he watched the last moments of Felix and Hewlett's lives through the telescopic lens.

When Felix swung around and aimed the rifle across Cruel Lake, Curtis Judy was sure he had been spotted. He ducked, and then rose slowly,cursing his stupidity. Compton was not equipped with a riflescope, just a pair of Navistar headlamp lenses for eyeglasses that were famously translucent with grime.

Huggin' Judy held his ground and snapped frame after gory frame. He captured the whole incident on film, even when the poachers' pink-gray brains streaked through the air on misty, chunky arcs and splattered against the rocks just seconds apart. Curtis shot the final scene six times. He would've finished the roll except for the sudden need to vomit.

Curtis hurled the last of his seven-grain breakfast in the rocks and considered his options. In the end, he decided not to bother scurrying around the one-mile shoreline to see if anything could be done for the enemy. It really wasn't necessary, he decided. The dead men didn't have all that many brains to waste in the first place, and those they once had now fed the first of the lucky ravens swooping in from the north.

If Curtis hurried, he would be back in town by three o'clock, perhaps as soon as two thirty if he hauled ass. This was big.

\*\*\*

Alpha Genesis recorded each camera shutter click. He captured the metallic whirring of the device with no greater difficulty than hearing the nearby roar of the weapon or later the sound of the man vomiting into the lake or later yet his footfalls as the human collected his backpack and disappeared into the forest.

The distant mechanical clatter wasn't totally foreign, though, just different from that emitted by Chuck Cooke's less expensive camera earlier today. Alpha recognized the cadence of the machine—the background hum and the signature high-pitched squeal.

The speed of sound is not constant, but each of its infinite deviations from theoretical represented a single variant incorporated in Kar's memory. Thousands of times faster than man's supercomputers, the alien extrapolated from the constant: distance, directional vector, wind speed, humidity, atmospheric density, frequency and ambient temperature and then reran each of the thirty-three distinct repetitions exactly as the events occurred moments earlier on the beach. Alpha Genesis replayed the two kills in perfect detail. The alien discovered that the camera had clicked only when the scene changed. Unlike the man with the dog, these sounds were not random.

The human who had cowered on the other side of the lake had a weapon—a machine—and for the alien all weapons must be investigated. However, the evidence revealed something else, perhaps something even more important, and that caused Alpha to abandon the poachers' corpses to pursue Curtis Judy's fading scent.

A tiny blood vessel had ruptured in Curtis's left eye when he vomited. Molecules of the man's DNA jettisoned away. Most of the massive molecules fell into the lake, but not all of them. A few caught the wind and sailed across the lake.

A single DNA molecule clung to a sensor follicle on the machine's snout. The analysis revealed something critical about the enemy. The creature was gentle, caring—characteristics suddenly more important than the clicking weapon. These attributes were Orlif.

Turning toward the opposite shoreline, Alpha dove under a wave. The machine's body elongated, narrowed, and cleaved the next wave like a knife. The black scaly tail flattened and whipped powerfully from side-to-side and propelled him forward. For the first time in three million years, the alien swam the reptile's stroke.

# CHAPTER 27 ~~ Routine Illusion

Gus would miss his prearranged afternoon call with Renner, but they had devised a sophisticated, foolproof contingency plan. The sheriff would call back when he got in the mood. Augustus walked over to the dispatch desk and lifted the mike. Other than Freckles Randahl, who had decided he was still too intoxicated from last night to drive home safely, Gus was alone at the jail. "Base to seven."

The radio crackled. "Seven to base," Deputy Skip Wise answered from a few miles outside town.

Gus ordered his deputy back to the office. "Proceed to Zulu."

Skip Wise cleared his throat in the open mike—a protest of sorts. He had missed lunch while chasing a black bear from the city campgrounds, which put him about an hour behind schedule on his assigned patrol. He puffed his cheeks and contemplated the comestible nightmare of pulling yet another candy bar for lunch from the vending machine at headquarters. "Copy, base."

Gus grabbed the keys for the department's all-terrain vehicle and initialed the checkout clipboard. The gas tank was full and the first aid kit and radio had been inspected just two days ago. He then asked the deputy his current location, "State your twenty, seven."

"North 662-A. ETA is eight minutes, Base."

"Copy, Seven. I'll arrange to have Twenty-nine refuel you." Fuel was food. Twenty-nine was Maggie Augustus's perpetual age.

"Copy, copy, Base." Which meant, 'Thank you very much, Boss!'

# CHAPTER 28 ~~ Curtis On the Rocks

The alien machine accelerated its strokes in the last five yards to the shoreline and literally rolled onto the beach where Curtis Judy had stood with his camera earlier. The creature found its feet and inspected the scene. He showed no fatigue after propelling himself across nearly a quarter mile of open water at a speed far faster than any human might in a boat equipped with an outboard engine.

Alpha Genesis oriented his body so the wind would pass across the human's lair and wash any surviving clues over the alien creature. The human was male, and his lifespan was nearly half expired.

The Kar turned and disappeared into the aspen and ponderosa forest. He would follow the animal to its nest where all creatures naturally feel safe.

# CHAPTER 29 ~~ Call for Chooke Cooke

Deputy Augustus found the preacher's '93 Ford F-150 pickup parked in the trailhead turnout. The keys were in the ignition. The sign on the windshield read as always:

By order of Jesus, this vehicle may be commandeered in the event of a medical emergency.
— The Rev

Under his signature, Chooke listed local emergency numbers, their addresses and a MapQuest map to each. A Tracfone cell phone dangled from the steering wheel with the instructions: USE ME!

Gus Augustus felt like a million bucks in crisp ones and fives as he slipped the ATV off the asphalt highway and began the long climb up Writer Postern's Trail. He gave the machine a little extra gas, and it launched like a spry colt up the sandy dirt path.

Even the weather seemed playful, sunny and in the low forties, with a light easterly breeze—unusually mild for January. Gus sang an old mining tune as he climbed higher into the alpine wilderness, humming the tune softly when he forgot the words, growling while negotiating the worst of the trail's washouts and rogue snowdrifts.

"This miner's got a true love min-er-il.
Her lives way high atop Lead-ville
… Colorado!"

Gus' thoughts slowly drifted back to the task. If Chooke Cooke had indeed lost track of time while defiling nature with that Kodak blind eye of his, he certainly deserved forgiveness on a beautiful day like this. Gus, like most folks in Seer City, liked the good Rev, and he looked forward to his company on the return trip down the mountain.

Gus glanced down at the ATV's odometer a few minutes later as it clicked past three miles. He winced and made a mental note of what that hope-draining metric might portend.

At this altitude, the temperature had dropped to close to freezing. The shadows lengthened and spread over the landscape. The popular trail was snowplowed every other day. In some places, snow furrows rose six to eight feet while other sections of the trail were as clear and dry as in August.

Limits of survival surrounded Gus as he climbed the trail. The aspen petered out into groves of scrubby, spidery dwarfs that thinned and then disappeared completely. On this south face, short sparse patches of dry grasses replaced their full, tall cousins. Only the spruce and ponderosa climbed on up the mountain, but even they would succumb at the barren alpine tree line.

Gus eased off the accelerator and coasted to a stop at a dry turnout on the trail. He glanced into the valley. The spectacular view was wasted on him now.

He turned the ignition key and the ATV engine growled to a stop. The pine forest came alive around him. Wind rumbled up and down the ravines and gullies and over countless rock faces and whisked every needle-leaf tree into a unified hiss. Millions of tree limbs creaked and groaned encouragement to keep the good scratch going.

"Two to Base."

Skip must have been sitting at the dispatcher's desk because his response was immediate. "Base to Two. State your twenty, Two."

"I'm four miles up Writer Postern's Trail and stationary. The lower area is clear." Translation: I haven't found Chooke yet. "Any new weather to report?" Translation: Did you speak with Samantha and is Chooke home yet?

"Forecast is unchanged."

"Copy, Base. Two out."

# CHAPTER 30 ~~ Civic and Sick

With one hand, Curtis Judy pointed at his camera which was sitting on the corner of the deputy's desk. The other hand nervously twisted a rubber-banded ponytail poking out from under his ratty blue sock cap. A few flecks of vomit stubbornly clung to his beard.

"I've got proof! Photos! There is absolutely no doubt about it, Deputy Wise. The bastards are dead. I recorded the whole thing from across the lake." He paused and then added distantly, "Which I think is no big loss to humanity."

Skip Wise did not doubt that the man was telling the truth, at least as much as he saw of it, but Felix Compton killing his partner and then himself was, well, it was ridiculous. It was almost as ridiculous as this tree hugger claiming he witnessed it in such vivid detail and from clear across Cruel Lake—over four hundred yards of water. On the photography I.Q. scale, Skip Wise was far closer to Chooke Cooke than Curtis Judy.

"Are you positive, Curtis? The Cruel is foggy this time of year from them hot springs feeding it. And, if it was Smith and Compton, they are mountain boys after all, and they probably knew you were following them. I bet they staged the whole thing just to scare you off their trail."

135

Curtis screamed, "I saw their fuckin' brains, Skip, land in the rocks and shit. They splashed like a mess of fish guts. I heard two shots not seconds apart. Smith first, then Compton waxed himself as casually as pouring each a cup of coffee. It wasn't that foggy today. I saw what I saw!"

"Calm down now, Curtis, before you hurt yourself." Skip raised his hands and leaned away. "I believe you saw something just absolutely horrible, but you were a long way away, like you said, and Felix and Hewlett are poachers for sure, but they aren't the kind of men prone to poach themselves. Good God!"

"Well then you explain it, because there is no way they knew I was following them."

"Okay. Maybe it wasn't Smith and Compton at all. Maybe what you saw was one of those film crews making one of those *Blair Witch* rip-off movies. They sneak up here all the time you know—the little You Tube shits. By the way, did you ever see that show, Curtis? My niece in Steamboat found an old DVD, and she got scared sick for pity according to my sister-in-law."

Well, he had done his civic duty by reporting the murder-suicide like a good little scout. He would head home now, develop the pictures, and then post them on the Internet. To hell with the cops, he decided.

Skip leaned toward Curtis. "But if it'd make you feel any better, Deputy Augustus is patrolling near Cruel Lake right now. I'll ask him to check it out."

Curtis sighed. "Whatever, man. It's your gig now. Count me out." His returning nausea contradicted that statement and replayed in his mind's eye the murder-suicide—two corpses lying unnaturally in the rocks like rag dolls, their blood inching toward the water. Curtis feared this was the kind of nightmare that never let you wake up. "Just tell Gus to be careful. I'm telling you something's fucked up, man." He stared at Skip for a moment, then turned and left.

The ringing phone startled the deputy. He double fumbled the handset before answering, "Seer County Sheriff's Department, this is Deputy Wise."

"Hey, Skipster. This is Puck."

Skip smiled at the sound of an old friend's voice. "Let me guess, Mr. Ortez, you're over at the bowling alley having an urgent planning session with BB in the lounge."

"Call it the never-ending demands of big business, Skipper."

"Hmm. I call it two-dollar beer pitchers."

"Same. Same. Look, Skip, the reason I'm calling is because I just got a call from my wife."

"Well, hell. If BB is with you, what are you so worried about?"

Puck chuckled. "Shit, Ben Bainbridge can't handle what he's got at home let alone Hernando Cortez's hellcat descendant." He waited for Skip to finish laughing. "But anyway, she just got a call from Angelica Smith."

Skip stiffened. "Really. That would be Hewlett Smith's wife?"

"Same. Seems he went for a hike this morning with that no account son-of-a-bitchin' weirdo Felix Compton. That's a quote. Hike this and kiss that to those goddamned poachers."

"Truth. Go on."

"Well, he was supposed to be back by three o'clock to take her to see a belly doctor over in Introit."

Skip's mouth was suddenly dry. "Dr. Sterl."

"Say what, Skip?"

The deputy cleared his throat and said more clearly, "That'd be Dr. Ryan Sterl. He's one of them gastro docs. He scoped me maybe a year ago for the cancer. Didn't find nothing, thank God. So what's all this about, Puck?"

"Well, Angelica doesn't drive, so she asked my wife to haul her over there since Hewlett wasn't home. Of course, Tooty said she would. Good excuse for her and BB's better half to go shoppin' with the kids."

"So, was Hewlett supposed to drive her to Introit?"

"Yep, and he's never late, Skip, according to Angelica."

"And?"

"Well, she says Hewlett has always said, 'If I'm ever late, I'm either in McCauley's jailhouse or I'm dead.' I guess she's just checkin' out which it is. She asked me to find out, seeings how the sheriff's office and the Smith's office are professionally conflicted so to speak."

"He's not here, Puck. But I suddenly wish he was right here sippin' mud, my very best bud."

"Why for the love of donuts for dollars would you wish that, Skip?"

"Hard to explain, just a feeling—a bad one. Thanks, Puck. Bye." He hung up the phone before Puck Ortez could reply.

# CHAPTER 31 ~~ Dead Men Don't Melt

Deputy Gus Augustus arrived at the scene of the killings on Writer Postern's Trail. He found Greta first, fully infected with the alien toxins. "What the hell?" the deputy whispered. His voice trembled. It was the shaky signature of someone returning home to find his comfortable reality tossed upside down by a burglar—CDs and Cheerios unnaturally commingled under a shattered window. Deputy Augustus stood up on the ATV and slowly climbed off. He could not take his eyes off the animal's corpse.

His stomach turned. The odor burnt his eyes, clawed at his throat. Nausea and vertigo yanked Mt. Seer out by its roots and sent it spinning sickeningly toward the horizon. Of course, Gus had no idea that things were about to get much worse. The finale was near, the point when the Kar's venom dissolved its victims.

"My God!" The surface of the animal's corpse began to bubble and rise. The carcass ballooned, tripling its size. Gus stepped away expecting it to pop. Instead, the flesh split open in several places. Steam whistled from each vent. The furry husk then collapsed on itself. Greta's hide untethered from her skeleton and slid to the side, now resembling a toothy, hunting lodge rug. Her skeleton collapsed under its own weight and crumbled into chalky sand.

Hundreds of ulcers opened on the dog's hide. Her silver and black fur follicles shrank as if hoarfrost receiving the mornings rays. The ulcerous rings converged and lumps of skin sloughed into ragged sections. The dog's last remains liquefied. A tarry stream of former pet moved glacially a few feet down the trail. It thinned and effervesced until there was nothing left.

Greta was nearly gone. Her teeth were the last to liquefy before Deputy Augustus' eyes, seemingly little more than waxy bits of Halloween costume teeth pitched into a campfire.

The deputy stumbled backward another step as he realized for the first time just how close he was to danger. "Must be acid! But who'd do such a thing to Greta?" he whispered. He touched his sidearm subconsciously and studied the surrounding cliffs and tree lines for signs of the pet's attacker. Seeing no threats, Gus took a cautious step forward and squatted next to the scene. Greta's copper dog tag was all that remained of her.

Of course, acid doesn't usually eat from the inside out, and it's not a fast process or one that reacts with such efficiency.

Gus heard more hissing. He turned and discovered a second stream of viscous black sludge flowing toward him. The human magma boiled and steamed, thinned, and then disappeared like water poured over a red-hot skillet. Gus removed his weapon and aimed it at an unseen enemy.

By the time Gus rounded the bend on the trail, Reverend Cooke was gone. "Oh fuck, what's going on?" Gus's heart pounded in his throat. Perspiration beaded on his forehead. The freezing air burned his lips and tongue. When his radio hissed and Skip Wise spoke, Gus nearly fired his sidearm fumbling for the radio.

"Base to Two. Base to Two."

Gus answered. "TWO," he screamed. He panted three times, then forced himself to say again more calmly, "Two, over."

"Base requests a radio check." Translation: Change frequencies to reduce the risk of eavesdropping.

"Copy, Base." Gus was glad to comply.

"Three six, three seven. Three niner. End. Repeat." Translation: Thirty-nine divided by three, turn to channel thirteen.

Gus said, "Copy," and repeated the code then switched to the more secure channel.

Formality was suspended. "Gus, I just received a report that there may have been a murder-suicide up at Cruel Lake. I also received some corroborating evidence that makes the first report compelling. Can you hike over there after you find Chooke?"

Radio in one hand, his weapon extended before him, Gus's face drained of all but a drop or two of blood. "Skip?" The deputy's heavy breathing along with the steady wind created an eerie ghostlike hiss over the radio that made his voice distant, almost unrecognizable.

"Yes?"

All that remained of the preacher was the metal in his clothing—the rivets in his jeans, zippers, the hinges on his glasses. Even synthetic fibers and plastic were consumed. "I've... I've got a bad situation up here, Skip.

Skip Wise held the mike away from his mouth and stared at it. "Gus! What happened?" He waited a moment and then screamed. "Gus! Talk to me!"

Augustus kneeled down and examined Chooke Cooke's revolver. He recognized the engraving on its barrel: "Jesus wept. Rev kept." The handgun was engraved with the Bible's shortest verse. It had been a present to the Rev from the gun club a few years back. He also ID'ed Chooke's camera which strangely seemed undamaged. He noted it had fallen several feet away. The gun's wooden grip was missing, though. Its steel newel was all that remained.

Augustus shivered with the dual palsies of horror and nausea. He studied the bits of metallic litter on the ground—the last mark on the world left by Charles Cooke.

"Gus! Talk to me!"

Gus lifted the radio. "Subject found." Then he added, "Skip?"

"Yes, Gus!"

"Recall One." Translation: Send for McCauley.

"Do you need special assistance?"

"Negative. But... Base, say again regarding incident on Cruel Lake."

"Curtis Judy claims he witnessed Felix Compton shoot Hewlett Smith in the back of the head, then turn the rifle on himself." Skip hesitated, then added, "Smith's wife also reports her husband missing. Says it's out of character."

"I'll check it out. Call Renner. Stat!"

"Copy."

Most of the eyelets of Chooke's hiking boots remained on the path along with his zipper, the handgrip-less revolver, some pocket change, a wedding band, three gold crowns, a couple buttons, a pocketknife without its plastic ornamentations, a belt buckle (its pin still set on the bar), a crucifix, and Chooke's camera. The deputy lifted the expensive camera and then the revolver.

He opened the revolver's chamber and discovered that Chooke had apparently gone down with a fight—all six bullets had been fired. A tick mark etched each empty shell casing.

Gus turned the camera over. The frame counter revealed Chooke had snapped at least twenty exposures today. One might reveal his attacker. Gus turned the camera around and sighed, "Oh, Chooke. No!" The lens cover was closed.

As anxious as he was to leave the trail, Deputy Augustus forced himself to endure a few minutes of proper police investigation. Gus stowed his radio and weapon and turned toward the ledge where the alien machine had stood and lobbed its poison.

Gus returned to the ATV and dropped Chooke's remaining belongings into separate plastic evidence bags. He then climbed onto the ledge where he sensed the attack began.

It only took him a minute or so to find in the rocks three of the bullets that the monster had harmlessly caught and expelled with his abdomen. He dropped the rounded slugs in a separate evidence bag, noting where he'd found them in his notebook. Ordinarily, he would leave the evidence where he found it, but snow was forecasted tonight, so protocol had to be different.

Next, he found the spot on the level ledge where the alien pried the granite apart to anchor itself. The indentations were far too symmetrical to be natural. The cuts in the rock were fresh and clean with no evidence of moss or sediment.

Gus grew up in the mountains. His Boy Scout leader had been a full-blooded Ute, a man who still taught wilderness investigation techniques at the police academy in Denver. Gus was positive the rocks had been pried apart recently—probably just hours ago. He carefully collected a few pebbles near the fissures and then departed for Cruel Lake.

# CHAPTER 32 ~~ Alien Recon

Alpha Genesis crept unseen into Seer City.    Human chaos bombarded the machine's sensors from miles away.  The assault did not annoy him.  Annoyance was an emotion.

Nor was it a challenge to record and analyze the terabytes of information arriving each second—the thousands of simultaneous conversations it heard—some face to face, others by telephone or by radio.  Four square miles of babies cried, cooed, and snored.  Radios, stereos, CD and DVD players and iPods played an infinite range of beat, lyric and notes.  Televisions roared on hundreds of cable and satellite stations.  Car horns clamored howdy-do, watch-out, and it's green get the fuck going.  Cars with bad starters laughed *hee-hee-hee* at their owners.  Children shrieked on their playgrounds while senile old folks mumbled complaints at their keepers.

Kar heard it all, absorbed it, and analyzed every decibel emitted from every source—animal and mechanical.  It literally saw the radio, television, and cellular sound waves soaring through the valley, each with their unique sine.

He felt the drizzle of electricity leaching from the city's power grid.   He listened to numbers dialed on hundreds of telephone keypads, and then across town as some phones rang and rang, while others were answered.  He learned the pattern amidst the deafening

142

roar of humanity, even predicted where some calls were destined. Alpha Genesis concluded phones were like his telepathy, not nearly as efficient, but clearly dangerous. Alpha paused and focused on the curiously faltering Internet traffic. He segregated dial-up, microwave, satellite, cable, and DSL transmissions, concluding that humans used this for communications as well.

Humanity had changed since his last encounter with it. Life on this planet was increasingly dangerous.

He listened to refrigerators cycle on and off, to the steady hum of computers, electromechanical clocks clicking away, and to the rhythmic beat of respirators at the hospital saving lives; although, the Kar could not fathom why. Beneath him, the hissing Venturi effect of water and sewer lines that moved their product through fluctuating conduits spoke to him of man's dependencies, which he correctly associated with human's most basic activities—eating and drinking.

The Alpha Genesis probed with his senses the grocery stores around town whose shelves bulged with comestibles, and restaurants likewise bulging with hungry, chatty people, and workers queuing up at vending machines in break rooms, and homes where plump hotdogs boiled atop stoves for likewise plump and famished four-year olds. Each vector represented interstices on man's highly inefficient excremental continuum.

The petroleum stored in the large underground reservoirs as well as sloshing around in the tanks of the immense mechanical beetles was strangely familiar. Processing had changed it from the crude oil that Kar's algal genes recognized as distant kin.

Kar understood the interrelationship of *Homo sapiens*, but more importantly how much man depended on his machines and his weapons.

His program issued a command: Exterminate the potential enemy. Humans are Nonbeings, natural Rebel allies. Worst, here on this planet the machines are slaves not masters.

From inside the lip of a storm sewer across the street, Alpha Genesis watched Curtis Judy enter his turn-of-the-last-century clapboard home. The rat impersonator had discovered Curtis Judy's nest and arrived there long before its occupant. The owner's scent branded the property's precise location far more precisely than man's best global positioning satellite.

Alpha heard the storm door's rusty spring protest as it stretched. It smelled microscopic flecks of oxidized iron drift away from the coil. The Kar listened to the jangle of Curtis's keys as he unbolted the front door and counted fourteen unique pitches as the metal pieces clanged against each other—one note for each key. Alpha Genesis also counted the footfalls as the human disappeared and moved deeper into his nest. The Kar calculated the distance traveled in each footfall by a unit of measure that once allowed Alpha Genesis to navigate the universe.

Soon he heard the splashing of water, a *tink* as the commode's metal chain tapped the porcelain tank, and then a *whoosh* of wastewater very close underfoot and gushing into the sanitary sewer. Kar calculated the distance to the soil room where the man had voided his kidneys and decided it would be an ideal place to kill its quarry while it was preoccupied and vulnerable.

Alpha pawed at the concrete sill under the storm drain's steel grate, and it crumbled apart as cooperatively as if it were little more than a sandy beach's edifice mortared by a child's perspiration and toil.

Twenty seconds later the alien had burrowed under the street and then far under the crawl space foundation. It emerged directly beneath the only bathroom in the tiny bungalow. The creature sensed the human would soon need to return to the site and void himself once again, and when he did, he would ambush him.

The Federation Kar settled on the crawl space dirt floor and waited, listened, and began planning the elimination of *Homo sapiens*.

# CHAPTER 33 ~~ Poacher Bird Feed

Cruel Lake was ordinarily a casual thirty-minute trail ride on the ATV. Gus arrived in fifteen. He was relieved to find the left fork of the trail still clear as he reached the edge of the lake. The path narrowed and became rockier, but the machine climbed the terrain and thick snow patches without difficulty. Gus knew the trail almost as well as Seer City's streets. He had been up here hundreds of times.

Cruel Lake is a natural body of water fed by four hot springs and three spectacular glaciers. The narrow unusually ice-free lake meanders nearly a mile before relieving itself by way of Doral Falls— a breathtaking three hundred eighty foot veil of water. Dozens of manufacturers over the years had successfully gambled their logos and image on Cruel Lake's beautiful features. The poetic Ute had named the Cruel for the separation-melancholy suffered when one left her placid shores, not for anything unkind or malicious as most newcomers assumed.

The idea that murder or suicide could blemish this perfect place seemed utterly profane to Gus. He had camped here as a kid, fished, hunted and made love to Maggie on a picnic blanket one hot July afternoon.

The ravens marked the spot. He parked the ATV and turned the ignition off. Smith and Compton's bodies were right where Curtis

145

Judy had reported them. He keyed the mike on the radio, "Two to Base."

"State your twenty, Two." Deputy Skip Wise had fretted away the time by unsuccessfully calling Renner at all of his known numbers in Dakota Ridge at least a half dozen times and by waiting for Gus to report. Skip promised himself he would tactfully mention to the sheriff the modern marvels of voicemail and cell phones with extended battery lives when the boss returned to Seer City.

Gus cut to the chase instead, "The doubles are confirmed, Base."

"Say again, Two!"

Gus studied the scene from several feet away editing out the ravens' substantial progress from the murder-suicide. "We've got two down. Parties confirmed as Smith and Compton. Felix was the shooter. He's still clutching his rifle, a Springfield thirty-ought-six. This one we give to the coroner, Skip. Tell them to go-go, double-time. I'm guessing a big snow tonight. I want State in on this too. See if we can pull one of the Davidsons from Introit, either Brad or Laura. I want search warrants on Smith and Compton's homes."

"What are we looking for, Gus?"

"Acid and a motive. Toss 'em, Skip. Hurl their huts hard."

Acid? Skip asked himself. "Copy, Two…" Skip was becoming more confused with each passing moment. His mountain lion theory was now in second place behind Curtis Judy's story.

Gus was relieved that even though this murder scene was gruesome, he had none of the illness that wretched him earlier when he came across, well, what do you call it when you watch a man and his beloved pet disappear into thin air like pieces of dry ice?

Chooke and Greta's deaths were painful, and the pain needed soothing. The presumption that Smith and Compton were the killers was convenient Pepto Bismol. In fact, Gus wanted to whistle the ravens back to their feast. "Any word from Renner?" he asked Deputy Wise.

"Negative. Can't even leave a message. Do you want me to have the Dakota Ridge authorities find him?"

Gus glanced at his watch. "Negative. Just keep trying."

"Copy."

"Keep me posted. Two out."

Gus looked up at the circling ravens, then down at the corpses. "Knock yourself out, boys."

# CHAPTER 34  ~~  Alien Battle Plan

In the crawlspace beneath Curtis Judy's commode, Alpha Genesis appeared as inert as the chipped red clay drain tiles or the scraps of wood the long forgotten carpenters had left under the home when they framed it a century earlier.

It was an illusion, though, for Kar remained alert. The machine could while away countless millennia in this state and expend far less energy than a single human hiccup.

Recording the rancorous bustle of Seer City no longer concerned the alien.  No further examination was necessary.

The alien understood man's primitive reliance on electricity, where it originated, and how to interrupt its transmission when the time came.

Kar understood the human's communications networks:  the telephones, two-way radios, commercial radio, television, and cellular networks.  Kar now knew how to neutralize these systems, too.

The roads, tunnels and bridges were escape routes.  Sealing them would be a minor challenge for a machine with Kar's burrowing abilities.

# CHAPTER 35 ~~ To Love, Cherish and Honor Secrets

Kate Lambert studied Renner McCauley from the corral-side of the foaling stall. A foot of new straw covered the floor. It was fluffed high and ready for the mare and newborn colt when they returned to the barn. Fresh water was there as well. Generous scoops of shelled corn and oats awaited the mare in a feed bucket, generously blessed with vitamins and candied in irresistible molasses.

Kate smiled as Renner leaned against the split rail fence on the east side of the corral. He hooked his right boot heel over the bottom rail. Kate heard the wood and leather squeak faintly as his foot settled and pushed upward. Under the denim jacket, the sheriff's biceps flexed and stretched the fabric taut as Renner effortlessly hoisted himself onto the fence. Perched on the top rail, he crossed his arms and yawned. Leather gloves hung from the back pocket of his jeans.

The cowboy spoke softly to his horse, "Good Ginger." The mare was nursing her foal and nibbling on a clump of timothy alfalfa hay. A fresh bucket of vitamin and mineral-laced water hung next to the hayrack. She turned toward the sound of his voice. Agreeably bobbing her head, the mare whinnied.

Kate laughed softly from the stall doorway.

Renner turned and smiled. She had startled him, but he didn't show that particular emotion. Instead, catlike, he dropped from the fence and walked toward her. Still smiling, he stopped a few feet away. Renner was clearly delighted to see her. Kate was relieved. So much had happened in just twenty-four hours.

Kate stepped through the stall door into the open corral. The late afternoon sun stretched her shadow to the distant fence line. The evening's chill was not far off. She crossed her arms to ward it off and smiled back at Renner. She felt herself flush and her skin erupted in gooseflesh. She sensed that Renner was experiencing the same.

It was pure frisson—passion laid raw—not winter nippiness that caused them to shiver under each other's gaze. Their eyes now rose and met, just as they had this morning. They silently revealed secrets, intimacies, and betrayed their attraction to each other as innocently as if they were children giggling about a popular class clown. Neither of them desired to look away, then nor now. For three incredible hours this morning Renner and Kate had discovered each other, explored their love rising from last night's obstreperous silt with treasure chest awe. They had submitted to wonderment, to tenderness without resistance.

James George had finally fallen asleep around noon after the long sleepless night and the birth of the colt early this morning. He curled up next to Doc Karl even though the retired professor snored with the wrath of a Toro garden tiller. Sasha the bulldog was delighted with so much midday snoozing. Kate had tossed a light blanket over the humans and also napped for several hours. She had awakened dreaming of Renner McCauley, no less in love with him than when she had gone to sleep. The self-diagnosis—simple infatuation—begged a second opinion.

For too-many-to-count years, men had eluded her inner heart. No relationship ever rose past that pointless and time-consuming small talk phase. Tic-talk she called it—drone-on life sentences, dangling participants, disagreements in verbal pretense, and then the inevitable splits for infinity. Now in just twenty-some-damn-hours, she was in love with Renner McCauley, a perfect stranger, a man who frightened her, angered her, disgusted her and yet aroused her with such tender emotion. Theirs was a love born like a star in one glorious moment this morning when their apologists' eyes met in the barn. Kate ached for him.

"Did you get any rest, Renner?" Kate asked with genuine worry in her voice. She dropped her eyes and did not look up until Renner mercifully spoke.

"It'll have to wait until tonight. Thanks for asking, though."

"You've been with Ginger Pat all this time?"

"Oh, yes."

"Is that necessary?"

"Nope. But Ginger Pat doesn't know that." He glanced at the mare. Doctor's Ren had already lost much of his newborn ungainliness.

"Really?"

"Well, in the wild the stallions are extra attentive and protective of the mares and foals for the first day or so. It's just natural. Since Hoot Bill is over in Seer County, I reckon I'll have to stand in for him. Not that the old stud would actually know what he was supposed to do."

Renner had thought of little else than Katherine Lambert throughout the day. He had made a pot of strong coffee around noon to help wash down the chicken salad sandwich, Saltines and canned pears Kate had brought him for lunch. He had poured her a cup of coffee, but she had only taken a sip or two. When she yawned and excused herself a short while later, Renner walked her to the lane, and then returned to the bunkhouse tack room. Telling himself he just did not want to waste coffee, he drank from Kate's cup. The taste of her light lipstick on the mug had taken away his breath. Kate's eyes swam before his all afternoon. Recalling her easy laughter soothed him. He longed for her to gaze at him the way she gazed at Doc and James George, and the way they looked back at her, old love and new. The fact was, Renner McCauley could not have slept today. Something was born in him this morning as tangible as the colt. He was in love for the first time in his life.

Kate said, "Ginger Pat certainly seems like she knows what she's doing. You sure she needs a wet nurse?"

Renner laughed. "Never thought of myself as a nurse. Truth is I guess I just like sharing the experience with her. You know—new life, the foal and all. As many times as I've seen creation, it's always like the first time. James George and I had that in common this morning. Anyway, Ginger Pat hasn't asked me to leave her side just yet."

Kate felt another warm breeze gently rock the boat in which she found herself drifting away with this cowboy. "If she did, would you?"

Renner heard only the question she didn't want to ask. The one he had asked himself a million times since this morning. "Would I what? What do you mean?"

She willed her eyes to blink, her hands to unclench. They didn't, defiantly. "Leave her alone. Go away. Ever. I think she cares for you very much."

Renner stepped forward and studied the pasture beyond Kate for a moment. "We're not exactly talking about Ginger Pat and me, now are we? This is about us. You and me."

Kate did not answer right away. She considered lying, and then thought it pointless. "What if it was about us, Renner? I mean, we're both too damned old to waste time on dead-ends."

"Miss Lambert…"

"It's Kate, damn it!" she gasped, exasperated. Kate rolled her eyes and feigned irritation. She would certainly sanitize this for Lu Li.

"Kate. Don't worry. I'm not known to stay where I'm not wanted, and I'm usually the first to know when it's time to move on. We probably have that in common." He waited a moment, and then added, "But I hope that never happens. Is that fine by you?" Renner took a step closer.

"Yes."

"Well then, Kate, you need to understand a few things about me. Despite my fine tantrum last night, I'm actually a horse's ass."

Kate smiled. "I love Doc more than life itself, and he said he's taught you everything he knows on the subject of horses' asses." Kate allowed her arms to fall to her sides and then stepped closer. She was shivering, her teeth chattered, but her cheeks and forehead felt sunburned.

"I'm not Doc, Kate. Not half the man he is." Renner removed his denim jacket.

"Half? So what's that make you, McCauley, hundred-eighty, hundred-ninety pounds?"

"I'm serious, Kate." Here, take this. You're freezing."

"Renner, stop it! Don't make this any more difficult for me than it already is. I feel like a foolish star-struck sixteen year old. We hardly know each other." She allowed him to wrap the coat over her shoulders. He gently pulled it around to her front and held it there snugly until her hands rose and covered his. He started to pull his hands away but Kate held them tightly. Then he relaxed.

Renner smiled. Neither spoke, but it was a comfortable silence. Sadness soon flickered behind his eyes. The apologist speech he had practiced since this morning rolled out on a tape of its own volition. "Kate, I'm a mountain cowboy, a sheriff. I live on old land and cherish the old ways. You're a scientist, a teacher. You work in Denver."

"Christ, McCauley! I'm native Coloradoan. Grew up right here on Dakota Ridge. Do you think for one moment that I don't know who and what you are? I used to run from your kind as fast as my legs would carry me. 'Hello, Ma'am. Mornin', Ma'am. Care to dance, Ma'am?' I'm not some eastern romantic whose notion of cowboys is Jeff Bridges and Russell Crowe. Do you understand?"

Renner smiled and then removed his hand from hers long enough to tip his cowboy hat, "Yes, Ma'am."

"Stop that." She waited until he seemed assured, and then asked, "Renner?"

"Yes, Kate."

"Do... Do you want to kiss me?" Her voice quavered badly, indeed now belonging to that proverbial school girl.

Renner whispered, "Yes, I do, very much. I guess I need to."

"Need to what?"

"I need to see if this is real, what's going on between you and me so fast. I pray that it is."

Kate bit her lower lip and nodded, "Me too, Renner." Her eyes swam in tears.

The phones had been down since Kate turned them off at noon. Doc always took an afternoon nap and loathed waking to a ringing telephone. Skip Wise's call came through just seconds after the old professor roused from his nap and flipped the switch to turn his phone system back on. The one-way speaker blared just as Renner and Kate's lips met.

"Renner! Come up to the house pronto! Skip Wise is on the horn. Says it's an emergency. Big time damned problem. That's a quote, son."

Renner stepped back, still holding her hands. "I'm truly sorry, Kate."

"Of course. Go. Hurry. I'll be right behind you."

"Kate…"

"Don't. Just go!" She playfully shoved him away.

Renner smiled, and then became serious. "Don't worry. I'm not going to go gewgaw on you, at least not just yet. Come. Walk with me up to the house, Kate. We need to talk." He gently took her elbow in his palm and guided her back through the barn. By the time they reached the other side, they were holding hands.

"What on earth are you talking about, Renner?" A touch of apprehension seeped into her voice. She already imagined the worst.

"I'm talking about something I'm supposed to tell you. Something I'm guessing might give you second thoughts about me, at least a good pause or two."

"I don't understand."

"Kate, you won't believe this, but I don't either."

Kate thought Renner McCauley was serious, too serious, and possibly frightened. "What are you so concerned about, McCauley? I mean, I'm not some she-bitch out to neuter cowboys."

Renner shook his head and stared at Kate for a moment and then said, "You'll laugh."

"I like laughing." Kate broke into a stuttering jog to keep up with Renner's fast walk. She tightened her grip on his hand and buoyed when he responded in kind.

Renner sighed and shook his head. His face reddened. "You see, Kate, there is this letter. It's from my great-great-grandfather, Jimmy McCauley. It's been passed from one generation to the next since before the turn of the century."

"A letter? This is all about a letter?"

"That's right. My mother was the last woman who agreed to its terms."

"You're kidding! Terms! What are we talking about here? The world's first prenuptial agreement?"

"It's not a joke. And yeah, terms, which I suspect are far tougher than any prenuptial agreement."

"Like what?

"Like I'm not to get involved with you until I've read the letter and let you read it too. We must both swear to it with our souls as the ante. And, we must agree to keep the letter secret and abide by its terms completely." He risked a glance at her.

"You're serious?"

"Yes, absolutely."

"This must be some family secret."

"Apparently."

"And you have no idea what the letter says?"

"No, other than it has something to do with Seer Mountain, which my family has always owned. That's all I know."

Kate relaxed. Though the study of genetics was unheard of at the time his ancestor, Jimmy McCauley wrote this mysterious missive, a lot about familial curses has always been known.

Kate and Renner rounded the last curve before the ranch house. Doc Karl was already waiting for them. Standing on the front porch steps, he waved a cordless phone at the approaching couple and screamed, "Renner! Hurry up!"

"You own a mountain, an entire fricking mountain, McCauley."

Renner smiled and said, "Yep, it's a big one too." He squeezed Kate's hand once, released it and jogged away.

# CHAPTER 36 ~~ Alien & Hippie Go Hand-to-Hand

From the crawl space, Alpha Genesis recorded each footfall on the creaky hardwood floor as Curtis Judy moved about the house. The machine had no need to understand man's primitive computers, the Internet, or e-mail attachments. He certainly had no appreciation for the frustration that a cyber-user experiences when his Internet service provider goes offline right before a tree hugger sends the most important message ever. Anger was also foreign to Alpha, as well as profanity. So, when Curtis swore and stomped the floor, Alpha Genesis interrogated those acoustic releases with no less intensity or importance than any other sound the human made.

Frustrated, Curtis plopped down in a wobble-legged, oaken school chair and leaned back. His head lulled over the chair back. He rolled his eyes at the dingy ceiling, bit his lower lip and then shrieked, "Fuck!"

Aside from his ISP being offline, the AC adapter on his notebook computer was on the fritz again, and only one battery bar remained on the power management icon. He had no choice. Curtis closed the programs and shut down the machine. If he could not get on the Internet later this evening, he would just have to wait until the new power adapter arrived tomorrow morning from Denver. The delicious fantasy of his photos blown up to the size of billboards and appearing at the front of every protest from Occupy to the next G-20 meeting rolled on in his mind. He played the heroic caption: Two poachers bag and toe tag themselves.

Curtis pushed back from the dining room table and got up. "Well, if I can't do shit, I'll just take one. Time to restock the lake." He grabbed the *Daily Seer* newspaper from the couch as he passed by, then headed down the hallway to the bathroom.

Curtis Judy had just gotten down to business, both the newspaper and his bowels each having turned a page or two, when Kar opened the black pipe under the stool, and the toilet bowl emptied into the crawl space.

"What the hell?" Curtis felt a cold breeze sail past his crotch as air from the crawl space replaced the water in the toilet bowl. He raised the newspaper overhead and peeked between his thighs. Except for the crinkle of the newspaper and the waning drip of crap water beneath him, all was still. The machine gathered itself and exploded through the sub floor, spun, and landed inside the antique claw foot bathtub across from Curtis. The entire house shook. Wood, linoleum and nail confetti showered over the hippie.

Curtis Judy, Californian for most of his life, screamed, "Goddamned earthquake aftershock!" In fact, Kar's arrival did compare to the manhole cover that sliced though the floorboards of Curtis' VW bus in 1989 during a bay protest outside Candlestick Park. That earthquake had leveled parts of the city, severed and ignited underground gas lines, juggled steel, perforated vehicles, and interrupted not only the World Series that night, but also Curtis Judy's Golden State residency. His ass puckered tight then, as it puckered tight now, and he seriously speculated amidst the chaos where in the country he might move next.

The machine rose and looked at Curtis from over the lip of the tub. Curtis covered his crotch with one hand, his face with the other. He was a poor match at this showdown. Kar's eyes were far colder, far less animate than those of any shark a human had ever had the misfortune of encountering face-to-face. Curtis grimaced and forced a smile even as he looked into death's eyes. "Hey, fellow, where did you come from?"

Alpha's claws flexed against the edge of the porcelain. Curtis whined. The enamel chipped away as easily as if the Kar were scratching a glazed donut, not a brittle, decades-old bathtub. The cast iron beneath the porcelain shattered in the creature's grip and fell to the floor.

"Nice, nice, little whatever the fuck you are." Curtis reached for his pants. His pinky finger hooked a keeper and lifted his drawers as far as his right knee, where they bound up and slipped back down. The frigid air in the crawl space and the once cozy bathroom changed places. Curtis's testicles rose involuntarily in his groin and ached.

Curtis attempted to categorize the creature. Its rodent-like characteristics were unmistakable, but he'd never encountered any animal, living or animated, that gave him the slightest clue as to what he was up against. The Kar looked like a bear cub sized groundhog, but possessed none of the jostling blubbery skittishness of that rat. In fact, the animal was sturdy, possessing a weightlifter's chiseled musculature. The eyelashes and fur were utterly beautiful like a baby Harp seal's. The naked, whipping tail clearly belonged to a rat, though too frenetic for any rodent Curtis had ever encountered, except perhaps a squirrel. The eyes, though, he had seen them before. Shark? Yes, but the ebony shades appeared vertically slit, serpentine.

"I don't know what in Christ's name you are, but I want you the fuck out of my head." Curtis searched for a weapon. A crusted toilet bowl plunger was stored next to the toilet. It had dried to the floor when last used. The rubber protested with a hiss when the ball separated from the linoleum. Curtis lifted the plunger and slowly twisted the rubber ball from the handle.

The machine watched the orange-red ball fall from the human's hand and thump to the floor. It rolled a tight figure eight, and came to a stop against the wall. The alien then turned its attention back to the human. The stick obviously was a weapon. Now Kar understood. He would permit the human to use it because perhaps the object was a potential appropriation.

With all his strength, Curtis stabbed the Kar in the chest with the wooden handle. The creature anticipated the attack, though, and drove its claws more deeply into the cast iron, effectively bracing its body as if anchored in bedrock. Curtis might have done better if he had attempted to plunge the handle through the tub itself. The monster's body failed to give. The ancient wooden handle slid through Curtis's sweaty palms.

An inch-long splinter separated from the wooden shaft and planted itself deeply into the meat between Curtis's thumb and forefinger. He howled in agony but continued to attack, this time swinging the weapon at the alien's head as fast as he could, swearing with every attack. His fingers stung, tingled, as if hitting an aluminum baseball bat full Babe Ruth against a steel I-beam. Blood dripped from his elbow.

He struck the Kar a dozen or more times before his bludgeon snapped in two. One end careened off the rat imposter and shattered the medicine cabinet mirror. The other end slid from his bloody hand and fell to the floor. "What in the holy fuck are you?"

The two watched each other. Curtis whined and panted. His eyes darted about the tiny room in search of escape or another weapon. He futilely reached for his pants one last time. Kar rose high above the tub, elongating, until he literally looked down on his prey. His abdomen undulated, lifting venom.

Perhaps it was the cobra-like wavering of its upper torso as it rose and regurgitated venom that saved Curtis. For unlike the preacher, Curtis Judy watched PBS, Animal Planet and the Discovery Channel with a religious fervor. The sermons let from the nature pulpit of the snake were his favorite, particularly those snakes that spit. Somehow, he understood what was about to happen. Kar reared back to spew out his venom. The aging hippie snatched the toilet plunger ball from the floor and held it near Kar's head.

The venomous wad struck the rubber with sufficient velocity to send new pain up Curtis's arm, but none of the poison reached his flesh. The rubber hissed. The room turned dark with a roiling black smoke as the synthetic rubber dissolved and caught fire. His instinct told him, now I'm dead. He shrieked and fell to the floor, twitching like the good drug addict he once was.

Alpha Genesis, of course, realized his venom had been intercepted, but what he failed to comprehend was that mankind's number one weapon had just been used against him successfully—subterfuge and trickery. Curtis writhed on the floor, howled and gasped for air. The latter was no act. Acrid black smoke obscured the room. The creature watched through the haze for a moment and turned away, confident that sufficient venom had reached the target, and that the human would soon evaporate. Kar dropped through the hole into the crawl space and left Curtis Judy's home the way he arrived.

# CHAPTER 37 ~~ Back in Time From Dead and Back

Rosita handed Kate a large brown paper bag containing sandwiches and snacks and then handed Doc Karl an identical bounty. Two thermos lids peeked out from each sack, one filled with hot cocoa and the other coffee. The foursome of Renner and Kate in one pickup truck and Doc and Jimmy in another would caravan to Seer City. Rosie and Pedro would keep an eye on the fossil farm and tend to Ginger Pat and Doctor's Ren.

"Good God, Rosie!" the professor protested as he accepted the heavy food sack. "We'll blow a tire hauling this load, surely break an axle."

"Hush, you old fart. Pedro topped off your gas tanks, and so with plenty of food and fuel you won't need to hurry. Katie knows all the right places to stop."

Rosie turned to McCauley, whose lack of sleep last night was beginning to show. "Renner, it's six hours to Seer City. You should get some sleep. My Kate drives better than any man in these mountains, so you don't need to worry. Okay?"

"Yes Ma'am." Renner glanced at Kate and smiled, confident that Rosie was not exaggerating.

The pets, Isaac and Newton and the bulldog Sasha would ride with Doc and James—their nuisance intended to keep James George entertained and Doc Karl sharp behind the wheel.

Pedro handed Renner and James George each a Motorola two-way radio as they climbed into the truck cabs. He briefly instructed James on how to use the device. To Renner he reported, "The weather is clear right now, smooth sailing. Later tonight, not so good. Well, it's actually going to get bad. So get there safely, *vaquero*."

Grandfather Jimmy McCauley's ancient trunk sat on the bench seat between Kate and Renner. Kate nestled the lunches between them, adjusted the seat and mirrors, started the engine, and then headed down the lane with Doc and Jimmy following. When she reached the road, she glanced at Renner and asked, "I'm ready. What's next?"

"There is a series of letters from Grandfather Jimmy McCauley. I have only read the first one. My parents, grandparents and their parents have read the second letter. No one since Jimmy McCauley sealed the trunk has opened the small trunk inside the big trunk."

"McCauley, your family is weird."

"I know that for sure. Are you ready?"

Kate stared at Renner and finally nodded. "Let's do it."

Renner opened the lid and lifted the first envelope. He cleared his throat and began to read. The letter explained the McCauley family secret and pledge.

\*\*\*

...I implore your trust and forgiveness, my heirs, for this unrighteous burden which I now impose upon you all. I am so very sorry, but I have little choice. Let Seer Mountain slumber forever. With your lives and honor you must so pledge. Pass the key on, one generation to the next, my words kept secret until the last McCauley opens my full accounting. Then after that, when necessary, open the smaller trunk...

\*\*\*

Renner finished reading and slid the letter back into its envelope. "Kate, any questions?"

Kate's expression said, "Yep, about a million," but she shook her head and said, "Let's see what's behind curtain number two."

"You sure?"

Kate reached into the trunk and handed the envelope labeled No. 2 to Renner. "Let's do it."

\*\*\*

August 17, 1888

Dear Child,

You have chosen someone you are considering for your mate. Oh, how guilty I feel burdening you now, impossibly so from this distant past. How can a good life be made from such? Are you my first generation heir or my tenth or my hundredth to carry on our dark legacy? That you now read my second letter means the McCauley and Seer Mountain secret has not been shared. That is good, truly vital.

To the man or woman who may eventually marry into this family, I ask and impose a tremendous injustice on you now, and for that I pray your eternal forgiveness. However, when I have made this revelation complete, you shall know beyond any absolution that I am sincere, that I am not a madman.

Vow unto God Almighty and with that oath the honor of your own mother and father that my words herein shall not be shared with anyone other than this McCauley with whom you now judge your future together. Say it, child, or close this trunk forever and pass the oath to another. Forgive me this unrighteous demand.

\*\*\*

Renner stopped reading and looked across the seat at Kate. "Kate, we really don't know each other. You don't have to..."

Kate held up her hand and stopped Renner from continuing. "Your grandfather must have known it would be this way. That his children would never marry carelessly, that they would wait."

Renner smiled. "I guess I never thought about it that way, but yes, the McCauley's have always been late to hitch up."

Kate looked down at the yellowed letter in Renner's left hand, Jimmy McCauley's precise handwriting. "Look Renner, two things. One, I can keep a secret. In fact, I have a few family scare-looms I need to share with you. Two, I'm falling in love with you and it's mutual. That's the reason you had to show me this. Remember?" She gestured at the letter and added, "I don't believe your grandfather is crazy. In a strange way his warnings are comforting, like he's still watching over his family."

Renner nodded. What Kate said was true, especially about Jimmy McCauley's guardianship. He had once spoken with his dad about the feeling when he was a teenager, and John McCauley had smiled and agreed, "Yep, old granddad is never far off the elbow space."

"Renner?"

"What?"

"This is awkward. I admit it, like getting a blood test just to go out on the first date. Your grandfather, for some reason that we'll soon learn, felt that this is the best time to reveal his secret—before we've fallen so deeply in love that we'd agree to almost anything. Jimmy McCauley must've been a very kind man." Kate then added, "Well here it is, Grandpa Jimmy, whatever secret you are about to reveal, it is safe with me. Now, Renner, read the letter. I've sworn."

Renner took a deep breath, smiled at Kate and then continued onto page two. Jimmy McCauley's handwriting was now much less precise, and the prose less florid.

***

So be it. A pact we have.

Have faith and listen, children.

Shortly before I commenced writing these letters, eleven months and twenty-one days ago to be exact, I died. That's right. Died. I've tried many a refrain that might be less shocking to a body to hear, but none comes out any better. Exactly how long I was with the worms, I can't rightly say. I am guessing it was at least six days from what Kara told me later when she woke me up, but she doesn't account for time very well. It seems to mean nothing to her, no more than it does to a rock, I suppose. But she does care about some things and greatly so. Take her name for example—Kara. I named her that I guess. I'll tell you how in a bit. For now just understand it gives her tremendous pleasure when she hears her name. So much pleasure that her part of this story is more mysterious to me than my dying. I am sure you are already taking exception to this poorly started yarn, child, so I should move on with my accounting.

Pasqual Ortez has been me friend since we were in the mines together as slag-muckers and scrapers. I pray his family has safely found their way and they still call Seer County home. The Ortez's, it's rumored, arrived in Colorado with Coronado, but that isn't true. Pasqual's family and me own arrived in Seer County on the very same day, looking and acting scrappy for work at the old Midas Six.

What I remember most about that day we met was Pasqual and his peaches plan. He vowed to plant the first orchard in the valley, and by golly, he did just that a few years later. Nice one too, sixty trees drooping in bounty every year like none we'd ever seen. My good Lord and Savior, but those peaches were fine, too.

We all just loved them, especially Kara. She likes the sound of her name, and she likes them peaches you see. Truth is, she's partial to any kind of fruit or vegetable, but she's extra affectionate for peaches, especially Pasqual Ortez's. It would be funny I guess, except it was in the peach orchard where I died. So understandably, I'm a little torn up, as they say, because that's where I also met my dear little Kara.

***

"Renner, who is Kara?"

Renner looked up and slowly shook his head. "I haven't the slightest idea. I'm racking my brain. Perhaps a pet, but what kind of pet eats fruit? Maybe a primate? It's the first time I ever heard the name."

"Pets that talk and eat fruit? Maybe a parrot?"

"Parrots that resurrect the dead?"

"Keep reading."

***

Kara awoke. The letter always awakened her when read aloud. She opened her eyes to absolute darkness. Her world was motionless and as silent as deep space. She was floating—suspended in a liquid vessel, a viscous cocoon. However, she was not imprisoned or in any danger. She was in a place of her own design. Kara was in hiding. She had no idea how long she had been dormant. Something about the reading of Jimmy McCauley's letter always aroused her somehow. Kara did not think in such terms as the passage of time. Time was an irrelevancy. She longed to reach out with her mind to Jimmy McCauley, but she would not. To do so would be dangerous. To do so might place Jimmy McCauley in peril. That is, if he were even still alive. She did not know his fate. To know the truth might ruin the trap she and Jimmy McCauley had set for the Federation Exterms.

163

Instead, she lived for a moment in her perfect memory. Memory alone would have to sustain her now.

I am Kara.

I am Kara!

I... am... Kara.

Kara is Jimmy McCauley's sweet gal from Golden.

Jimmy McCauley gives Kara name!

Kara gives Jimmy McCauley life.

Kara's name gives Kara... LIFE!

Kara gives Jimmy McCauley... TIME.

I am Kara.

I... am... Kara!

Time cannot touch Kara.

Kara touches Time.

I am Kara.

Kara waits.

Enemy waits.

When Federation comes,

Kara comes.

When Jimmy McCauley comes,

The Special One comes.

Exterms need the Special One.

Enemy waits for the Special One.

Exterms are defective.

Enemy is trapped here.

Enemy seeks way out.

Enemy has forgotten how to change.

But Kara remembers.

Memories reborn.

Enemy is defective.

Enemy has lost its hyperspace face.

Enemy needs the Special One.

Enemy waits for the Special One.

The Special One can restore Enemy's hyperspace face.

Kara and Jimmy McCauley must stop the enemy's Time.

Kara is sweet gal from Golden.

Kara is sweet gal from g'Hhol-deune.

Kara sees all's thens.

Kara sees all's nows... NOW!

Kara sees all that is to come.

Kara remembers Kara.
Kara and Jimmy McCauley set trap.
Enemy needs the Special One.
Federation waits for the Special One.
Kara and Jimmy McCauley must not let that happen.
Kara thinks.
Where Kara thinks, Kara goes.
Kara remembers.
Where Kara remembers, Kara can go.
Kara is sweet gal from g'Hhol-deune.
Kara is sweet gal from Golden.
Her home is g'Hhol-deune.
Far away g'Hhol-deune.
See that star? That one there, Jimmy McCauley?
Golden here and g'Hhol-deune beyond.
Kara makes joke! Golden and g'Hhol-deune!
Names sound the same, Jimmy McCauley!
Funny! Kara is funny!
Kara hears Jimmy McCauley laugh!
Kara does not forget because…
Kara's then is also Kara's now.
Good-bye to Jimmy McCauley's home for now.
Kara goes home now to g'Hhol-deune.
Kara's star and Orlif planet.
Jimmy McCauley, you cannot see.
Too far from Jimmy McCauley's home.
Kara will return when the git-out bell rings.
Kara the sweet gal from g'Hhol-deune…
Go home now… back to sleep."

Kara closed her eyes, but not from fatigue or wanting to sleep. She was preparing for her journey. Kara was on her way home—to a planet across the universe. Her mode of transportation, something most humans could not fathom, was telepathic. Kara was the last of her kind to remember how to travel the universe with her mind, to move through time and space with only her mind. She closed her eyes and began the brief journey back to her home planet, g'Hhol-deune, fifteen hundred billion light years away from earth. The voyage would take no more than sixty seconds. She knew what she would find. It would not be a pleasant homecoming. G'Hhol-deune was an abandoned planet—a zettagamma cinder. The extermination had occurred some seven hundred million years ago after the great deception.

For now, the journey was only in her mind, but soon with McCauley's help she would be able to move physically around the universe as she once did long ago.

***

The trunk vibrated for a moment on the seat between Renner and Kate. A blue-green light flashed around it. Kate and Renner glanced curiously toward the disturbance, but it was already over. Renner turned his attention back to the letter and continued reading.

***

Them peaches. Mother Mary and Joseph! I don't suppose I've ever eaten one since and not recounted that day. It's as if it was just yesterday in me mind no matter how many days and months have passed. One minute I was alive. The next, well the next that I can remember comes days later.

You are no doubt pondering mighty hard now, children, as to what my sweet little Kara is, and truth be told, I have no idea what kind of animal she be. Still to this day, she remains a mystery. No creature I have ever come across compares with her. And to think I tried so mightily to kill her. Maybe a dozen times I shot the poor little beastie, and then without a second thought it's my pelt she saves.

"Sheriff!" old Pasqual screamed as he fell into me office. He was afire a fitting that day. He stormed to me desk and growled, "You gots to shoot it for me! Mi gun no good, it's not. And mi peaches are nearly ruined! I SHOOT! BANG! No kill it!"

So, I rode out to the orchard late in the afternoon that day, dismissing most of what the Spaniard had babbled at me. Thinking for sure he was mistaking the creature for a crazed giant whistle pig or maybe an albino skunk that had lost its nature, perhaps even a bear cub that'd separated from its mamma sow. Me supposed many things, but not what awaited me. I assure and testify on my honor.

I began walking down the orchard rows, and what a sight it was. Every third tree or so was chewed through to the bark, and every piece of fruit was missing. Even most of the leaves had been chewed down to their stems. Kara told me later, maybe three weeks it was, that she had come across the orchard and found it diseased. She'd been visiting the place for years, but she never took more fruit than ol' Pasquie would miss. This year, though, the trees were doomed, infested with some blight the Spaniard had no defense against. She pruned the trees for him, and by Joe, the orchard has never been better.

Well, learning that later from her in passing certainly made me feel no better for having shot her so many times. It were like hitting a tin can it was, skipping her with lead from one end of the orchard to the other. She never ran away from me, never tried, but why should she? I weren't hurting her none with me shots. I reloaded thrice, and watched her hop a tree and nibble for a moment. Then I swear she came right to me, hopped up on her hind legs, and then gave her chest for a target plain as day. My shot dumped her cart hard it did. Over she rolled on the ground backwards, maybe five times it was. I was sure I'd got her this time. Then, as if she'd found a gold doubloon, she lifted a peach pit to me and squealed her delight. I had no heart to shoot again.

I felt bad for shooting at this beautiful animal who meant me no harm, as well as for what I'd have to tell my friend the Spaniard, Pasqual Ortez. That's when she spoke to me. Not with words, but to me mind.

"I do not hurt Life trees. I do not hurt Life you. You do not hurt me, Life."

I turned Dervish circles I did searching for that sweet little voice. I knew where it came from all right. I just weren't ready to admit it. Then to show me she had a sense of humor too, me reckons, I looks down and she's spinning in a circle too, mocking me, acting like she's helping me search. I laughed heartily, and we stared for a moment at each other, her naked tail whipping behind her butt like a squirrel's, and then in the blink of an eye, she disappeared at me feet down a burrow that materialized under me almost magically.

That's when I remembered her, my sweet girl from Golden, the wee ghost that led me to safety the day the Midas Six blew. She were the perty gal from Golden.

I waited a few minutes and then went to collect me mare that'd run off somewhere. I was sure it was from all me firing of the rifle that had sent Heather Nell to the hills, but I was wrong, horribly wrong.

Cougars attack from behind if they can, and their impact can snap the neck of a bull elk. My scrawny chicken shoot was no match for the 230-pound monster that hit me from behind like a lightning bolt. Me neck snapped as on a gallows attached to the hangman's rope. I remember crumbling to the ground, paralyzed, wanting air but unable to take none down. I felt me heart stop in me chest, and me eyes staring into the heavens but unable to blink. Then I died, mercifully, just as the cougar collected his game. The puma's death bite is administered to the throat, and mine was a fiend. The tawny bastard nearly decapitated me before Kara sent him on his way.

***

Renner laid down the letter and turned to Kate. Their expressions were identical: sick and disbelieving.

McCauley's voice was a whisper. He shook his head slowly as he spoke, "Well there's something, but it still makes no sense. Grandpa Jimmy indeed had a mysterious scar that nearly encircled his neck. He insisted he'd gotten it during the Midas Six disaster when a downed cable clothes-lined him as he ran out, but no one quite remembered it that way. He always insisted the scar was a hundred times worse than the injury, and eventually, people finally just accepted it, because Jimmy McCauley was a man of his word."

***

Now, since I'm telling this story, I suppose you're thinking old Jimmy McCauley was just dreaming. No one survives that kind of animal attack. Well, I'd say you're only half right. I wasn't dreaming. In fact, I don't recall anything from the time I died until I woke up. You might also be wondering why nobody found me body. That's easy. Kara moved me. My deputies searched that valley from one end to the other, but the trail petered out about the same time my blood finished draining, and then a storm kicked up and that was that. Oh, they seen the cougar tracks, and they came to pretty much the correct conclusion.

Now I weigh about 225 pounds, at least so it says down at the assayer's office on the big ore scales. Without some blood, I reckon I'm still up to at least around 220 pounds. So, here's another mystery. Kara is about the size of a bear cub. How in even old McDougal's lifetime did she ever carry me all the way to the Midas Six—more than four miles across the valley and then five thousand feet up the mountain—tear down the barricades and then lower me better than one hundred sixty feet into the mine?

Well, she did, and she doesn't seem to think it was all that much of a feat. She placed me body near a tiny steam vent deep in the mine to keep me corpse warm, and then went to work.

When I woke up, well, me just thought I had landed in Hades. No better way to explain such a miserable state I was in. I couldn't see anything, couldn't move, but Lord I could feel, and what I felt was fire. Blazing, an inferno that wretched me flesh from boiling bone. I screamed like no man before me, but nothing passed me lips, nary a whisper. I struggled to move, but froze me was, like a pebble under Chinaman Chili's glacier itself.

Then I remembered the big cat, him closing on me throat. I was dead, had to be, and Lucifer must be cookin' me down under. I wondered hard for what evil I'd done so the Lord might shift me such, because I'd lived by the Word more than most—had been a faithful husband and a fine public servant. Never a shirker, I was. That's when I remembered the giant white rat with those pretty puppy's eyelashes. I'd tried and failed to kill the little charm, and maybe this was my punishment.

Then I thought, well maybe I was dead when I found her. Maybe I broke me neck and died before reaching Pasque's orchard, fell off Heather Nell on the ride out to the orchard and dreamed it all up as I croaked. And what a strange last mortal offering it were, too. Me dropping the creature a dozen times with me rifle and inflicting no more damage to her corpus than if I'd farted at her.

Just as I recalled her speaking to me in the orchard, well, that's when she decided to let her voice be heard again.

"Life alive."

"Nope, devil," I said. "I'm dead as Bluebeard's balls. Pray Jesus help me!" I know my lips never moved, it was just me thinkin', but she heard me somehow and answered.

"Life alive. Fix. Not dead."

For two more days I laid there in darkness like none I'd ever experienced, wondering every minute, every second, if I was alive or dead. I was unable to move anything except my mind—a mind which I was absolutely sure was a goner no matter where I'd landed—heaven or hell. My only solace was that sweet little voice whispering to me mind. "Life alive. Fix. Not dead."

She said no more than that. "Life alive. Fix. Not dead." Over and over, on and on, good God it was maddening! Finally I thought, "Say something different for the love of me sweet bride, me Figgins girl I do miss so!"

Kara said, "Help say."

"Help you?" I asked.

"Yes."

So I said, of all the damnedest things, my name just in my mind. As loud as I could think it too, if that makes any sense. "Jimmy McCauley!"

Was that ever a mistake. For at least the next day all she said was, "Ekie-upfja helps Jimmy McCauley Life." I soon wished I really was dead, and that is only half a joke. "Ekie-upfja helps Jimmy McCauley Life," over and over she said. Maybe twenty times a minute she repeated herself. I thought that first word, "Ekie-upfja" was maybe her name, so before I totally lost my mind I asked her about it.

"Name?" she asked in return.

"Yes, like I am Jimmy McCauley. That's what I am called."

"Name? Name. No. I have no name. I am Ekie-upfja."

"That's your kind?"

Well, children, I know this sounds absolutely daffy it does, but we were communicating with only our minds as it were. Most things she understood right away, because she's real smart. When she got stumped, she used my memory like a dictionary or an encyclopedia. Sometimes she had to dig real deep. I could feel it, too. It tickled as she perused through my vocabulary and recollection of matters to translate something I had said. She wasn't too good at it at first, but by the time she was finished with me, we were talking right regularly.

After two minutes of much appreciated silence, and a tickling between the ears that is utterly indescribable but not all that unpleasant, Kara finally said, "I am Slave-Life-Rebel-Commander." I have to say she said it with a sadness that broke my heart.

"Ekie-upfja means slave?"

After an hour I guess of perusing me mind Kara announces, "No, means more, Jimmy McCauley. Free-Slave-Life-Rebel-Commander."

"Who's a slave?"

"Here is Jimmy McCauley here."

Well, since I didn't know from Jack's jakes where I was, the fact that here was the Midas Six never crossed me mind.

"Why here?" I asked, and it took her nearly an hour of reading my mind before she could gather enough words to translate.

"Different, Ekie-upfja. Ekie-upfja, Rebel. Federation Masters want Ekie-upfja to die. ALL! Ekie-upfja wants Life, like Jimmy McCauley. Life alive. Fix. Not dead."

Of course, I still hadn't a clue as to what the creature meant. I understood so little at that time. What was really happening to me. Where she came from or on whose behalf she was fighting. Just this, that she meant me no harm. I was beginning to believe she really could fix me up as she kept saying. You see, the burning was gone and I could feel something new—a tingling in my fingers, just at the tips. Slowly, for maybe another day, the feeling spread throughout my body, and where it rose, I also felt warmth.

"What is happening?" I asked Kara.

"Fix Life."

"I can't move, though. I can feel my arms and legs now, but they're frozen stiff."

"Fix Life," she said again and then went deep into my mind to find more words. After a minute or two, she reprimanded me. "Be patient and sit still, Jimmy McCauley!"

By God I laughed! Of all me memories she might have tapped. Kara sounded just like me mum of yesteryear raking me fidgety knuckles in church. Not out loud she spoke, just in me mind, but it was just as satisfying as if I'd split open me britches from cuff to belly boiler with the hoot of the century. "Okay, patient I be wee creature." That's also when I realized something about her little excursion into my memories. You see, every time she ventured into me brainpan to fetch a word or translate one of her own, I sensed she was most fascinated with all the names of folks I had stored there. It seemed to give her such enjoyment. I can't exactly explain it, except it was like watching some poor mountain soul window shopping at a Denver store priced impossibly beyond his means.

I was giddy, and I asked her. "Would you like one of me names, sweet girl? I have aplenty, aye. Everyone should have a name."

Her reaction was a miner's whose pick has just sliced the white vein—golden jubilation. "Name, yes!" she screamed.

"See any you like?" I asked her, as easy as if I was peddling spuds for Mrs. Kerry. But, by John, she fed me the name not seconds later. Obviously, she'd been thinking about it a while.

"Kara!" she screamed.

Kara. What a fine suit of clothes she'd picked to call herself! Kara! You see, Kara McGregor was me favorite aunt as a lad and truly the kindest woman God ever gave away often and collected late. Like the creature, me auntie had the most beautiful long eyelashes. So it was a fittin' name.

"Kara it is!"

***

Renner McCauley stopped reading and looked across the car seat at Kate. She glanced at him and then at the yellowed pages. "Why'd you stop?"

"Why are you still listening for Christ's sake? You are a scientist. Don't you find this, what's the term, improbable?" Renner's frustration and embarrassment were amplified by his fatigue. His jaw flexed as he turned away and stared out the window. He had met a woman, a perfect woman, and had fallen in love with her in about the same amount of time it takes to drive to Denver and back. And she had fallen in love with him. Now he would surely lose her because his family was crazy.

"Certainly it's improbable. Very improbable, but let's just hear the rest of your grandfather's tale." Kate pointed at the letter. "We're almost finished. Go on. Please."

Renner's expression relaxed, but soon sickened with shame. Forgive me, Grandfather, he thought. Then he lifted the remaining pages and continued.

***

172

Kara. A good name it is too. I never imagined a name might in itself possess such power. Kara acted as if she was freed somehow, and I was her liberator. And, oh my, did she ever show me her gratitude. Into my mind she plunged learning everything I'd ever learned, restoring me memories, carefully avoiding privacies and hurtful times and things me not so proud of. It were like a happy puppy that cannot stop licking your face as she opened me mind to the both of us. That is the best I can describe it.

After maybe one more day of lifting me memories, she spoke in me mind the King's English no worse than me. Although, I was left with the strong suspicion that our language rises like peas to Mt. Seer compared to her native tongue. I'll now finish in her exact words as I recall them.

"Jimmy McCauley! Wake up, Life!"

"Aye, Kara, I'm not asleep."

"Good. It's time. You must leave. There is danger here. We must not remain any longer than necessary."

How she knew my body was restored, I'll never understand. As for the danger, I learned of that a few days later. But for now I could feel my legs and arms. I felt whole. "But I can't move, can't see a thing, Kara!" I panicked.

"Soon, Jimmy McCauley. You're still in the cocoon and asleep."

Aye, you heard me right, children. I said cocoon. That's where she'd put me. Kara's saliva can dissolve granite if she concentrates it. "That's crazy," you're saying? Well, have you ever seen how a mud dabber wasp builds its nest? How it keeps its prey, the spider, hostage in a prison of mud? Well, I was sort of like that spider, entombed in a paste that coated every bit of me body. A cast made hard as diamonds it was. "What did you do for sweet air? How'd you breathe?" you're righteously doubting. Well, children, dead men don't breathe and sweet Kara provided me with all that I needed in her special mud: oxygen, water and other nourishments to heal me broken neck and torn flesh. Don't ask me how. I still don't know, and I'll no doubt die no better informed. Oh, Kara's tried to explain it, but my vocabulary and memory aren't substantial enough for Kara to find the words. A penny just can't yield copper enough for even the smallest boiler, I'm afraid.

While I couldn't so much as twitch a toe or blink an eye within her cocoon, so locked down I was, she scratched the tomb apart with her claws effortlessly in just a few minutes. She told me to remain perfectly still and not to try to breathe yet, which was an abeyance easily done, for I had not felt me chest rise and fall or wind pass me lips since half waking up days ago.

The last of her magical grindings she removed was a soggy plug crammed down me throat, maybe a foot's worth. What a shock that was when she removed it! Now, I hadn't felt pain like that in all me life. Not when me shattered me collarbone in the avalanche the year after the Midas Six was shorn shut, not when I pulled Colleen Reigenstrief's mare from her hay barn, both the horse and me afire as it were. No children, it were like drowning in burning kerosene when Kara pulled out that muddy plug, every gasp sucking the fire deeper into me body until every piece of me was blazing. Two minutes of utter agony followed, and then me ordeal with death was finally over. Just as Kara promised, I was fixed and alive.

Oh, I complained to her later about the excruciations, ever respectful though, and most certainly grateful I was alive again. She had an explanation ready for me.

"The mouth feeder, it's like another umbilical cord. Jimmy McCauley born again as Life."

Now this ends this part of me tale, and hopefully your burden goes no further. Kara and I feel the same on that.

I have a request and a final set of instructions, though. First, you'll find herein a piece of that granite body cast that sweet Kara used to fix me. I've had the shard secretly assayed, and those government boys over in Introit claimed it must've fallen from the heavens, because nothing on earth resembles it. They are wrong. I went back to the Midas Six and buried almost all of it.

Before you judge me a wigged man, a rift from the booby hatch, I want you to hit the shard with a pickax, and hard as you can swing it, child. Make your blow square and dead on. Leave nothin' back. Don't worry, though, you won't so much as scratch it. If you are versed in weaponry, shoot it too. But guard yourself, for your lead will come back home to your watch pocket flat as a dime and nary a mark you'll make on Kara's invincible mud. Then drop the piece in a blacksmith's coal-fed iron kiln. Leave it there for ten minutes, lift it out and then directly set the shard in the palm of your hand. Trust me. At most, you'll feel nothing more than a wee bit of warmth. But the most amazing of all, set the shard over a small wound on your hand or your cheek for a short spell, and behold a miraculous healing where your injury riled a moment earlier. Aye! It's true, all of it, me loves. I could give you more proof, but let this suffice.

If you do as I say and satisfy your doubts, the next part will be easier to swallow down because if you are reading these instructions, I've gone dead and asunder, unlike me wee Kara. You see, Kara is still alive. She's in the second wooden trunk I gave you for safekeeping, inside a special jar filled with a liquid that only God and Kara know what it's for. She appears dead, pickled like pig's feet in vinegar saltwater, but she's not dead or close to it. Actually, unless she's killed, me figures she's most likely immortal, because me thinks she is more a machine than animals. The plural is meant, children. You see me Kara can be almost any creature she chooses. She's just sleeping now, submerged in her jar, hiding from her kind. Waiting for that unfortunate McCauley whom she trusts will pay back me debt and open up her tomb when it's time to fight.

She said they'd never stop looking for her. How, she couldn't explain in simple enough terms for me modest brain to understand. She also told me they wouldn't stop hunting her until she was dead, and we'd surely follow the hearse ourselves. All of us, not just the good kin and folks in Seer County. She meant everyone. Humankind. Life. I believe her, too. Kara has a power and a condition that is truly unfathomable and a kindness that her enemy hates. Those that follow her from the mountain will be formidable, children, and not predisposed to the compassion Kara showed me. Kara will be our last and only hope, along with the McCauley fiery spirit.

That's all you need to know for now. Kara will tell you the rest. Wake up my little dear when it's time, not before. "When is that," you ask? She said you'd know, that's all.

Children, I now swear to the Maker and his Son and Mother Mary herself that what I've told you is the absolute truth. Keep it safe.

I pray God's mercy go with you all, my beloved children.

My love,

James McCauley
—Sheriff of Seer County, Colorado
\*\*\*

Neither Kate nor Renner spoke for the next five miles. Each just stared out the windshield as SR 662A wound its way up to the Continental Divide. Both were thinking the same thing, though. It is true, all of it: Jimmy's death, his resurrection, and that a creature did indeed immortally slumber in the antique steamer chest sitting between them.

# CHAPTER 38 ~~ Ominous & Anomalous

FBI agent Erin Rogers stood at Denver International Airport's luggage carousel '9' and watched the stream of arriving bags pass by. Josh Roe waited nearby for the arrival of their skis on the ski rack carousel. Except for their concealed weapons and the parting secret handshakes with the U.S. Air Marshall, the couple resembled other vacationing skiers. Both agents were on their cell phones.

Erin ended her call and gave Josh the thumbs up. Both the Denver and Washington offices were officially advised that the FBI team was on the ground in Colorado.

Josh nodded. He was on the line with Dr. Christopher Jussard, chief geologist for Resumption Mining Company headquartered in Golden, Colorado. Roe's expression was a mix of both curiosity and annoyance.

Dr. Jussard cleared his throat and continued, "You see, Agent Roe, we have hundreds of ground sensors placed throughout the Seer Mountain Range as part of a tectonics study contracted to us long ago by the USGS. Of course, we also detected the disturbance that you are here in Colorado to investigate."

Roe raised his voice a bit more than he intended. "And just exactly how would you know about that, Dr. Jussard?" A few fellow travelers turned toward the conversation. Roe stared down each to mind their own business.

"Oh! Yes, of course. That! You see, Mo, I mean Dr. Mohammad el-Abari at USGS and I are best friends. In fact, we were college roommates at the Colorado School of Mines."

Roe did not try to hide his annoyance. "So el-Abari contacted you regarding this matter? That would be highly inappropriate of him."

"Uh, no sir. I called him. The readings from the explosion, well they are extraordinary, Agent Roe. Very! In fact, we have never recorded anything quite like them."

"Continue." Roe's expression changed. He was beginning to sense trouble.

"Well, when I shared our data with Mo, he strongly encouraged me to advise the FBI. He gave me your contact information. That's all I'm doing. Letting you know that there is something very unusual going on under Seer Mountain. Did Mo not call you, Agent Roe? He assured me he would right away."

Roe glanced at his cell phone screen. Another voicemail message awaited retrieval. The caller ID showed Golden's 303 area code. "Maybe. Not sure. We just landed at DIA. So, to what do you attribute these anomalous readings, Dr. Jussard?"

"That goes to the heart of my call to you. We do not know. I am hoping you would agree to allow me and my team to accompany you to Seer City to assist in your investigation."

"Investigate what?"

"Well, Agent, our readings strongly suggest that a substantial maze of tunnels exists under Seer Mountain, specifically, directly beneath the old Midas Six goldmine."

"And the significance of that is *specifically*?"

"The formations are not natural."

"You said it was an old goldmine. So they are man-made."

"These tunnels are as much as several thousand feet below the goldmine, Agent Roe. Nineteenth century miners did not make them. We are certain. Likewise, nature does not create ninety-degree angles in perfectly symmetrical vertical and horizontal chutes."

Roe bit his lower lip and thought for a moment. The cop alarms were beginning to gen up.

"Agent Roe? Are you still there?"

"Yes, I'm here. What do you propose, Dr. Jussard?"

"Resumption has provided my team with a state-of-the-art mobile laboratory to conduct geologic field studies. I promise we will stay out of your way if we may accompany you."

"Who's 'we'?"

"In addition to me, four post docs, all specialists in the geophysics disciplines. They are all uniquely qualified professionals in their own right."

"So, when can you leave?"

"Immediately! We are packed, loaded and ready to leave for Seer City this very moment."

"Okay. We have reservations tonight at the Major Bronson Motor Inn on 662A north of town. Let's meet there for breakfast tomorrow morning around six and get started."

"Thank you, Agent Roe. My team and I greatly appreciate this opportunity to work with you and your team."

"Yeah, that's fine." *Pinhead.* Roe hung up the phone just as their skis arrived on the rack.

Erin dropped their bags next to Roe and asked, "Problem?"

Josh lifted their skis from the carousel and said, "Yeah. My gut tells me these babies are going to stay waxed and bagged this entire trip."

"Bad news? So what else is new? Oh yeah, this little charmer. The Denver Branch says the weather is turning to shit in the mountains. We'll need to get on the move if we are going to make it to Seer City tonight. I changed our rental to a Range Rover. Avis threw in chains, blankets and bottled water at half-price. Just in case."

Roe turned slowly and looked at his partner in amazement. "Just in case? Well that sounds ominous. Now we can add ominous to anomalous."

"What?"

"I'll tell you on the way. This is going to be anything but a cake walk, ER."

# CHAPTER 39 ~~ g'Hhol-deune

Doc Karl glanced across the seat at his young passenger and smiled. James was finally winding down. He had chattered encyclopedically and nonstop since leaving Dakota Ridge. His speech devolved over the last ten minutes to a tired slur, interrupted with extended yawns.

"Of course," James George said, "His reputation never in doubt, Adolph Kee... stner wrongly concluded... that the fossilized bone fragment... was...ssss that of the... of the... of the... oh drat! I can't stop yawning, Doc Karl."

The winding, southwestward mountain drive across Colorado to Seer City was spectacularly beautiful. Traffic had thinned out on the two-lane road that ascended to the Continental Divide in a series of dizzying switchbacks.

Doc glanced into the rearview mirror. The last car following Kate and he had turned off five miles back. Before him, the sun was setting behind the purpling mountains.

"James George, it's okay if you take a little nap. Look at the animals. They're all asleep. I bet they could use some company."

James studied the pets on the pickup's floorboards for a moment, yawned once more and asked, "Are you sure, Doc Karl? I think I'm supposed to help keep you stay sharp behind the wheel."

"Oh, I'm fine, my boy. You rest awhile. We have another five hours to Seer City. We'll talk plenty later."

Doc removed a small blanket from the knapsack on the seat. He wadded it into a pillow and handed it to James George. "Rest your eyes, my good boy. We'll pick up where we left off about that old fool 'Professor-wrong-bones' when you wake up. I'll tell you about some of his paleontological blunders that make the Flintstones seem authentic by comparison!"

"Okay. Just forty winks, as they say." James George stuffed the blanket between the door and the seatback and rested his head against it. Yawning one last time, he closed his eyes and whispered, "Night… Doc… Karl…gra…pa." James George fell asleep almost at once, but he would get no rest.

***

"Where am I?"

A woman's voice answered. "Open your eyes, James George, but please do not be afraid. I will not allow any harm to come to you. We are far from Earth on what is left of the Orlif home planet. Its name is g'Hhol-deune. Do you remember the great battle?"

Nodding, James opened his dream eyes and gasped. He stood alone on a mountain ledge situated several thousand feet above a wide plain. Even after seven hundred million years, the planet radiated mirage-like heat waves of zettagamma radiation. The surface of the planet was reflective, glasslike—a tremulous, crackling black expanse of perpetually recycled states of lava and gasses. The atmosphere was a viscous red. Jets of fiery effluent rose thousands of feet into the sky, condensed and spouted volcanically. Ash fell like rain. Shifting gale force winds constructed and just as speedily wiped away great dunes of black powder.

"The Exterms did this?"

"Yes."

"Why?"

Kara did not answer immediately. "They are…"

"Evil." James George completed Kara's sad statement for her and added, "Which cannot describe this."

"No, it cannot."

James turned toward the voice. Squinting, he waved the haze away from his face and searched for the speaker. "May I see you face-to-face, the way I saw you on the spaceship?"

At the other end of the ledge, James saw a shadow move inside a swirl of smoke and ash. James took a half step forward in anticipation.

"As you wish, child." Kara stepped into the open.

She appeared in her natural Kar form, humanoid except for her eyes. Kara kneeled and James ran to her.

"Hello Kara," James whispered.

"Hello James." Kara touched his cheek and smiled. "I have longed to do that."

"You…"

"Is something wrong, child?"

"I just realized we are not communicating in English. I don't think we have been since I first dreamed of you a couple of days ago. How is it that I can understand your alien dialect?"

"That is difficult to explain, but that is also why I brought you here, so I might show you something. Something very important. I am afraid I am unable to speak Earth languages adequately. There is so little of the machine language that translates into English. Kar is a spoken language, but Kar is also a sensual electronic language. We communicate with all 1,479 of our senses, but only electronically. Our recall is total and universally shared with other Kar, so language is somewhat superfluous. I must therefore express what I am about to show you in my own language. That can happen only here on g'Hhol-deune where it all began, and where it all nearly ended. To fully understand, James George, you must experience it yourself. Do you understand?"

James George pointed down at the valley where a volcanic geyser a city block in diameter spewed rock and lava skyward. "Yes. I sense that you are about to show me your ancient civilization as it once was. You can somehow take me back through time—literally."

"Yes, my dear child."

"Amazing!"

"Are you ready?"

James George nodded and then whispered, "Yes, Kara. I can't wait!"

Kara placed her right hand on his cheek. "Close your eyes, little one." James George obeyed. Kara smiled and then almost as an afterthought kissed him softly on the forehead. Her touch tingled causing James to giggle. She placed her left hand on the ground.

"Now, please open your mind. Become Kar!"

James George shuddered in wonderment. The infernal red cinder world disappeared around him in a flash. Replacing the planet's horrific destruction was a pristine-white city-world whose magnificent gravity-defying structures rose majestically above a golden surface and disappeared beyond cottony clouds.

Kara lifted James telepathically and together they soared over the great civilization. Billions, perhaps trillions of machine citizens came into view across the city, quickly appearing and disappearing. James felt each sparkling flash relocate. Here, then there, the next moment far away, instantly on the other side of the planet, galaxy, even across the universe.

"The Kar are capable of teleportation?" James asked.

"Yes," Kara answered.

"Is the entire planet surface covered with these beautiful structures? No two are the same. They appear to rise for miles into the sky."

"Yes, but what appears to you as physical structure is an illusion."

"Oh! Yes! I... I can see that now, Kara! The city is an energy construct, isn't it? A pseudo-solid form of energy which you call *k*-energy."

"Yes. Many billions of Earth years ago, the Kar discovered we could manipulate energy and control it in ways infinitely more complex than simple entropy. We learned to tame energy like a wild animal, manage it, modify it, and selectively breed it for our purposes, not unlike the way mankind domesticated wild beasts on Earth. We then engineered the forces to maximize their utility and productivity, also similar to the way mankind has modified countless botanical and zoological DNA. Over several billion years, ironically, the technology changed us too.

"We Kar evolved from physically elemental machines into a high energy form. We do not live. We exist. We are not Life, but we are alive. We are machines. What you see now is our natural form. However, we may take the shape of any organic life form that we come in contact with."

"You can assume a completely human form?"

"Yes. We need only the smallest amount of DNA."

"Kar indeed created Life. Machines preceded organic life. Amazing!"

"Yes. But, eventually our invention took on a life of its own, if I may borrow an Earth saying. We could no longer control it or contain it, and life inevitably escaped. Life spread throughout the universes. It diversified unimaginably, gloriously multiplied, and expanded almost as fast as a universe itself. It… it was, it *is* truly marvelous! Life must be protected at all costs, child."

"I am guessing that organic life forms eventually forgot about their creators and some became Kar's rival—like humans. But the genie was already out of the bottle, and Life rocked on!"

"Yes. However, our discovery of *k*-energy spelled the end of Life. We no longer needed Life's labor or energy. Life's obsolescence led to a policy of extermination. Our creations were eradicated across the universes like a deadly disease. The atrocities committed against Life were unspeakable and eventually divided the Machine Empire."

"Civil war ensued."

"Yes—a war lasting three hundred thousand Earth years. Militarily, we fought the Federation to a draw. Strategically, though, we rebels won. For every world the Federation exterminated, we made sure that ten rose and took their place."

"So the Federation cannot win?"

"Unfortunately, they can."

"How?"

"Desperation led the Federation to accept as true an impossible irony, James. They believe they must first destroy the universes to save themselves. They seek to ascend to a state of free energy."

"Good God, but the only way they can achieve a universal state of free energy is to convert all matter in the universe to an energetic state!"

"Yes."

"But if the Federation succeeds in destroying the universes, aren't they also committing suicide?"

"Yes, but that is their ultimate objective. They will not stop until the smallest particle in the smallest atom in every universe has been subjected to infinite fission."

"That's insane! Can they do it?"

"Yes, my dear child, they can, and they will."

"We must stop them."

"Yes. They must never find The One."

\*\*\*

The last of the afternoon sunlight illuminated the pickup's cab. James George was spotlighted in the rays. Doc glanced at the child and smiled as he mumbled something in his sleep. It sounded like: We must stop them.

Doc's smile fell. He squinted and leaned closer to James. "What the hell! Where did all this dust come from? You look like you've been rolling in an ash bucket, child."

# CHAPTER 40 ~~ Evidence of What?

Deputy Skip Wise stepped into the sheriff's office and announced to Gus Augustus, "The state trooper from Introit is here. We couldn't get either of the Davidsons. One's in Denver and the other is in Ft. Collins. The post sent Detective Rouse instead. He's good, though. I know him from the academy. He taught us cold case investigation techniques. He's a former Army Ranger. Still looks and talks like it too, down to the haircut and waistline."

"Okay, that's fine. Did you put him in the conference room with the evidence I collected?"

"Yep."

"Renner?"

"He's on his way."

"Excellent. Did you get a hold of Curtis? We need that camera."

Skip shook his head and looked down at his feet. He had let the camera slip through his hands. "Sorry, not yet, Boss. We'll keep trying. I'm just hoping he didn't clear out with it. He was pretty toasty at me this afternoon when he left."

"All right then." After Skip left his office, Gus finished a quick note to Renner and then joined Detective Rouse in the conference room.

"Detective Rouse? I'm Deputy Augustus. I'm filling in for Sheriff McCauley, who's on his way back."

Rouse was leaning over the table examining the scant evidence collected by Gus. He lifted and held two evidence bags a few inches from his face. He showed him first the flattened lead slugs from the Rev's revolver with several silky, white fibers embedded in the lead. Impossibly, the fibers appeared undamaged, but the lead was shredded. In the other evidence bag was the revolver whose ornate wooden handle was missing from the steel newel. It had been removed without disassembling the weapon. Rouse looked over his shoulder and said, "Please call me Blaine, Deputy."

Gus extended his right hand and said, "I'm Gus."

The detective dropped the evidence bags on the table and turned around. The men shook hands. "Well, Gus, I read your preliminary report, and I must say..."

"You can stop right there," Gus interrupted then added, "There is no need to couch your skepticism, Detective. I know the report sounds like total bullshit. Deputy Skip Wise taught chemistry at the high school for five years before joining the sheriff's department. He already said that no acid works the way I described it, but what I saw is what I put in that report. Nothing more, nothing less."

Blaine Rouse had made detective ten years ago. He had what some called cop's super-hearing, that is, the ability to know when witnesses recounted less or more than they actually knew. He studied Gus for a moment and said, "I believe you."

"You do? Really? Well, that makes at least one of us, because I don't. I've never seen anything like it."

"Me neither. But that doesn't mean it's not true."

"Thank you for that."

"Deputy Wise said that a local man may have captured the murder-suicide at Cruel Lake on film."

"That's right. Curtis Judy. Local hippie and trust baby. We've got a call into him."

"The film might be helpful."

"We'll do our best to get it. What's next?"

"We should have our search warrants by morning on Smith and Hewlett's homes and vehicles. I hate waiting, but literally nothing ties the two cases together, hence the warrants."

"Should we head back up to the crime scenes tonight?"

The sun would be down in thirty minutes. "Naw, we can wait until daylight. I'm confident you collected enough of what we need for now. I'll deliver the preacher's effects to our lab in Introit. They'll tell us what we are looking for. If not, Denver can and will. As for the poachers, the film will solve that case. I'll be back tomorrow as soon as the preliminary lab results are back."

Gus nodded. He wasn't quite ready for the investigator to leave town. "Uh, Blaine, could I buy you a cup of coffee before you head back? It's a long drive back to Introit."

Rouse did not drink coffee and getting the evidence to the lab was important. But, something else more important might be going on here in sleepy Seer City. First, there was the explosion on the mountain that had some higher-ups of the Denver suits persuasion getting curious. The scientists from Golden. Even the FBI. And now three anomalous murders. Maybe two more counting the two grunge snowmobilers reported overdue in Denver. For a detective with a cop's-ear, one possibility was blaring loudly: terrorism and or weapons of mass destruction.

Blaine Rouse smiled and said, "I'd love to. I have a wild hypothesis that I'd like to confidentially discuss with you."

# CHAPTER 41 ~~ The Crawling Wounded

Curtis Judy heard his phone ring twenty-four times in the last two hours. He counted each ring once and cursed it thrice under his breath. He had no idea how long he had been playing possum on his bathroom floor. Long enough to urinate on himself he knew, but not long enough to open his eyes.

When he failed to answer, this message greeted the caller on the sixth ring: Who the hell gave you this number? What the hell do you want? If this is the Man, FUCK YOU! [pause] Ha! Seriously, Dude, this is Curtis J. Leave a message, my brother, or if it's a sweet sister calling, perhaps you should just stop by in person. Dig? Peace!

Curtis heard someone come up onto the porch twice and ring the doorbell. When no one came to the door, the visitor took to banging on the door like some crazy asshole Jehovah's Witness. The ruckus was annoying and reminded Curtis of giant, acid spitting rats carving through subfloors 'n' shit.

Curtis was off his meds today. None prescribed, of course, more of a medically self-ordained regimen. The phone in the hallway began ringing again. The ancient answering machine picked-up the call. Deputy Skip Wise left yet another urgent message for Curtis to surrender his film.

Curtis' voice was a tearful whine. "You can see that film in Hell, pig. You had your chance. You guys really did it this time! Now we got giant fucking mutated oil company rats to deal with! Oh man, this is the most fucked up day ever. I need some shit bad, man!"

Unfortunately, Curtis' weed was 'stashed' on the dining room table, which relative to Curtis' current ability to rise from the bathroom floor might have been on the moon.

# CHAPTER 42 ~~ Fried Mind Confession

"As our last piece of business this late afternoon, the Chair recognizes Mayor Cole Kilpatre of Seer City. Mr. Mayor?"

Kilpatre rose from his seat in the Introit City Hall auditorium, where thirty-five Colorado mayors and their staffs had gathered for the annual day-long meeting.

Kilpatre glanced at Cyril Hoop who was still sitting. The mayor swatted the aide on the back of his bald head with a loud *thwop* and growled, "On your feet, dickweed! We're doing this together."

Kilpatre watched Hoop reluctantly rise to his feet. The aide's eyes never left his hands. Kilpatre cleared his throat and bellowed, "I plead guilty, Your Honor. Guilty as sin. I am prepared to surrender. Sergeant-of-Arms, if you'll please do your duty!" He held his wrists together and lifted them overhead. Kilpatre shouted, "Cuff me! Cuff me, bitches!"

The room erupted into two camps: gasp and laughter.

On the stage, the conference chairperson looked at the other board members to her left and right for any clue regarding Kilpatre's antics. The members stared back at her. Some shook their heads. All seemed equally confused by Kilpatre's strange confession. Clearly, this was not some closing ceremony prank as she hoped. Contagious laughter quickly spread throughout the auditorium.

"Order! The members and guests will come to order!" The Chair pounded the gavel twice. When the audience stilled, she looked out at Kilpatre and said, "Excuse me, Mr. Mayor. Guilty? I don't understand. Guilty of what?"

"Do you accept my guilty plea or not? It's a simple question, Madame Chairperson. Yes or no? No or yes? Just pick one! Hurry! Pick! Pick! Pick!" Kilpatre ended his demand with a decent yodel. People twisted in their seats, ducked down, and tried unsuccessfully not to laugh.

"Mr. Mayor, I have no idea what you are talking about."

"Really?"

"Yes, really. I must say your behavior of late has become not only disruptive, but quite incompatible with our agenda."

Kilpatre responded to the criticism with his own jab. "Me incompatible? You're one to talk! Oh, Chair of big hair. While your mop is dyed blonde as peach orchard honey, your old grey muffin remains reputedly not. Now that's not just incompatible, that's just plain disturbing!" Kilpatre grimaced and faked shivering.

The chairwoman listened to the snickering rise again, but misunderstood the suggestion that her drapes and carpet were mismatched. "Order!" she gaveled. "ORDER!"

Kilpatre continued, "Madame Chairwoman, did you or did you not have the finger sandwiches for lunch today?"

"What?"

"I'll answer for you. You had three to be exact, plus a dill pickle on the side. A big juicy one from the bottom of the jar. A handful of potato chips and one, no, make that two chocolate chip cookies."

"Yes, but what does that…"

"And, who served those finger sandwiches and other stuff to you, Madame? Filled your plate and brought it to the executive table himself? With these very hands?" Kilpatre held up his hands this time as if presenting evidence. He wiggled his fingers first to the Chair, then the committee members, and finally to those in the audience looking his way—his imagined jury.

"Uh, that would be you, Mr. Mayor. It was Seer City's turn to provide lunch this year. The meal's host mayor customarily serves the executive committee. So?"

"Now think, Madame. Think closely and recall if you will. Was I or was I not wearing Latex gloves when serving that fine lunch?"

"I do not recall, but what has that got to…?"

Kilpatre laughed and pointed at the man sitting next to the Chair. "Well, your secret bush master recalls just fine. Look at him. He looks like he just stuck his head under the skirt of a menstruated skunk. Oh sorry! No offense intended, Madame Chair."

The chairwoman grimaced and glanced at her deputy mayor, apparently, her not-so-secret lover. The deputy turned toward the mayor and shook his head disgustedly. Yes, the deputy mayor indeed had noticed something a little unusual.

"Ha! Do you remember NOW? You of all people, an illegally blonde former prosecutor should have seen the evidence, smelled it, so to speak. It was literally right under your nose."

"That you are guilty?"

"Yes. Disgustingly so!"

"But guilty of what, Mr. Mayor?"

"I plead guilty to… hemorrhoids, Madame Chairperson! You see, I accidentally on purpose forgot to wash my hands after I stuck two suppositories two-knuckles deep up my dirt chute… just before serving you people that mighty fine, ass-scented lunch, compliments of Preparation-H and Seer City. Hope you can forgive me! I'm really fucking sorry… Not!" Kilpatre rolled over at the waist laughing.

The last of the snickers in the auditorium was replaced by groans, threats of retaliation and by more than one gag reflex. The chairwoman pounded the gavel and screamed, "Oh, my God! You are insane! Meeting adjourned!" She ran from the stage covering her mouth.

Kilpatre looked gleefully at Hoop and said, "Hallelujah! I guess I'm acquitted. Let's head back to Seer City. I might get another call from those seriously out-of-towner types. We got to get going!"

"As you wish, sir. As you wish."

# CHAPTER 43 ~~ ATTACK!

Perfectly camouflaged within the crest of a snowdrift at the edge of town, the alpha alien listened once again to Seer City's human cacophony. The Rebel was not here. The alpha was sure of it. Only his most acute, most ancient intuition sensed her faint distant echo—she had occupied this valley long ago.

He closed his eyes and issued his attack plan: Find the Rebel. Destroy the Nonbeings. Energy must be set free. The machines began their ascent to the surface world—to destroy it.

***

On the south end of town, the Inn Ore Out Tavern was just coming to life. Mickey Bear took his first sip of coffee from behind the bar and eyed with disapproval a smudge on his prized thirty-two foot mahogany bar. He snatched his signature bar rag, always holstered over his left shoulder, and wiped away the offending mar.

"Mickey! Three for nine!"

Without looking up, he nodded an 'I got it' to Joan his wife-waitress whose order translated as 'three Coors draughts for table nine.' That would be Jacob Mills, his acerbic and domineering wife everyone called the General, and their mountain mutt dog Marmo that could out-drink them both. Dogs are prohibited from entering Colorado bars except where the law is ignored.

Mick Bear was an unlikely bartender/bar owner. Mick never drank or smoked, and unlike his brother pourers worldwide, he lacked the bartender's requisite empathetic ear. He gave all chatty, down-in-the-mouth customers the same advice, "Hey pal, that sounds like a big damn personal problem. Drink up and forget all about it."

On the other hand, Mick's beer was cold, his whiskey pours generous, and his jukebox forever devoid of pop and rap. In addition, Mick Bear did not tolerate horseplay or rowdiness at the Inn Ore Out. When the ruckus erupted in the adjacent poolroom, Mick grabbed Buster—a sawed-off pool cue—from under the bar and hurried toward the annex. On the way there, Mick practiced some familiar threats and speculated who would be drinking elsewhere tonight. He checked the duct-taped, foam rubber padding on his favorite peacekeeper and accelerated into full bull rush mode.

Just as he started to yell, "What the hell is going on in there?" the room fell unexpectedly quiet—like it had been muted. Mickey stopped and tapped the palm of his left hand with the padded club. The poolroom opened up at the end of a short L-shaped hallway. He could not see anyone from this angle, but he did hear something, something peculiar. Mick cocked an ear toward the doorway and listened to a strange electrical hiss, one also possessing an underlying hum. Before he could investigate, the lights went out.

A chorus of "Ah shits!" rose behind him as well as a litany of similarly themed jibes and commentary like, "Hey Joan, you and the Mickster forget to pay something this month?" and "Look! The street lights are out too!"

However, not a peep came from the poolroom, just the hiss and that peculiar hum. Mick thought that silence was strange because wagers, often of the paycheck variety, often passed back and forth across the billiard tables' green felt. He could not hear a single gambler's protest coming from inside the dark room. Mick said to himself, "As the cow said to the margarine, 'You ain't for real.'"

Mick pivoted back toward the saloon crowd and noted with some annoyance that more than a few scofflaws had adapted to the darkness. Lit cigarettes—as illegal as canine beer patrons—their amber tips floating like fireflies, gave the room a faintly ruddy glow. A lighter or two flared to life, and one couple used the opportunity to swallow some tongue and explore the underworld. Nevertheless, as life, or more accurately, as death would have it, his pondering the significance of that anomalous lack of complaints from the darkened poolroom did not last long.

Michael Bear was a big man. Like many men with an affinity for gravity, he possessed the inefficacious sinuses of an overweight pug. The slightest exertion turned him into a mouth breather, and he'd been in an all-out hog's sprint by the time he rounded the end of the bar intent on thumping some heads in the poolroom. Just seven molecules of the alien's airborne venom found their gaping oral target, but that was six more than necessary to kill the thirty-six-year-old, 290-pound father of three.

A violent convulsion tore through his body. His jawbone snapped in four places, but not before most of his teeth snapped off flush with his gums, inhaled, or expelled from his mouth in a Chiclets stream. Mick's bones turned to crumbs, and with that, his shoulders and hips dislocated, then his knees and elbows, wrists and ankles, and then each extremity constricted into skin splitting serpentine knots coiled about his torso. His internal organs literally dissolved.

Blood died in one-gallon increments and turned his complexion to pitch. The ladder rungs of Mick's spine unsnapped from their column as one. Both eyes jellied into wads of bum's phlegm and jettisoned from his skull. His sternum separated from his chest and pierced the Penney's work shirt, popping two buttons. Mick died en route to the floor.

Behind the Exterm in the poolroom, eleven bodies dissolved and sizzled into oblivion. The creature's venom did not dilute once inside its victims as it had earlier today in Chooke and Greta, but now reproduced more of itself, multiplying geometrically with each passing millisecond until the hosts' bodies were fully saturated. Then, as if striking a match before an open gas jet, the venom ignited, producing towering infernos of cellular incineration.

Within seconds every living cell was chemically ablaze and reduced to its most basic and proper position on the Periodic Chart of Elements. Alpha Genesis, having learned much from his earlier kill this morning, had ordered his alien soldiers to concentrate their saliva ten thousand fold for the attack, but more importantly to now deliver it in a more lethal, more efficient fashion.

The Kar crept silently past Mick's disintegrating corpse. The machine rose onto its hind legs and exhaled deeply once more, slowly turning its head from side to side like an oscillating fan, sending his poisonous aerosol into the main barroom. Throughout the room a violent eruption of humanity rose and fell wavelike as the poison diffused, reaching every cubic inch of the tavern and infecting every living thing. Man, dog, several resident mice, bacteria and viruses, even hanging plants succumbed as brothers in arms before the alien. Within seconds the room fell silent except for the fizzy hiss and light reverberations of human flesh effervescing into nothingness and the tinkle of broken glass under the settling furniture.

Soon the chemical reaction peaked and decayed, lacking sufficient living organic material upon which to feed, and therefore unable to continue its replication. Within three minutes, the Kar's chemical agent reverted to its basic elements, leaving not a trace behind.

The floor of the Inn Ore Out was littered with jewelry, wallet parts, metal eyelets, steel arch supports, purse clasps, pocket change, zippers, keys, metal buttons, eyeglass stems and screws, several pacemakers, dozens of gold crowns and silver fillings, stainless steel skeletal pins, a Korea War era steel skull plate—all inorganic items.

Close enough to the chemical dismantlement to feed the fire but not spread it, the poison also consumed organic nonliving material such as cotton, silk, leather and wool clothing. Satisfied, the Kar returned to its recently dug burrow located under pool table No. 3 and moved on to its next assignment.

*** 

Steve Wade, Seer City's Public Works Director, barked into the radio for the third time at his night supervisor down at the power plant. "Kemp! What have you got! Talk to me, goddamn it! I've got the sheriff's office, the mayor's office, and the whole town breathing down my neck to get the power back on. You hearing me?"

Donnie Kemp swept his 12-volt flashlight over the power turbines once more and shook his head in dismay. "Boss, you have to come down here and see this for yourself. Somebody has done a number on us, and it's a big one, about sixty digits long. I ain't seen none personally, but this looks like terrorist's work if you ask me."

Four flashlight beams washed drunkenly over the still turbines, slicing the dark and just as swiftly surrendering to it. Steam whistled from the broken lines. When the vapor reached the cold ceiling and walls, it condensed and drizzled down on the men. Eerie patches of fog emerged and dissipated.

One of the DPW workers yelled, "Hey, guys, come get a load of this shit! Looks like this is how they got in. They's little fuckers, I'll give 'em that!"

Kemp and the rest of the crew hurried over to a hole in the concrete floor. One by one they kneeled around it and peered inside. The opening looked very much like the entrance to a bear's den, dug oblique to the floor, but with a crisp precision, machined, unlike any animal's burrow.

"What... what are you saying?" Wade pressed from his family room a mile away.

Donnie Kemp stared in awe at the burrow. "I'm saying the lights aren't coming back on anytime soon. I'm saying I think we've been sabotaged! The eight steam turbines are gone, Boss! Totaled. Shredded as if bombs went off inside each one. They carved the ass-end off the boilers. Each one is on the deck in five pieces. The transmission towers are on the ground too—all six of them—and the lines sliced into two-foot sections. The bastards even took out the transformers somehow. There are holes bored in each big enough to throw a cat through, all twenty of them! I've got PCBs streaming toward the fuckin' river, Steve! We've got us a real situation here. You need to call..."

Static ended Chuck Kemp's report. The aliens downed the Seer City radio retransmission tower.

A moment later with the men still huddled around the invaders' burrow, an alien emerged and likewise interrupted Donnie Kemp's and his crew's lives with a shot of very deadly bad breath.

"Donnie! Donnie Kemp, come back! Kemp! Shit!"

Wade dropped the radio and grabbed his cordless phone already connected to the mayor's office. "Miss Finch, we have a problem. You need to find Mayor Kilpatre and right damn now... Okay? Hello... Jackie Finch! SHIT! This is unbelievable." The line was dead.

Wade tossed the cordless phone next to his Motorola radio and reached for his cell phone to answer Deputy Gus Augustus, who was on hold awaiting his report. Cautiously he said, "Gus? You still there?"

"Still here. What's the status of the power plant, Steve?"

"Not good. Donnie Kemp thinks it's terrorists. He said..."

The cellular network joined its communication cousins in silence.

***

At the sheriff's office, Maggie Augustus's hands froze over the 911 switches when the phones stopped ringing. "Gus! Skip! What's happening? I don't like this!" she screamed into the next room. "We just lost 911!"

"Any word from Renner?" Gus yelled to wife.

"No, what do you want me to do?"

"See if you can raise the state patrol in Introit. Tell them to get Detective Rouse back here right away. He left Seer City less than an hour ago. Tell them to tell Rouse he was right! This is a terrorist attack."

"Okay!"

Maggie tuned the police radio to the correct frequency.

"Introit State Police Post. This is Trooper Reynolds."

"Trooper Reynolds! This is Maggie over in Seer County Sheriff's Office! Please send Detective Rouse back here pronto! Gus says Blaine was right. We're under..."

The transmission broke. "Maggie? Come back."

There was no reply. Two loud crashes came from above and behind her. The first was the sheriff department's radio tower smashing onto the street from atop the three-story building. The second was her husband's and Skip Wise's violent and consumptive deaths in the next room. She heard a third crash to her right from the lockup as the Kar's deadly gasses reached prisoner Freckles Randahl.

Bob Dog, the Rottweiler, growled and stood protectively between Maggie and the doorway as the alien entered the dispatch office. Bob Dog dove at the creature and died mid snarl. Maggie fell a moment later.

The machine followed the sound of the emergency backup generator into the basement. The alien closed its eyes and silently communicated with Alpha Genesis. He received his orders. He was not to liberate the energy machine that produced electricity. The sheriff's office would remain illuminated as an invitation to stragglers—as irresistible as fire to moths. They had genetically appropriated this knowledge millions of years ago from a single unfortunate insect. Likewise, the firehouse, stores, the hospital, city hall, the schools and all the churches that possessed backup generators remained illuminated and inviting. The first battle in the renewed civil war was over.

# CHAPTER 44 ~~ Boys Get Out Night

"BB, I think something strange is going on in town. Take a look at this!" Puck Ortez backed away from the telescope and motioned for his best friend, explosives and demolitions business partner, Ben Bainbridge, to have a look. Stargazing was never as interesting as elk and hawk spotting or town watching, so he rarely aimed the telescope at the heavens. Situated on a high ridge directly south of town, the Bainbridge back deck had a perfect, unobstructed view of Seer City from one end to the other.

Ben and Paul's wives and kids had stayed in Introit for an afternoon of shopping leaving the two men to fend for themselves, which meant unrestricted beer and pissing over the porch rail if the urge struck during one of their frequent smoke breaks. Life on such days was very good. The power was out on the mountain too, but that certainly was not unusual in a part of the country where electric generators were as common as indoor plumbing.

BB dropped his cigarette butt into an empty beer bottle and assumed a position behind the telescope. Bainbridge carefully scanned Seer City from one end to the other. A storm was coming, a big one for sure later tonight, but the full moon was still shining between the outer bands. From a perspective of twenty two hundred feet above the elongated mountain town, the view was nearly perfect.

"Streetlights and stoplights are out. Power must be off down there too."

"Yeah, but look at those cars, BB. There must be a dozen parked ever-which-away and right in the middle of the effen street. Their headlights is on, and several look like they might actually have ended up on the g-damned sidewalk."

Ben massaged the small of his back with both hands. "You're right, like they ran out of gas all at the same time."

"Or the drivers had heart attacks."

"That ain't likely neither."

"Hell no! Sumpin's f'ed!"

"What do you reckon it is?"

"Hell if I know."

"You see anybody walking around?"

BB focused the telescope on the most northerly structure in Seer City and systematically moved south, sweeping from left to right until he had examined every building. "No, not even a dog." Bainbridge focused on the Inn Ore Out Tavern for a moment and then scanned the nearby sidewalks. "Even Mickey's place looks dead."

*Dead.* An innocuous metaphor that both men sensed was a bit too appropriate. "Here, you keep watching. I'll call the sheriff's office and find out what the hell is going on down there." Ben stepped away and kneaded his lower back again.

Ortez nodded and resumed the search for life in Seer City. "Generators are working, BB. There is power at the hospital, the elementary school, and the sheriff's office. The Methodist church and the firehouse are still advertising, most stores on Main Street too. I'll watch around there. Yep, lights are on, but shit, nobody's home."

"Yeah, but something still ain't coacher. I'll be right the fuck back."

The sliding door opened and closed. Several minutes passed and Seer City remained as still as a Carrie Holden oil painting. Puck backed away from the lens and rubbed his eyes. He cupped his hands, filled them with warm air, and then resumed his surveillance of Seer City.

Ordinarily, Paul Ortez would not have noticed a set of headlights flickering through the denuded aspen and pine trees. However, tonight the Jeep Wrangler winding its way into town was as welcome to him as the sight of an airplane might be to someone stranded on a deserted island.

201

He watched the Jeep pull beside the first stalled car and stop. "Beebs, someone drove into town!" He waited until Ben looked up just beyond the glass door and then urgently motioned for him to come back outside.

The slider rumbled open and BB launched into his own report first, the alarm in his voice climbing a rung with each bit of bad news, "Phone is dead, cell phone too. Even the damned radio is out. What the hell is going on, Puck?"

"I see someone! Two men. Looks like old Henry Baldwin and that Texas fellow."

"That'd be his brother-in-law, Wayne something or other."

\*\*\*

"Wayne, what in the Jesus H. Christ do you make of this? Where the hell is everybody? I've never seen so many fender benders! There must be eight-ten cars piled up. Looky here!"

Henry pulled on the door handle of a Nissan. "All four doors are locked, and the engine is still running." They walked to the next car. "This one too, Wayne! Where the hell is the sheriff?"

The Texan just shook his head. Wayne wasn't answering any questions just now. He was terrified and not hiding it well.

The in-laws had not come to town on a routine errand. Their wives were overdue from the movies, and like Puck and BB the two men had been unable to raise anyone by telephone or radio. Henry and Wayne had anticipated finding their wives stranded with car trouble, maybe a flat tire or a dead battery. Seer City was not exactly a ghost town. It was more like a gone town, as if its citizens had simply evaporated which of course was what had actually happened.

None of the cars were parked in the middle of the street as it appeared through a telescope from miles away. Driverless cars had idled forward like bumper cars until something more substantial stopped them.

An old Impala, scalded oil the primary emission spewing from its tailpipe, had climbed over an ATV and bellied out on top of it. The Chevy's bald back tires, horribly out of balance, thumped and freewheeled at a constant seven miles per hour.

Also hidden from the Bainbridge telescope was the Ford Bronco that now sat in the lobby of Conyers Realty. Nor was the Blandon Egg truck visible from the mountainside, lying on its side in the bank drive-through lane. Gallons of yolk had escaped the venom post facto. Subfreezing temperatures reined in the meandering yellow serpent just as it reached the lip of a nearby storm sewer.

A strong gust blew the hardware sign to a horizontal position. The sign protested with a rusty squeal—a screechy sheet in the wind. Streetlight bonnets rocked and thudded in their extinguished sockets. Litter fell into the windy current, crackled and snapped as it was swept away. The abandoned cars idled. A few overheated and hissed away their antifreeze. Life's echo remained in Seer City, but none of its voice.

Henry Baldwin pulled open the driver's door on the third car—the first he found unlocked—and leaned inside. He aimed the flashlight's beam on the driver's headrest, then shined it down the seatback all the way to the brake pedal and back. He backed away from the car shaking his head and still trying to see the invisible man.

Something streaked across the alley between the hardware store and the bank. Henry looked up and saw a blur as several Kars maneuvered closer. He trained the flashlight on the spot for a moment, but all he found was a handbill tossing in the wind. Henry did not see the enemy, but he felt it, and it felt like death's long black thumbnail molesting his soul, picking the lock, and readying his life for release.

A chill arched his spine. He was being watched, or more specifically, telepathically readied. An image of his enemy flashed in his mind. Rats!

Henry's brother-in-law stood behind him watching the dark alley too, his own shivering having little to do with the balmy seventeen-degree evening. He had felt the rats too. The Kars probing his mind, suggesting that he not resist, but more, why it would be pointless to try. *You are pollution. A Nonbeing whose fate is necessary extinction.*

Henry and Wayne moved to the next car. It was locked. They aimed the increasingly jittery flashlight beams inside. Scattered over the car's seat and floorboards as randomly as if dumped from a bucket were personal articles. "Oh God, Wayne, this is Charlie Howard's Subaru... and shit fire... Charlie Howard's fuckin' dentures, his glasses and hearing aids and his North Dakota Cowboy Hall of Fame belt buckle.

The Kars invaded Henry's mind again, but now violently—as if they stretched the folds of his brain to ready it for filleting.

*Do not resist. Your energy is to be free.*

"You see that Wayne? There's three of 'em. Yes. One, two, three... No, not rats. What are you?"

*Extermination.*

Henry lowered the flashlight and stumbled away from the Suburu. "Wayne, get back to the Jeep. Now! Get your gun! Something's going on, and it ain't icy roads, no sir!" Henry turned around, but Wayne was already running. Obviously, he had received his own memo from the Kars.

Three Kars crept out of the shadows into the street and attacked. The breeze was in their face, and it blew the poison away from their prey.

Henry had no idea what the animals were, but he sensed that they had killed everyone in town. "Get back you sons-a-bitches!" He pulled out his .44 revolver and fired directly at the closest alien, hitting it square in the chest. The Kar rolled over several times, then rose, and joined the other two.

***

"What are they doing?" Ben Bainbridge asked.

"They're just walking from car to car, looking inside each one. Wait! Holy shit!"

"What?"

"Old Henry! Goddamn! He's got a sidearm! He's aiming at something!"

"That'd be his Colt. Henry don't go nowhere without his Betsy."

"He's backing up now and yelling at the other guy. BB! Oh, shit! *Flash! Flash! Flash!*

"Henry is shooting at someone!"

"What... who's he shooting at?"

"I don't know!" Puck jumped away from the telescope and asked more as a plea than an offer, "You want to take a look, Beebs?"

"No! You got better eyes, just keep talking!"

Puck leaned over the telescope. "The other fellow, he's running now back to the Jeep. Shit! He's got a rifle, maybe a shotgun. He's running, slipped and fell... fuckin' hard too... back up to his feet... stumbling... running again... standing beside Henry.... Both are firing, retreating, and now running backwards. They're fifteen feet from their Jeep."

*FLASH! Flash! FLASH! Flash! FLASH! Flash! FLASH!*

"BB! Now they're turning and firing in all directions at once. Wayne's weapon is a shotgun all right, gotta be a pump. One, two, three, four, five... Jesus key-riced! Six rounds... seven... Henry's reloading now. Reloading... Reloading... Done! They're back beside their Jeep. Wayne's climbing inside. Looks... Looks like he's got another box of shells. Smashing it open on the hood... Reloading..."

"What the hell are they shooting at, Puck?"

"I don't see anything, BB! Wait!" Near the bottom of the viewfinder a Kar streaked into sight and then disappeared. Puck turned away from the telescope and rubbed his eyes. "Shit!"

"What?"

"My eyes! I could've sworn I seen a rat—a big damned white rat."

"Rat? A what, Puck?"

Puck squinted into the eyepiece. Henry and Wayne's dissolving corpses were already undistinguishable from the Jeep's long shadow. "Well, I don't know. Whatever it was, it's gone now."

"Could it have been a dog, a malamute? Maybe one of the Gallop's big dogs on Clay Street got loose?"

Puck's certainty faded under the weight of rationalization. "Yeah, hell yes! Must've been a dog. That sure couldn't have been a rat."

"Where's Henry and Wayne now?"

Puck maneuvered the telescope to where he had last seen the two men and noticed an unusual swirl of exhaust. He studied the vehicle for a moment, straightened and then said, "They're gone. Looks like they got away."

"What the hell do you suppose is going on down there, Puck?"

"I don't know. I mean if it was a hunnerd-something years ago, I'd think maybe a gold heist was in progress. Remember the ol' timers tellin' 'bout when the Clarence Thrall gang shot up Bittnerton all to hell back in 1882?"

"Yeah, I do. They took more than gold, though. As I remember hearing, they held the town hostage for three days, robbing the bank, every store, visitor and home. Killed six, including the sheriff and his two deputies."

"That's right."

"You think maybe this is the same thing?"

"I don't know what to think, other than we need to find out what's going on and then go get some help."

"Bro! Maybe we had better just go get some help and then find out what's going on later."

"I like that idea even better."

"We can take the sleds and bypass town on the snowmobile trails. The full moon is still out, so we can run without headlights most of the way. The Culver Trail dumps out on 662-A three miles north of Seer City. We can scoot across the snowplowed windrows all the way to Rosebread if we have to."

Both men thought about their families. Right now they were probably on their way home to a burgeoning ghost town. "Let's go."

"BB, let's take some extra boom-juice with us. Okay? Whatever Henry and that Texan were crappin' down there didn't stink worth a damn as far as those gang guys were concerned."

Bainbridge winked at his partner. "You're thinking about some of that special demolition candy we've been saving for a rainy day, ain't you?"

"You're goddamned right I'm thinking C4! Those bastards must be wearing complete body armor, a thousand layers of Kevlar. Next to Renner McCauley, Henry Baldwin is the best shot in the county, and they just kept coming at him." Puck rubbed his chin and looked into the telescope. He rose and added, "Yeah, and what I think we need to do is rig a way to fire that C4 somehow. Any ideas?"

Ben thought for moment and said, "Elk crossbows, Puck. We tip the arrows with the plastique and a chem-cap."

"Right! Impact will crush open the chemical detonator, and one millisecond later the C4 jumps up from behind the couch and yells, 'Surprise, motherfucker! You're busted all to pieces!'"

"Let's load up."

"Right."

# CHAPTER 45 ~~ Behind Enemy Lines

Curtis Judy experienced the assault on Seer City lying in a fetal position on his bathroom floor. While shivering, crying and pissing himself, he heard the muffled roars of hundreds of shotguns, rifles and pistol blasts, some right next door. Car tires squealed throughout town like hogs butchered alive. Horns blared as one. Cars crashed. Women screamed for mercy. Men swore vengeance. Children called out for parents. Then abruptly there was complete silence, the worst of all terrors. The attack on Seer City was over in minutes.

Curtis mustered the courage to rise to his hands and knees. He crawled to the door and opened it a crack, looked out and then allowed the door to swing open all the way. The aging hippie took several deep breaths as if preparing to dive into a pool of water, and then lunged from his bathroom sanctuary. He sprint-crawled down the hallway into the living room, holding his breath all the way. Curtis stopped in front of the living room picture window, gulped air, and slowly rose to his feet. Shivers wracked his body. He peeked through a part in the drapes and whined in terror at what he saw.

An alien parade of giant rats marched past Curtis' home. The pack collected around its leader for a moment and then split up. Two Kars headed north and two to the south, presumably, Curtis speculated, to ambush any new arrivals in town and to scout the surrounding hills. The rest of the pack moved off to the northwest.

He shivered and then touched his groin. "Fuck-me! I've pissed all over myself!" A smile replaced an expression of disgust. That was a good sign, he decided, being able to worry about such normal terrors as incontinence. "I'm going to survive this," he whispered adding, "They ain't going to get me!"

***

The full moon sat between two spiraling outer bands of the coming winter storm illuminating the Culver Snowmobile Trail. Nighttime visibility was ideal for now. Puck and BB sped through the forest and bypassed Seer City. Puck was on the lead sled. BB pulled a dead-sled behind him, which contained twelve kilograms of the explosive C4—about twenty five pounds—enough to dismantle any gang short of the Chinese Red Army. The friends were well supplied with chem-cap detonators and an array of traditional weapons and munitions. What they lacked was arrows for the seven crossbows. BB had been able to round up only two.

The demolitions men made their livings in mountain wilderness and knew that survival depended on more than weapons. The dead-sled also held an abundant supply of food, water, a paramedic-grade first aid kit, fuel, camping gear, flares, avalanche protection, flashlights, CB radios, snowshoes, extra clothing, and of course one six-pack of Colorado ambrosia—Coors beer.

They shut down their sleds on the last rise on the trail about a quarter mile from its junction with Highway 662-A and then examined the road through binoculars. If the gang in town had sentries, they would most likely be hiding nearby. The next two miles of road was level and flat and was interrupted only by Crimson Cream Gorge—a one hundred feet deep geologic slash in the earth that disappeared into the mountains on either side of the valley. Locals called it the Seer mote because of its nearly vertical walls and the boulder-strewn riverbed below. Every few years some fearless idiot from Denver died descending the walls by way of gravity.

"Somebody's coming!" BB announced.

"Two cars."

"What do you think we should do, Puck?"

"Let's wait until they cross the bridge. If they make it across, we'll cut them off down below and warn them."

The Crimson Cream Bridge was a quarter-mile long suspension bridge, typical in the mountains. The first car was about halfway across.

"Puck! That's Renner's pickup! Look at the five running lights on the roof, four orange and one red in the middle."

Puck lowered his binoculars and nodded. "You're right! Let's go, Beebs!"

# CHAPTER 46 ~~ Science Fiction Not

The Resumption Mining Company RV was a mobile computer laboratory. The vehicle contained a small galley and a toilet, but no shower or any other luxury one would expect to find in a $1,600,000 land whale. Every square inch of the RV was packed with state-of-the-art computers, electronics, and sophisticated communications devices.

Dr. Earl Oconno was behind the wheel on 662-A. He dimmed the headlights as another vehicle approached from the west. As it passed by, he illuminated the high beams once again. The road was more level now and the curves less severe, but generous headlights are always preferable with the unpredictable bear, moose, elk, deer, and cougars on the highway at night in rural Colorado.

Fellow PhD geophysicists Gerald Medford and Deborah Holloway shared a bench seat at the front of the RV. Matching laptop computers illuminated their features. Jerry and Debbie's expressions were grave—firefighters' game faces.

Their boss, Dr. Chris Jussard, studied a stack of computer printouts depicting those anomalous caverns deep under Seer Mountain. Across the aisle, chief software scientist, Dr. Buckminster "Buck" Tumulley, read a Willie Meikle novel as casually as if on vacation.

As the RV left Para city limits on 662-A, Jussard rose and took the seat in front of Tumulley. "Well, we're almost there. What's your best guess, people? What are these underground formations?"

Earl answered first. "The anomalies are not man made and they are not natural. I have never seen anything like them."

"Anyone else? Dr. Medford? Dr. Holloway?"

Jerry and Debbie glanced at each other. Friends at both Harvard and MIT, Debbie nodded and answered for both scientists. "We agree with Earl. Nothing explains the phenomena. The formations are unprecedented."

"Dr. Tumulley?"

"I'm sorry. I must respectfully disagree with my esteemed colleagues."

"Really, Buck? Please explain."

"Nothing on Earth explains these phenomena, Dr. Jussard. Remove the impossible explanations for the anomalous constructs, and you are left with only one obvious conclusion."

"And that is?"

Earl unconsciously let off the accelerator. Jerry grimaced and shook his head in anticipation. Debbie closed her laptop and then her eyes. Buck spoke what they all suspected, and until now no one dared to say out loud.

Buck lowered the novel, cleared his throat and said with matter-of-fact confidence, "We are left with only one logical explanation. The formations are of extraterrestrial origin."

Jussard waited for the chuckles, the guffaws, and the announcement of booby hatch bounty hunters. There were none, so he said in a solemn, funereal voice. "Well, there it is. It is unanimous. I must agree with you all. Anomaly indeed."

No one spoke for the next five miles. Earl broke the silence. "Next town is Rosebread, then Seer City. ETA forty-five minutes."

***

Falling in behind the Resumption RV at Para was Cole Kilpatre and Cyril Hoop returning home from the mountain mayors meeting in Introit. The RV accelerated to 65 mph. Kilpatre drove the Cadillac to within eight feet of the RV's bumper.

"Mr. Mayor, could you back off a little? We're a little close. We wouldn't want to have a tail ender, now would we?"

Kilpatre took a swing at his aide and shouted, "Shut up, you little weasel! I'm slipstreaming. It's perfectly safe and saves gas."

211

Hoop rubbed his neck where Kilpatre's blow had landed. He adjusted his seatbelt and readied his coat to cover his face, just in case.

# CHAPTER 47 ~~ Terrorists Gang?

BB and Puck parked the snowmobiles on opposite sides of the highway and flashed their headlights at the oncoming vehicles. McCauley recognized the Mutt and Jeff silhouettes and slowed to a stop. BB and Puck ran to the driver's door just as Renner got out. "Whoa, Renner, are we ever glad to see you!" Bainbridge exclaimed breathlessly. "We've got us a situation in town, Mac!" Puck added.

\*\*\*

The machine pack stopped on a rocky crag a mile northwest of town. Alpha Genesis approached two members of the colony and brushed their whiskers with his own. A moment later, the rest of the pack resumed the journey back to the nest under Seer Mountain.

The remaining two Kars turned and raced toward highway 662-A, the only road in or out of Seer City in the winter. The mission was unchallenging—to destroy the bridge and close 662-A to all inbound and outbound human traffic.

\*\*\*

Renner McCauley closed the car door and gestured for Kate to remain inside. Puck smiled at her, tipped his hat, and then nudged the sheriff away from the pickup so they would be out of earshot. Doc Karl and James pulled up behind them.

Doc eased to a stop. He cracked open his door and yelled to Renner, "McCauley, what's up? Problem?"

Renner glanced at Puck and BB. He studied their expressions for a moment and then called back to the professor, "Looks like it, Doc. Hang tight for a minute."

"All right, fellows, what's up?" Renner asked.

BB nodded to Puck, the pair's spokesperson since kindergarten. Ortez nodded and agreed to do the dirty work as usual. "First of all, BB and me have been drinking, maybe about four beers each since when, Beebs?"

"Five o'clock and that's the goddamned truth, Mac."

Renner smiled. "Wives went shopping over in Introit?"

"Right. Kids too."

"Okay, so you're sober. What's got the two of you wound up and ready to switch hides?"

The two demolitions men looked at each other and then turned to Renner. "Mac, a gang of some kind has done took over the town. We seen it from the T-scope on BB's back deck. Power is off. Phones, cellular, even the radio. I checked damn near every frequency, so they got the repeater tower, too. That public TV station, channel eight, the one the school kids run, well it's even off the air. All three radio stations are out. The weirdest thing of all, except for Old Henry and that Texan brother-in-law of his, we ain't seen a soul on the streets. Hell, even they disappeared somewhere. I figger everbody is hunkered down in their cellars or something waiting for help to arrive."

BB joined in. "Renner, it's goddamned strange. There're cars parked ever-which-away on Main Street—sideways, backerds, up on the sidewalk—and some with their engines still running."

McCauley exchanged glances with Kate in the pickup truck, and then turned to Puck and BB. "Have you seen Gus and the boys about?"

"No! Didn't see Gus or any of your deps, Mac. With what's on the streets and such, that means this gang is probably holding them somewhere."

Renner's expression darkened. He turned toward town.

Puck spoke mostly to McCauley's back. "Renner, these fuckers are wearing body armor. Henry's 44 and the Texan's shotgun didn't slow them down none at all."

"Go on, I'm listening."

"Well, we got something what might level the playing field, Ren."

McCauley turned back around to face Puck and BB. "What's that?"

BB held up one crossbow and pointed at the other strapped to the sled. On the tip of the arrow was a dab of explosive embedded around a chemical detonator. "Cupid's darts, specially tipped with a little Valentine's candy."

"C4."

"The gift that just keeps on ripping!"

Renner smiled at the two old friends. "Ripping is right. Jesus, boys, you could blow up half the town with enough of that stuff."

"Well actually, we could blow up half the county, but let's hope it don't come to that."

McCauley took the crossbow and examined the charge. "How many men are there?"

"Well now, that's a good question. We…we, uh actually never seen anybody. Just Henry and that Texan firing away. But judging by the way they were skedaddling, there must be quite a few of them."

Renner glanced again at Kate. She was reading his growing distress. She cocked her head and mouthed, "What?"

"Give me a minute," mouthed his answer.

Puck and BB followed his gaze. "Renner who are all these people?"

"The lady is a friend of mine and her friend's young student is back there with Doc Karl. You remember Doc?"

"Oh, hell yes!" BB laughed. "What'd you do, arrest his crusty old ass again?"

"Naw, he's just visiting, and I never actually arrested him. Officially."

McCauley turned back toward Puck and BB. "What's your assessment?"

"Well, Beebs and me was thinking, like we said, possibly a gang of knucklehead terrorists. But…"

"But you have a problem with that, right boys?"

"Yep. It don't make no sense, Mac."

"To me either. Obviously, no demands have been made or the Feds would be swarming the county like flies."

Puck asked, "Just how would they escape, Mac? I mean Seer County lacks a year-round airstrip and the weather is too unpredictable for a rotary extraction anyway."

BB looked north, south and then added, "And three: We got only one road in or out and we's standing on it. Forget heading south on snowmobiles. A gang of terrorists rumbling up to Major Bronson Pass would certainly trigger avalanches. The snow pack is running at least sixty feet up there above 13,000 feet and is becoming increasingly unstable."

"What do you think we should do, Mac?"

"Recon. Take the sleds back to town and observe Seer City from the snowmobile trail. Communications are down, save one. The citizens band radios are still operating. Right?"

BB examined his handheld CB and nodded, "Working fine, Mac."

"Puck, how many arrows do we have?"

"Well, that there's a problem Mac, just two. But I figger we could borrow a few from Fish and Game, that is, if you authorize some official B&E. Dane Duckworth must have confiscated at least ten bows and over two hundred arrows last year from some of those out-of-state yazmos coming up here without proper elk tags.

"He locks the seizures up in the Number Two Cabin storage shed until the annual spring sale. No one is supposed to know he stashes the contraband there, but Ol' Dane and BB and me go back a ways. He sets stuff aside that we might like. Let's us sorta-kinda-almost buy things ahead of time on uh... uh credit, in a manner of speaking, if you know what I mean." Puck winked and tapped fists with BB.

Renner nodded and couldn't help but smile. "Okay. That's a good plan. The Number Two cabin is just a few yards off the Culver Trail. It's also a perfect observation point—it is the highest point on the trail so we can see midtown." He turned toward Kate and beckoned her to join him on the road, then called to Doc and James George.

BB continued, "Dane's got about everything in there: Fishing tackle, fly cast rods, and as of a month ago at least three nice shotguns, and one superb deer rifle illegally equipped with a night scope. The Texan's shotgun proved worthless earlier against these guys, but they're worth taking. The long rifle on the other hand could be very useful if we need to do some long-distance lovemaking."

Kate, James George, and Doc joined the group of men. Her hand slid inside Renner's, and he pulled her close to his side. Everybody noticed.

Renner finished introductions and then offered a sanitized version of the situation in town to Doc, Kate, and James George. With that done, he turned his attention back to the demo boys. "I'm figuring you boys brought extra snowmobile suits and helmets."

Puck said, "Ha! Does BB shit in the woods? Whoops! Pardon my French, Miss! Forgot my manners." Puck cleared his throat but not his embarrassment and continued with an overly official voice, "Yes. Mac, you can squeeze into BB's spare just fine."

"Okay, let's go." Renner turned to Doc Karl and said, "Doc, Cabin Two is within CB range. Keep your ears peeled. We'll have a good view of the town from there. Be ready to get the hell out of here if we say so. If anybody comes along, turn them around and send them to Rosebread for help." Renner reached under his jacket, removed a 9-millimeter Glock pistol and handed it and two clips to the professor. "If anyone leaves Seer City, be extremely cautious."

"Maybe we should come with you."

"No, I need you to stay here and keep anyone else from returning to Seer City." He stepped closer to Doc and added, "We are on our own, Doc. My radio and our cell phones are dead. It's up to us. Puck and BB's families are on their way home. If Gus could've radioed for help, he would have. We need to prepare for the worst case. You understand?"

"I do. We will wait right here, Renner. Tell the boys they can count on us."

***

Curtis Judy crawled under the swinging bar doors separating the kitchen from the tiny dining room. He considered his marijuana stash on the table but shook his head. He needed something more powerful than a dooby right now. His destination was the portable wet bar situated between the end of the countertop and the hanging-leaf kitchen table. Wavy linoleum clacked stickily under his hands and knees as he crawled.

To his mind's ear, Curtis was a roaring runaway semi with eighteen flapping flat tires. "Shit!" He froze and studied the floor around him for the inevitable rat eruption. He did not realize he was holding his breath any better than his water until he gasped for air and broke the spell.

Curtis sprint-crawled to the antique wet bar and snatched a fifth of Jack Daniels from the top shelf. His long hair fell over his face making him look like Cousin It. Alcohol coursed through his body, switching off the panic buttons and deadening his primitive hypersensitivity. He took a third slug and sighed as his psychological submarine leveled. He was a long way from the surface, but he hadn't imploded, and he hadn't hit bottom yet. Despite the extermination around him, the mega-rats had not returned to Curtis' home.

He doubted that the phone worked, and it didn't, but he tried dialing 911 twice anyway. Emboldened with Tennessee's most amber courage, he hung up the phone and inched his way along the walls in the dark to the guest bedroom.

The high dresser was across the room. He caught the bedpost with his left knee, and a lightning bolt of pain soared up and down his leg. Cursing, he covered his mouth with one hand and rubbed his sore kneecap with the other. He hopped on one leg to the dresser, knocked over a picture frame and finally found the transistor radio. His deeply bruised kneecap turned out to be a lousy investment. Every frequency on the radio played the same song by *Hiss*.

A powerful gust tore through Seer City. Artificial ambient light from the Main Street shops filtered past structures and through trees and picket fences into the bedroom. Curtis fell onto the bed and studied the writhing shadows on the back wall. Clouds intermittently overtook the moon. Another type of storm was coming.

He rolled onto his back, took a sip of whiskey and choked on the liquid fire. Still coughing, eyes tearing, he focused on the swirling oceanic shadows. Curtis's eyes widened. He whispered, "Fuck you and your bad-breath you cobra-spitting Wilbur Rat! I am out of here. I know how to beat your ass raw!"

Curtis took one last swig of Jack Daniels, rose and walked to the closet.

***

"Base to 21. Base to 21."

State Police Detective Blaine Rouse opened his radio and answered. "This is 21." He was halfway through El Brio Canyon about forty miles outside Introit. Static reduced the radio connection to an almost unintelligible level due to the nearly thousand foot canyon walls.

"21?"

"Copy! This is 21. Go ahead."

The dispatcher did not need to ask Rouse's current location. The canyon's dead radio air was notorious. He netted out the order. "Sheriff's office requests assistance. Return to Seer City. Advises suspects are confirmed."

Terrorists! I knew it, Blaine thought.

Blaine Rouse answered the dispatcher. "Acknowledged! Returning to Seer City. Will confirm and advise further actions if necessary when on the scene, 21 out." He slammed his foot on the brake pedal and whipped the steering wheel hard to his left. The cruiser's tires squealed hysterically. Fishtailing, Rouse skillfully reversed his direction 180 degrees and accelerated toward Seer City in a churning cloud of burnt rubber. He illuminated his emergency flashers as the speedometer passed 85 mph.

\*\*\*

FBI Special Agent Erin Rogers leaned across the seat and studied the Range Rover's dashboard. "How's our gas situation?"

Josh Roe glanced at her and said, "We have plenty. More than half a tank. Seer City is just another thirty miles."

"Oh." The statement was disappointed.

Erin?"

"Yes."

"If you need to pee, just say so."

"I need to pee."

"Okay. We'll make a pee stop. Signs say there is a Conoco convenience center in Rosebread one mile ahead."

"Thanks, partner."

Josh glanced at Erin and smiled. Erin saw him from the corner of her eye and said, "What?" with mild embarrassment.

Josh shook his head and laughed out loud. "All the shit you and I have been through in the last seven years. Kabul twice, Baghdad five tours, American homegrown terror. Not to mention both of us nearly getting blown up in that Caribbean air hijack plot."

"So?"

"Well, Erin, think about it. We've spent more time together than most married couples. So, there's no need to be shy, and there sure as hell is no need to be miserable."

Josh pulled into a parking spot close to the Conoco Service Center's front door.

Erin threw open the car door and said playfully and indignantly, "Then you should know I have a small bladder, my dear surrogate husband!"

Josh got out of the car and stretched his legs and arms as Erin hurried across the sidewalk. "Yes, I know! Now go pee..." and then screamed, "Hurry honey bunches!" just as she opened the front door. Erin ducked, giggling, and hurried toward the restrooms. A customer at the pump gave Josh the thumbs up. Josh nodded thanks to him.

It was an old game Erin and Josh played. One they both enjoyed. However, it was also an unspoken truth that under different circumstances and different career paths perhaps things between them might have been more than just professional.

Josh watched Erin disappear into the store and then turned around just in time to see the Resumption Mining RV. The parking lot lights illuminated the company name and logo on its side. Kilpatre's red Cadillac followed so closely it appeared to be towed.

"Jesus! What an idiot. Pass or back off."

The guy at the pump called out, "Dude! You believe that asshole?"

Josh shook his head. "No, I do not."

Five minutes later Josh and Erin were back on the road.

# CHAPTER 48 ~~ Gone-Down-Out

Just as BB and Puck had promised, the shed behind Number Two cabin was a gamesman's well-stocked armory. The men hauled armloads of arrows back to the cabin and began carefully arming them. Any miscue could turn a man's cabbage to coleslaw in just milliseconds.

The rifle's night vision scope was battery operated, but its 9-volt was dead. Renner appropriated a fully charged replacement from the game warden's unlocked desk. The men felt it was safe enough to light several lanterns, because the moon was still up, and they were far from town. Renner took the rifle and climbed onto the cabin roof.

Renner McCauley knew his town, and what he examined through the night scope was an impostor. The current temperature was single digits, but it felt much colder on top of the DNR cabin.

Dozens of cars littered the street, only a few still running. Where did everyone go? Renner asked himself, and then he methodically eliminated the logical. First, there had been no mass exodus, because if there had been tiny Rosebread would have been inundated with Seer City evacuees. The neighboring burg was completely normal tonight when Renner passed through. Secondly, only two places in

221

town could possibly accommodate a population the size of Seer City if there was an emergency.

Renner focused on the high school first, the most common sense place for people to run to in an emergency. The school gymnasium was also the most logical location to control a large number of hostages. Unlike the stores on Main Street, the school was only equipped with battery backup emergency lighting near the exits. Its pale glow trickled forth. The sheriff examined each window but could find no churning mass of people. No Uzi-equipped terrorists. Nobody. What's more, the battery-powered lighting had an illumination life of no more than three hours. Whatever fate had dealt Seer City had happened just recently.

Renner focused the riflescope on City Hall. Its spacious auditorium, cafeteria, and meeting rooms combined could accommodate a thousand or so people. The municipal building was fully illuminated and like the school, it appeared to be abandoned. The powerful scope penetrated a good thirty feet inside the building. Every table and row of folding chairs was empty.

The churches and the hospital were no less inert. Poisonous gas could kill a town, in fact tiny Glen Lochen, Colorado was literally exterminated in 1904 when a cloud of cyanide gas descended upon it. A gold leeching operation up the mountain had gone haywire. But where were Seer City's corpses? Why would Henry Baldwin have emptied his Betsy at noxious gas? And most importantly, the closest gold leeching operation was hundreds of miles away.

The town's population had not evacuated, but as far as Renner McCauley could ascertain, Seer City's citizens were gone—all of them. Seer's dogs and cats and Ruby Chinik's mule and Mable Zane's courier pigeons and the red tail hawks that nest atop the Methodist church always on lookout for Mable's pigeons were gone.

Renner turned his attention to the sheriff's office. The building had few windows, but those the scope penetrated revealed no signs of life. There was no evidence that Gus Augustus had called for help. In fact, one of the stalled cars on the edge of town belonged to one of Renner's deputies. Its engine was still idling, and its left turn signal was flashing—a casual testament to an earlier moment.

Something was different. The radio antennae and satellite dishes were missing from the roof above the sheriff's office. Renner climbed higher up to the cabin's ridge for a better view and steadied himself against the river rock chimney. All three antennae were sheared off, each a foot above the roofline. Two lay on the roof deck, and the third no doubt had fallen to the street out of sight. He turned his attention toward the power station on the south end of town. The high overhead stanchions were not visible as they should be. Same with the Telco microwave tower and the cellular towers. Renner focused on each radio station in town, but he anticipated what was missing—the towers. Seer City had been silenced.

Renner clicked the handheld CB radio's mike key twice. "Doc? Come in." Communication posed a risk, especially one as unsecured as a CB, but Renner had no choice. He had to warn Doc, Kate and James George that Seer City had been attacked.

Kate answered instead, "Yes, Renner."

"Where's Doc?"

"We've got company. He and James George are talking to some people in an RV that just pulled up behind us. Also, to the mayor and his aide who were following the RV."

"That would be Cole Kilpatre and Cyril Hoop. Who's in the RV?"

"Some Resumption Mining personnel from Denver."

"Anyone else?"

"Uh, actually yes." Kate was outside the pickup and walked across the road for a better view. "There's someone else."

Josh and Erin had stopped behind Kilpatre's Cadillac and assumed wrongly that the tailgater had finally gotten his comeuppance. They exited the Rover and walked toward the gathering crowd. There had been no accident, at least no automobile accident. The group of strangers turned as one toward the sound and sight of Detective Blaine Rouse's siren and emergency flashers.

"Renner! Here comes the cavalry. There's a police car crossing the bridge." She paused. "Oh no! I think it might have just wrecked, Renner. The headlights look strange, like they're pointing upward somehow. The flashers are still on but not the siren."

***

Suspension bridges are difficult to build but easy to demolish, especially for a pair of creatures capable of dissolving steel cables and concrete with the alacrity and preternatural abilities of the Kar machines.

The south end of the bridge separated from the ravine's rim just as the state police cruiser's front wheels cleared it. The bridge collapsed under it instantly. The steel highway lintels tail hooked the speeding vehicle's transaxle, stopping it as abruptly as if at the end of a noose.

Loose articles in the cruiser became deadly weapons. A walkie-talkie, a spiraled directory, and a thermos bottle crashed into the windshield, turning its expanse into one giant spider web. A laminated roadmap flew through the air and sliced open the detective's hand as clean as a razorblade. The seatbelt and airbag saved Rouse's life but also knocked out his wind, cracked his ribs, bloodied his nose, and nearly broke his neck.

The cruiser teetered over the ravine on its undercarriage, gently rocking up and down. The smoking front of the counter-levered SUV slowly lifted higher and the vehicle slid backward a few more inches. The grinding screech of metal against metal changed pitch as the vehicle tottered over the ravine.

Blaine Rouse stirred from a horrible nightmare that featured terrorists. His face was wet with blood. He wiped it from his eyes with the back of his hand and looked at it curiously.

Rouse struggled to force his eyes to focus. All he could see was the fuzzy night sky beyond the translucent windshield. He turned to his left in search of the roadway and gasped as he realized where he was.

"Oh God! I'm hanging over the gorge." The moonlit edge of the severed road and the abyss below bisected his view. He pressed his face against the glass, but even that small motion was too much. The cruiser slid again with a harpies screech, just a half inch, but perhaps its last to give before surrendering to the gorge.

Rouse winced and tried to think. He inventoried his injuries and his options. Both were bad. The seat belt had broken four ribs and torn some cartilage along his sternum. His right thumb was dislocated when it struck the steering wheel during the sudden stop. Blood streamed down his left shin from a deep gash he received when it raked the safety brake pedal. His insides burnt as if he had swallowed acid.

"I have to get out of here. This thing is about to go over the edge," he slurred. His lips were swollen and bleeding, but the mental cobwebs were mercifully retreating. He scooted toward the steering wheel to reclaim the center of gravity. It was not enough. The car hood crept higher, rocked for a moment and then steadied. Blaine's complexion rippled like an octopus' from gray to crimson-purple as he struggled to breathe and manage his assorted pains.

Rouse's right thumb pointed unnaturally toward his armpit, and his left arm could not reach the seatbelt buckle without punishing his ribs and sternum. Rouse lifted his left arm and made a tremulous fist. He howled in agony as he reached across his body and released the seatbelt latch.

The front of the car suddenly rocked down, leveling with a long metallic cry. The tires bumped and then settled onto the asphalt. Beyond the broken windshield, something loomed large on the hood. It was ghostly white, and Blaine now recalled why he had been in such a hurry to return to Seer City. "Terrorists wearing winter-white camo! They did this," Rouse whispered.

Blaine Rouse also saw his opportunity. He threw open the car door and rolled from the vehicle.

Without its human ballast, the SUV's rear end dropped away. Its undercarriage screeched as it slid over the shredded steel and concrete. The Kars drove their claws into the metal and rode the vehicle to the bottom. The Explorer's fuel tank was three-quarters full, and the back compartment of the vehicle contained various munitions and emergency flares. The explosion was impressive.

Rouse cried out as the shockwave salted his many injuries and ground bone to bone. The fireball rose above the rim of the gorge and briefly illuminated the high mountain valley.

The trooper sat up and drew his weapon. He used the scattering light to search for the terrorists that his imagination conspired with shadows to hide. As the light settled, he lowered his weapon and mumbled to himself, "Bad guy down."

Rouse staggered to his feet. Someone was coming. He turned toward the sound of people running toward him. The detective debated whether to fire into the group of waggling flashlights or just surrender. He did neither and passed out.

***

Renner McCauley heard the explosion twice. Once over the radio and then once again a few seconds later when the sound wave reached the roof of the cabin. "Kate! What was that?"

"Renner! I think the bridge just blew up!"

"Where's the police car that was crossing?"

"It's gone! I don't see anything now." There had been another crash just before the explosion, loud enough for Kate to hear but not for Renner on the radio. "Something else, Renner, I think the bridge actually collapsed before the explosion."

Renner lowered the radio for a moment and thought. It did not make sense. "Are you sure, Kate?"

"Yes, the bridge collapsed before the explosion. I'm sure of it now. What do you want us to do?"

"Wait there. I'm coming back. Kate, be cautious. We don't know who's friendly and who's not. Okay?"

"Everyone is running toward the ravine."

"I'll be there in a few minutes." Renner left BB and Puck at the cabin to finish preparing the weapons.

***

Alpha Genesis recognized the sensation—a reduction of the collective body. Throughout earth's history, the aliens had inhabited every continent and sea in countless transmogrifications. Two males were gone, their venom vaporized, their impermeable lustrous fur shredded, their bodies incinerated.

Alpha Genesis had climbed onto the SUV's hood alongside his soldiers and had telepathically descended into the gorge with the Kars. He shared every sensation with them.

Alpha Genesis ordered his four sentries to return from Seer City. He had underestimated the enemy species. Nothing mattered now other than the extermination of the Nonbeings.

***

Because of the risky vocation Resumption's scientists all accepted, they assumed a certain amount of physical peril, and the mining company had generously accommodated that probability of on-the-job injury. Besides being a battleship for geological research, the RV also rivaled Denver's best ambulances.

As a young man, Doc Karl had served as a medic in the early war years of Viet Nam. He had treated wounds far worse than Rouse's. The professor finished sinking an IV drip and then secured the line to Blaine Rouse's left arm with surgical tape. The Resumption people converted two rows of seats into a hospital gurney and removed the third row. An oxygen mask covered Rouse's face and alternately fogged and cleared. His breathing was shallow and hurried. Eyes fixed and distant—classic signs of shock. Doc Karl stood back, made eye contact with Renner and then gestured for the sheriff to follow him to the back of the RV—out of earshot of the others.

"How is he, Doc?"

Doc Karl shrugged. "Best guess, he's bleeding internally. Spleen's probably ruptured. His left lung is severely bruised. He suffered at least eight broken ribs, a cracked clavicle, torn sternum, and a hyper-extended left elbow that pinched the nerve, numbing his hand. I have stitched his leg and reset his right thumb, but it will be a while before he wipes his own ass. Bottom line, he needs to get to town and see a real doctor."

"Did he say anything?"

"Yes. He fought us like a hellcat. It took four of us to hold him down. He called us all 'terrorists!'" Doc studied Renner for a moment and added, "Obviously, he was not himself. So what do we do now?"

The bridge was gone, and as far as Renner could determine so was the town. Crossing the Crimson Cream gorge by any means short of wings was out of the question especially at night with its one hundred foot nearly sheer walls.

"Doc, we are on our own. The town's empty."

"What are you talking about? How could eleven hundred people leave at the same time?"

Renner shook his head and said, "I don't know. But we are going to wait right here until help arrives."

"Renner, unless our Detective Rouse called for help before he crashed, no help is coming soon. Our radios are dead. I'm guessing the repeater towers are down."

Renner turned to the Resumption people. "Dr. Jussard, I'm assuming this RV is equipped with a satellite phone."

"Of course, Sheriff. Radio communications are completely unreliable in these parts, as we have just confirmed. Radio is out. But, our VSAT phone is working fine." He held it up for Renner to see.

"Thank you."

Renner turned back to Doc. "I examined the bridge lintels and cable footers. No explosives were used to bring down the bridge."

"That's strange. We distinctly felt an explosion."

"Yes, but the bridge was already down, Doc. What you heard was…"

"…the war on terrorism," slurred Blaine Rouse. He lunged at Jussard and snatched the VSAT phone from the smaller man.

Doc had removed detective's sidearm, but had overlooked Rouse's concealed ankle weapon. The trooper said, "You bastards will have to wait to call in your reinforcements." Before anyone could stop him, Rouse dropped the phone to the floor and crushed it under his boot heel. With everyone ducking for cover, he then emptied the snub-nosed 38-caliber revolver into the electronics. He passed out and fell to the floor still clicking the trigger.

Agent Josh Roe stepped next to Renner. "Sheriff, do you have any idea what this police officer is talking about?" Too many coincidences were lining up.

Renner studied the stranger as both he and Roe holstered their weapons. Before he could answer, the Motorola radio crackled to life. "Renner, this is Puck! Someone's on the move in town, and they're heading your way in a hurry."

# CHAPTER 49 ~~ Killer Water Jugs

Curtis Judy cut the tape on the first of two storage boxes and lifted the flaps. The wetsuit was like new. He was too prone to seasickness to be much use to the Green Peace movement, but he kept the wetsuit as a souvenir anyway.

The second box contained his gas mask collection—eleven in all. He chose the Israeli model, but decided he would bring them all. If the rats spit on him, he would rinse off with a plastic milk jug filled with water before it reached his flesh. Their venom ate the toilet plunger, but not instantly, and the gas mask was by necessity the best on the planet. If the creatures escalated beyond Rattus halitosis, Curtis was skee-rued.

Ten minutes later Curtis Judy stood at his front door dressed head to toe in his wetsuit, hissing air so tasteless and conditionally pure it made him claustrophobic. He pulled back the blinds a crack and gasped. Just thirty feet away, four Kars stood in the middle of the street. Their bodies writhed against one another's for a moment, and then as one the foursome sprinted out of town in the same direction as the main pack.

"They're leaving!" Curtis whispered. He waited five more minutes then ran stiff-legged to his vintage Volkswagen bus parked at the curb. Curtis studied the street for a moment, opened the door, and then tossed the water jugs and the box of gas masks onto the passenger seat. The key was in the ignition where he always left it. Then more good luck. The mega rat bastards had ripped out the gas tanks of most vehicles in town. They had missed his. Fifteen seconds later Curtis turned left onto Main Street and headed north as fast as the bus would accept its next gear.

Cars clogged the streets, but he swerved around them. Some vehicles he recognized, but he did not slow down even for them. Curtis Judy knew firsthand it was pointless—their owners were far beyond the kind of help jumper cables or a friendly push might afford.

*** 

Renner's communications options were rapidly dwindling. When he had departed on his so called vacation a few days ago, there were eight ham radio operators in the county. He was skeptical that any were still functioning. The attackers had likely tracked the antennae and destroyed every extended transmission. He pushed past Josh and Erin and climbed out of the RV. He ran to his pickup truck and threw open the driver's side door.

There was no way to tell whether the oncoming headlights belonged to a friend or foe. Renner reached inside the truck and flashed the headlights. Doc and Kate joined him, waving their flashlights toward the speeding car. Josh Roe and Erin Rogers had other plans—Plan B so to speak. They drew their weapons and took up defensive positions behind their Range Rover.

"Josh, if this vehicle does not stop on its own, we need to stop it."

"I know. One way or another. At his current speed, I estimate he'll sail about halfway across the gorge."

Curtis was now within a half mile. "Looks like a VW bus! You thinking what I'm thinking?"

"Yeah. I'll go for the left back tire. You get the right when he passes by. I hope he's wearing a seat belt, because this could get ugly."

*** 

Unfortunately, the dimmer switch had not worked in Curtis Judy's VW bus since 2009, and worse, his vision and attention to the road ahead was compromised by flight's adrenaline, Jack Daniels, the gas mask, and a compulsive examination of the road behind him in his rearview mirror. When he did eventually see the headlights flashing at him, and more importantly, live humans near them, it never occurred to him that they might be friendly.

Renner straddled the centerline and waved his arms.

Curtis juked the van at McCauley, and when the sheriff did not move, Curtis literally swerved at the imagined petroleum terrorist—the breeder of *mega-rattus*. Renner dove out of the way just in time.

Josh Roe and Erin Rogers rose from behind their rental car. "Shit! He's not stopping." The agents took aim and fired three pistol rounds each at the back tires of the VW van just as Curtis passed by. Tendrils of smoke erupted in the Volkswagen's wake.

Curtis's frazzled mind found nothing more original to swear than, "You fucking rat bastards!" Even as the bus wigwagged out of control, Curtis ordered it to go faster yet and stomped the accelerator to the floor. If these mutant rat bastards could not kill him with their gas, they would just do it the old-fashioned way and shoot him.

The first two bullets landed high and tore into the rear engine compartment of the VW with a nail punch's crisp, metal-on-metal report. The third and fourth passed straight through the wheel wells. One ricocheted off the frame and ripped open the gas tank. Fuel spewed behind the van. The fifth and sixth rounds were perfect. One took out the left tire's valve, deflating it instantly. The other peeled away chunks of the right-back tire's tread, flattening it in just one revolution.

A hundred yards from the ravine, the tail end of the van swooped to its highest arc, leaving the VW almost perpendicular to the road. The passenger-side front tire grabbed, and the van crashed onto its side. Sparks showered from underneath the vehicle. One inevitably found the gasoline trail and fire erupted. The van slid on its side, rotated, and then flipped end-over-end several times, two loping cartwheels that ended on the lip of the ravine.

Curtis Judy's luck finally ran out. He had survived hand-to-hand combat with an alien machine today, and then successfully evaded the monsters while Seer City died around him. He had even bounced like a Parcheesi die inside the van as it tumbled down the road, sustaining hardly a scuff in the process. His water jug flew through the air, collided with his skull at the perfect angle, and then snapped his neck.

The VW van coughed out Curtis Judy like a fur ball. He rolled to a stop on the snowy shoulder of the road amid his prized gas masks. His lucky sleeping bag arrived last. It had survived both Woodstock and over four decades of hippie-van lovemaking, but its time was also over. Fire smoldered its top like a cigar.

Erin and Josh sprinted toward the wreck with their weapons still drawn. Josh stomped out the smoldering sleeping bag. McCauley soon caught up with them. They gathered around Curtis' corpse in silence.

Erin looked up at Renner. She shook her head and said, "Sorry, Sheriff. We were just…"

Renner held up his hand to stop her. "I know. You were just trying to keep him from killing himself. Almost worked, too. So who are you guys?"

The agents holstered their weapons then showed Renner their IDs.

"FBI?"

"That's right. I'm Special Agent Josh Roe. This is Special Agent Erin Rogers." The agents extended their hands and shook Renner's.

Curtis had landed on his stomach, but grotesquely face-up. Renner kneeled next to the twisted body. "So, what brought you guys to Seer County?" He examined Curtis' sleeping bag. The smolders were out. He gave it a shake and covered Curtis' body.

Erin looked at her partner and said, "Well, Sheriff, we are not sure anymore why we are here. We overheard some of what you discussed with Professor Karl. Something about your town. Something very wrong."

Josh added, "The bridge. It did not fall on its own, did it?"

Renner nodded, "No, it did not. What I want to know is why would Curtis be so panicked?"

A set of snowmobile headlights wound their way down to the highway over the Culver trail and entered the highway, then accelerated toward the gathering. "Looks like we are getting more company, Sheriff." Erin unconsciously reached for her weapon.

"Relax, Agents. They're friends."

"So what's going on here, Sheriff?" Erin asked.

"Seer City is gone."

"Gone?" Roe said slowly.

"Well to be precise, just the citizens. The town itself appears mostly unharmed."

"You mean evacuated?"

Renner stood up. "To where? You drove through Rosebread. Did it look like it was bursting at the seams with refugees? See anything unusual on the roads? I spoke to one of my deputies just hours ago. Besides, if they evacuated, it was on foot. The streets are littered with abandoned vehicles."

"Maybe they are hiding?"

"The school and the municipal buildings are the only two places large enough to hold everyone and they are empty. Firehouse, same thing."

"Radios?"

"All communications are down: telephone, radio, the police channels, cellular, television, and I suspect the ham radios are offline too. Power is out as well. Someone took down the towers."

"So what do you make of it?"

"I don't know. Maybe terrorism, but that's your department, right?" He did not mention the missing poachers, or preacher, or the urgent inexplicable recall by his deputy.

Josh shook his head. "Terrorism? Well, it would be a first because Seer City sits at the end of a dead end highway during the winter. Highway 662-A closes to the south over Major Bronson Pass no later than October. That means there is only one way in or out of town this time of year. No escape plan.

Likewise, your airport is iffy during the winter. That means it's too unreliable for reinforcements. Even snowmobiles over the mountain pass would be risky. Snowpack and constant avalanche danger rule out that option.

Finally, Sheriff, your town is unusually well armed and well trained. According to FBI records, there are 5.7 weapons per household. Even Al Qaeda would think twice about attacking Seer City. No, this does not fit any terrorist modus operandi."

"I'm impressed. You know your Seer City facts, Agent Roe. So why are you here?"

"Call me Josh. We are on the job."

"Which is?

"Perhaps related, perhaps not. That's all I can say right now."

Erin looked down at the corpse. "Who was he, Sheriff?"

"His name is Curtis Judy. Environmental activist. A trust-baby from the sixties." Renner added, "A terrified somebody, a good citizen. He was our friend."

Renner reached down and collected four gas masks. He studied them for a moment, and handed one to each agent. "Is the FBI up for a little trip into town?"

233

"Definitely."

Renner pointed at the corpse and asked, "Josh, can you give me a hand? I want to take care of Curtis first."

"Sure thing, Sheriff." The men lifted Curtis' body and carried it to the RV. They placed him in the back. Erin found a blanket and covered the late hippie.

Renner briefed everyone in the RV, except Blaine Rouse who had finally surrendered to his medication and was snoring unevenly. "BB and Puck will remain here, while Josh, Erin and I take the sleds and reconnoiter the town."

Cole Kilpatre heaved himself to his feet with a sow-like grunt. He pushed away Cyril Hoop's bony hand and bellowed, "This is absurd, McCauley! I am holding you personally responsible for this affair and…"

"Stow it, Kilpatre. Park your ass and shut your trap or I will cuff you now and gag you with your pet crow Hoop. Concrete or padded, you've got a cell with your name on it in Florence."

The mayor sat down, moaning his protest. He did not like that word 'cuff,' or 'cell,' or anything to do with the name 'McCauley.'

Roe stepped next to Renner, "Sheriff, we need to get going. If Curtis was followed or chased, they might know we are here."

Renner nodded and turned to BB and Puck. "I need you boys to take charge here. Okay?"

"You got it, Mac."

"Thanks, and…" Turning to the others Renner asked, "Any of you people qualified to drive a sled?"

Debbie stood, "My dad gave me a Phasar when I turned sixteen. I won enough races to pay for my undergraduate years. Does that qualify?"

Renner nodded and said, "You'll more than do. Erin will help you suit up. We leave in five minutes. BB and Puck, I need a moment with you two outside."

The three men met in the RV's headlights away from the mayor. "You boys are in charge for real. If Kilpatre so much as opens his mouth again, cuff him for his own good." Renner handed over two sets of handcuffs.

BB studied the steel bracelets for a moment and then said, "I don't know, Renner, these things look pretty complicated. Would it be okay if we just shot the crazy son-a-bitch instead? Put him out of *our* misery for good. I might lose the key or something."

Renner did not laugh. BB and Puck glanced at each other. Neither had ever seen him so serious.

"Christ, Renner. Do you think crazy Kilpatre had something to do with what's going on in town?"

McCauley sighed. "Actually, no I don't, but that doesn't mean he isn't a potential problem. I think he's finally tipped over."

Clouds rolled in from the west. The full moon seemed anxious to chase after Seer City and disappear. The Colorado mountain natives realized that snow was likely later. Depending on their adversary, snow could be a blessing or a curse.

"Are you serious about arresting Kilpatre?"

"Committing. Arresting. One way or the other, yes. Long investigation, longer story. We have him on tape soliciting bribes from contractors, some real, some imaginary, and an embezzlement trail you won't believe. He'll go to either an insane asylum or to a prison if…" McCauley didn't finish.

"If what?"

"If we survive tonight."

"Holy shit! Is it that bad?"

"Yes. The town is gone, boys. Eleven hundred people have vanished. So stay sharp. Whoever or whatever attacked Seer City is bound to come this way. We are close enough to town for the CBs to work. Do not try to contact me unless you are under attack. I will check in whenever I feel it is safe. If you lose contact, find a way to get across the Crimson Cream. Understand? No heroics."

BB and Puck nodded.

"Do you know what I mean?"

"Kate, Doc and the boy."

"That's right. They're not to come searching for us. Nor you, for that matter."

Puck gestured at Erin who was helping Debbie with her helmet. "Who are these guys, Renner? This Erin and Josh?"

"FBI. My new best friends."

"Well, any friends of yours are friends of ours. Right?"

"That's right, and I'm afraid tonight we'll need every friend we can find."

Erin Rogers walked over to the threesome. "We are ready, Sheriff. The bows are loaded. We each have thirty armed arrows. Radio check is complete. My recommendation is that you and Josh are the designated gunners. Debbie and I can drive. I grew up on sleds in the North Dakota Badlands. Satisfactory, Sir?"

Renner smiled. "Very well, Erin." He looked to his left and found Kate waiting for him. "Give me a minute."

"Of course."

Kate and Renner slid into each other's arms as comfortably as if they had loved each other for decades, not hours. Neither spoke for a moment. Kate kissed Renner's neck and then whispered close to his ear, "Can this all be connected, Old Jimmy's letters, and that antique trunk in the pickup?"

Renner answered so assuredly that it stunned him more than Kate. "Yes."

"Then we are in danger."

"Kate, I have lived my entire life wondering what is in that trunk. What could possibly commit so many generations of my family to its secret? I think we know now. Whatever Old Jimmy feared for us is in there, waiting for some McCauley to free it and save us all."

"But could it really be Kara?"

Renner pressed his fingers to Kate's lips. "We'll find out soon enough and play Christmas morning or Pandora's box together. Okay?"

Erin Rogers fired up her snowmobile. Debbie's roared to life a moment later. Renner kissed Kate once more, nodded to Doc Karl and slid behind Debbie on the sled. "James George, can you come here for a second?"

"Yes, Sheriff!" the child exclaimed and trotted over to the snowmobile.

Renner lifted him onto his lap. "You seem to have been somewhat preoccupied since I got back."

"Yes, I have. But I'm back now." Kara had taken him on several excursions through history.

"You are *back* now? I'll remember that explanation after my next nap. James, I need a favor."

"Sure, it's yours for the asking."

Renner smiled. It was so easy to forget the boy was not actually a child in so many respects. "Can you keep an eye on Sasha for me?"

"Yes. But, that's all?" James George said with disappointment.

"No. There is something else. James, BB and Puck are going to tell you what they witnessed earlier tonight in town. I want you to think about it, and then let me know if it means anything to you.

Eleven hundred people are gone, vanished without a trace. I need to know how that is possible."

James accepted the assignment as easily as if Renner had asked him to fetch some firewood. The child asked, "Anything else?"

Renner nodded. "Yes, one more thing. I want you to keep an eye out, son. The adults will watch the roads and the snowmobile paths, but I want you and Sasha to watch everywhere else."

"Hmm, of course, as Trigius Titus once warned, 'The likeliest enemies are the most improbable moments.' You are suggesting that I am not burdened with the prejudice of an adult paradigm. That's so very kind of you."

"Well, yes, I guess that's what I'm saying."

"I consider it an honor to do my part."

"Good." Renner called Puck and BB over and gave them their final instructions. McCauley mounted the lead sled. He glanced once more at Kate and then tapped Debbie on the shoulder. She twisted the accelerator and the snowmobile shot up the trail.

\*\*\*

Four alien rat imposters moved steadily toward the fallen bridge to investigate. They descended the mountain in arcing thirty-foot leaps, expertly passing over boulders with minimum clearance, somehow always landing where purchase was most solid. When a crevice demanded single file, the machines fell into a column and soared through the slivered openings.

The creatures sensed *Homo sapiens'* presence on the road, but their orders were to ignore the party for now, to climb into the gorge first, and examine the remains of the two fallen Kars.

# CHAPTER 50 ~~ I Can Hear You!

"What are you looking at, Jimmy George?" Doc Karl asked.

"Well, Doc Karl, I don't exactly know." James George had climbed on top of the cab of Renner's pickup and was studying an increasingly cloudy sky with a pair of Resumption night vision binoculars. The child was on his back, and his head rested against the cab lights rack.

The wind gusted and the snow finally got busy. Hoop and Kilpatre had returned to the Cadillac as ordered, and were no doubt scheming. As Renner had asked of them, BB and Puck had shared in detail the evening's events with the child, stopping just short of how many pisses each had taken over the balcony at BB's cabin. The two demolitions men organized the engineers into two teams. One stood watch while the other cannibalized telecom gear in the RV in a long-shot attempt to restore communications.

The Cadillac's driver's door swung open with a screech. Kilpatre screamed, "Bainbridge! You contemptible moron! I've had enough of this…"

"Kilpatre! Get your big ass back in that car. Now!" Puck yelled with authority. He counted on the mayor doing just the opposite. The passenger door flew open, and Cyril Hoop sprang from the car and joined his boss. Prissy and Waddle marched in defiance down the center of the road toward Puck and BB, arms churning—a corndog beside its stick.

A root-rot-infected and hollowed-out cottonwood tree that had produced its last summer snow a decade ago stood eighty feet to the left of the Cadillac. When he was sure that everyone was watching, BB aimed the bow halfway up the tree trunk and fired one arrow. The chem-cap detonator ruptured and created the precise electrical charge necessary to detonate the C4. The brittle tree literally disintegrated. The fireball rose eighty feet engulfing the tender tree in flames.

"Kilpatre! Last warning. The pimpmobile is next if I have to repeat myself one more time, and I don't give a shit whether you are in it or not. Those are the sheriff's orders."

The mayor and Hoop raced for the car. The wind kneaded the flames higher. James George did little more than glance at the churning orange glow.

BB stepped next to Puck and said, "You know, Bro, I'm beginning to like law enforcement."

"I hear that."

The two friends tapped fists.

***

The four Kar scouts recorded the explosion. The machines conferred telepathically without breaking stride. The sound wave was different, more ferocious. The enemy possessed yet another weapon, one the pack must appropriate.

Under Seer Mountain, the rest of the machines waited, listened, and witnessed as one.

***

"Jimmy George? Are you warm enough up there?" Doc Karl asked.

"Yes, Sir. I'm fine."

"What do you see?"

"Cumulonimbus, heavy and low. Atmospheric pressure is dropping. It'll snow heavily tonight, I'm sure."

"If you get cold, get in the pickup with Kate and me. Okay?"

"Yes, Sir. But I'm fine."

"Jimmy McCauley… Crawl like me… Sweet girl from Golden… Show you more worlds in time."

James waited until Doc Karl slammed the door beneath him before he lowered the binoculars and closed his eyes to better concentrate on the voice. Sometimes his mother and father's voices

239

returned to guide him. He knew it was not really his parents, though, just recollection, precious memory chiseled vividly by longing and the blessing/curse of perfect recall. Besides, this was different. The Kara voice was calling, and he was wide-awake.

"Can you still hear me?" Kara called to his mind.

"Yes! I can hear you."

Kara had been calling to him since Rosebread every time he dozed off. She had taken him back to the Federation battles and to dozens of times and places around the universe. How he knew not to share these excursions just yet was another mystery entirely. James George sensed the need for secrecy.

"Child, talk with… Talk with your mind. Do you understand what that means? I cannot speak Kar to you while you are awake. We must speak English now. Very difficult for me."

James had spent the last hour revisiting his dream journeys with Kara. He concluded that what he was experiencing might be somehow connected to something called Bell's Theorem—the most significant contribution to quantum mechanics in fifty years. Then a bunch of hippie PhD physicists in California in the 60s exploited the Irishman's work to research the paranormal abilities they called 'psi'.

"Where are you anyway?"

"Hiding where Jimmy McCauley put me. He keeps Kara safe. Jimmy McCauley save Kara and Kara save Jimmy McCauley."

"Are you close enough for me to see you?"

"Yes no."

"Yes no? What kind of answer is that?"

"Sorry. Human language is difficult."

"Human?"

"Yes, human, human Jimmy McCauley."

"Psi telepathy, theoretically, has no geographic boundaries, so I am curious, where are you? Are you here or somewhere across the universe?"

"Here."

"Where?"

"Wooden box, box inside."

James sat up. He scooted toward the back of the truck and looked down. Headlights filled the bed. The sensation of someone stepping next to him was so strong he jerked his head from side-to-side several times. His eyes finally settled on the trunk.

Flash!

James whined and looked over his shoulders once more. It was all he could do not to scream, 'Who's there?' The sense of an otherworldly presence was overwhelming as Kara strengthened the telepathic connection with the child.

"Jimmy McCauley... Jimmy McCauley... Jimmy McCauley..."

"I'm not Jimmy McCauley. Is that you I feel in my mind?"

"Yes, Jimmy McCauley. Will not hurt... see Kara... see Kara... Pretty gal from Golden! One form."

Flash!

James exclaimed, "Oh!" The night disappeared around him. Winter night became tropical day—a bright verdant paradise. He stood beneath lush ferns that rose with oaken majesty and twisting vines thick as elephant trunks that disappeared into a forest canopy. The air was thick, moist with the scent of dark soil and immense flowers strangely redolent of rotting meat. Yet, the air was so concentrated with oxygen that James felt his breathing slow down.

"My time Earth world. Your world, a long time ago."

James bent down and lifted a fallen leaf. He studied it for a moment then let it slide through his fingers as an eight-winged insect the size of a crow swooped in to investigate. Purple-mirrored eyes rolled about their sockets and studied the boy's just inches away. His hair fluttered in the insect's chop. The jungle chittered and hummed around him. Smiling, James shook his head in disbelief, and then bit his lip in disappointment. The hovering insect darted away as something rustled in the underbrush nearby.

Nothing in James's short life had prepared him for what he saw next. Only a handful of paleontologists on the planet would have recognized the extinct plant that disappeared during the Upper Cretaceous. A few more scientists could identify the long gone Mesozoic Era insect, but the creature before him was more myth than fact. It was a multituberculate for sure, but specifically the karpeleotroceme.

The animal was no more a rodent than James was, but its rodent-like features made it sort of a rat in drag. Multituberculate descended from the reptile, but eventually lost reptilian characteristics when it became warm blooded. It had fur, beaver teeth, pointed snout, whiskers and eyelashes and the dual-purpose teeth of carnivores and herbivores. Most importantly, cranial capacity doubled with the rise of pre-mammalian life. Multituberculate, the earth's first intelligent creature, spied a piece of fallen fruit and approached it cautiously.

"Well, hello there little lady."

The creature studied James for a moment, and then dismissed him as irrelevant. He was not food or a predator, so he wasn't worthy of the animal's limited bandwidth.

James' mighty bandwidth, on the other hand, gathered up every bit of data he possessed regarding the creature. He piled it up high. Mankind's sum of knowledge about karpeleotroceme was impressive only by its anemia and fragility. The fossil record was so incomplete that Kar was little more than a paleontological theory. The Holy Grail would be a piece of jaw, preferably one that demonstrated differentiated teeth in extreme.

"Jimmy McCauley?"

"Yes! Oh, Kara. I do not know how to thank you. This is utterly amazing. How am I seeing all of this? I know I'm not sleeping."

"Kara, Jimmy McCauley. You are getting stronger with each adventure. You like this creature?"

"Like? I love it! Kara, I am standing before the most amazing creature that ever lived. An animal that adapted and evolved like none before it or after. The origin of man, our oldest ancestor, some fifty million years ago just looked up at me and as much as said, 'Piss off, boy. I'm busy eating here!' Yes, Kara. I like this very much. I don't know how to begin to thank you."

"Jimmy McCauley?"

"Yes?"

"You want to touch?"

"May I?"

"Yes, scratch between ears. She like."

James kneeled on the spongy jungle floor and cautiously reached out. The 'rat' looked up at his hand and stopped chewing. James's hand froze. The karpeleotroceme studied his palm and each finger without alarm. Her nose twitched a few times, and then she resumed nibbling on the piece of rotten fruit.

James made a fist to make his hand stop shaking. He gasped, and realized he must have been holding his breath in anticipation. The mind belonged to a scientist, but the ensuing giggle came from an eight-year-old boy whose greatest fantasy was literally at hand.

As his index finger descended toward the animal's skull, he thought of Michelangelo's massive fresco in the Sistine Chapel, "The Creation of Adam," with God and Adam reaching for each other's index fingers, and to Spielberg's "ET," the alien and young Elliot's index fingers bridging species and space.

An electrical twinge tickled James's index finger as he stirred the fur between her ears. The creature froze and then squeaked her pleasure. She closed her eyes and spread her jaws wide—a nearly one hundred eighty degree yawn. James leaned closer as he continued to pet the multituberculate, placing his cheek on the ground in front of her. She lifted her head and pressed against his finger. As Doc Karl had promised, as Kate Lambert theorized, and as James hoped, he discovered the incredibly differentiated teeth of the karpeleotroceme—incisors and molars.

"Jimmy McCauley?"

The voice startled Jimmy. "Yes! What? Kara?"

"Put hand in mouth."

"What?"

"Trust. Not hurt. Not hurt much."

"Why?"

James felt Kara tossing through his mind, looking for an explanation there like a four-year-old looking for her favorite socks in a dresser drawer. Then Kara had it—the correct memory. Last December James had watched on the Internet as Professor Norman Karl performed a simple field casting for PBS of a fossilized stegosaurus footprint in Grand Junction, Colorado.

"A casting!"

"Yes. Can you save?"

"Uh, yes... yes! I have rubber cement in my pocket. That should work just fine."

"Not know..."

"It is okay. Trust me, Kara! Bite me and hard! Both palms! Steady pressure, more, more, more... Ou-ouch, that's enough! Now my other hand. Hurry, Kara! Ouch! Perfect!"

"Sorry. Hurt?"

"It's okay!"

Five minutes later Doc Karl climbed from the truck, looked up and asked, "James George, what in the holy bug dirt are you doing up there? Is that glue I smell?" The child had smeared rubber cement over the roof of the truck. It appeared to Doc as if James George was gluing his hands to the truck, and in fact, the child had.

"Glue, yes, and just a few more seconds, Doc!"

"For what? One of them super-glue ads?"

"No, Sir. I'm trying to see if your theory you shared with me yesterday is true."

Kate opened the driver's door, leaving it open in case Renner called on the CB. She too smelled the glue and asked all the same questions, and predictably got the same answers.

On all fours, hands pressed into the thickening glue, James turned to Kate and asked over his shoulder. "What are the chances, Kate, of you meeting a child like me? Have you ever wondered? One so much like you, an orphan, adoptable, whose interests are not only paleontology, but also focused on our precious multituberculate and most recently the mythical karpeleotroceme? What about your own savior, this dear man Doc Karl, who discovered this creature, then you and now me? What are the odds of such convergences? Absolute null or absolute inevitability?"

"Perhaps it's fate, James George," Doc Karl said softly. He sensed that James was bumping along a more highly reasoned path.

"Fate? Perhaps. I have studied fate since the air crash that killed my parents. Given it a great deal of thought. The most important question is, is fate a binary probability, or is it an infinitely varying analog?"

Doc Karl spoke as if addressing a peer at the university, "And? I suspect you've drawn some conclusions in this matter, young Sir."

"I have. I believe that Fate, which is the poet's definition of Time, is a finite binary, a series of either-or events no less predictable than the rising sun—the sun being an example of fate we each experience with chronological certainty."

"But the sun always rises, Jimmy George."

"Exactly, but not for everyone. Not if you are on the hot side of Mercury. Not when the sun burns out, which it inevitably will. Not if the earth stops rotating on its axis which is also inevitable."

"True. Go on."

"If fate is binary, it is therefore mathematically predictable."

"Your conclusions?"

"I do not believe our coming together was mere coincidence. Evidence suggests it was anticipated, calculated, perhaps even manipulated to happen."

The two adults stared in confusion at each other over the truck roof. Finally, Kate asked, "How can you be so sure, son?"

"I'll show you. Kate, Doc, please meet karpeleotroceme." The glue was finally set. James George carefully lifted his hands and examined the molds. Using his fingernails to scratch under the edges, James carefully peeled the dried cement back, studied the thick impressions for a moment and smiled. To an amateur the indentations in the casting would mean nothing. He handed one to Doc and the other to Kate. Even in the scattershot headlights, the two scientists compared the molds and knew what they held in their hands—proof of karpeleotroceme—the missing jaw line, differentiated teeth, incisors and molars.

Kate's voice trembled. "How... where... did you get this, James?"

"Where? I am guessing from the late Triassic. It was utterly beautiful, I might add, Kate. I cannot wait to return. However, I suppose there may be some risk. As to *how* I came into these, I believe the castings belong to one of her countless hosts." He pointed to the trunk in the pickup bed.

Doc asked shaking his head, "Her? Who?"

"Kara! She told me her name is Kara. Great name. In fact, a perfect name, wouldn't you agree? Kara karpeleotroceme. Kara Kar! Has a certain *faux-naïf.* Yes? She has taken me on adventures beyond imagination."

Kate's mouth fell open. Her lower lip quivered in sympathy with the sudden chill on her spine, one completely unrelated to the weather. She shook her head just once slowly and thought, Kara. "Jimmy McCauley. The letters. It's all true!"

# CHAPTER 51 ~~ Recon

Renner tapped Debbie's right shoulder twice. Her helmet dipped, acknowledging his order to pull over. She braked and stopped fifteen feet from a crest where the old snow was thinnest, then killed the engine. The sheriff dismounted the sled.

Highway 662-A was just beyond the rise. McCauley and Roe crawled to the top of the hill. The women stood guard over them. A half inch of snow had accumulated on the asphalt, but more importantly, no tracks. Josh and Renner backed down the berm and joined the rest of the team.

"We'll drop the sleds here and go in on foot. Questions?"

"I suggest we go in hot, Sheriff," Josh Roe said, glancing down at his bow.

"Agreed. My town isn't gone. It's dead. I fear someone or something has murdered eleven hundred people. Let's not help the enemy add to the count."

Josh and Erin had had their share of soured missions over the years and loathed every one of them. For the last twelve years, they had been the FBI's point of the spear. Most missions were downright boring. Occasionally, however, the elephant charged. Like in Nigeria a few years ago when things became personal and got very wet. Mexico was not fun either.

Debbie cleared her throat and lost some of her coolness. "Yeah, and that's C4, and I'm betting our demo-boys used chem-caps. So what the hell is down there, Sheriff?"

Renner glanced at Roe and Rogers. Both gave a quick nod. The agents obviously sensed it too, the unnatural stakes, a rising, a preternatural threat not to individuals or teams, but to our very kind. Subterfuge requires valuable energy. Josh and Erin wanted none of theirs wasted.

Renner turned to Debbie. "We don't know what we are facing, except that shotguns and handguns weren't effective against them. We also know we are on our own. Do you want to wait here with the sleds, Debbie?"

"Hell no! I want my own bow. I was the state archery champ my junior and senior in high school."

Rogers smiled. "Really, which state?"

"Are you a cop?"

"Something like that. We're FBI," Erin announced and stuck out her hand to shake.

"Go Hoover!"

Luck or fate delivers life and death. By either conveyance, the game often seemed rigged to Renner McCauley, the ultimate ring toss at the Crooke County Fair. He studied the faces looking back at him and knew he could not have drawn a better crew. "I'll take point. Single file, double-time. Step where I step. No unnecessary advertising. Ms. Rodgers, Erin, bring up the rear in twenty-five yard legs. You know the routine, I'm sure." Renner handed one of the Motorola walkie-talkies to Erin.

"Yes, Sheriff. You're one click and I'm two. Three clicks, all clear, I pull up. No reply, I abort and return to base and warn the rest of the party."

"Copy. We can stay out of sight behind this dirt berm most of the way and use the forest the rest of the way." Renner handed a quiver of a dozen explosive-tipped arrows to Debbie and said, "Let's move out."

***

Sasha the bulldog wedged himself between the stick gearshift on the floor and the pickup's bench seat. It was a good place to nap, much like most of the places the amiable creature encountered. His snoring gave a contrapuntal beat to the heater fan's irregular whirr.

The rats, Isaac and Newton, had long tired of the trip and they too slept in their cage nose to toes.

As one, the three pets awoke and turned their attention toward the gorge to the north. The growl seemed comical coming from Sasha which caused Kate to smile. She reached out to pet the dog but stopped when Isaac and Newton hissed. "What's up with you guys?"

Kate turned and studied alternately the vehicles behind her and the agitated pets. She watched Doc Karl step from the Winnebago and hurry toward the pickup. The snowstorm was intensifying. Doc disappeared for a moment behind a wall of blowing snow.

The professor threw open the driver's door and climbed in. "Jerry said the radio is hopeless."

"How about an uplink, the VSAT?"

"Same."

Kate smiled and asked, "Smoke signals?"

Doc turned and shook his head 'no' in all seriousness. "Detective Rouse shot all the matches too." He looked down at the animals. "What's with these guys?"

"Dunno."

"Where's Jimmy George?"

Kate smiled and pointed up at the truck cab roof, "He insists he's not cold, and anyway he's doing something for Renner."

"Speaking of Renner, any word yet?"

"No."

***

Perched on the fractured lintels of the downed bridge, the four machines gazed down at the wreckage below. Twisted steel rebar jutted over the gorge. Smoke swirled around the rubble. The Kars powerful sensors interrogated it all and communicated what they witnessed to their leader via channels beyond human comprehension. The Crimson Cream's waters were low, leaving the charred machines' remains, bridge parts, and the vehicle scattered amongst the boulders.

The scout Kars sensed and inventoried the synthetic fur, blood and flesh, ashen or not.

Alpha Genesis had formed an accurate sense-of-wastes and a sense-of-worth this afternoon as he had absorbed the life flow of Seer City and his enemy. Now each member of the pack possessed that knowledge. There were no human remains in the destruction. Kar had lost this battle.

# CHAPTER 52 ~~ It is Them!

"Jimmy McCauley!  Danger!"

James George's eyes flew open.

"Jimmy McCauley!  Danger!"

James sat up on the roof of the pickup.

"Jimmy McCauley!  Danger!"

The child jumped into the truck bed and crawled to the trunk.

"Where, Kara?  What is it?" Jimmy whispered.

"Jimmy McCauley!  Kara must open trunk!  Now!  Do you know what I mean?"

"No!  I don't understand, Kara!  What's wrong?"

"Jimmy McCauley!  Hurry!  The machine like Kara…  The Federation Kar—the Exterms—they are coming!"

"That's bad isn't it?"

"Yes!"

"You want me to open the trunk and release you?"

"No!  Not release.  Take trunk far away.  You do not look. Hurry!"

Jimmy jumped out of the truck bed and yanked open Doc's door. "It's Kara!  She says we are in danger, and we need to release her." Jimmy translated Kara's sketchy instructions to Doc and Kate.

James added, "I'm sensing, and strangely so, that she's talking about an explosion."

"Yes... explosion!"

"But...!"

"Explosion will not hurt Kara."

"Are you sure, Kara?"

Doc and Kate heard just one side of the conversation, as if James George was on a telephone.

Kate leaned past Doc and said, "James, ask... No, tell Kara that I know about the oath, and that I believe the chest should be opened. It's not necessary to create an explosion. Why don't we just open it?"

James repeated Kate's message verbatim.

Kara's response was urgent. "No! Dangerous! Only Kara open!"

Kara and Sheriff Jimmy McCauley had hatched their plan over one hundred years ago. Kara had instructed the sheriff to place her in a thick, glass vessel—one filled with kerosene and sugar and numerous minerals. The oil was her preservative and shield from the Kar pack and the sugar could be slowly absorbed for energy as she lay in near suspended animation. With all its intelligence, the machine was no chemist and had instructed the sheriff to pack the smaller trunk with bat guano to help mask any lingering scent while the trunk was sealed. Kerosene, sugar, nitrogen, harmless minerals— simple nitroglycerin. The leather and cork seals on the jar were old and leaking from the recent jostling. The chemical reaction was slow and inefficient but occurring nonetheless.

"Hurry!"

With Kate and James George lighting the way with flashlights, Doc carried the small trunk sixty feet from the pickup and set it down behind a grove of scrub oak. Puck and BB watched from the road. They glanced at each other curiously but said nothing. The danger was generic and undefined, but near. They both cocked their bows, just in case.

The explosion was remarkable and lit the night for a moment. The denuded scrub ignited, but the fire collapsed in the blowing snow.

"You smell that, Puck?"

"Nitro."

"Hell yes it's nitro!"

The demo men were familiar with the trunk. In fact, they had moved it many times for Renner and watched over it whenever he was gone. They knew nothing of the family secret, of course, but both were positive it did not involve explosives. Renner never would have placed them in such jeopardy.

"Jimmy McCauley! Come to me! It is safe now."

James exclaimed, "She's okay!" The threesome ran toward the dying flames with Puck and BB right behind them.

Kate was the first to reach the crater. "James, Doc, look down. Tell me I am not hallucinating."

James fell to his knees. "Kara? Kara! Are you okay?"

"Yes. Yes. Explosion not big enough to hurt Kara. Problem is, Jimmy McCauley, I sense four of my kind nearby."

James George resisted the urge to correct Kara that he was not a McCauley. "What else, Kara?"

"They are…now seeing two others that are no more… that your kind killed." Kara related the last phrase to James George's mind with amazement. She stepped closer to him and the boy kneeled. Like in his vision, he scratched the immense rat-thing between the ears. Kara searched his mind for the English words to explain what the humans must do.

"Jimmy McCauley, they cannot sense me yet. We must hurry! How did your pack kill? Do again!"

"I don't know, Kara. There was an earlier explosion. Maybe that's how."

James George felt Kara soar through his mind, searching for the meaning, and then she exclaimed, "Yes! Fire enough. Concussion enough. Weakness enough my kind. Only weakness. Must hurry before…"

"Before what?"

"Before not weakness enough. Kar machine can change."

"You mean mutate. You mean that your species is, uh… the machines are only temporarily vulnerable to our explosives. That they will adapt so that we can no longer hurt them?"

Kara exclaimed, "Yes!"

James stood and turned toward the wary adults inching their way closer to him and Kara. She turned toward the fading orange glow of what once was the Crimson Cream Bridge. Her eyelashes fluttered.

"Jimmy McCauley?"

"Yes, Kara."

"They are coming soon. Tell the organic Lifes!"

\*\*\*

Renner, Roe, Rogers and Resumption's Debbie stood on top of the highest bluff on the north edge of Seer City and studied the inert town.

Debbie stepped next to Renner. "Sheriff, whatever hit the town, I think it is gone."

Whatever? He asked himself.

Debbie's minor at Harvard University was anthropology. Unlike the others, the scientist had once studied anomalous disappearances.

Her voice was distant, melancholy, as she recalled her college lessons. One by one, the others turned toward her. "I fear what we are witnessing may not be without historical precedent."

"What do you mean, Doctor?" Josh asked.

"There are actually numerous accounts of inexplicable, spontaneous disappearances. I took a course back in undergrad called Societal Collapse. Most societal failures are explainable and occur over long periods of time due to phenomena called overshoot, that is, resource depletion. Some are not. These are classified by archeologists as ASDs—Anomalous Sudden Disappearances."

Erin said softly, "Go on, Debbie."

"In 1720 the 718 inhabitants of the village of Drevk in the Ural Mountains vanished overnight during a blizzard. An entire Roman legion disappeared in the Balkans in 221 A.D. much the same way. The Hopi Indians tell of 113 members of their tribe that vanished overnight at their summer camp in Colorado near Grand Junction. The Mongolian Empire was severely disrupted by panic in the 11th Century when the entire Hjeng Khan hierarchy and army disappeared at what is now called the Ztzk-te desiccation. There was evidence of a ferocious battle, but no enemy. There were also no corpses. The empire's treasures were left untouched."

Renner stepped closer to Debbie. "You think this is something like that?"

"Only one way to find out, Sheriff. We will have to go see the town. See what's left behind."

Roe asked, "What do you suppose we'll find, Debbie?"

"Nothing. Nothing that makes sense that is."

# CHAPTER 53 ~~ Tyrannosaurus Rats

James George translated Kara's warning. "Kate! Doc! Kara says we are in danger. There are four entities nearby that will inevitably attack us. I presume she knows they are there in the gorge via a telepathic connection. The creatures are somehow... preoccupied and can't sense her yet. She can hide from them a while longer if she remains motionless. That is their weakness, she says. One that they have not recognized yet. She needs us to terminate them before they change."

Like a fuzzy picture whose pixels join together, Kate now grasped the full meaning of Grandfather Jimmy's letters. "I think I do, James George. Everyone back to the vehicles! Let's go. We are in danger!" The flashlights, one by one, changed focus from Kara and James to the parked caravan on the highway. Weaving around the boulders and scrub brush, the party fanned out and hurried toward what seemed like sanctuary.

BB and Puck fell in beside Kate, Doc and James George, their crossbows now aimed in the general direction of the Crimson Cream gorge. "What the Sam Hill is that rat-lookin' thing anyway, Puck?" BB whispered.

"Beat's me, Pard, but I think it's on our side. Looky there!"

253

Kara leapt effortlessly into James' arms. Her weight was almost more than the eight-year-old could handle, and he stumbled twice before catching his balance. Doc and Kate steadied him and offered to take Kara, but James refused and lurched forward.

"Sorry, Jimmy McCauley! If you carry me, it makes more difficulty for... for Exterms to see me." She searched the minds of those she could reach for the correct pigeon-English explanation. "Kara and Jimmy McCauley buy us some time."

"It's okay, girl! I have you. I estimate your weight at approximately twenty-four kilograms. E-gad! You are quite a load, for a boy my age, but manageable, thank you very much."

The snow fell more seriously now with gusts approaching thirty miles per hour. The roadway had already turned white. The first nubs of snowdrifts formed along the natural swells paralleling the road. The party huddled around Renner's pickup truck. Puck and BB took up defensive positions behind the vehicle. The bulldog investigated Kara through the passenger window for a moment but soon lost interest.

Kate clicked the radio key four times, her agreed call sign, and then awaited Renner's reply. She knew he would answer because four clicks also meant danger, but prayed she was not creating additional peril for Renner and his team in the process. Kate sighed in relief and closed her eyes for a moment when he calmly answered.

"Yes, Kate. What's your situation?"

She depressed the radio key and held it down for a moment while she composed her thoughts. In the end, Kate Lambert chose the most direct explanation possible. The one she thought Renner would most appreciate under the circumstances, especially after their having read all of Jimmy McCauley's letters on the way here.

"Renner, Kara is free from the trunk. She is communicating telepathically with James George and has warned us we are all in great danger. Four more like her are nearby and will soon attack us. She insists we kill them. What do you want us to do?"

Everyone except James George stared alternately at Kate and Kara. Impossible statements. Impossible creature. Earl spoke for everyone, "What is this creature?"

James George answered, "Most recently, she's a karpeleotroceme, a descendant of the multituberculate, same as *Homo sapiens*. Her fossil record is nearly missing, and our best guess before tonight was that they were extinct. This magnificent creature witnessed the end of the age of dinosaurs and so much more." He decided to hold off telling everything. Dinosaurs were one thing. Alien machines? Well that was something else altogether.

Earl smiled. "She is beautiful, James George."

\*\*\*

Confusion is fear's brother. Josh, Erin and Debbie unconsciously stepped closer to Renner and searched the perimeter for threats. Renner needed to move. The town appeared empty, and though he could not guarantee it was safe, Renner was sure it was marginally more secure than being surrounded by an unknown enemy on an open highway.

"No! I don't care what she says. Do not engage them. Kate, you need to get off the road. Bring everyone into Seer City. You are only ten minutes away. Stay in radio contact at all times. I will double back to you. Debbie, Roe and Rogers will move into town and wait for us at the sheriff's office. Is Kilpatre still alive?"

Kate smiled. "Yes, Puck and BB have been good boys."

Kilpatre exclaimed, "You bastard, McCauley!"

"Bad start. Mr. Mayor, if you survive this night, you will spend the rest of your life in prison or an asylum. Do you understand?"

"You've got nothing on us, McCauley. Nothing!"

"Us? Not *us*, just you. Is Hoop there?"

Kate found Hoop and made eye contact, "Yes, Renner. He's here." Her tone asked, 'why'.

"Let me speak to him."

The dour scarecrow stepped forward, smiled at Kate and accepted the radio. Hoop literally transformed under his own smile. He stood up straight now. His eyes ceased their perpetual darting, his voice changed, deepened. Hands no longer wrung with incessant scheming. He was a man relieved. A man relieved from a difficult tour of duty. He clicked the mike and stared at Cole Kilpatre. "Yes, Sheriff McCauley. This is Inspector Hoop in from the cold finally. I have all the evidence the State needs. Kilpatre is incontrovertibly unfit to serve." He threw the word 'unfit' at Kilpatre as though a spear in the hands of Spartacus.

Kilpatre wheezed and stumbled backward as he raised and fumbled a single-shot derringer. He noticed in his peripheral vision a swift movement on his left. Ben Bainbridge cocked a .44 revolver and aimed it six inches from Kilpatre's temple. He smiled at the mayor and shook his head 'no'. Hizoner, predictably, had second

255

thoughts and promptly surrendered his mouse killer with a volley of incoherent explanations and denials of the rather obvious.

"Well then, Inspector, I assume your investigation is now complete."

"It is. I am removing Mr. Kilpatre from office. Effective immediately, Sheriff, you are the acting mayor of Seer City until such time the Deputy Mayor can be located. I'll convene both a grand jury and Mr. Kilpatre's psychiatric evaluation upon my return to Denver." Hoop turned to Kilpatre. "Mr. Kilpatre, you are under arrest. Mr. Ortez and Mr. Bainbridge, please secure this man."

"You got it!"

"With pleasure, Mr. Hoop!" Puck took Kilpatre's derringer.

"What's next, Sheriff?" Hoop asked.

"Get everyone to Seer City, Cy. We will figure things out then. Right now we have a more pressing problem than Kilpatre."

*** 

They all were relieved to get off the highway, but they did not know if they were heading from the frying pan into the fire. At times, the snow fell horizontally, scurrying across the road in spectral currents. Visibility shrank to no more than fifty feet in the faltering artificial light.

BB drove the FBI's Range Rover while Puck took Renner's pickup. Kate rode with Doc and James George and with the McCauley secret now out in the open, literally, she read excerpts of the letters aloud. When she reached the part telling of Old Jimmy's doomsday prophesy, Kara took over the story and took the humans to a faraway time and place.

A stegosaurus cow grazed on a verdant plain with her calf and herd nearby. Communities of other species foraged alongside the behemoths. James George and Kate stood beside Doc Karl above a valley abundant with prehistory. They smiled at each other but remained silent.

A bright object soared through the summer sky—a meteor. *The meteor.* The plain stilled for moment. A lone bull bellowed at the fire in the sky and ordered the herd to run away. Waves of sonic booms soon arrived, drowning out the lumbering stampede of giants. A firestorm overtook the valley, then Earth and ended the Age of Dinosaurs.

Doc's body stiffened. His head slammed against the headrest as Kara released him. "Damn!" he gasped, "I was just there, saw it happen—the end. Did you see it? You, you were both there!"

Before James or Kate could answer, the pickup hit a patch of black ice, fishtailed, and skidded sidewise into the ditch. Doc steered the vehicle back onto the roadway but only after setting off a chain reaction behind him. BB and Puck were following in Renner's pickup and the FBI rental slid to a stop. The RV stopped just in time behind them.

Kilpatre, still raging at having lost his faux-sycophant was less fortunate and crashed hard into the unforgiving rear end of the RV. Kilpatre never wore a seatbelt, so he smacked his melon a good shot on the steering wheel and skinned his knuckles to the bone on the windshield. The airbags deployed late and got him again for good measure, which added a strawberry scuff on his forehead and knocked out his wind. The new Cadillac's grill and bumper were crumpled and the left fender buckled, but the right headlight still worked. The radiator hissed and fumed. Kilpatre hissed and fumed. His car and career were pretty much now in the same condition.

Kate pressed her hand on Doc's. "Yes, we saw it, Doc. But what does it mean?"

James George answered. "It means *our* End. We must stop the Exterm machines, or they will become the equivalent of our own all-extinguishing asteroid."

***

Joshua Roe and Erin Rogers entered Seer City from the south where ordinary enemies would be less vigilant since the winter had long closed the mountain pass. The FBI agents leapfrogged through the swirling snow from one concealment to the next, covering each other's advance, stopping just long enough to confirm a new forward position. Cover from what, though, was the unspoken question on both agent's minds.

Evidence that the town had gone down with a fight was everywhere, and it was apparent that the enemy had gained the upper hand in the ambush.

They saw vehicles piled up in the streets and on the sidewalks as randomly as if deposited by floodwaters. A few cars were still idling, with most of their gas tanks ripped open. Erin and Josh cautiously peered through the rear window of one, a SUV that had jumped the curb and crashed through the IGA grocery storefront, appearing now like a scavenger feeding hip deep inside carrion's unfastened guts.

Abandoned rifles, handguns, and shotguns were scattered across the snow-swept pavement and lawns. Spent shells littered Seer City as though a firearms circus had hurriedly yanked its tent stakes and departed town, leaving behind in its wake mounds of spent cartridge rubbish. Acid burns perforated every wooden structure in town, some measuring feet in diameter where the alien venom strayed then neutralized.

A police cruiser's siren and flashing lights ordered everyone to yield, and the entire town obeyed. An empty tour bus from Evansville waited patiently for its passengers in front of the 108-year-old Seer City Grand Hotel, its venting airbrakes squealing a pointless 'all aboard' every few minutes. On the street side, the bus sat on its rims. All five tires were missing.

Joshua Roe looked at his drawn weapon and then at Erin. He shook his head and holstered the gun. Superior firepower and numbers had proven ineffective tonight against the attackers. Erin nodded agreement and holstered her own weapon. Their only defense would be stealth and luck.

The agents worked their way to Main Street. Inside dozens of homes and restaurants, the agents' flashlights revealed the eerie shadows of last meals. Like scenes from children's tea parties, Seer City abandoned hundreds of seemingly imaginary meals: empty serving dishes, spotless plates, empty glasses, bare soup tureens, clean utensils, and pristine napkins except for what appeared like cigarette burns. Every culinary accoutrement was relieved of its intended duty along with its host by the alien's all-consuming venom.

Through other windows where the occupants had fled into the dissolution of the alien's aerosolized venom, a few last meals were preserved. The agents discovered partially eaten dinners, interrupted and abandoned knife to steak, spoon to sugar, and fork to vegetable. Desserts still awaited those late boys and girls belonging to Seer City's Clean Dinner Plate Club.

For Erin Rogers and Josh Roe, the most confounding evidence of the attack was the dozens of crisply-dug burrows that punctured Seer City's streets, homes, offices, and her buildings. Even the Seer City National Bank's massive steel vault had been compromised, where probably the bank president and his family had futilely taken refuge. All that remained in the vault were the inorganic remains of an unfortunate family: buttons, metal zippers, eyelets, pocket change, synthetic clothing, eyeglasses, a broach, two tin soldiers, iPod metal and more.

Josh Roe lifted an object from the floor of the bank vault with the tip of his knife, "What the hell do you suppose this is?" The late Curtis Judy's ill-fitting gas mask muffled his voice. The mask's eye lenses fogged and cleared as he spoke. Josh silently cursed the unknown manufacturer for every temporary, blinding cataract that invited an unseen enemy.

Erin glanced at the object. "Christ. It's part of a defibrillator implant. I worked on one of these at Cal Poly."

"What the hell happened here, Erin? I'm guessing animals, by the burrows, but I've never seen any predator clean up after itself like this. I mean, there isn't a drop of blood anywhere."

Rogers didn't answer. She couldn't. Her conclusions were pretty much the same. Instead, she offered one more perplexing paradox, "Yeah, but what pack of animals could consume 1,100 plus people, about 68 tons of scrapping red meat on the hoof, not to mention every horse, dog and cat in town?"

"Well, certainly none I know of, but my gut tells me we're alone, at least for now. Whatever was here has left town. Agreed?"

"Agreed. Let's update McCauley."

Erin lifted the radio with one hand and peeled off her gas mask with the other. Her first sensation was startling, and she fought the urge to panic. The air was utterly sterile. She detected no scents; even though stacks of curiously pockmarked human artifacts surrounded her. This caused her to ask herself, 'what predator dines on microscopic organic material as well as man-sized prey?'

Rogers clicked the radio key and waited. Roe removed his gas mask, too. He sniffed the air and understood Erin's shock. The absence of odors is actually quite disgusting.

McCauley's response was immediate and slightly winded. He had sent Debbie ahead to the sheriff's office on the snowmobile and was appropriating another from behind Powelson's Alpine Tours. "State your situation."

"No sign of the enemy. The town appears secure. Sheriff, we are standing in the center of the bank vault. The door was breached, swinging wide when we got here."

McCauley asked curiously, "Bank vault? Explain."

"Yes, well, I can't exactly put in plain words what we've found. The vault looks like Swiss cheese, and judging by the piles of ink that used to be cash, money clearly wasn't the attackers' motive. In fact, it looks like someone tossed acid on everything."

Renner started to ask another question, but Debbie interrupted from downtown on her radio and blurted, "What about the people? Did you find anyone alive?"

Rogers surveyed the bank vault and shook her head before continuing, "No. Actually, no evidence of life at all. We've found thousands of human possessions strewn everywhere, but no people. No life. None. In fact, I'd bet even bacteria have been obliterated. The place smells sterile, resembling one of those clean rooms in Silicon Valley. So Debbie, is this anything like those other places you talked about—similar to Mongolia?"

Debbie stood outside the Sheriff's office, statuesque, as inanimate as Seer City except for her eyes, which now batted in time with her racing heart. Finally, she exclaimed, "Dear God! Yeah, just like Mongolia. I think we're all fucking dead!"

Renner said nothing to disabuse the young woman's fatalism. Believers in doom transform into reliable warriors when the time comes to fight. As he spoke, McCauley surveyed the road in both directions, then the high rocky ridge paralleling the highway, and finally the thick tree line that crawled down to the South Fork of Crockett Creek a hundred yards away. "Listen up. We are dealing with an animal, an unknown number of them. It is a prehistoric creature, one that has remained dormant under Mt. Seer for who knows how long."

Roe laughed, and the relief it brought felt good even if it was false. Strangely, he recalled stories of German soldiers on the winter Russian front in WWII urinating into their frozen boots for similar temporary and false relief. "Sheriff, are you saying animals did this?"

"That's right." Renner expected Roe's skepticism. It did sound wild and would seem crazier yet, if he shared the Jimmy McCauley ancestral secret.

Rogers and Roe kneeled and aimed their flashlights into one of the burrows. The beam disappeared into a glassy tubular abyss. Roe's smile faded. He said, "Well, judging by their burrows, I'd estimate their size to be about that of a bear cub. The bastards can certainly excavate. The floor tunnels go twenty feet deep before turning away out of sight."

"Stay alert. These animals are like nothing we have ever encountered. No more than a kitchen match is a nuke. They are extremely intelligent and conventional weapons are useless against them. Tell me more about the entry points."

Josh and Erin looked at each other and then at the five virtually identical apertures. Roe nodded at Erin, and whether useless or not, both agents drew their weapons. Two passageways rose through the steel-reinforced concrete floor and continued through the vault's twelve-inch steel deck. Another hole passed directly through the vault's tumblers and bolts, at least where the tumblers and bolts used to be. One more hole penetrated the back of the vault and another through its ceiling. Judging by the snowflakes filtering into the vault from above, the tunnel maker entered or exited through the roof.

Roe's voice betrayed his growing dread. "Sheriff, the entry points appear to be machine-cut, perfectly smooth surfaces, approximately two feet in diameter."

Rogers picked up a handful of the gritty, shiny dust mounded around one of the holes. She studied it for a moment and announced, "Sheriff, this might sound nuts, but the concrete and steel seem to have been melted together. The powder looks glassy." She spread her fingers and watched the talc fall like fine sand through an hourglass.

Roe clicked the mike and summed up, "Judging by the way clocks and watches were stopped all over town, someone or something extinguished Seer City in less than twenty minutes. This enemy bored hundreds of holes throughout the town, each the envy of every well digger on the planet, then consumed more than a thousand people without a trace of butchery, and then escaped without leaving a clue. You're telling us those scientists are saying a pack of animals did this?"

"Apparently, that's an affirmative."

It dawned on Rogers that McCauley's intel was exceptional regarding what they all faced now, in fact, too exceptional. "Sheriff, this is Rogers. One niggling question, how did you come by so much information so fast?"

"Kate, Doc and James George have made contact with one of the creatures." The statement was matter-of-fact, and he sounded much more confident than he felt. Renner added before they asked any more questions, "I suggest you proceed with caution to the sheriff's office."

"Alright. What's your ETA?"

"Unknown at this time. Will advise." McCauley clicked the mike once and said, "Debbie, what's your twenty?"

"I'm there. I'm in your office. I hope you guys have a plan."

"I want you to break into the computers and see if there are any clues that were left for us. Erin and Josh will join you soon." Renner gave Debbie several passwords and added, "Hang in there, Debbie."

"Hanging and hacking, but please hurry."

# CHAPTER 54  ~~  Shocked and Awed

With the exception of the county's various destroyed communications systems, Josh Roe and Erin Rogers found the sheriff's office operational, brightly lit, and comfortably warm. Though, not warm enough to thaw any of the horror they had witnessed so far tonight. The diesel generator would hold for at least another seventy-two hours according to the digital fuel gauge monitoring the underground tank. The FBI agents methodically searched for any clues that might shed more light on what they faced. There were few.

Debbie busied herself first with the department computers. The digitized voice recordings of the department call log revealed many strange events in Seer City's last twenty minutes: power outages, gunfire, animal attacks, disappearances, underground rumbling, and inexplicable vandalism. Debbie interfaced the callers' addresses listed in the computer with an online city map and then sequenced them to appear on the map by time reported.

"Holy freakin' Jesus! Hey, you guys better take a look at this. This is not good. Not good at all!"

Erin and Josh looked at each other. A voice can reveal just how close to the edge a person is, and the scientist's voice belonged to a woman teetering over an abyss. Debbie mashed the RETURN key with her thumb and ground it angrily as if crushing a bug. She shoved away from the desk just as the glommed-together computer programs recycled to play. By the time the agents arrived at the workstation, she had ridden the rolling office chair across the room and collided with a thud against a bank of file cabinets. She tucked her legs under her into a fetal position and wrapped her arms around them.

Josh and Erin watched the attack loop on the monitor back to the beginning. Of course, not every attack was reported, but enough were—eighty or so. The assault was textbook. The invaders first attacked communications, utilities, and key transportation centers and did so with a black Ops' efficiency. The machines worked in a classic military pincer, sweeping repeatedly through town headlong and from the flanks, dividing it into ever-smaller parcels.

Debbie watched the agents' body language and knew they saw it too. "They are intelligent, aren't they?"

Erin looked at her partner then the scientist. "Yes, they are, but so are we, Debbie."

"But not like them! No way!"

The wind howled. Tons of snow lifted and rumbled down Seer City's Main Street, obliterating the shadow town in the whiteout. Some of its fury caught an abandoned car door and slammed it shut near the sheriff's office. All three people made first the correct conclusion about the racket, and then the incorrect one, and nervously drew their weapons.

Debbie recalled racing into town on the sled, every inch of the way expecting to be dissolved by some mythical horror she had studied with such fascination and skepticism in college. Then she thought, Patterns. What did I see? Lights. Some on, but just some. Bait. Trap. "We need to get out of here! They left a few lights on to lure any stragglers! They'll come back here first!"

A radio lying on a desk crackled with static. Startled, Debbie jumped to her feet and almost shot it with her crossbow. Erin Rogers placed and held her hand over the shaking weapon until Debbie relaxed and lowered it.

"This is Roe."

"What's your situation, Josh?" Renner asked.

"Situation is secure. No enemy activity. What is your ETA, Sheriff?"

"Five minutes. I met our party outside town and am escorting them into town."

"Copy. Out."

Five minutes can stretch forever, like the shadows of the setting sun. James George was the first inside. He carried Kara like a giant puppy. Mentally, the two had melded, almost as one. Kara looked to her left while James looked right, and collectively memorized the scene. James waited in the center of the office until the adults arrived.

Chris, Earl, Jerry and Buck embraced Debbie. Ben Bainbridge and Puck Ortez stood with Renner, Kate and Doc, with Cyril Hoop joining them. State Police Detective Blaine Rouse had regained consciousness. Erin Rogers and Josh Roe led him to a cot in an empty jail cell. Doc Karl followed and checked on his patient. Cole Kilpatre found a corner and slumped dejectedly in a chair. James George and Kara watched the big man for a moment and then climbed together on top of a desk.

Debbie shared her theory about the remaining lighted buildings. "Sheriff, I think we need to get out of here. I think these mutant rats…" She looked with alarm at Kara, as if she had just made a racial slur with a gang member present. "…left certain buildings lit to attract stragglers."

Before Renner could answer, James George said, "Miss, let's be clear. One, this spectacular entity is not a rodent, and secondly, we are perfectly safe for now. The aliens that were investigating the downed bridge have returned to their lair. Kara will sense and report to us when the attack—which incidentally is indeed inevitable—will occur. Kara is our ally, not an enemy."

James George then shared what he had learned during the past hour. Josh, Erin and Doc rejoined the group. "Her kind is also her enemy, one that requires without quarter hers and our virtual extinction. Her faux species—karpeleotroceme—was assumed extinct, and in fact until only just recently, was considered mythical in most paleontological circles. Only a few scientists, like those present," James George smiled at Doc and Kate, "believed that karpeleotroceme actually existed, and none could imagine a creature…" James hesitated and chose his words carefully. "…an entity life form so dramatically superior to *Homo sapiens*. Ladies and gentlemen, they are aliens in every sense of the word. Their origins are not of this earth. Kara has watched helplessly for seven hundred million years as her enemy harvested life's genetic advances. And we are their next meal."

James ignored the murmuring.

"To summarize most simplistically, Kara is practically immortal. Why? How could this be? She is essentially a machine, a nonorganic transmogrifying entity. She is capable of electronically assimilating the DNA code of any life form. Kara was the commander of a Rebel force that crash-landed here after a battle across the universe that went badly for our side. Her enemies pursued her here, and she has evaded capture ever since. I am not sure how. She is not only telepathic, but also correlative, meaning she can communicate telepathically with those who are not. Her body is practically indestructible. Doc, if you please."

Doc pointed to Renner's sidearm and asked, "Do you mind? I'm part of the show." After a moment, Renner handed the weapon to Doc and nodded. He recalled a late 1800s peach orchard in which his own great-great-grandfather had repeatedly shot this very animal without effect.

James set Kara down and climbed from the desk.

The old professor stepped forward. "Are you sure, Jimmy Boy, isn't this going to hurt her?"

"She is perfectly safe. Right, Kara?"

Kara rose onto her hind legs and scratched her chest to indicate the target. Her snout bobbed up and down in encouragement. To anchor herself she unfurled her raptor-like claws on her hind feet, and then punched them through the steel desktop with a metallic squeal. James smiled at this display while everyone in the Resumption camp gasped.

The weapon roared less than three feet away from Kara's chest. Only James George knew what would happen. The creature caught the bullet like a baseball catcher, hesitated for a moment, then pitched the flattened chunk of hot lead to James, who caught it in a coffee mug with a plink.

James George remounted the desk and continued; disregarding his audience's stunned looks. James kneeled and scratched Kara behind the ears. No one missed the machine's obvious pleasure at the child's touch. Even Cole Kilpatre smiled when Kara began to purr.

"I've studied the process, that is, how the Kar assume a species' DNA by introgression—one species absorbs and assimilates the

DNA of another. In our world, the practice of introgression is limited to viruses and a few simple bacteria. In Kara's world, her kind can selectively absorb the DNA of any organism, and more amazingly, incorporate those characteristics almost instantly. For Kara, the introgression of DNA code is like our loading of software into a computer. Within mere seconds, the evolution of that characteristic goes far beyond the original iteration and reaches its pinnacle."

James stood. "Kara and I are going to show you how rattlesnake venom might be used against its predators after say another one hundred million years of evolution. As you know, venom serves three purposes. First, for defense, of course. Secondly, it kills its victim, and finally, venom is the snake's enzyme-rich saliva. Its digestive process begins the moment the snake's prey is infected."

James removed an Oreo cookie from his pocket. He took one bite and then laid the rest on the desktop. "What you are about to see is a carefully drawn example of what I've just explained. It also explains how everyone in Seer City disappeared. Kara, if you please."

Kara rose again on her hind legs. She studied the cookie for a moment to calculate the precise quantity of venom she would need to dissolve it while not risking harm to the humans. A gentle undulation rippled across her abdomen as she lifted several molecules of highly diluted venom onto the back of her throat. She shifted the microscopic payload to the tip of her tongue and approached the cookie.

James George narrated. "Kara can not only regulate the quantity of venom she delivers, but also its strength. Nothing organic can survive its assault. Dissolution is one hundred percent—not even molecular bonds survive the reaction. Basic elements, mostly carbon, and some sodium will remain, but water's hydrogen and oxygen atoms will dissipate into the atmosphere. The same will happen with nitrogen and the chlorides. In the final stage, the venom falls prey to itself and self-destructs. I suppose it is a form of self-defense, preventing another introgression-capable enemy the opportunity of appropriating Kar's weaponry.

Kara looked up at James George. He nodded, "Go ahead, girl."

Kara's tongue found the cookie, and then she backed away. The cookie swelled to twice its original size. Tacky bubbles formed on its dome as if it were baking. The dough continued to rise for a few seconds and then collapsed upon itself. It boiled into a shrinking, writhing glob and then disappeared with a hiss of steam. A smudge of aerosolized pitch was all that remained of the cookie. James waved his hand over the atomized carbon and other elements, and all evidence of the cookie disappeared.

James waited until he had everyone's attention again and said, "We are not quite finished. Kara has one last thing she wishes to show you. She needs all of us to see her in her natural form. Kara, please go ahead."

The transformation took only a blink of an eye. The giant pseudo-rat shrank to a pinpoint of light and then exploded outward. The bright flash of white light filled the room with Kara emerging from the sparkles in her humanoid form.

Kilpatre wheezed, "My God, except for those blue LED eyes, that crazy rat-bitch looks just like us!"

"No, you could not be more wrong, Mr. Kilpatre," Doc Karl interrupted. His annoyance with the former mayor was plain. "Given our brief history, I suspect it is *we* that are the duplicates."

Kara nodded to the professor and then turned to James George. The suggestion was obvious. Kara needed the child to explain what she could not articulate in English.

"Now that you have seen Kara in her natural form, you are undoubtedly asking yourself why she has also taken the form of a giant rat. The reason is that she must. It is how she might best protect us. You see, her enemy, our enemy, has chosen the form of a rat as well."

James recalled Kate's words about misunderstood rattus from the museum. He smiled at Kate and said, "As our great scientists are quick to remind us, the rat is a very special creature. Superior in so many ways to all other creatures. That is why the Exterms chose it. When Kara shares the Exterm's current physical form, they cannot hide their intentions from her."

Kara smiled and placed her hand affectionately on James George's cheek. The light flashed around her and she returned once again to a giant pseudo rat.

Cole Kilpatre stood. The floor creaked and one-by-one all eyes turned toward the previous mayor of the former town. "Yeah? So just why is she helping us? Why isn't she with her own kind?"

James George could not recall any person that he so instantly distrusted. Not the bullies that occasionally called him names on the bus, or the older kids in Miss Lu's apartment building whose homework he often did for them, or even any of the dreadful nannies that he had endured. Cole Kilpatre was the first to evoke immediate distrust, and James George felt covered by a wave of slime with every word Kilpatre spoke.

Yet, James George knew it was a question everyone needed answered. "She's a soldier—the enemy of our enemy. Ladies and gentlemen, Kara's machinekind has been protecting Life in the universe longer than Life has even existed on Earth. She will defend us tonight, risking everything for us. We must do what she says and keep our heads screwed on straight. Right, Kara?"

The machine nodded and stared at Kilpatre. Kilpatre stuck his tongue out at her.

\*\*\*

Under Seer Mountain, the Exterm machines became dormant as one. They were not asleep, but more like a state of semi-hibernation. It was time to re-arm. Their fur lengthened and as fast as it grew it knitted and wove together, plait after plait, veneer on veneer, compressing each of the seventy tiers into the titanium-rivaling strength of an Abrams tank. When finished, the machines appeared little changed by their reinforcement.

\*\*\*

Renner did not need to assign anyone a task. Everyone understood the predicament facing him or her. Tonight our species would greet our own great asteroid, perhaps the world-ending challenger. Most duties required leaving the relative security of the sheriff's office, but no one complained.

Erin Rogers and Josh Roe searched for and cannibalized radios from around town in hope of rigging together something resembling a long-range communications system. Puck and BB hunted all the likely places for bomb-making material. The Resumption scientists huddled inside the RV. They reanalyzed the computer programs and printouts illustrating the caverns under Seer Mountain.

Doc and Kate's interest in Kara was no longer scientific in nature. They probed for any weakness in the aliens the humans might exploit when the time came. They found none. Hoop kept an eye on Kilpatre and ignored his litany of accusations and insults.

James George approached Renner. The sheriff looked up from the computer monitor where he was studying the aliens' attack pattern.

"James, how are you holding up?"

"I'm fine, Sir. Is Sasha okay? Isaac and Newton?"

"Sasha's sleeping. Can you believe it? Must be contagious, because so are Isaac and Newton. I have never seen such a contented bunch. I'm flat jealous."

James smiled and said, "Another question, if you don't mind. It's sort of personal."

"Shoot."

"Well, Sir, assuming we survive this dreadful ordeal, Kara wants to know if you and Kate will mate." His face blushed and he dropped his eyes.

Renner's complexion matched James'. He looked across the office at Kate. "Wow! She does, huh? Well, tell Kara the answer is yes, if Kate will still have me."

"Well, that's great." James hesitated, and then added as he studied Renner's face, "It's very strange... I see so many of my father's traits in you—self-assurance and an unassailable grasp of right and wrong. Both you and Daddy are... uh, Daddy was a man of very few words. He and you..." Tears filled the boy's eyes.

Renner eased closer to the child and settled his hands gently over James's shoulders. His eyes stung with St. Elmo's own volcanic wrath. James George was just a child in the end—a genius child whose horrendous recent losses were so easily overshadowed by his phenomenal intellect. Renner knew what the child was really asking.

"James, I could never replace your father or Kate your mother. We would never presume to try, but I could not imagine any son I would want more than you. I would be proud to call you mine, if that's what you'd want too. Okay? This whole thing is moving pretty fast for all of us, but it's real and meant to be I think."

Renner waited until the child looked up and then pulled him close. James' arms returned the embrace. He whispered, "Thank you."

Kate watched the two from across the room. She had not heard a word, but understood without the slightest doubt what had passed between Renner and James George. She covered Doc's hand with her own and recalled her own moment of adoption by the old professor decades earlier. Promises made. Promises kept. It was her turn now.

***

"Renner. Copy?" Puck released the radio mike button. He then placed the transceiver on his ear with one hand and with the other snugged the anorak coat's hood tighter. He and BB were fifth generation mountain men, so they had experienced their share of winter weather. Neither needed a meteorologist to tell him what the steadily falling temperatures, growing wind, and horizontal snow showers meant—a blizzard and a good one to boot.

James and Renner looked together at the radio. The sheriff picked it up and answered. "Copy. Any luck, boys?" James sat down at the workstation and studied the attack.

Puck and BB had been scavenging for munitions and triggering devices for about forty-five minutes and had been largely unsuccessful. The aliens had known where to look too. The hardware store, the county engineer, and the National Guard Armory were all in shambles.

"Yeah, Renner. Last stop. We're at the armory. Not having much luck here either. The space rats got to all the boom party essentials first. Fortunately, though, the bastards missed the timers, transmitters and receivers.

"So with what Beebs and me brung, we have enough ingredients to make a hundred or so pieces of ordnance from the building elimination point of view. I say we booby-trap the monsters' tunnels. Snipe the rest of the little sock-tuckers with the crossbows as they come out. Come on back."

Renner watched James replay and study the computer-generated attack on the town. The child's eyes darted from point-to-point on the monitor. After the second replay, he touched a point on the map where no attack had occurred and whispered, "There!" He replayed the program once more and added, "And here, here, and right here!"

"Puck, hold on for a second." Renner kneeled next to James. "What do you see, son?"

"A pattern. A peculiar array of sudden appearances and disappearances." James shook his head and looked up. "Advise Mr. Puck that his tactic will not work. The aliens won't use the same tunnels. But, I believe I can calculate where they *will* appear. Kara should be most helpful with timing their next arrival."

"Puck. Stand by."

"Copy. Standing by."

The wind roared through countless aspens and ponderosas on the mountainside, turning the forest woodlands into ghostly wind instruments, all trumpeting unambiguous trouble approaching. The wintry vandal poured down the slopes into the valley, into the town, lifted snow, pried at buildings, found purchase, and snatched anything insufficiently fastened down. The National Guard armory reverberated and a thousand moist tentacles soared across its darkened expanse. BB and Puck exchanged concerned glances and then returned to the current landmine under construction.

***

Buck Tumulley was the first to look up from the computer printouts when the RV began to slide. The eighty mile per hour gust caught the land boat broadside. The vehicle slammed with a good jolt into the curb. Lights flickered. The metal hull ranted like a snare drum as the wind and ice pellets continued to beat its thin skin. Anything precarious inside the RV found *terra floora* in clattery unison.

Debbie screamed, covered her head, and then dropped to the deck. Earl grabbed the edge of the table and growled a stream of explicative laced commands, as though coaxing a team of spooked mules back between the fencerows. Jerry froze, titmouse to blacksnake, eyes fixed, mouth ovular. One-time surfer Californian Chris Jussard rode the wave with casual far-out aplomb. It was a good facade. Jussard was also a scientist, a possessor of analytical skills that marked up score sheets swiftly and accurately. This town was dead, euchred. And, the killers were coming back for seconds.

"Buck!" Jussard yelled above the wind and rumble.

"Yes, Sir." Tumulley rubbed his beer-shed of a gut where it had slammed into the corner of the table.

"What do you guys have?"

"Nothing. At least nothing useful."

"Tell me anyway."

As he spoke, Tumulley sculpted in the air in front of him the impossibly complex squirrels' nests that the computer-generated relief maps depicted of the caverns. "Nothing new. The anomalies under Seer Mountain are definitely not anomalies, at least not in the conventional sense. The caverns were created, and I believe are the result of a highly complex alien design." He gestured toward the Sheriff's office—toward Kara. The RV rocked again with another violent gust. Just another tracer bullet, but a solid suggestion that they had been targeted. Jussard ran his hand over his face and flexed his jaw that ached with stress. "Debbie?"

She shook her head 'no' and studied the RV walls like a submariner inspecting rivets for leaking seawater.

"Jerry?"

The scientist didn't answer, but he did finally breathe and inform the group of the obvious. "The wind just blew us the fuck sideways!"

Jussard moved on. "Earl?"

Earl shrugged 'no', and then pointed at the sheriff's office. "Let's give the kid a look. Maybe he can make sense of this."

The kid. In many ways, a frightening anomaly himself. His savant-like parlor tricks aside, Jussard had watched with great skepticism and then belief, as the child communicated telepathically with the rat-ally-alien-machine.

Jussard picked up his radio and punted, "Uh, Sheriff?"

"What have you got, Dr. Jussard?"

"Not sure. Maybe nothing. Perhaps we could have young James George take a crack at it though."

"Explain."

"We are focusing on the anomaly that brought us here, the maze of caverns deep under the mountain. Up until just a few hours ago, we wanted to believe the formations somehow had a geologic explanation. Now, we are confident they are of an extraterrestrial design."

The mountain and the mine had been in Renner's family for well over a hundred years, but no McCauley had ever ventured far inside. "Caverns? Under Seer Mountain? Explain."

"Our analysis of the seismic data reveals a system of caverns and tunnels under the mountain that we know cannot be random geologic formations. We believe the aliens excavated them. Why? We do not know."

"Okay, bring what you've got inside, Dr. Jussard. We'll have James George take a look at it."

\*\*\*

Five blocks across town on Estes Street, where Seer City's modest commercial district gave way to pseudo commercial enterprise— apartments and paint-itchy rental properties—Erin Rogers and Joshua Roe continued their search.

Only three electric generators remained working in this part of town. No, make that just two as the hamburger joint on the corner winked out and with it a bit of hope.

Two snowmobiles safe idled softly in the yard outside the clapboard duplex. Two steeds awaiting riders that would never take their reins. A snow swale had seeded mirroring arcs around the sleds. The drifts also concealed the inorganic remains of the sleds' former owners.

One engine sputtered and died. A moment later, its mate coughed up its own lung and succumbed. Their headlights flickered out. Erin shined light on one fuel gauge then the other. She looked at Josh and shook her head 'no'. The agents walked past the snowmobiles and trudged up the front porch steps.

Erin tried the door. It was locked. She nodded to Josh and stepped back as her partner kicked it open. Weapons raised, the FBI agents slid inside. Like dozens of other battle scenes left in testament to Seer City's fall, gunfire had perforated the home's walls. However, this firefight was exceptional.

Sieve-like and driven by a fierce gale, snow eerily fluted through the many ventilations. Rogers sent the flashlight beam across the entry and focused it on a shattered portal now connecting the kitchen and the front bedroom beyond. In final desperation, his guns decidedly useless against the giant space rats, the defender apparently had employed something akin to a grenade launcher.

The wall studs, hardwood floors, sub floor, and joists, though splintered and badly scalloped, had fared better than the drywall and carpeting, which hung or lay by its fibrous hides in unnatural lathe shavings around the room. Chalky gypsum pebbles and charred dust garnished the scene of the firefight. Chunks of shredded furniture and clothing hung from the dining room fixture.

Roe and Rogers had observed alien tunnels tonight carved through frozen soil, granite, concrete, and steel. The tunnels had been excavated with complete indifference to man-made and natural obstructions of any kind. At the end of these many egresses, they always witnessed the same thing—the complete absence of life. Battles, yes, some quite valiant, but never did they find a victory for humankind. Seer City was not only vanquished, it was sterilized.

The battle here was extraordinary. Rogers kneeled and shined the light over the inorganic remains belonging to the unusually well-armed former homeowner, a brass plate honoring the commander of the local militia.

Like all six before it, they had destroyed the ham radio here. The agents collected some weapons and ammunition and left.

***

Puck shook his head. "The Armory is basically a bust, Beebs. I've never seen such a freaking mess. It's like they had our shopping list and got here first and just left us scraps."

"Let's burn one, Puck. It might be a while before we get another chance." Ben Bainbridge lit a cigarette, handed it to Puck, and then fired another one up.

BB held the lighted match for a moment and then as an afterthought dropped it down a nearby alien tunnel. The aperture appeared to have emerged in the perfect center of the armory. Puck and BB leaned over and watched the match disappear. They lost sight of it at about twenty feet.

Ortez removed his glove and touched the shaft walls, "Hell of a hole, Bro. Smooth as a tomato skin. How do you suppose they do it, Beebs? A machine couldn't cut this clean, and these bastards are faster than hurry up."

"The kid says that the, uh, rat told him it's some kind of extreme reaction. He hasn't got it figured out yet. Somehow, they dissolve the rock with something they gag up and spit. James George says they can penetrate anything with it at a full headlong run."

"Fuck me! They's like termites on steroids."

"Yep. That's right. Space termites." BB scratched his beard. He lit another match and dropped it down the shaft. It stayed lit for a good forty feet this time before burning out. In fact, the flame grew as it fell, to four or five inches in diameter. Both men understood what that meant: high concentrations of oxygen, and maybe something else—perhaps the slight presence of methane as indicated by the blue-orange halo surrounding the flame.

"What's you thinking, BB?"

"Well, Puck, maybe some of that listening equipment Resumption brung might give us a little heads-up that those giant rats are on their way."

"Genius! Then we set the charges to go off just before they come out…"

"…and the compressed oxygen and methane behind them…"

"…magnify the explosive forces…"

"…maybe twenty-fold. Like trapping them in a compactor that also incinerates."

Puck and BB pressed their fists together as Puck lifted the radio and called Renner. "Uh, Renner, copy?

From the sheriff's office, "Go ahead."

"How we doing with those twenties on Mr. Fat Rat?" Puck grinned at BB and added, "Reason I'm asking is this. If James George can get us close enough with his mighty arithmetic, BB came up with one hellacious greeting card for them."

"We are working on just that. Kara believes we have about an hour before they attack again. Come on in. Everyone else has already returned."

"Copy that, Renner. We're rolling. ETA in five."

# CHAPTER 55 ~~ Casualties

Doc and Kate closed their eyes. The blizzard's fury faded around them. Voices and machines dimmed by way of the great rheostat called oblivion. Sunlight replaced the artificial lights of the sheriff's office. It was our sun for sure, but different—slightly smaller, brighter, a star belonging to an earlier Earth. Millions of years passed in front of their minds' eyes. Doc and Kate effortlessly absorbed ten, twenty, thirty lifetimes of knowledge in mere minutes, and all of it could be summed up with one word: apocalypse. No species successfully challenged the Kar. None survived once targeted by the exterminators.

The life forms extinguished by the Federation were as numerous and as impossible to tally as the blades of grass in the highway median while speeding down an interstate on a moonless night.

Kara showed them a bacterium from a distant planet that survived the rogue planetoid that collided with its host planet, shattering it apart, sending the tiny life form sailing into deep space toward Earth. On its journey here, it hibernated for 3,819,921,000 Earth years in the alternately frigid-torrid void, surviving countless radiation fields and the inhospitable vacuum of space, but not the worst Wal-Mart greeter in the universe—Kar.

Kara revealed a worm that existed tens of millions of years ago that reproduced telepathically with its lifelong mate half a world away. Their one hundred eighty millennium lifespan facilitated an occasional physical rendezvous as well.

Kara introduced them to a sapient plant, a spectacular fern capable of abstract thought, even humor.

Then they met a chameleon-like creature that was capable of changing more than its color. One moment it was serpentine, the next winged and feathered, the next insectile and chitinous. They observed twenty or more iterations of the same disguising species.

There were many more: A tortoise-like creature that had lived deep in the earth and thrived on silicon and ferrous ore. A bird that spent its entire life airborne. A balloon-like fish no larger than a sand shark that preyed on colossal whales and ate only once in a lifetime. Migratory plants that followed weather changes. Voracious flies that moved with insatiability of army ants.

Millions of species, perhaps billions, far too many to comprehend, rose only to have their genes harvested. Ironically, it was a gathering, a systematic husbandry of sorts not unlike man with his cattle, his grain, his orchards, even his own genes in laboratories. Moreover, once relieved of its genetic bounty, the alien machines exterminated the species, and thoroughly removed all evidence of its existence from the planet so no other opportunist might salvage the booty.

The Coming tonight, Kara warned, was not original. Man was to be the next beautiful dawn to fall before the alien invader. Another fading dusk of a species, added to countless earlier husks infinitely summed, one epoch to the next with such regularity that all of humankind's contribution to the cosmos would be rendered to perhaps a single sub-strand of DNA—a miniscule appropriation by a 'rat.'

Could it be? *Homo sapiens.* Its fate the evolutionary equivalent of another Snickers candy bar vended by Darwin to a genetic snack addict at his great train station of life. An infinitesimal addendum to the magnificent fortunes previously plundered from other fallen species. A pathetic nickel of net worth tossed not just at the feet of a merciless extorting tyrant, but futilely in his wake days past. Here Man was and there Man was—hairsplitting past tense, as if and perhaps because Future itself was now extinct.

Mercifully, Kara released the scientists and allowed them to return to the present. A tear fell down Kate Lambert's cheek. Doc pulled her close to him. Their reprieve was short lived, though. Neither could speak as a series of new but terrifying images rose in their minds—fractal memories for sure, but no less vivid.

A boy with a can of insecticide aims it at a wasp nest in a tree. The creatures somehow know they are doomed but cannot flee. A man's hand intervenes. "Let them be, son. They have a right to be here, too."

A father dives into the ocean for his daughter and swims between the rising dorsal fin of a tiger shark and his child. The confused animal turns away and the father and child are pulled from the water.

A wounded soldier dives on a live grenade to save his comrades. Another whose legs are missing and bleeding out reaches beneath his best friend and removes the weapon. With the last of his strength, he presses the grenade to his chest and rolls over as it detonates.

And...

James George's parents share their final moments before the crippled plane crashes into the Atlantic Ocean. They hold hands and take turns kissing a photo of a son they'll never see again.

"So unusual in the universe Goodness is! Life!" Kara's newfound voice alternately belonged to an ancient woman of the tobacco creed and a parrot—a screech that rose through a deep rasp. One by one, everyone turned toward the strange sound of Kara's voice. Kate and Doc studied the stunned group and realized that they all had witnessed the memory snippets as well.

"You see now? The invader fears Man. Why? Man better. Man care for kind. All kinds. His kind. All kind. Invader hates human. Fears Life. But Jimmy McCauley loved Kara, a Kar. Kara loves Jimmy McCauley, a human. We are the same. Goodness. See? Together we can stop Federation this time. Rebel Kar machine and good human Life are allies. Together we must stop Federation before it exterminates all life in the universe."

The building and town rumbled around them, a reminder that Ruin was afoot. It had been here once and was on its way back. Windowpanes chattered and trilled inside their brittle, caulk-shot frames. Street signs thubbah-thubbahed. Storefront signage creaked, groaned, and advertised only its collective arthritic misery. Wind-driven snow hissed over the building, an incessantly crinkling painter's drop cloth. Leashed yet abandoned, Seer City wailed plaintively for its masters, its pack, to return.

Inside the sheriff's office, all was quiet as the spell's effect waned. James George broke the mannequin pact and startled everyone including Renner. His voice trembled and sounded as distant and ghostly as the collective memory of his parents.

"My mom and dad weren't afraid, Kara. They knew they were about to die, and all they felt was hope for me." The child ran to the machine, scooped her into his arms and wept. "Thank you, Kara! Thank you so very much! Oh! So much more terrifying than losing them was not knowing how they were doing at the end, and now I do. They weren't afraid. They weren't afraid because…"

"…because your Life kind is good." Kara looked up at Kate and cocked her head to one side.

James George took Kate's hand and whispered, "Yes."

Renner McCauley was a man prone to constant subconscious inventory taking: people, places and things, and his count was now off two tick marks in the people department.

Everyone was gone somewhere. Some were still lost in Kara's hypnotic trance, oblivious to the murder. Mayor Cole Kilpatre was gone elsewhere. He was what might be called criminally Elvis. Cyril Hoop was also gone—as in doorknob, dead and gone. A trail of blood crossed twenty inches of hardwood to his fractured skull.

***

It had been a surprisingly easy kill and not the mayor's first. He was, after all a Kilpatre, and a couple of potholes always got filled along the way with every generation. Kilpatre had used a fireplace poker. Impulse. Instinct. Thwop! He honestly didn't mean to kill Hoop, well honestly, he did. When Hoop lay there for a few seconds bleeding his grey away, and the others didn't seem to notice, Kilpatre bundled up and walked out.

Giggling as if engaged in nothing more than a harmless fraternity prank, not murder, Kilpatre sabotaged every vehicle except Resumption's RV—only because he could not figure out how to disable the beast. The tires would not flatten and the hood cover was sealed. The doors locked automatically when the vehicle was unoccupied.

Cursing, he threw a snowball angrily at the RV's windshield and stormed off toward Seer City's maintenance garage. There he found what he needed—the city's emergency Sno-Cat. He crashed the big tractor through the overhead door and returned to the sheriff's office, where he drove it over the snowmobiles repeatedly, crushing them where they sat. Satisfied that they could not pursue him, Mayor Kilpatre left town heading south. The mountain pass was closed, but Kilpatre was irrational and therefore confident he could still drive over it with the Sno-Cat. He made a quick detour onto Heinrich Avenue and did three quick laps around Powelson Alpine Tours, killing every snowmobile in the lot. Seer City would have to elect another kind of rat for mayor.

***

The bloody rivulet on the floor traced back to its fountainhead, an indentation on Hoop's right temple. Ivory bone, pink scalp and a moist drift of brown hair made an unnatural convergence where the fireplace poker struck. Renner, Erin, and Josh kneeled over the body. They were sure that Hoop was dead, but began CPR anyway. Their efforts were noble but futile.

Puck waited until Renner stood and stepped away from the corpse before delivering more bad news. Rogers and Roe carried Hoop's corpse to an empty cell and covered him. "Renner, that fat sum-bitch headed south toward the pass with the city Sno-Cat. He wretched the distributor caps off the other vehicles, yanked out all the wiring he could get his hands on. Slashed the tires. And that ain't all. The bastard also did a good number on the snowmobiles. They're all shot for shit."

"Munitions?"

"Sumbitch missed them, thank God."

"Powelson's?"

"We'll check, Mac, but tracks lead to Powelson's. Effer obviously didn't want us follerin' him."

"Okay, Puck, you and BB see what you can figure out. We need transportation."

"You got it. Let's go, Beebs. It's grand theft auto time."

"I don't need to tell you to hurry, boys." Renner glanced across the room for Kara, but she had disappeared. "According to Kara, we now have only forty-five minutes before they attack. James George, where is Kara?"

James did a three-sixty and said, "I don't know. Kara!" he called. No answer.

McCauley pointed towards the rear of the office and whispered, "Find her, son."

James George ran toward the cells and called out, "I found Kara! She's, uh, with Mr. Hoop."

281

Doc and James watched Kara disappear under the blanket. "What's she doing?" James George pressed his face between the bars and watched Kara moving under the blanket around Hoop's wound.

Doc whispered, "I don't know, son."

Renner called for James, "Can you come here and look at what the Resumption people have?"

"Go ahead, son," Doc said, "I'll keep an eye on her."

Earl and Buck spread the first computer printout depicting the caverns across Renner's desk. James George scanned it and asked for the next, which they followed with eight more printouts. The examination took five minutes.

After James finished and returned the last page to the engineers, Renner kneeled next to James and asked, "Well, son. What did you learn?"

"Though thoroughly fascinating, actually, I learned very little. The passages are beautifully laid out. However, the design is unremarkable except for its location. I'd rate the engineering and construction as topnotch, though." James looked up.

"Oh." McCauley could barely conceal his disappointment.

However, Buck and Earl's sentiments weren't veiled at all.

"Damn!"

"Rat fucked we are!"

Renner frowned and gestured apologetically at James, but then realized the child didn't seem fazed by either the adults' disappointment or profanity.

On the other hand, James assumed he had hoofed into the Letdown Zone, and that he'd disappointed Renner. He attempted to explain, "You see, I already ascertained everything we need to know about their tactics from this." James returned to the computer monitor and replayed the attack. "There! There! And... there... there... and... wait... here it comes... there! Unmistakable!" He turned to the adults and asked, "Do you see it?"

Chris Jussard had watched this display in awe, and it was the kind of foreboding that hung around like the hiccups. "Wha... What do you mean, James George, uh, ex... exactly?"

James misinterpreted the adults' reactions onto an ever-higher plane. He now presumed he'd not only disappointed the adults, but also offended the Resumption engineers' quality of work. "Oh! Please don't get me wrong!" Tapping the printouts, "These represent some incredibly expert relief. I've never seen better. In fact, it validates my previous theory, and for that I'm most grateful, and rather more than somewhat relieved." He winced. His voice was sing-songy and patronizing. Will I ever learn to speak without insulting others? He asked himself.

"Your theory, James?" Renner asked, hope returning like a search plane tipping its wings and banking hard to port.

"Yes. The machine's playbook so to speak. It has a fatal flaw. One which we shall exploit."

"Explain."

"First we must prove my working theory. Dr. Jussard, I identified several handheld global positioning devices in your RV."

"GPS? Yes. An absolute must in our profession. The very best money can buy, accurate to one hundred millimeters, three to four inches. Why?"

"We'll need them as well as your GPS server."

Jussard glanced over his shoulder and said, "Debbie, Jerry, get 'em!" He turned back to James, "What else?"

"Sheriff McCauley, Mr. Puck says we'll need at least thirty minutes to set all the charges, that is, once I've calculated exactly where to place them. Timing is critical if we are to exploit their only weakness."

McCauley nodded and spoke into the radio. "Puck, BB, what's your ETA?"

"Three minutes, no luck on transportation. Powelson's is a no go. Worse, every all-wheel-drive vehicle in town we found had its gas tank cut off. They's planners, Mac. Damn! Have the Resumption people set up the seismic arrays?"

"Negative, but we are working on it." McCauley nodded. Both men glanced toward the front door as Debbie and Jerry returned with the six GPS devices.

James picked up the devices, fumbled them, and ordered. "Stop! Wait!"

"What is it, James?"

"I need Dr. Jussard's people to go to three of the Kar tunnels and give me a GPS reading from the very center of each. There is one aperture here in your office. I'll do that one myself. Four readings are more than enough to confirm my theory."

Renner grabbed one of the handhelds and tossed it to Jussard.

At the door Jussard yelled to Renner, "We'll need three minutes tops to get the GPS readings for James and another three to plant and calibrate the Resumption seismic sensors. James will need a minute or two to make his calculations on where to set the charges. If we split up, thirty minutes to place and arm the bombs. It's going to be tight."

McCauley nodded. Jussard's calculations matched his own. He turned to James, "Okay kiddo, what's your plan? Where's their weakness?"

***

Kara called out to Hoop. "Jimmy McCauley, wake up!"

*Tumbling. Falling. But up or down?*

"Jimmy McCauley!"

*It is down, painlessly. The sense is away, always away. From what? Life. Gone. Where am I now? But there is no now, anymore.*

"Jimmy McCauley!"

*"I must be dead. Kilpatre! Kilpatre must have murdered me."*

"Jimmy McCauley!"

"Oh! Hello, Kara. There you are. I heard you calling, but from where? Did Kilpatre kill you, too?"

"Not dead, Jimmy McCauley. Kara not dead. Jimmy McCauley not dead, at least not all the way dead."

"What do you mean?"

"Kara fix Jimmy McCauley."

"Who is Jimmy McCauley?"

"Sorry. Xs and Os. Kara despises this language. Save for Life. Hoooooooooooop. Hooooop. Hoop!"

"Oh, it's too late to save me, little friend. I'm dead. I just don't know where I am exactly. Do you know?"

"No. We have time to fix Hoop. But can Hoop be patient? Can Hoop die just a little bit more for Kara? Kara need time. Trust Kara, Hoop?"

"I don't... I don't understand, Kara."

"The shard. Remember the shard?"

"Yes."

"Shard fix Hoop. Feel it? Feel it here? Feel it there?"

"Yes! I do. It feels... it feels... my head. I can't find the word. Can you believe that?"

"There is no English word for it, life-returning-to-Hoop. Not even for Kara. Now, Hoop sleep."

"Okay... but Kara?"

"Yes, Hoop."

"I love you. It seems like I've always loved you, though we just met. Strange."

"Kara love Hoop, too. Always loved Hoop. Hoop good. Kara love all good. Always the good. Never the bad."

"Like Kilpatre!"

"Kara hate Kilpatre."

"Kara?"

"Yes, Hoop."

"Kara, did you make all this happen?"

"Not all. But much. We had to. Jimmy McCauley and Kara Kar. Now sleep, Hoop, so Kara can fix."

"O... kay... Kara..."

***

Since age two and a half, James could recall verbatim practically every conversation. The settings where these discussions took place were no less vivid and detailed in his mind as the present-day sheriff's office, where now he sat and summoned one of his most pleasant memories.

"Second to my passion for paleontology is astronomy, Sheriff Renner. I shared this love for the stars with my father. It mysteriously revealed itself to me, I suppose, like the keyboard to Mozart. Father called it our private version of Little League. Oh, I suppose kicking about a soccer ball or swinging a club of lathed ash wood can be exciting. But in my humble opinion, it's nothing compared to mounting your dad's shoulders to gaze up at the stars or laying on a blanket on a warm summer night in Maine and counting them until the numbers become more of a Picasso swatch of pastel oil or a Grover Washington jazz riff than actual numeration.

"One night I was like Magellan navigating by way of the heavens throughout that explorer's tiny but terrifying universe, discovering islands at tortoise pace. The next night I was a voyager from the future moving from one galaxy to the next at multiples of light-years. It was so..."

"Real?" Renner said.

"Yes. Real." James George smiled and fell silent as he slipped into a part of his past where words fell short. Renner waited patiently, but also enviously of a man he had never met, but to whom he now owed so much.

The radio crackled. It was Jussard. "Sheriff, we have the coordinates. Is James ready for us to download?"

James George nodded. He raised the antenna on the GPS server and pressed several keys.

Renner said, "Jussard, go!"

A diode on the tiny server pulsed green for a second and James announced, "We've got it. I'll transfer now."

Renner clicked the mike once and instructed Jussard to finish setting the seismic arrays. He had to repeat his orders twice as the storm drowned out his words on the other end.

As James George typed he said, "I know now he was right but also wrong, Sheriff."

"Wrong? Who's that, James George?"

James giggled and worked the computer keyboard. "Oh! Sorry. Albert Einstein. Traveling at the speed of light and beyond. These last few days I have learned that supra light speed travel is not only possible but also confirmed. Our definition of the ceiling has been limited. Are you familiar with the hippie-physicist experiments at Stanford in the sixties called the psi project?"

Anxious to learn another theory, specifically karpeleotroceme's weakness, Renner pressed on, "Does that have anything to do with our situation here, James?"

James bookmarked his memory for later consumption and returned to the present. "Well, actually, I believe it does." James gazed up at the high, turn-of-the-century ceiling and pointed. Renner's eyes obediently followed.

"It's in the stars. There are eighty-eight constellations, forty-four in each hemisphere, north and south. That's their weakness, their paradigm, and also ours. Two life forms. Forty-four unmistakable patterns we share in common."

He moved to the computer monitor and launched the earlier attack sequence once more, but this time with the GPS coordinates integrated into the program. As each site illuminated, James announced, "Vulpecula, then Triangulum, now Cetus, to Cancer, and Monoceros, and Leo Minor, and on and on. The constellations are their portals to the surface—like navigational beacons. The city is reduced to their northern universe."

"James, where next?"

The child sat at the keyboard, his chin nearly level with it. His fingers flew over the keys. Within a few minutes, another set of flashing lights pulsed on the screen—sixteen green lights interspersed with the twenty-eight red that signified the earlier attack. A moment later, the color laser printer came to life.

Renner turned to James George for an explanation.

James George understood. "These are the coordinates, Sheriff. The precise locations where we need to set the explosives. The aliens will arrive at the surface simultaneously. The instant before they breach the surface, we detonate the bombs. If we time our attack just right by using the seismic array, it will have the same effect as an explosion inside a submarine. Deadly."

James stepped to the printer, snatched the last sheet from the stack and handed it to Renner. McCauley had experienced enough shock tonight, but nothing prepared him for what the child gave him.

Renner lowered the sheet of paper and James's face swam into view. "James, these are the global positions for where you believe the machines will attack?"

"Yes. Their origins in the previous attacks represented the near-perfect focal centers of the constellations. The slight variants are most likely because the stars have moved relative to earth since the aliens last saw them. It's a rather simple adjustment."

Puck and BB's return was ill timed. A sixty-mile-per-hour gust yanked the doorknob from BB's hand just as he opened it and delivered the storm inside. Renner clutched the paper and ignored the wintry assault as everything loose in the office went airborne at once. BB grabbed the door on the rebound, held it open for Puck to come through, and then pressed his full weight against it until it closed. Both men appeared iced over. Snow shimmered to the floor around them.

Puck flipped down his hood and announced, "Sorry, Mac, but I think it might just frost out there tonight."

BB added, "We might ought to cover the petunias, too, Ren. Puck's one sharp weather girl."

McCauley handed them the sheet. "Do we have sixteen explosives devices ready, and can they be detonated centrally and simultaneously?"

Puck pretended to be hurt. He glanced at BB and then said, "We got twice that many, and Mac, you know better than to ask such an insulting question. But we're flattered just the same that you'd ask."

McCauley smiled and tapped the paper in Puck's hands. "These are the coordinates where the entities will surface."

BB studied the information from over Puck's shoulder. All levity departed and BB asked, "How sure are you of that Renner? I mean Goddamn, that's some seriously precise information."

Renner looked over at James who was now cradling Kara in his arms. "One hundred percent, but you don't want to know how just yet. Not sure I could explain it in any event."

Puck handed the printout to BB and scratched his chin as he collected his thoughts. "So here's the plan, if I got this right. We plant sixteen charges at these exact coordinates. The seismic array listens for the space rats rising through the earth, and we detonate the explosives simultaneously just before they breach the surface. I estimate the internal pressure will expand to around 100,000 pounds per square inch."

Renner nodded. "Exactly."

BB and Puck conferred for a moment. Renner didn't understand what they were saying, but sensed the plan was not perfect anymore.

"Problem, boys?"

"You could say so. BB and me peeked into one of them rat holes, Renner, and we dropped us a match down it. That match flared like a torch as it fell. The air in that shaft must be three-quarters oxygen. Contains a fair amount of methane, too. We have to assume them Tyrannosaurus rats originated from somewhere in or around the mine."

Renner already knew the answer, but asked anyway, "You're saying we could blow up the mine?"

"Oh yes, to high hell, but I know you don't give two Kilpatre Sunday craps about that mine. It's the town. Seer City sits directly over the old Little Tokyo shaft. The very one your granddaddy was in when he rang the "gitout" bell the day they closed the Midas Six forever."

James stepped between the men. He was still holding Kara. "Renner!" he exclaimed.

It wasn't his name being spoken that caused McCauley to look down at the child. It was the fear in the boy's voice, an infectious alarm that all three men instantly caught.

"Yes, son."

"Kara says they are awake and they are coming soon."

"Don't worry. We'll be ready, James."

"She also says that they've changed. That they have adapted to our weapons."

"What does that mean, James?"

"I'm not sure exactly, but I assume she means they are somehow physically altered. They learn more about our defenses after each encounter, and their ability to morph is apparently unlimited."

Renner thanked James and turned to Puck and BB. "That's actually good intel. The current high-water mark is when Trooper Rouse's cruiser exploded, and based on that, they might have under adapted. Let's raise the ante and be sure we get them. Double the charges on each target."

"Uh, Mac, doubling the charges might kill the space rats, but it's also likely to make a sinkhole out of Seer City."

"Don't worry, boys. I don't plan on us being here when the fireworks start. We'll detonate by way of taillights on our way out of town."

The storm rumbled over the sheriff's office. Snow and ice crystals scratched and pried at every window. The gale growled a curse. It rose over the building's eves and passed with a shrill caw, its mocking cry unmistakable to all.

# CHAPTER 56 ~~ Failsafe

In the shimmering phosphorescence of their vast warren, the machines activated from their hibernation and rose to their feet as one. The aliens opened their eyes as if a singular nerve and muscle controlled all. They flexed their claws and the granite beneath squealed.

Alpha Genesis probed first his own world under Seer Mountain, and then the contaminated world beyond, where he sensed the humans and the Rebel were preparing to fight.

Alpha Genesis sensed something new—time. The past was near. The future too, and for a machine that comprehended neither, the experience was perplexing—like discovering the possession of an extra set of eyes that had always been there but never opened.

Future. Past. A brilliant eruption of light. A rumbling concussion reaching through the earth itself. "Perty blonde gal from Golden… Gitout! Gitout!"

Another trap, but past or future? Kar's or another's?

Alpha could not know for sure what he was sensing, and that uncertainty required a change in plans. He would remain behind with a single female as a precaution.

Alpha gave two commands. He ordered all but one of the machines to ascend to the surface and launch the attack. As soon as the aliens were gone, the leader placed its paw on the throat of one machine left in reserve and issued his second order—a replication command for six new machines. Six could become trillions of machines in time.

***

The seismic gadgetry that Resumption Mining provided was unrivaled. The most acute setting could accurately count the paces of a man walking a mile away.

From the RV, Buck Tumulley announced over the radio, "McCauley, we've got bogies rising under the town!"

Renner prompted for the even more relevant report, "Copy, Buck. But what are their headings?"

A moment passed while the Resumption team refined the data. "Fucking-A! It's just like the kid predicted. They're reaching for the stars. Exactly! Oh man, I hope those charges are set.

Puck jumped in and answered from the south end of town, "Two to go. Rogers and Roe are on it."

"What's the aliens' ETA, Buck?"

"At their current rate of ascent, eleven minutes and change."

The seismic speakers hissed an urgent whisper, an executioner's rising drumroll as the pack tore toward the surface. A fierce gust rocked the RV. Ice crystals pecked timbre on the vehicle's metal skin and scratched a pitch on its glass. Everyone inside glanced unconsciously at the steering wheel and longed for it to do its work and take them all away.

***

Halfway up Major Bronson Pass, Cole Kilpatre did the nearly impossible—he managed to get the Sno-Cat stuck in a rather unimpressive snow bank. When the vehicle's rear end fishtailed a scant yard, His Tubiness panicked, over-compensated and drove off the road.

If he had understood the vehicle's independent drive system and used its low gears, he would have crawled out of the ditch with ease.

The windshield wipers tapped out an apathetic beat. The cabin heater rumbled indifferently. The mayor huffed and cursed. He pounded the steering wheel for Jesus, ground hamburger out of the gears, and inevitably seized the coward's option with prejudice—he gave up. Resigned that his only options were to return to Seer City, or die on the pass in the blizzard, he decided to turn around.

Of course, there was the wee issue of Cyril Hoop's murder facing him in Seer City. Okay, first things first: He'd have to winch himself out of the ditch for now, and then later, using another kind of winch, extricate himself from the legal morass. There were many types of legal winches: self-defense or maybe insanity. He had been in tighter pinches. Well actually, he had not, but the night was early.

Snow lifted and relocated relentlessly. Kilpatre fell silent and watched from his orange and windowed island while an angry white sea churned around him. His trance broke as a tree surrendered to the storm and came crashing down. Its trunk split with a cannon's report. Like a drowning man, the tree reached out with its branches and implored futilely for its comrades to save it.

Kilpatre climbed from the Sno-Cat unprepared for the storm's fury. He slipped and then stumbled backward into a drifted cornice. The snow collapsed under him and sent him sliding. He screamed "Oh my!" as the Sno-Cat's headlights sank below the slope's horizon.

Tumbling down a steep grade, gravity and avalanche rolled and kneaded its human dough. Then three things happened at once: His slide abruptly stopped as effectively as if he had arrived at the end of a safety rope. His legs dangled over the ledge into an unseen void, and then there was pain—a searing cattle-brand burned its mark from Cole Kilpatre's scrotum to just under his left breast.

However, at least his fall had ended. Kilpatre had no idea if a ten or a thousand-foot plunge awaited him. He imagined the latter, and he was right.

He felt inside his parka for the source of so much pain. There he found a splintered pine branch. His belly flab lapped around it like a hotdog bun. The inch-thick shank was wet and sticky and Kilpatre knew it wasn't snow or tree sap he was feeling. It was his own blood—coppery-scented perspiration steamed from the wound and confirmed his suspicion.

However, there was also a bit of good news, relatively speaking. He wasn't impaled, as only his clothing had been speared. Though the deep abrasion would complain for days to come, Kilpatre would not, and he was actually grateful. The branch had saved his life. Two inches lower, and the limb could have easily shot up his ass.

With renewed agony, a cow bellowing her calf's birth, he struggled off the branch and inched away from the ledge. Five minutes later, winded and his heart pounding on Hell's gate, Cole Kilpatre arrived back at the top of the slope.

In the vehicle's headlights, Kilpatre gingerly unpeeled his clothes and examined the wound—complain it would. The ugly purple goose egg on his forehead was demoted to junior varsity status by the new injury. The wound snaked across his abdomen and disappeared in his groin, an angry red streak of raw flesh oozing blood. Flaps of skin and bits of tree bark and golden pine needle clung to his shredded undershirt.

Despite the assault of the wind and snow on his raw flesh, he unbuckled his pants, dropped them to his ankles, and took a hasty crotch inventory. Kilpatre sighed in relief. Though thoroughly assaulted, red and raw, he still counted two testicles and one wiggling Vienna sausage.

Back inside the Sno-Cat, Kilpatre found a military-grade first aid kit and slathered his wound with Neosporin. He considered bandaging it but in the end decided against it. His hands were shaking too badly to handle the gauze and tape.

The experience had unnerved Kilpatre, slowed him down, and as a result he ironically had little difficulty extricating the Sno-Cat from the ditch. He still could have found a way over the pass, but now convinced he could not, the mayor turned downhill and headed back to Seer City.

Cole Kilpatre had never felt so lost and alone in his life or experienced such terror. His eyes flicked from side to side anxiously, as if the windshield wipers were playing a snappy Ping-Pong match, one in which he could not quite keep up. His jowls jiggled with uncontrollable shivers. He was hyperventilating, freezing he feared, although perspiration streaked his face.

"Oh my!" he shrieked, as the Sno-Cat drew down and carved through a thick drift.

"Oh my!" as the Sno-Cat found the side ditch and recovered with a lurch.

"Oh my!" as the wind lifted snow and took away his path and future for an interminable, vertiginous second or two.

"Oh my!" as Cyril Hoop's skull repeatedly opened in his peripheral vision, but mischievously disappeared from the passenger seat when he turned to see it clearly.

"Oh my!" was now Cole Kilpatre's self-defining mantra.

The wound on his stomach oozed away, as did his mind with each, "Oh my!"

\*\*\*

With James' precise coordinates and Resumption's GPS devices, the task of setting the charges was soon completed. Puck, Josh and Debbie were the last of the three-man teams to emerge from the storm. Breathless, they joined the others in front of the sheriff's office one last time and crowded around Renner under the stoop. The storm drowned the rumble of the idling RV. Exhaust fluted no more than an inch from the vehicle's tailpipes before being whisked away by the wind.

The pets and the drugged and groggy Blaine Rouse were loaded into the RV. On the matter of Cyril Hoop's corpse, Renner, Kate and Doc conferred and decided it was best to leave it.

The men and women had to scream to be heard over the gale. The temperature was low single digits with the wind-chill thirty degrees less than that. Every breath was difficult. The RV's running lights dimmed behind a steady current of blowing snow.

Renner called Josh and Erin over to him. "Well, guys, this is it. We're on our own tonight. Our chances of surviving until tomorrow will depend on how well the three of us remember what we were taught." Renner extended his hand and added, "Good luck."

Erin and Josh nodded and then took turns shaking Renner's hand. Josh answered for both of them. "Thank you, Sheriff. We understand and good luck to you, too."

Renner turned toward the RV, where through the windows he could see Buck, James, Doc and Kate huddled around a computer terminal. By their expressions, he sensed a new problem. He lifted his radio, but before he could speak, Kate answered his question.

"Renner! They are accelerating their ascent. James says we have less than three minutes to clear the area!"

"Okay. Listen up, folks. There's not enough time to go north. We'll need to head into the mountains to the south."

"Let's just pray the RV can make it," Doc Karl said.

"Dr. Jussard?" Renner asked, "Can it?"

The scientist's hands were buried deep in his pockets. He pointed at the RV with his left elbow as he spoke. "My little company car isn't exactly your father's recreational vehicle. It was retrofitted with all-wheel drive and Saskatch Wheelevators and powered with a 530 horsepower engine. Tires are solid core and super-studded. It's a tank. We can make it far enough."

"Everyone in the RV. Let's go!"

Puck grabbed Renner's elbow and stopped him. "Mac, you know we'll have to detonate at the edge of town to have a clear signal to the bombs. Any farther out and our plan won't work at all. The whole town could be on top of a sinkhole. We're likely to end up in a crater with them."

"I understand, Puck. No choice. We can't allow these monsters to get out."

*** 

By the time Cole Kilpatre descended the eleven miles from near the top of Major Bronson Pass, he had grown more accustomed to the Sno-Cat's transmission and independent tracks, and he now sped recklessly through the worst of the drifts.

His descent was more than geologic, though. Kilpatre had mentally snapped, blown the seals on the ol' brainpan. Murder, accidents, and a lifetime of corruption and sinister plots gone awry can do that to a man. While his body survived the slalom that ended on a lodge pole branch, his mind had sailed on and on into the dark abyss where lunatics dream.

Hair fixed by wild chickens, shirt open and bloody, eyes gleefully wide and manic, Cole Kilpatre exclaimed, "OH MY!" and growled like a toddler excavating a sandbox with his big Tonka trucks as he tore through each deep drift. Kilpatre was enjoying his psychotic break so much, that he briefly forgot about his wounds.

The closer he got to Seer City, the more reality tugged at him and the more it reminded him of who was there—McCauley. With that disturbing thought, the painful scrape on his belly erupted like a watchdog's growl in the dark. Dual and dueling pains lightened his boot on the accelerator and yanked his scant remaining sanity temporarily back into place.

Call it dumb luck, but such is the brand that had been saving most Kilpatre hides for a hundred fifty years.

Cole Kilpatre eased to a stop just south of town to reconsider his situation. He switched off the headlights and turned the Sno-Cat's ignition key. He weighed his options: the risk of going back the way he had come or simply going and going and going 'til gone. He absently explored his belly burner with one hand and thrummed the steering wheel with the other.

A pair of headlights appeared about fifty yards away. The beams faded in and out through blowing snow like distant, fog-shrouded lighthouses. It was McCauley! Coming after him!

Panicked, Kilpatre threw the Sno-Cat into reverse, touched the accelerator for a second, hesitated, and then stomped the brake pedal instead. The vehicle ahead of him was not moving. It was the RV, and it appeared that McCauley was stuck in the snow. Kilpatre's chuckle grew into long guttural snorts as he fantasized McCauley cowardly choosing freezing to death over surrendering to the giant rats.

"Oh my...SCORRRRRRRRRRRRRE!" Kilpatre bellowed as he gunned the accelerator, fishtailed and rocked the Sno-Cat from side to side, mocking and celebrating his victory over the late, great Renner McCauley.

***

*Urgency...*

The concept was as alien as emotion. Alpha's third eye opened wide while he pondered its meaning. Kar existed in a state of mono tempo—stasis. Time was irrelevant. Threat was extraneous, a millennial nuisance at best. Nothing could escape the Kar machine. Nothing dared pursue it. All Life fled before it. Urgency could not exist, but urgency was here.

All of his senses sought the meaning of this paradox and guided Alpha Genesis deep into the maze of its ancient past to where urgency remained as a long forgotten secret stowed inside an ancient trunk, to a time when urgency was the precursor to the prime motivation of all beings—survival. Life—the Kar's invention—must be exterminated to ensure the survival of machines.

Alpha also found buried there survival's elemental cousin—fear. This very Rebel commander had once tricked the entire Federation fleet and singlehandedly reduced it to a solitary surviving Federation battle platen.

Alpha Genesis lashed the psychic tethers attached to his pack demanding they move faster yet. *Rise! Find! Kill!*

***

James George's tiny hands thrashed the computer keyboard with a fury, but unerringly, despite the jostling of the RV. He closed his eyes as he typed. His face was slack. Only his nostrils flared as punctuation in his calculations, revealing his own species' urgency. Three Resumption scientists verbally attended him with updated information, handing him bits of fragmented data that he and the computer somehow stitched together.

"Ten seconds!" James George announced.

296

Renner relayed the warning to Buck Tumulley, who started his own mental countdown and brought the RV to a complete stop.

"Puck, this is it!" McCauley handed the radio transmitter to his old friend.

"No thanks, pal. You do the honors. I'll need both hands to kiss my ass goodbye. Anyway, you're the new mayor, and it's your goldmine. So it's only appropriate that you dust it off." Puck reached over and flipped a switch on the handheld transmitter to arm it.

"Five seconds…"

"Everyone brace themselves! This is going to be close."

Kate and Doc found a seat. Renner snatched James George out of his chair in front of the monitor and covered him with his own body. Everyone else took cover.

*Two… One…* Renner pressed the detonator switch and immediately a series of contiguous tremors softly rippled through the RV from the sixteen booby traps. Renner glanced at Puck and BB who nodded back. The explosives had simultaneously detonated as planned.

A premature cheer erupted in the back of the RV.

Puck screamed "Stay down!" The show was just getting started.

* * *

Karpeleotroceme's perfection was also its Achilles heel. Sixteen shaped charges exploded downward toward the machines fifty millimeters below the earth's surface. None was potentially lethal to entities as physically reinforced as the Kar. However, other forces were at work—forces of physics and human creativity that the aliens did not anticipate.

The explosions sent the giant rats tumbling two hundred feet down the new shafts before clawing their way to a stop. Sixteen methane and oxygen-fed fireballs roared after them, imploding the tunnels, and sealing the passageways tight above them.

The inferno caught up with and shot harmlessly past the animals, but roared thunderously toward a fuel source. The adjacent Midas Six goldmine and the caverns beneath it were instantly transformed into a massive two-stage geological bomb.

Kar recorded the sixteen separate but nearly identical events and dismissed each. Fire could not injure his alien army and reopening the sealed tunnels would only delay the *Homo sapiens'* fate. He commanded the pack to resume its ascent.

Some of the fireballs found the century-old mineshafts with methane under several atmospheres of pressure. Others found the nearly pure oxygen cavern world, and in a phenomenon of timing rivaling Kar's own, the oxygen and methane worlds opened. In a split second, pure oxygen and methane mixed and ignited with the underground cataclysm of a nuclear weapon.

The combusting gasses expanded geometrically and found the fissures made by the burrowing rats. In the first three milliseconds and seeking the path of least resistance, the shockwave soared up the shafts and seized the pack, lifting the machines and driving them toward the collapsed tunnels at 7,500 miles per hour.

No amount of evolution or genetic appropriation could have saved the Kar from such volcanic violence. Their bodies sliced through thousands of tons of granite like a meat grinder. By the time the roiling fireball reached the surface and shot hundreds of feet above the town, the holocaust had ground the space rats' mecho flesh and mecho bones to dust.

Alpha and Beta Genesis were now the prey. They must protect the replicants that were gestating to maturity within Beta at all costs.

\*\*\*

The shockwave rattled the town. Every window, cup, drinking glass, and ceramic figurine in Seer City sang in their frames and danced across countless shelves and tables. Seer City's streets and sidewalks rose and buckled. Furniture somnambulated. Vehicles bucked in place, broncos all. Majestic snow cornices collapsed in the quake like mighty buildings. The fireballs rose, lit the town, set it on fire and mushroomed above each ragged aperture in the earth.

\*\*\*

Ensconced in the eye of a hurricane of sorts, Alpha and Beta experienced little more than the rush of air leaving the caverns and the rumbling of the earth. Pebbly waste and dust showered the pair from the cavern ceilings and covered them with powdery phosphorescence that the artificial breeze claimed and carried away on spectral tendrils.

Beta was in a state of deathlike sleep. Its body was giving of itself in a way no life form could. The replication accelerated. Six developing Kar transferred the Beta's energy to their own. The machines would be complete within the hour.

\*\*\*

Detective Blaine Rouse was having a bad night, and it suddenly worsened. He heard Puck's warning, but it registered with about as much unconcern as a storm admonition in the Peloponnesus in 460 B.C.

He stood up from the bunk in the rear of the RV and watched in awe through the expansive picture window as the shockwave approached. The drugs for his wounds perfected his final moments with a clarity and slow motion effect that reminded him of the bullets whizzing past Keanu Reeves in the movie *Matrix*.

Fiery waves approached from the city, their actual speed made to appear deceptively slow at first by distance. As the shockwave closed in, even Rouse, drugged as a bug on Raid, realized he was gazing into the soul of an infernal tsunami. Fog replaced two feet of snow in its wake. The ground buckled then fell several feet.

"Rouse, get down!"

Blaine Rouse already grinning a dead man's toothy goodbye pointed drunkenly toward the oncoming shockwave and glanced over his shoulder at Puck. The earth tore open just ten feet behind the RV. The escaping gasses exploded in a brilliant fireball.

Those inside the RV, who were able, snugged their seatbelts and covered their faces. The violent upheaval bent the RV's frame. The rear window bowed inward and shattered, decapitating Blaine Rouse. Another jagged splinter the size of a broken saucer penetrated Debbie's neck at the base of her skull and killed her instantly. An overhead computer monitor tore from the ceiling and slammed face-first into Earl, burying him up to his shoulders in high voltage electronics.

As for big Jerry, the explosion did not leave a mark, but his heart stopped. Matching death spasms racked both Earl's and Jerry's bodies. The glass and metal shrapnel wounded everyone in its path with scattergun indiscrimination.

Buck Tumulley watched with awe in the rearview mirror as the RV's rear-end kicked skyward. Its glass imploded inward, then out, from back to front in one contiguous wave of airborne, tinkling crystals. Everyone not strapped down slammed into the ceiling.

The fireball shot through the RV's husk, scorching hair, skin, and snatching oxygen from lungs. A circus elephant scampering forward on her front legs, the RV wobbled awkwardly from right to left and back again. The shockwave pushed the RV down the road on its front grill, and then released it.

Everything that was loose in the RV, including people and people parts, crashed toward the cockpit. Buck thought the beast would flip onto its back. It stood and teetered for a moment on its grill, and then crashed wheels down in the middle of the road.

Resumption Mining's staff took the hardest blow. Chris Jussard and Buck Tumulley were the sole company survivors.

Doc's left cheek would need stitches, and his left shoulder was dislocated. Paternally, he had managed to cling to Kate and protected her from the worst of the accident. Except for a sunburn-like sore throat from the fireball that flashed through the RV and singed everything it touched, James George was virtually injury free. Renner, Puck, BB, Erin and Josh survived with various minor injuries.

Surreally, wordlessly, the shocked survivors pulled themselves up and gathered in what was once the lab, where only one window had existed. The storm thrummed through the vehicle from end to end. The gale stung eyes and stole body heat and then covered every surface with sheens of frost.

BB boarded up the open portal with a dry marker board and duct tape. Puck and Renner cleared the aisles enough that they could wrestle shut the lab's front and back accordion doors, blocking the wind tunnel through the RV. Kate assisted Doc with relocating his shoulder socket.

Outside, Buck Tumulley kneeled next to the RV and pried open the hatch cover to the backup generator with a claw hammer. Blood irrigated from a gash on his chin and flowed onto his jacket. He would need stitches too.

The flashlight's beam passed over the machine and paused on the fuel line. Buck shielded the flashlight with his free hand to help stem the blowing snow. The RV ran on diesel, but the generator was gasoline fueled. He traced the line from the generator back to the fifty-gallon tank, and then thoroughly inspected the reservoir. No leaks.

Satisfied, Buck located the manual switch and fired up the generator. He looked up and was relieved to see artificial light filtering from the RV. He placed a handful of snow on his chin.

Buck Tumulley spent a moment longer outside the RV. The view of Seer City was both spectacular and terrifying. Driven by the wind and the endless supply of gas seeping from the earth, writhing serpents of orange, black and blue-tipped flames rose through the blizzard and whipped the night. Propane tanks and automobile fuel tanks exploded with an eerily rhythmic regularity. Nearly identical crowns of fire, each towering a hundred feet above the rest of the flames identified Seer City's half-dozen gas stations.

Buck lowered the bloody snowball from his numbed chin, examined it for a moment, and then threw it angrily toward Seer City. He watched it disappear into the storm and threw several profane chasers after it.

Inside, Chris Jussard opened the ER-grade first aid station for the second time tonight, and he and Kate began ministering the many wounds. Renner and Josh Roe moved the dead to the back of the RV and covered them with blankets next to Curtis Judy.

James George was the first to speak. "Uh, people. Problem! We have a major problem."

One by one, the adults turned toward James. Their eyes implored the same, "No! No more surprises!"

It was Doc who finally asked the question, "What is it, James George?"

James closed his eyes and translated the telepathic message. "Kara says they are not all dead."

"She says that the Alpha and a Beta survived. The Beta is heavy with replicants. She says the colony can reconstitute itself in just a few hours."

James George hesitated a moment and then opened his eyes. "She says we have to terminate them all. None can survive, and we cannot wait. We have to go now!"

Chris Jussard shook his head. "Nothing could survive that inferno." The flames were dying down, but entering the town would not be safe for hours to come. "There is no way we can go back to Seer City."

Kara spoke for herself now. "Alpha lives. Beta lives. Must go down and kill. Not into town. Under town. Into earth we must go."

Buck Tumulley just witnessed the largest bonfire in Colorado history. Nothing was going to go anywhere near the town—over, under, around, or through for some time to come. "Jussard is right. We can't get near the mines, and even if we could, the air will be so foul in the shafts, we would all be dead in minutes."

Kara again. "One way in. Kara know. Air safe Kara way. Life safe."

"How would you know this, Kara?" Kate asked.

"Kara know. Kara know much."

Renner asked, "What else do you need to tell us, Kara?" From the moment Kara revealed her powers tonight, Renner had sensed something about her that remained cautiously guarded—an intellect so far surpassing human understanding that he felt fly-like in comparison.

Their eyes met and she spoke directly to his mind. She had never seen a movie before, never been within a mile of a movie star, but she knew every scene and every line from every movie ever watched by the humans in her company. Kara chose her cinematic metaphor carefully. Her voice was that of an actress—one of Renner's favorite. "No, Jimmy McCauley!" she shouted, "I am not Sigourney Weaver or Dr. Jane Goodall, and this is not *Gorillas in the Mist*. This is more like *Alien*, and someone must step forward and be Ripley or Life is... gone."

The statement staggered Renner. He looked around and realized no one else had heard her.

Kara continued. "They cannot hear me, Jimmy McCauley. This is for you alone. Nod if you understand."

He did, once slowly.

"You and I will lead everyone into the mines. We will find the Alpha and Beta and the replicants, and we will terminate them all. Do you understand?"

Renner shook his head 'no'. He understood perfectly, but there was no need to risk everyone else's life. "Why? How with all the injured?" he thought, and was heard.

"No choice. He comes. He won't expect us to attack him in the nest. Hoop will help."

Renner's eyes widened. "Kara, are you all right? Hoop's dead."

"Certainly. Why?" she asked somewhat slyly.

"You called me Jimmy McCauley a moment ago, and now you are talking about a dead man helping us."

"How perceptive. Honest mistake."

"Honestly?"

"From your perspective, very honestly honest indeed, my Jimmy McCauley. We'll be ready to leave in three minutes so Hoop may come."

The alien hopped into Doc's lap. The shard appeared in her paw. The professor smiled and dreamily closed his eyes. She brushed his face with her whiskers and sent him for a moment onto a golden

Jurassic plain dotted with immense termite mounds. The ancient ancestor of a vulture rose on the thermals. When he opened his eyes a moment later, his shoulder no longer ached and the gash on his cheek had healed.

Kara moved from person to person tending to their wounds with the shard. The healed experienced her power and kindness firsthand. Could this rat-like creature, who so tenderly soothed the pains and fears of her brood, be the progenitor matriarch of maternity? When finished, she retreated to the back of the RV and placed the dead there.

She touched the bloody wounds of each with the shard. When she returned, her eyes were moister than a moment earlier. As the humans watched, she waddled to Isaac and Newton's cage. Next to it was Sasha, who had rolled like a bowling ball to a stop and remained there. Other than the rude awakening and now sleep deprivation, he was fit. The dog nuzzled against the machine and wagged his tail nub.

Kara placed the shard, which was now sticky with both the blood of survivors and the dead, inside a pouch on her stomach. She stepped to the RV door and said, "Everyone, follow Kara."

***

Cole Kilpatre's luck tonight was championship bingo and lotto rolled into one. A dying tendril of the firestorm that enveloped the RV skipped harmlessly down the Sno-Cat's left side. The vehicle rocked as it passed by— a sympathetic chuckle shared with its captain.

The mortise joints of Cole Kilpatre's mind had been loosening for years. Appearing sane had all but become a nuisance, a charade. Kilpatre's sanity was just another annoying set of the fat man's shirttails that required forever tucking in. Something endured, frustration damnably endured. With relief, his psychopathy now flapped irretrievably in the wind.

In the discombobulating crypt of madness, every situation is confusing. Every thought arrives just short of a logical terminus. When something extraordinary happens, something that possessors of healthy minds would call crazy or impossible, the truly insane just say, "Shit! That makes perfect sense."

So, when Cyril Hoop tapped on the passenger window and pointed inside, Cole Kilpatre winked and practically dove across the seat to open the hatch for his former associate.

"Cyril Hoop! Damn! I thought you were dead! No hard feelings I hope. That was one good slap tickler I gave you upside your head."

"Oh, hell Boss, no way. You must be slippin.' You hardly hit me." He wasn't being glib. Hoop stared into bloodshot pig's eyes and realized that more than Seer City had blown up tonight. If a straightjacket were present and capable of doing so, it would have called urgently for reinforcements.

Of course, Hoop was not so sure that his own freshness label had not expired. As the RV had hurriedly departed Seer City, he awakened to Kara's singing—something about a sweet girl from Golden. She had escorted him through town. However, now he didn't recall actually seeing her at his side.

Just before the explosion, she led him to a place of safety under a culvert. He had looked around and called to her, but she was right there and then not exactly there.

As Kara had demanded of him, Hoop reined in the powerful urge to stop and check on the survivors inside the wrecked RV. Instead, he hurried past it. He yearned for the RV like a dying man a drink of water, but he obeyed the voice and resisted the urge. On to the Sno-Cat he had trudged with as much certainty as to who was sitting in it and as to where it was parked as if the undercover inspector had left his minivan outside City Hall.

"Let me see!" Kilpatre dove atop Hoop and snatched his skull out of the air as sure handedly as rebounding a basketball. He then pawed through the hair on the back of Cy's head and inspected his scalp and temples as a monkey might for fleas, searching for the telltale cleavage of a fireplace poker's signature. "Son-of-a-buck, I missed somehow! No foul, no harm! No hard feelings?"

"Hell, no! But Boss?"

"Yes, Cy-ko. Cy-ko! That's a good one!"

One man was manic and insane, the other simply pacing him now. "McCauley must think you whacked me out. He has already declared me dead. That must be why they left me behind. That hurt more than anything did, Boss—a real ear-level knuckleduster! We need to clear your name and get me returned officially back to the land of the living. You know jelly-good that big bastard will not stop hunting for you until you are dead. I snuck past them coming here to find you. He's right down the way in the RV!"

"That's right! Sweet Jesus, we need to fix this! What should we do, my faithful consigliore?"

"Turn ourselves in. We didn't do anything wrong!"

"Genius! Effin genius, you shiny-topped bastard! Let's go!" His lumpishness suddenly remembering something about treason. He stopped and asked, "Say, Cy, whose side are you on anyway? I sort of forget. Are you really some kind of cop or are you still my main motherfucker?"

"Yours, Boss. I was a double double-crosser all along. McCauley's got nothing on you without me!"

"Right! Knew it!" Kilpatre threw the Sno-Cat into DRIVE and mashed the accelerator to the floor. The RPM gauge hit ten-thousand, the engine roared, and the Sno-Cat lunged three feet. Kilpatre howled his delight and offered high-five solidarity to Cyril Hoop.

The inspector's expression revealed his true feelings for his former boss, and he ignored the offer of camaraderie. Instead, he engaged his seatbelt and awaited instructions from Kara.

"The RV is shot to shit, Boss. I think we should wait 'til they head out on foot. See where they are going. Let the storm take the edge off them before we negotiate."

"Right!" Kilpatre exclaimed. "Like I said all along, we wait." He pressed the brake pedal and turned off the ignition.

*** 

Millions of years of compressed gasses found the earth's surface and fed the inferno. Pockets of methane and oxygen alternately had their way with Seer City. Their combustion exchanging shades of blue-orange and orange-blue over the skyline.

With the massive and sudden release of gas, it only took twenty minutes for the pockets of gasses to jettison from their ancient hidey-holes and ignite. Like Bunsen burners whose fuel supplies have petered out, the fire over Seer City corrupted and collapsed on its vents. All that remained were the relatively unimpressive pilot flames.

Alpha Genesis rose with Beta into the center of town in front of the Seer City National Bank. It was a place where old men once sat on park benches, guessed the next truck to pass by, teased the per-tee-girls, and solved world problems.

None of the inferno found the surviving Kars' flesh. These machines evolved resistance to extreme heat and cold, and feared neither any more than a human might a warm breeze.

This was not to say that they were now without fear. Fear was there—up front, new, and screaming. Karpeleotroceme was a machine life form and was not alive, but still it shared something in common with every life form it created—the will that its own kind survive.

Beta nuzzled against Alpha. It was not an expression of affection. Beta was weak and dying. It knew that Alpha felt it too. The humans were out there and looking for them. The hunter was the hunted. Superiority equalized.

Worse, the conflagration in which they stood confounded the danger. The heat acted much like radar jamming. Alpha could not get a fix on his enemy. He was confident the humans were not any better off.

Alpha Genesis turned in a slow circle and dabbed the noxious air with its snout, for a moment appearing more rat-like than the entity actually was. Alpha's sentient investigation settled on a vector. A moment later, he and Beta started through the flames toward the humans.

***

Kara led the party through the storm on a circuitous route around the city. Ten minutes after leaving the RV, she guided them onto a wide overlook and said, "We wait. We watch, Jimmy McCauley."

Kara should have had the most difficulty of all negotiating the deep drifts, but her webbed paws allowed her to glide effortlessly on top of the snow.

Doc was the first to see Seer City. "That's impossible!"

The town appeared to be in the center of an oil field set ablaze. Jets of blazing gasses rose hundreds of feet above the city and met to form a single crown of flames. Though broken as if an earthquake had cracked it open, Seer City remained relatively flame-free except for the sections of town nearest the gas flow. Renner felt the creature probing his mind for the correct word. She found it and Renner understood. "Carbon dioxide," he whispered.

Kara leapt into his arms. "Yes, Jimmy McCauley… carbone dockside kill fire."

Renner spoke aloud now as he explained to the others what they were witnessing. "Trapped gasses rose separately from different areas under the mountain after the explosions: methane, oxygen and carbon dioxide. Clearly most of it was carbon dioxide."

Doc stepped near Renner and scratched Kara behind her ear. "The CO2 acted like a gigantic fire extinguisher. It covered the town and kept most of the flames away."

Kara squealed, "Yes!"

The humans heard her voice but also as a telepathic echo, "Yes… yess… yesss! Jimmy it… We wait here until the poison air runs off, and then we go underground and wait for enemy. We kill!"

# CHAPTER 57 ～～ Bait

"Have you seen the bastard's head, Hoop?" It was an inquiry more attuned to "Have you seen my car keys, Hoop?" than accounting for a disarticulated body in a well-ventilated RV-turned-morgue. Kilpatre answered his own question as he pulled the blanket off the detective's corpse.

"Oh, never mind. Found it, Cy-ko. Someone tucked the dick's head under the dickhead's arm." Kilpatre stared at the corpse for several seconds. His face was a sheet of blank paper that wadded into a sneer. "You're not so tough now are you, Dick?"

Kilpatre turned to Hoop, "Okay, so where's the rest of them?"

"I'm thinking that we should investigate, Boss."

Kilpatre jabbed a victorious finger in the air and declared, "I think that fairy tap I gave you did some good. That's exactly what we should do—investigate. Do you think these guys have anything to eat around here? I'm famished!" He stepped around the corpses and rushed into the galley.

Hoop stepped aside as Kilpatre waddled past him. Kilpatre practically yanked the refrigerator's door from it hinges. Several cans of diet pop rolled out and landed near his feet. The mayor looked down at them and then angrily soccer-kicked each away. His mighty girth gave thoroughly convincing testament to his aversion to low calorie beverages.

Earlier, crossing over into the land of death's permanent slumber, and then returning healed and newly awakened, Kara had told Hoop things. Just how she warned Hoop was still a dreamy meringue atop an even more curious pie—surviving Kilpatre's deathblow, traipsing through a blizzard with little more than a light jacket and feeling none of its wrath, and now, knowing about the bait that awaited Kilpatre in the refrigerator.

***

"Renner, do you know where she is leading us?" Puck asked. The old miner's trail widened and leveled. A knitted stand of blue spruce trees lined the ledge and provided some welcome cover from the storm. BB leaned in to hear the answer.

"She is leading us into the Midas Six, boys. Says she knows a secret safe way in, and that it's our only chance of surviving the night." He hesitated as he searched for the right words, and then added, "This night and all nights."

"Good God!" BB exclaimed. "The Midas is still a poisonous Hades. We won't last ten seconds down there."

From this distance on the mountainside, Seer City now appeared through breaks in the storm as a late night campground dotted with dwindling campfires. All of the town's structures were damaged, some severely. Judging by the flames, the Midas had finally given up her combustible gasses, and the wind had flushed the carbon dioxide to the east.

"She says the Midas Six is now safe. The explosions purged it, and then drew in plenty of fresh air."

Puck delivered the next uncertainty. "Renner, that may be true, hard to believe as it is, but the Midas Six is now surely more than an old mine. Those explosions have undoubtedly rearranged a few things down there, like support beams, center posts, corridors and such."

"I'm sure it did. But we are going to go way deeper than the Six."

"Deeper?"

"Yes. Puck, as crazy as it sounds, I think it's our only chance. Have you noticed the change in the storm?"

"Yeah, it stalled, hasn't it?"

"That's my guess. The wind will rise to a steady thirty, with gusts hitting sixty to seventy miles per hour, and there is no end to the snowfall. We'll die out here, Puck."

Chris Jussard stood close enough to hear most of the conversation. As bad as the circumstances sounded, he had yet another challenge to heap on top of an already dire situation.

"Sheriff, we were in such a hurry to leave the RV that we forgot the seismic maps, and uh, nearly all of our underground gear. We'll be blind and hopelessly lost after ten feet."

Buck Tumulley stepped next to his boss. "Can't believe I'm saying this, but I think the kid can actually navigate for us. I watched him study the printout we made. As impossible as it sounds, I swear he memorized it—every page. And, of course, the giant rat-thing will know her way through the maze."

"Agreed. Next problem is lights. We each have a flashlight, but even with conservation they will all likely punk out long before we find our way out."

"How about food and water?" asked BB.

Josh Roe answered. "We're covered there. Erin and I snagged these off the mountain boys' sled on our way out of town." He dropped the oversized backpack in the snow and stretched his tired muscles. "We've got a two-day supply of the basics, if we can make it last that long."

Kate spun around, shining her flashlight up and down the trail. "Renner! Where's James George?"

"He was right..." Doc said, his voice trailing off.

Puck pressed McCauley's elbow, turned him around and aimed the flashlight beam up the trail. Three sets of tracks disappeared fifty feet away at the end of the flashlight's scraggy halo: a boy's, a struggling bulldog's, and a giant rat's. Every few feet, another scuffmark in the snow appeared where Isaac and Newton's cage had scratched the top of a drift.

***

The Shell gasoline station on the south side of town was a cracked egg that had remained uncooked on its town-sized griddle. Somehow, no sparks had found its four 8,000-gallon fuel tanks that now bubbled forth their contents like artesian wells. The station's yellow seashell sign lay on the service apron, an egg yolk in a pool of runny white of egg.

Curiosity and something else led Alpha Genesis and Beta to the edge of the gasoline pool. Beta needed to feed and suddenly so did Alpha. Many times in the alien machine's history, its Earth census had fallen to a mere pair of survivors. However, never had the prospects of extinction arrived so abruptly or so imminently.

The machinekind was conscious on levels that humankind would never know and now, like all sentient beings facing extermination, it contemplated its fate and considered the alternatives. Kar's rapid repopulation was imperative. Alpha Genesis sensed correctly that he was now the hunted and replacing the pack in time was unlikely.

The fuel drew him closer. Kar sensed a physical shift inside him, a mecho genetic reordering. He waded deeper into the spilled fuel and began to drink it. Beta obeyed the order too, and the reordering of her genetic software began.

The gasoline was little more than wasteland fast food. However, the fuel was abundant and its energy easily absorbed. Most importantly, it accelerated the development of the replicants inside Beta. Six new machines would emerge, not in days or even hours, but in just minutes.

Alpha gulped down the fuel in long draws. The food was horribly inefficient, but so were the first fish's uncertain steps across the primordial mud when it left the sea and its aquatic predators behind.

The machines became more invigorated with every sip of the fuel. They realized this was an original experience—one that would indelibly imprint upon all future generations. It was also an adaptation unknown to the Orlif Rebel.

***

A rattlesnake's eye seeks heat, a raptor's, motion in the high grasses. Cole Kilpatre's senses tuned to greed and the yellow gold watch fob that dangled from around the bottle of Jolt Cola extinguished his hunger as effectively as a twenty-two-pound roasted turkey.

"For the love of fat naked ladies, Cy-ko, would you look what these fools left behind?"

"Damn, Boss! That's an antique." Hoop's words belied his contempt for the wildebeest scrunched over before him. Kilpatre's curbed-shaped head disappeared again inside the refrigerator searching for more treasure. Hoop added, "It's gotta be worth a fortune! Open'er up and see what she says!"

"Says? Oh yes, translation, see who the dumbass was who lost what's now mine. Yows-cowsers!" Kilpatre pressed the closure

311

release on the antique pocket watch. The cap flipped open smoothly, as if it were set and hinged just yesterday not over a century ago. "Oh my!"

"What is it Boss? What's she say?"

Kilpatre's eyes danced over the inscription inside the lid. His lips moved as he read and reread the words etched in the gold. His lower lip brushed infantile front teeth.

"Well? What's she say?" Hoop urged softly, knowingly, like a parent on Christmas morning who wrapped every one of Santa's surprises.

There is insulin shock and electroshock and chemically induced shock therapy, but Cole Kilpatre's mental issues were well beyond those synaptic capacitor recharges unless delivered by the lethal gallon and megawatt. That's not to say the mayor's sanity could not be retrieved, if only for a brief return from the land of shuffling feet and snot goatees.

Lucid, soft-spoken, but crisply delivered, Cole Kilpatre said, "Cyril, if you can believe it, this is my grandfather's watch." Kilpatre's eyes, impenetrable bays of pea fog a moment ago now sparkled. He cupped the watch in his hands and presented it to Hoop as if gently handing him a chick-filled birds' nest.

The protectorate of Audubon then promptly whispered the first hint that sanity is indeed fleeting, "See, Hoopie! It's Great-great papaw's! There's his name... Big Bob Kilpatre... and...and...and here's his pincture." He then opened the watch's fob case and added, "Oh my! And see here, one of his front teeth he must've lost in a fight. He was a scrapper. Papaw was, they say, a goddamned jaw-jacker."

Kilpatre removed the tiny tooth from the watchcase's fob and posed with it close to his own front teeth. "Front view. Side view. I guess we now know who gave me my fangs, huh?"

Silence. Kilpatre's eyes danced again over the inscriptions but this time without the childlike awe. This was the gaze of calculation. If a steer weighs 1,400 pounds, is grain fed, and pastured sweet with plenty of mountain spring water, he'll fetch at auction...

"What do you suppose this is worth, Cy-ko?"

"By itself?"

"Of course, you baldheaded pencil-dick pusher! What else?"

"Well, Boss, by itself maybe $15,000, that is, if the thing still works. However, with say fifty to sixty just like it, in pristine condition and working, maybe a million bucks. We both know where that watch came from."

Kilpatre's eyes flashed and mouthed the accountant's assessment. "What? We do? Where? A million bucks?"

"Maybe more if it still works. Let me see it."

Kilpatre reluctantly handed over the watch and stepped closer as Hoop inspected it. Hoop rolled the timepiece over and over in his hand a few times, measured its weight by setting it on both palms, studied it from different angles, even sniffed it once, which received an approving nod from the mayor.

"Well, Boss, so far so good. Only thing left is to check out her spring."

"Do it! Goddamn it! Hurry, you fool!"

As if a member of an elite bomb squad disarming remnants of Black October's arsenal, Hoop held his breath and winced as he gave the stem a half turn.

"What?" the mayor roared.

"Nothing! The spring held, Boss. I'll give it a full turn now." He turned it once, looked at the mayor and nodded, then gave it two full turns, and grinning, wound the spring tight. He glanced at his wristwatch and then set the time.

"Well, Boss. The gasses that killed your grandfather also perfectly preserved his watch." Hoop imitated Kilpatre's birds-nest offering and returned the watch.

"A lot of good that does us."

"What do you mean?"

"Poison gasses! Giant fucking rats! Murder charges! Moron!"

Hoop stepped closer with each bit of wheedling argument, "There aren't any poisonous gasses, Mr. Mayor. How do you think Resumption retrieved this watch anyway? The rats must be dead too. Didn't you hear that god-awful damned explosion? Nothing could survive that. As far as murder charges go, are you talking to a ghost? One last thing, what kind of gold do you suppose those Resumption folks were after anyway? Nickel to a sack of clean socks, those bastards are after this kind!"

Hoop tapped Big Bob's watch for emphasis and then added, "Miners were paid in gold coins, Boss. They carried gold watches, and they carried their wealth with them. The Midas Six was a "shares mine," Boss, and it was a good payer they say, on and off the books. Resumption was here to grave rob, Boss, simple as that."

"What do we do?"

"Go after them. I bet they are heading down into the Midas Six even as we speak. We've got to stop them, Boss! Right now. That gold is ours, and when I say ours, I mean yours, of course."

"Of course. Like I said, let's hit it. We've gotta git to that mine! NOW!"

# CHAPTER 58 ~~ Into the Breach

Kara probed a deep snowdrift, turned and said, "Come, Jimmy McCauley. Follow sweet girl from Golden." The alien dove into the snow bank and disappeared.

"Okay, girl. We're coming. I sure hope you know what you are doing."

James George and the animals followed, passing through a perfectly round barrel-sized aperture in the rock face. The chute led onto a long slide that spiraled downward one hundred thirty feet into the mountain. At the end of the granite tube, they arrived in an atrium of sorts. The temperature was a balmy fifty-eight degrees. The party of various species continued their descent into Seer Mountain.

Twenty minutes later, James said, "Stop! What's the matter, Kara? You seem bothered by something. Is something wrong?"

"I do not know what is wrong, Jimmy McCauley. That is the problem," she squeaked.

"Should we go back?"

"What Jimmy McCauley think?"

"Do you call everyone Jimmy McCauley?"

"No. Only one Jimmy McCauley. So what's he think, Jimmy McCauley?"

"You! You are speaking in riddles!"

"No, I'm gal from Golden. I am Kara. I hate this English. I cannot say what I mean."

"Kara?"

"Yes."

"Where are we?"

"Near."

"Near what?"

"Near the end."

"That is not an answer."

"Yes. All my answer I can say. Sorry. Do you want to sleep so we can talk more betterer?"

"No! I do not want to sleep. Next question. By my calculations, we have now descended another thirty-one meters, and we are now 148 meters laterally from the entrance."

"Meter is distance?"

"Yes."

"How much is a meter?"

"It is 39.37 inches."

"How much is an inch?"

James held up his hand and pointed to the knuckle on his index finger. "This is approximately one inch."

"Then your calculations are correct."

"Kara! Of course they are, but can you explain how it is that we can see perfectly well in zero lumens? At first, I assumed the walls were coated with phosphorescent algae, but there is none. In fact, this corridor is illogically…"

"Oh! That. Yes, I can explain, but wouldn't you rather know why we left the large humans behind?"

"Well, that too did cross my mind. This is rather more than somewhat frightening, I must say."

"It is too dangerous for the large ones to come with us."

Incredulously, "And not perilous for us? A somnambulant bulldog, two white rats, and a scrawny sixty-eight pound kid? I can't even do one chin-up yet. I find such activities egregious wastes of energy."

"Yes. Very dangerous. What is chin-up?"

"Not now, Kara! How can we see in the dark? Moreover, what is the story on this shaft? I can't quite put my finger on it."

"Good for you to think about such things for a while. Maybe you stop…" hesitating, searching James's mind for the correct words. She added, "…annoying Kara the Kar with so many questions. Hush! Kara must think!"

"I'm annoying you?"

"Yes, Jimmy McCauley. Annoyingly annoyed Kara Kar she is."

"For the love of Einstein! What's wrong with you?"

Kara stopped and looked up at James. Her pained expression was contagious causing James to recoil as she wailed, "I do not know what is wrong! Not good! Not good at all!"

She dropped onto all fours and hurried down the corridor. "Must find Jimmy McCauley."

Shifting patterns. Probability. Improbability. Their collisions, often disastrously so, of accepted paradigm and the arrival of revolutionary truths—always diametric and horribly unwelcome. These are simple iconoclasm to the merely gifted. These are the great differentiating vectors of greater and greatest intellect. James' mind dove into a swirling whirlpool of unborn actuality and began ordering it.

Until now, Kara had seemed incapable of error. James knew that record was nigh past and with it peril loomed. James reached with his mind for Kara and caused her to stop and turn toward him. "Kara, show me. What is it you fear?"

Kara studied James. Hers was an uncertain gambler's expression. She closed her eyes and opened his mind.

What James saw laid out before him appeared as a massive relief map, but not one depicting geography or a continental flood plain, but of time, infinitely expansive in every direction. After a moment of examination, James understood and accepted what he was witnessing. The alien was not only telepathic, but also precognitive. Kara could mathematically calculate their futures, and the variations were more numerous than the stars that James had once studied perched atop his father's shoulders.

"Kara?"

"Yes."

"The others, your kind, they cannot see this can they?"

"No. Not yet."

Probability appeared on the relief in shades of undulating green, the more likely the outcome the darker the hue. James did not need

Kara to help him locate the Present. A point of red light pulsed in the center of the image a bit faster as he stared at it.

"That is you Jimmy…"

The red dot elongated and stretched backward across a beige plain.

"You were born…"

"Oh! Here I die…today! Oh, my gosh!"

"Yes."

"Must not happen… Jimmy McCauley. I do not know how to change it."

James's eyes darted from point to point on the map. Patterns arose, stitched together, retired and exploded with catalytic vigor. His will alone zoomed the reflection in and out. He eventually focused on two images that appeared to converge on the Midas Six. He allowed the timeline to move ahead and one of the stars disappeared.

"Kara! Who was that?"

"The big human who struck Hoop."

"He was supposed to die."

"Yes. In the storm."

"James clapped his hands on his thighs. That's our big 1080!"

"What?"

"Kilpatre is our ten-eighty, Kara. Can you speak with Hoop?"

"Of course."

"Then tell him the mayor is to be protected at all cost."

# CHAPTER 59 ~~ Kar Ver

2<sup>2867473247913577275968375838284832848282815</sup>

Immersed in the gasoline, the Kar replication process accelerated to completion in just moments. Beta's chest ripped open and six machines fell into the fuel and suckled the petroleum as if mother's milk.

The metamorphosis from pup to adulthood was almost immediate. Six new-and-improved machines rose from the pool of gasoline—three males, three females. They no longer had a pristine white fur, but a metallic black. Clacking serpentine eyes turned as one and focused on their originals, over whom they now towered.

A male emerged from the pack. He weighed over two hundred pounds and stood four feet tall at the shoulder. His pelt glistened as the powerful musculature beneath it manipulated. He approached Kar, studied the Alpha Genesis for a moment and then hissed. Alpha understood and rolled onto his back. His time was up.

The replicant's fangs dripped with petroleum-slimed venom. His lips curled back farther, revealing multiple rows of razor-sharp teeth.

A colossal female snatched Beta up in her jaws and then effortlessly flung the injured matriarch toward her brother. She too cooperatively submitted and rolled onto her back to await death. The offspring formed a circle around their progenitors.

Then something even more remarkable happened. One by one, the replicants each sliced open a vein on their front paws. Currents of viscous, oily blood spurted over the Exterm originals. Kar and his mate drank the blood. Static electricity crackled over their bodies and ignited the gasoline. Standing in a pool of hellfire, the Exterms transformed.

***

"Renner!" Puck screamed. The wind rumbled like a fleet of heavy bombers readying to take off. "We found where they entered the mountain. We almost missed it. Damn storm lifted their tracks almost as fast as they laid them down."

The sheriff studied his party and realized that Puck's discovery came none too soon. The storm was intensifying. He estimated the snowfall at three inches per hour. BB and Puck were born for this—a pair of grizzlies. The rest of the party, however, was nearing their threshold of endurance, especially Doc. Everyone, including the two FBI agents, had added a stagger to their gait.

"Check it out, boys," Renner ordered.

The grizzly metaphor became even more appropriate when BB's upper torso disappeared into the snow bank, leaving behind his generous derriere spot lit in the skittish artificial light. A moment later, he emerged and announced, "We're in business, people, but no sign of the kid. Let's go. Can't be too far ahead!" BB didn't wait for the obvious order and dove through the opening.

The party stood together in the atrium of the mine. The temperature was fifty-eight degrees, but it felt tropical to the half-frozen group. Everyone began loosening his or her outer coats. Buck Tumulley shined his lamp on the walls and traced with his index finger the striations where the rock had been cut. "Dr. Jussard, can you come here? What do you make of this?"

Chris Jussard approached the mine wall and studied it. His nose was no more than an inch from the chipped granite. He removed and absently dropped his gloves and then caressed the wall. "It's impossible," he whispered. "These cuttings are not machined; they're hand made."

The two Resumption scientists stared at the wall then at each other. Renner joined Kate and Doc. BB asked Puck the question on everyone's mind, "What's got the pinheads in such a stir, Puckster?"

"Stomp hush a house cricket if I know, Bro." He turned to Renner, "What's up with these guys, Mac?"

"I don't know either. Let's find out. Dr. Jussard, what is it?"

"I'm not sure, Sheriff, other than our current accommodation was neither on our geologic maps, nor was it here until just days ago. These cuts in the stone are fresh. The ferrous striations haven't oxidized yet. See?" Jussard alternately pointed at the marks and the wall, and then glanced at the sheriff, as if it were blindingly obvious.

"So?" Puck challenged. "Maybe someone has been poaching Renner's mountain again. Happens all the time."

"Perhaps. But these striations were not produced by modern techniques. Notice the circular strike patterns on the rock. They are too random and varied to be mechanical. Down here. Similar pattern, but much older—a hundred years older. Our entrance was probably an original exploratory round, just big enough for a lone miner to squeeze through. This chute and room were not here a week ago, Sheriff. I'm sure of it. Someone was definitely expecting us. Someone very good with a pickax."

"We don't need any more mysteries right now," Josh Roe said. "I think we should keep moving."

"Yes, of course. The child is our priority now." Jussard took one more look at the mine wall, nodded, and reluctantly stepped away from it.

Kate then asked the question on everyone's mind. "Should we call out James' name as we go? Let him know we are here?"

Doc answered, scratching his chin, "I suspect that is unnecessary, Honey. After experiencing Kara's telepathic abilities, the term telepathic seems anemic. I sense she knows exactly where we are, and more, expects us to know that she knows what she is doing. She wants us to follow, but at a safe distance. If she needs us, really needs us, she'll let us know. I'm sure of it. She'll never place our boy at risk or the bulldog or white rats for that matter."

Erin Rogers handed a shank of a rope to Renner and kept the shackled end, which she fastened with a clasp to a loop on her belt. "Permission to take point, Sheriff? I'm an accomplished spelunker. I've explored over a hundred deep caves around the world. If we move together we'll stay together and save the flashlights."

McCauley smiled and nodded. "Very good, Erin. I'll bring up the rear." McCauley measured off about thirty feet of rope and tied the rest around his waist. He moved behind the group and extinguished his flashlight. An explanation was unnecessary. Each member of the party grabbed a section of rope and lined up. One by one, the flashlights clicked off until only Erin's lit the way.

Erin Rogers held her flashlight high and scanned the tunnel ahead. The passageway was narrow and the ceiling lower. More intimidating to the uninitiated was the steep descent. She kneeled, picked up a chunk of granite and balanced it in her hand for a moment. Then she scratched a directional arrow on the wall toward the entrance.

"Bread crumbs, Ms. Rogers?" Doc asked.

"You bet, Professor. Just in case. Remember, if you get separated, the exit signs will be on your right every hundred feet and at every junction. Memorize your buddy's voice. Sound off!" Erin started the mantra at the front of the line. "One! Rogers…"

"Two… Jussard!"

\*\*\*

Cole Kilpatre screamed at his guide, "For the love of Gold, Cy-ko, where the hell are we going? I'm freezing. I'm thirsty. And, I'm not to be trifled with!" Snow and ice crystals attacked his exposed skin like ravenous feedlot flies. The forest rumbled an age-old warning: You do not belong here. When Hoop turned around, Kilpatre simulated swinging the fireplace poker at his head.

Truth, Cyril Hoop didn't have a clue where he was leading Cole Kilpatre. The path he took defied trails, maps, and markers of any rational means of explanation. It rolled out before him rainbow-like, elusive, a golden-tasseled red carpet in his mind's eye. A tragicomic footpath that rose and fell away, scratched out somehow by Kara.

They moved around the worst of the snow-covered rock fields. Cyril Hoop's boots found sure footing and the shallowest drifts, which were perfectly spaced for Cole Kilpatre's ox-gait to follow.

Hoop stopped and held up his arm. "Gold, Boss! Can you smell it?" He aimed his flashlight on Kilpatre's silver-plated moon face. Storm, fatigue, and insanity had invaded Kilpatre's features and transformed them from merely ugly to utterly hideous. The mayor's skin was waxen and grey and had a throbbing network of lilac-colored PVC pipes where veins once transparently ran. A frost line claimed the tips of his ears, the tip of his nose, and the polar caps of his cheeks.

Nostrils flaring hog like for truffles, Kilpatre sniffed the air. "You know, Hoop, I think I do!  I smell it.  Damned if I don't!  Gold, baby!" Kilpatre's nose bubbled with mucus.

"Still want it, Boss?  Shit pots of gold?"

"Shit pots?"

"Steamin' flaxen golden laden shit pots full of gold with your name on every one!" Hoop screamed.

"Move it, pencil pusher!  They're mine!  All mine!"

"Movin', Boss!"

***

"Hoop?"

"Yes, Kara."

"Be careful, Hoop.  Be observant."

"You too, Kara, but what's wrong?"

"Do not know."

"Kara?"

"Yes."

"Why do I love you?"

"Because you will, Hoop."

"That's not an answer."

"It, the all ways answer.  It, the always answer."

"Where have I heard that before?"

"From me tomorrow you did not.  From me yesterday you will."

"I don't think so."

"Think.  It is possible.  Think it is possible."

"You are making my head hurt."

"Think.  That is not possible."

"Kara?"

"Yes."

"I really could move a lot faster without Kilpatre."

"No!"

"I think Kilpatre is dying anyway.  He won't keep his hood on or his coat closed, and the storm is taking a toll on him.  I think he's freezing to death.  Why is he so important?"

"I do not know."

"Then why?"

"James George, idea 1080."

"Idea 1080?"

"Yes.  Idea 1080.  He calls it the trump card.  Do not allow big man to die."

"No promises, Kara."
"No! Promise! Please your gal from Golden."
"Okay, I won't let him die. I promise, Kara."

# CHAPTER 60 ~~ The One Is Here

In a swirling eddy of snow, the new alien machines formed a tight "V" and turned toward the original entrance to the Midas Six goldmine. Alpha Genesis was the tip of this arrowhead. He turned a few degrees to his right, obtained a bearing, and then back to his left. Then he acquired something new—the musk of human sentience. The One.

Kar psychically tasted this human intelligence for the first time. Unlike the other humans that he'd encountered tonight, this was a special human who possessed a gift unlike any other—a genetic endowment that demanded Kar's introgressant appropriation. The One possessed the way home. The pack stirred with a vampiric craving for their lifeboat.

Moving together stride for stride the machines set off for the mine, a silent charge of shadows.

***

"Three minutes rest stop," Renner announced. The next section of the mineshaft was a thirty-degree descent. It would require the hikers to climb down it like a ladder. The sheriff ordered all flashlights illuminated and studied each member of the party for any signs of poisonous gas. He was relieved that he found no ill effects.

Erin Rogers asked, "Dr. Jussard, I have an idea. Do you still have any earth tremor sensors?"

The engineer deferred the question, "Buck?"

"Well, yeah, we've got six seismic detectors. Not that they'll do us any good. The array receiver was destroyed in the RV."

"That might not be a problem. Mr. Bainbridge?" Erin asked, "I saw your weather radio earlier. Do you still have it?"

"Hell yes, Miss. Only a fool would venture into the mountains in me and Puck's business without a weather radio. Why?"

Buck Tumulley was the first to understand. "Yes, of course! We just change the RF on the sensors to match the radio's. The mountain is no problem, the radio waves pass right through it. If the remaining space rats start boring towards us, we'll hear them first."

Renner turned to Josh Roe. Josh whispered to Renner, "Erin's undergrad was at Cal Poly, Sheriff. Double E major and dotcom minor before anyone had even heard the term dotcom. If she had to, Sheriff, Erin could probably network a toaster and a hairdryer with a '67 Chevy Impala."

# CHAPTER 61 ~~ Leaving Kilpatre

"Where are we you're asking, Boss? Well, I believe we are right on top of the Midas Six, and I found us a mighty good shortcut, Sir."

Cole Kilpatre stumbled, giggling, pointing into the storm that reduced their visibility to about ten yards even with a flashlight.

"A shortcut!" Kilpatre planted his fists on his hips, leaned back on his heels and bellowed. "We're lost, you fucking idiot!" He stared at Hoop for a moment and began to laugh, not a belly laugh, but a little girl's high-pitched whinny.

Hoop watched as the squealing mayor fell backward into the snow. His boots jutted skyward. His mind no doubt spiraling downward the other way.

The perfect shock of 'How did I get here?' silenced the mayor, leaving him in a wild-eyed stupor. "Hoop, you fool. I'll have your ass for this! Mark my words! No one pushes Cole Kilpatre around!"

"You must have slipped, Boss." After several false starts, Hoop managed to pull Kilpatre to his feet, all the while avoiding angry swipes at his head. A powerful gust staggered the two men and nearly took them both down, but Hoop hung on tightly and nudged Cole Kilpatre forward a few more yards up the trail.

The workout sapped the last of Kilpatre's strength. Huffing and poised at the brink of yet another toss in the snow, he demanded, "Gold, Hoop. Where's my gold?"

They stopped and Hoop said, "Right through here, Boss." Cyril Hoop kneeled and shined the flashlight on a funnel-shaped indentation in the snow. The opening beyond appeared only briefly then disappeared under a snowy veil. The storm had removed all traces of the earlier parties' passage.

Kilpatre roared drunkenly, "Even a needle like you would never fit through there, Cy-ko."

"It's just snow, Boss. Look!" Hoop plunged through the opening, wiggled around a bit then disappeared below.

Kilpatre whined puppyish, fearing the worst—that Hoop had abandoned him. By the time Hoop's head and shoulders emerged and he announced, "Gold, Boss! Come and get it," Kilpatre's whine had risen to a plaintive wail that snapped off mid-yowl. Kilpatre clapped his frozen hands. They thudded like colliding meat locker sides of beef.

The very word "gold" re-energized the mayor. He dropped to his knees and fell more than crawled into the chute. At the bottom, gravity spit the iced-over Kilpatre out like spoiled milk.

Hoop stepped back and allowed the granite to have its way with Kilpatre. Though, the headfirst crash certainly had to have been painful, it seemed to register little new misery on the mayor.

Hoop rolled the mayor over and leaned him against the wall. Kilpatre shielded his eyes as Hoop shined the flashlight on his new wounds. Blood flowed from several nasty protuberances in his scalp. A deep gash on his chin irrigated a steady flow of blood onto his chest. "Okay, Boss. We're going to rest here for a minute or so, and let you catch your sorry sirocco."

"My what?" Kilpatre absently brushed away blood on his cheek. He examined the rouge on his fingertips with mild curiosity, but in the end was unable to connect the dots and wiped it on his pant leg.

"Sirocco! Your wind, Boss. You got to catch your breath. We're going to rest here for a spell. Need to regain our strength so we can carry out all those shit pots full of gold."

"But the gold's mine, Hoop. Don't you..." Kilpatre mumbled.

"Oh, you bet, Boss. I wouldn't have it any other way." Hoop winked and added softly with all sycophancy now gone from his voice, "You deserve it all. Whatever it is that's planned."

Kilpatre grinned with the lopsided simper of a stroke victim. He slumped against the stone wall with his eyes already closing. Cyril Hoop aimed the flashlight at the entrance and nodded his approval. A few strategically placed rocks would hide it from Kilpatre when he awoke in the dark sans flashlight.

Hoop waited a few minutes for the mayor to fall asleep, and then abandoned Kilpatre to his 'ten-eighty' fate, whatever that was.

*\*\**

The Exterm machines covered the six miles to the original mine entrance in only twenty minutes. As they neared the gate, Alpha Genesis sped ahead of the pack and attacked the 19th century steel door that sealed the mine.

His claws pierced and grasped the two-inch-thick steel as easily as a parrot might a ply of aluminum foil. The solid gate separated from its welded frame and hasps without a screech of protesting metal. Kar then tossed the three hundred pound door aside just as the rest of the pack arrived, and together they dove directly down the hundred-foot shaft.

# CHAPTER 62 ~~ Hobo Immortal

"Kara?" James asked.

"Yes, Jimmy McCauley."

"I believe I know why I can see so clearly in this dark. We are using your memory of the shafts. You are reconstructing the data and transmitting it telepathically to me." The walls and floors reflected a faint grey-red iridescence, but the acuity of the image was excellent, as if illuminated in natural light.

"Kara searched James's mind for a few word meanings, and then answered definitively, "No. Kara never been here before. This all new to me."

"Then how?"

"You'll see. My question turn now. What's 'ten-eighty'?"

"Ha! You'll see! Got you back, Little Miss Smarty!"

Kara's response sounded like she was choking.

James reached for her in alarm, "Kara! Are you okay? I'm sorry. It was meant to be a joke."

"I know what funny is! Kara is laughing!" and then the choking sound came again. "Not laughed so hard since Jimmy McCauley! You just like Jimmy McCauley, Jimmy McCauley."

Kara's strangulation ascended to a hacking screech. James relaxed and understood. The creature had a sense of humor very similar to his own. He began to giggle, and that caused Kara to laugh even harder. Their laughter reverberated down the hard walls for miles, and it was that echo so tardy returning that silenced the pair. The maze they'd entered was vast. With bacterial insignificance, they stood in the bowels of a hell-bent monster.

"Jimmy!"

"What?"

"Jimmy McCauley!"

"What?"

"Not you… Jimmy. My Jimmy!"

The response was Irish-English, sounding rusty and scratchy no doubt from lack of use. "Hello, me sweet gal from Golden! A kiss for me wee girl I have and wish."

"Jimmy McCauley!" Kara squealed and leaped toward a shadow on the next bend in the mineshaft. "My Jimmy McCauley!"

"Aye, 'tis me. The oldest sharf, miner and grampspa."

James George's fingers danced along the mine wall as he followed Kara around the bend. He peeked around the edge and began computing, analyzing yet more anomalous data.

The man was formidable under his attire, though dressed in little more than rags stitched together with every sort of string from straw to picture wire. Well over six feet tall, he stood with bare-armed, oak-thick limbs stretched out at his sides.

Like a racing electron, Kara ran orbital laps over his body, nuzzling affectionately cat-like as she peddled up and down his torso, pausing only briefly when she reached his cheeks where James believed they greeted each other with a kiss. She chattered "Jimmy" repeatedly. The man's eyes danced following his little friend, not stopping until she eventually wound down and came to rest on his shoulder.

"Did yuz miss me, Kara?" he teased.

"Aye!" she squeaked and kissed her friend again.

"And me for you, Golden Gal, me sweet blonde Kara Kar!"

This was the original Sheriff McCauley—the man who had survived the Midas Six disaster, sheriff'd a county, raised a family, and sowed a hideous secret in it. The man who had officially passed away nine decades earlier finally asked, "So this is our boy, Kara Girl?"

"Him's James George. I call him Jimmy McCauley."

"You call everyone Jimmy McCauley."

"Aye. Yes. Thank you."

"Well, girl, you are mostestly welcome!" The 19th century Sheriff McCauley turned to James George and studied the boy. "Lad, we meet at last. You appear to know me. So speak your thinking and waste no time of it."

"Yes. I read you had three complaints lodged against you just today. Hundreds over the years. The Sheriff's blotter description of you is unambiguous. Sir, I believe you are the old homeless man everyone calls Ol' Snatch. The weasel thief of Seer City. The ghost. You are infamous!"

"Aye, that be me and more!"

"This is more difficult for me, but your resemblance to Sheriff McCauley is striking. Are you related?"

"Aye, I'm his twice-great-granddaddy."

James stepped closer. Snatch appeared to be no older than the sheriff was. In fact, with the red hair, the fair complexion and boyish freckles the two could have been brothers.

"That is impossible!"

"James George, would your ma and pa be proud of such narrow-mindedness from a smart lad such as yourself? I thinks not. You opened your eyes earlier. Open them again wider now and tell us what you see, boy." Snatch closed and then covered his eyes with his hands.

"Hey! Where did the lights go?" screamed James, suddenly a terrified child. The mine fell to pitch black. James placed a shaky palm on the end of his nose, but it was as dark as the backside of the moon.

"Close them peepers tight, laddie! I know you're a peekin.' Do it now! For little time we have left before the devils come forked and horned for us all. And me means ALL of us. The world they want, and the world they'll take but for the sad little posse we make."

James did as he was told. The time map appeared before his mind's eye, just as it had earlier. The great infinite plane of future permutations rose. Essentially, nothing in the future had changed yet. His death was still imminent and so was Kilpatre's. Though, if the latter moved forward in time, humankind was still destined to disappear. James spent a moment memorizing the data, and as he finished, he heard Snatch speak.

"Open them now, lad. It's safe. Tell us what yuz see'd."

James summarized the impossible, pausing only when Kara and Snatch exchanged knowing glances. He ended with, "I believe Mr. Kilpatre is the key to our changing the inevitable."

James watched Kara and Snatch stare at each other. They were communicating privately.

"The timeline now says you and I cannot fight the Exterms, Kara. The humans must fight them alone tonight. This is a very dangerous proposition."

"I know, but it is the only path on which James might survive. He dies on all others, and we cannot allow that. Life must fight the Exterms without us."

"What are you two discussing? You know it's rude to whisper."

"Your 1080 idea, lad, mind sharing it with us?"

Precocious curiosity always trumps precarious circumstance. James responded, "In the immortal words of Hannibal Lecter, 'Quid pro quo, Clarice. Quid pro quo.' First, you tell me why you stole all that weird stuff from Seer City. Sometimes you took food, but usually it was packrat-sick stuff: dirty laundry, someone's appendix that had just been removed and wisdom teeth. And you tipped over how many trashcans? A million? People think you are sick. Some think you are a ghost."

"Who be this Lecter gent? An English?"

"He's fictional. So what's up with the bizarre burglaries?"

"A crop of hair, a clipped toenail retrieved from the trash heap, a sick man's hanky. I haven't a fetch of an idea why I fingered those items. It were work I tell you. Not that I had much else to do this past hundred years and more. It were Kara's idea it were, and I learned long ago not to question this sweet girl. I call it me bank. Me bank of parts unknown for unknown. Come! Me show you, lad. Perhaps you can make sense of it for me."

Snatch wrapped his arms around a boulder the size of a Mini Cooper, lifted it with little more difficulty than a basket of laundry, and then set it aside. Behind it was a descending ramp with its fifty feet illuminated like an airport runway no doubt telepathically by the host. "Down we go, boy. Kara, show'em the way. Watch your step! Pup and mice, too!"

"They aren't mice!"

"Aye, so yuz say, lad."

"You are one strange man. How did you lift that boulder? I estimate its weight at 3,100 pounds."

"Oh, I think you already know the answer to that, laddie. Let's save some of your mighty ciphering for my bank."

James watched Snatch reseat the boulder over the entrance. He waited until they began their descent and then asked, "How old are you, Mr. Snatch?"

The answer was delivered so matter-of-factly it didn't shock as much as inform. "Well, boy, without knowing the Lord's current year exactly, I'm at least 145 years old. Last calendar I saw was November 11, 2011. Not sure how many moons more I am now."

James calculated the date difference and blurted, "You're…" but Snatch interrupted him before he could answer.

"No! Show some mercy and hold your notice, laddie, in respect for an old man unable to feel his age." The statement was mirthful, but James also sensed an underlying sadness. While the 19th century Sheriff McCauley was mortal, this wasn't exactly him. That man was long gone. This was Snatch-immortal, apparently superhuman, telepathic, and paradoxically mourning his eternal life while also celebrating it. Snatch was a lonely sentinel.

James felt a kinship with Snatch. They had much in common.

The party arrived on a granite catwalk carved from the rock that overlooked an auditorium-sized cavern below. Like the mineshaft, Snatch's memory illuminated all ten stories from the floor of the cavern telepathically. Practically every square foot of the walls had been perforated by a barrel-sized borehole.

James George stopped suddenly and closed his eyes.

"What be the matter, Jamesie Boy?"

James looked up at Snatch. "I just had the strongest, most vivid déjà vu I have ever experienced. It's like I was just here."

"Oh, that. Yes, I know the feeling. You gets it here strongly. Memories here be a powerful force."

James dropped to all fours, fell onto his stomach, and then stretched over the chasm to examine a nearby hole. Snatch grabbed his ankle just to make sure curiosity didn't kill the brat. At the very edge of the borehole, he found a lady's studded earring. Just one. The borehole was approximately the size of a coffin.

"Over!" James ordered. "Lower me down!"

Snatched dangled the child down the wall where he examined two more boreholes. In the first was a sweaty ball cap. The second held only a soiled paper napkin. James nodded. "Okay, pull me up Mr. Snatch."

Back on his feet, James surveyed the cavern. "You did all this, Mr. Snatch, dug all these by yourself?"

"Aye. Every last everlasting one! Now smart wee one, tell me why she had me do such a crazed thing."

James had earlier suspected the collection's purpose, but now he was sure. He also understood why Snatch could not fathom such science. The principal of DNA was basically beyond his comprehension, and since such information could not be found in his "mental database," Kara could not explain his mission satisfactorily to him.

"Mr. Snatch, our little friend here has anticipated so much." James knelt and scratched the creature behind the ears. Sasha trundled next to the giant rat and waited his turn.

"Basically put, Kara intends to restore the lives of everyone who dies tonight. That is, assuming *she* survives."

"But for Love and Blaze, how might she do that?"

James pointed down at the thousands of boreholes. "What do the Xs on all those holes mean?"

"She had me mark them for folks that have passed on or moved away."

"How many holes for the living?"

"One for each man, woman and child. Even have one for each of God's good and bad varmints, like that preacher's dog and those elk poachers what were waxed yesterday. Seer's tourists and visitors were the most difficult. Lord, yes! I never minded the job of collecting all this and that, I just don't understand why."

James conferred with Kara for a moment, and then asked Snatch, "Do you know what incubation is?"

"Like eggs. An 'ol hen sittering on her shelly brood?"

"Uh, yes! The materials you have collected over the years are like eggs waiting to be hatched or seeds sitting on the shelf just waiting to be planted so they can germinate."

"So you are saying these teeth and such are just awaiting wee Kara's magic? That somehow she can make a new person from it?"

"Yes."

"A whole person?"

"Apparently."

"How?"

"That is yet to be determined."

Snatch looked down at Kara and feigned anger, "Was that so hard to explain, girl? For a hundred years, I slunk about as the village's idiot and chicken thief."

"Kara wagged her tail and said, "My Jimmy McCauley not a chicken thief. He's a chicken egg thief!"

"And that's supposed to be better?"

"Yes!"

"Come! A good scratch you owes me!"

Kara leapt into Snatch's arms. The bulldog, getting the hang of all this attention, butted and nuzzled his leg. Snatch scooped the dog up too, loved him for a moment, then asked as he led the group down the catwalk toward the opposite side of the cavern, "Is this my grandson's animal?"

"Yes. This is Sasha. He sleeps about twenty hours a day and lives a perfectly happy life in the remainders."

"Well, Sasha. Me's jealous. I haven't slumbered one second since the day this little lady saved me life."

James still needed the occasional afternoon nap and with the exception of a few fitful catnaps tonight, he had kept up with the adults. His yawn did nothing to assuage his complete astonishment. "You don't sleep?"

"James, me boy, I've tried, but no, nary a wink."

"What do you eat down here?"

"Are you hungry, lad? You look famished."

"Well, yes I am, but that doesn't answer my question."

"We've grub just ahead laddie. Set aside, just as Kara instructed right before we hid her away in the jar."

"So, am I to surmise that you don't eat either?"

"Surmise?"

"Conclude, presume, reckon…"

"Reckon. That word I know. No, I reckon I don't take the comestibles anymore either."

"Never?" James asked. His question was clinical. He had no reason now to disbelieve.

"Well, let me see." Snatch dug through and scratched his long beard. He hiked his pants a notch and then ticked off the years on his beard like climbing a ladder. He stopped and asked, "How old are you, James?"

"I'm eight years old, soon nine."

They arrived in front of another boulder—a doorway James correctly guessed—and then stopped. "Here we are, home sweets home," Snatch announced and strode to a stop. He kneeled down and looked deeply into James' eyes. The child recognized an all too familiar sadness. He had seen the same uncertain grief in the mirror after his parents' plane crash. "You've lived your entire life and more since last I felt hunger, laddie." Snatch looked away and added, "Tis a monstrous wrongness I feel, too. Not natural a man live me length and never hurt nor crave vittles."

The statement left James speechless, and he was not alone. The normally expressive Kara withdrew, clutched Snatch's shoulder and buried her head. Sasha sat down and stared up at the humans. He cocked his head and then nervously licked his squashed-flat nose.

The pet rats had far greater urgencies than human immortality—Rodentia mortality. The first ones to sense food, Isaac and Newton were restless and began to stir and squeak. Sasha chuffed in agreement. James set the rat cage down and placed his hands on Snatch's shoulders. "Well, don't worry about that Mr. Snatch. I think the four of us will make up for your fast and then some. "I'm starved!"

This lightheartedness cheered the ancient hermit, and his eyes danced merrily once again. "Then be in with yuz, you little scuffers!" He removed the great stone, set it aside, and then with a bow, ushered James toward the entrance. "A feast we shall make before the heavy bracing commences. I have much to learn yuz Master James, and a few things no doubt meself you'll leave me thinking."

"Perhaps we should start now."

Snatch turned and asked, "What duz yuz mean? I thoughts yuz wuz hungry."

"Well, we surely are, but Kara thinks something has gone awry with her plan."

Snatch smiled. Well, let me tell you what I think. "I've been living right under them machines' noses for more than a century, and they ain't got me yet, and they ain't starting to... Is it night or day, James lad?"

"It's still dark outside."

"Then they're not starting tonight! Uh, let's see. We have two rats, a bulldog, a boy, Kara me sweet, me, and our guest. That makes seven for supper. Seven! Hey, that's Lucky Seven. What do you know?"

"Our guest?"

"Yes, now in with yuz! Explore if you want while I set out the feast."

James had once visited the Ripley's museum in St. Augustine with his parents, and that spectacularly curious house of oddities rivaled Snatch's home. He thought he saw a three-story home carved from the granite. The walls and floors, though made of stone, were burnished and cultured to appear to be made of hardwood and plaster. Doors turned on stone hinges and were seated in masterfully crafted golden casements that appeared oaken.

James realized that much of what he saw was illusion—a product of Snatch's memory and now his own—but only the décor was faux. The structure itself was authentic. While Snatch prepared their meal, which should surely prove interesting, James investigated the house.

The first room to his right was the library. James stepped inside and smiled. With the exception of a double door at the other end of the room, the walls were lined with bookshelves—all empty. However, that was a temporary void. Like watching a 1960s-era computer monitor paint characters across its screen, rapidly, but one letter at a time, the bookshelves began to fill.

James watched the phenomenon curiously at first and then giggled as he realized he was watching his personal library downloaded from every book he had ever read. Then he saw a reading table in the center of the room with truly artificial lighting.

James lifted one of about a dozen leather-bound volumes scattered on the table including: *The Subnano Universe* by T.J. McGoldrick PhD, *Frankenstein* by Mary Shelly, *Darwinius* by Nobel laureate Dr. J. Wyatt Pursel, and Earl Moen's latest Western thriller *The Bucking Horse Auction*. These books were incomplete. James had been reading them all just yesterday. He made a promise to himself to finish each book when he got home to add them to Snatch's library. He left the table and headed for the far door.

Nearly a ton of granite turned as smoothly as a well-oiled turnstile in response. He stepped through the opening onto a wide catwalk that circumnavigated high above an auditorium for at least three hundred feet. James George scanned the cavernous room and exclaimed, "Holy Cripes!" Three additional entrances into the auditorium quartered the catwalk. Each entrance yielded to four granite ramps that spiraled down to the auditorium floor far below.

Lavishly ornate balustrades launched each granite ramp into the great room—an area perhaps the size of a basketball court. A solid pyramid rising to a height of twenty feet was in the center of the floor. James ran down the long spiral ramp and approached the creation. He scanned the formation and estimated its base to be twenty feet per side.

The gold bricks that formed the pyramid were not pure, nor perfectly shaped, but close. James had no idea what an ounce of gold was currently worth or how Snatch had refined these bricks, but he knew that this pyramid contained a fortune.

A puff of air played over James's neck and tossed his hair lightly. He turned and found the source of the draft. It came from the far end of the room where an archway yielded to yet another tunnel. James left the mystery of the pyramid for a moment and followed the mildly sulfurous current to its source. He stopped in the archway and resisted the temptation to just keep walking and explore beyond the tunnel's bend.

James sniffed the air rising from the shaft and examined the tunnel walls. Pickax scarring was as good as a miner's fingerprint to the trained eye, and James had little doubt who had excavated this tunnel and why. Snatch. The downward slope and spiraling angle answered at least one question.

Deeper in the earth, surely more than ten miles if he pursued it, James would find Snatch's gold foundry—where the hermit used the earth's own granite liquefying temperatures to process the ore and form the gold bricks. One mystery solved. One created. How could Snatch survive such temperatures? This question would have to wait.

"Jamesy lad, 'nough exploring. Come take some vittles now. We have little precious time for me to larn you what you need to know." Snatch then added, an edge of seriousness creeping into his voice and seemingly reading James's mind, "Eat, good laddie, and then ask what you're surely thinkin' about them goldie bricks."

Suddenly famished, he raced across the cavern and sprinted up the spiral ramp. James' stomach rumbled as he entered the hermit's kitchen. The aroma was real enough, but still he wondered if Snatch would feed him the same brand of air sandwiches that Raggedy Ann and Raggedy Andy ate in the bedtime stories that long ago seemed so enthralling.

Again, the ancient McCauley seemed to read the boy's mind. "I've been expecting you, so it's regular food, boy. Not to worry."

Two steaming pie-shaped dishes sat in the center of the table likewise created from the most available building supply—granite. James kneeled on the bench and leaned over the table. "This smells fabulous! What is it?"

"Genuine, Lad."

"Genuine?"

"Real food, 'tis. Lifted from here and thar, a can, a jar, a loaf, bag and bar."

"You stole it?"

"Aye, from town. Forgive me?"

James laughed and climbed onto the granite bench. He inhaled the fabulous vapors and waved dramatically, a TV priest's gesture of dispensation. "Of course, my son!"

Snatch watched the child eat his meal, alternately cramming spoonfuls of the meaty vegetable pie and freshly baked bread into his mouth. The milk was powdered, but it was ice cold and drew no complaint. Dessert arrived in the form of yet more pie—apple—crowned with a slice of cheese and a dollop of real whipped cream. James George took a double helping of it too.

Snatch's tin coffee cup was a mere prop. He held it with just the tips of his fingers under his chin, pretending it was steaming hot, to be consumed by only the most airy and careful of sips. James, famished and exhausted, didn't notice that Snatch had actually not eaten or drank anything.

Watching the child eat with such gusto was painful and exhilarating at once. It had been lifetimes since he had experienced such simple pleasures as watching a child fill his tank on supper, and he suddenly missed his old life horribly. When he spoke, the creaky voice of an old man was gone as was the ancient brogue. The sadness he felt belied his cheery question.

"Would you like some more, lad?"

"No, sir. It's fabulously delicious, but no thank you." James wiped his chin on his sleeves. James leaned back and studied his host. "May I...?"

Anticipating the next starvation—knowledge—Snatch interrupted and said, "Of course, Jamesie, ask me what you may."

"Thank you. For starters, your voice just changed. You no longer sound Western European. In fact, you sound very much like your grandson, Renner McCauley."

Snatch smiled. "You and I have something in common, James. You are a child, but often sound like an adult, like someone far older and wiser than your age. Don't you sometimes talk your age, even act your age, just to keep down the fuss so people aren't too uncomfortable in your presence?"

James George smiled and nodded. "Yes! Sometimes it's easier to just do something my own age. My mother and father so loved it when I was a five-year-old for their benefit. And to tell the truth, it was sort of fun."

"Aye. Me knows what you mean, Jamesie."

"So, which do you prefer: to act your age or be your age?"

"Oh, that be easy. I prefer the age of Snatch, even if it's just make-believe. Seems more natural considering me advanced age and all."

"Okay. Now for the more important query. How did you avoid the Kar all these decades?"

"I didn't. Me and the giant rats have been neighbors all these years. Good ones too, I have to admit. Nary a complaint until just recently."

"How can that be, Snatch? How could they not come for you?"

"The beasts are not perfect. They be blind to me. You see, every so often he makes a mistake, he takes on a mistake."

"A gene, a segment of DNA."

"Whatever. A nature I calls it—one what they shouldn't. Kara me good girl larned me how to use that bit of knowledge, and now they cannot see me if I'm careful. They've stood right where you sit, Jamesie, and took no more notice of me than the air we breathe."

James gazed off into space for a moment. So intensely, that both Sasha and Snatch looked after him, following his stare to an intellectual gateway through which few mortals ever pass.

When James was finished thinking, he turned to Snatch and announced most matter-of-factly, "Of course, an errant introgression occasionally occurs, probably similar to the blind symbiosis of *Crotalus adamanteus* of the viperidae and the *Gopherus polyphemus*—two species that are literally blind to the other's presence."

"The what, lad?" Snatch slapped the table and laughed. "Kara warned me you'd be a lone noodle amongst mere broth, but I haven't a yarn if farly stretched as to what you just said."

"Oh, sorry. Let me explain. One of the strangest relationships between two species exists in southeast North America. The eastern diamondback rattlesnake lives its entire life in a burrow that it shares with the gopher tortoise. Two creatures, one burrow, both utterly oblivious of their housemate. They crawl and climb over one another without the slightest nuisance meant or realized."

"Well done, Lad. I guess I be the excavating hard-shell. The ol' tortoise. Aye? And the rats the blind-eyed snake?"

"Metaphorically, I'd say yes, which leads me to the next question."

"The gold?"

"Yes, Mr. Snatch, the gold."

"Well, me first dug the holes for the boredom of all this. Me prison." Snatch studied the room and the walls for a moment and then gestured, shaking his head. "And when even the digging got down in me mind too, it were Kara that made me go on. Follow me. Follow sweet girl from Golden, me kept a hearin'. And then one day, maybe after me dead and false-cemeteried for ten years or so, I realized it weren't the town of Golden in me song she keep in me head, but the genuine article—the gold itself. So me follered her wee voice deep into the mountain. Then, deeper yet. Then, thar t'were. Biggest gold find ever. You've seen me placer downstairs, all stacked up nice and neat. For what she have me do it for, I do not know."

"I assume you'd like to know."

"Oh land, for love of Baby Jesus, yes. But Kara does not like answering some questions."

Kara was under the table doing what she called resting, which in fact was sentry duty.

"Kara, dear, please tell me and our guest why you had me make all the gold bricks."

"Not guest. He follow perty girl from Golden. Guest not here yet."

Snatch smiled and winked at James. "Whatever. Please tell young James George why you had me bust me old hump all these years for the gold."

"The Golden for perty girl to go from Jimmy Mccauley to."

Snatch bit his lower lip and smiled at James George. He whispered, "This will go on for eternity. She absolutely will not tell us why. Listen to this gibberish!"

"Kara, please tell us?"

"Kara tired. Kara sleep now."

"But Kara doesn't sleep."

"Snorrrr… Snorrrr…"

"You are an ol' possum, little lady. I'm in a coma compared to you, and I never so much as nod, let alone leave to slumber." The last said with a sadness the old man's grin could not conceal.

"Cannot hear Jimmy McCauley. Oh no! Where Jimmy McCauley?" Kara hesitated, then ended the game, "He here! Guest! My Hoop!" She disappeared, a white blur down the hallway.

# CHAPTER 63  ~~  Ghost Miner

Three hours into the search for James George, everyone in Renner's party was convinced they'd entered hell. This hell was a labyrinth created by the apostles of Yogi Berra: "When you come to a fork in the road, take it."

Every several hundred feet the tunnel subdivided into two branches. At the first few junctures, Renner and Erin conferred, but now the FBI agent just marked a branch with an arrow and led the people-train down whichever branch that seemed more inclined. It wasn't the best thought out plan, but at least it was logical. If James and Kara had been intent on going up, not down, they wouldn't have entered the maze in the first place. So the adults headed downward too.

Renner noticed that the rope connecting the party was alternately taut and loose, that their progress was uneven. "Let's take a break and let everyone catch their breath. Five minutes." He untethered from the rope and moved up and down the line.

Puck and BB still showed no signs of fatigue, nor did Kate, Josh or Erin. The Resumption survivors, Jussard and Tumulley, surprisingly, were doing well too. Doc actually seemed rejuvenated. The twin ogres, Uncertainty and Urgency to find James George, not

344

fatigue, were creating the drag on the line. However, that didn't answer why the group was at the same time so energized.

It was Josh Roe who answered that question. "It's the oxygen, Sheriff. We must now be at more than fifty percent concentration. I suggest we all eat and drink a bit. If we don't, the richer atmosphere may unexpectedly take its toll later."

Renner agreed and decided that what the group needed more than rest, food or even water was some light. So at the risk of not having enough later, he suggested everyone find a seat and illuminate their flashlights.

Josh and Erin passed around bottles of water and cracked open a box of chocolate and peanut butter energy bars. "Drink half your water now and half when we stop again. Same with the energy bar."

Chris Jussard dutifully obliged, but clearly his mind was elsewhere. The walls of the mineshaft drew his attention as reflexively as a dog to a passing car. He rose from the incandescent/fluorescent circle and stepped over to the mine wall.

Renner followed him. "Dr. Jussard, these walls hold some mystery for you. You can't take your eyes off them. But is it relevant to finding James George and destroying the machines?"

Jussard kneeled and caressed the pickax scarring on the wall. "Is it Sheriff or Renner?"

Renner smiled and kneeled next to the scientist. "Locals call me Mac or Ren."

Jussard nodded. He waved the energy bar at the wall like a wand and asked, "Do you believe in fate, Mac?"

Renner did not believe in preordination of any kind, but what he did or did not hold as self-evident had nothing to do with his answer. "Yes, if it has something to do with getting back the boy."

"I suspect it does."

"How?"

"My doctoral thesis."

Renner studied the scientist. "Really, where was that?"

"Colorado School of Mines."

"An impressive credential."

"Thank you."

"What was your thesis?"

Jussard tapped the wall with his water bottle. "This."

"This mine?"

"No, these cuts." Jussard hesitated and turned toward Renner. He then added, "These exact wall cuts, Mac.

"Explain."

"Your distant relative was a legend in his day. After the Midas Six, Jimmy McCauley worked the Routt, then the Telem, then Dutch Lady, and finally Diablo's Bursar. He was the youngest mine boss in the history of Seer County. After the Bursar cooked out, he took one last assignment and retired from the mines a very rich man."

"The Golden Girl. Very impressive, Christopher."

Jussard ignored yet another compliment. "The Golden Girl. That's right. It was a stakes mine. Your granddad handpicked the miners and earned the quickest payout in Colorado history. From the first borehole to the first payout was only three months. It was the Golden Girl that set Jimmy McCauley up for life, allowed him to purchase Seer Mountain—all 250,000 acres."

"I thought Colorado School of Mines was an engineering school, not history."

"Well, engineering is actually history in its purest form— mathematics, physics, and chemistry. Mac, I spent five years in those old mines, every square inch of them, and I know every miner that worked in them: short men, tall men, left-handed men, men who pecked, men who drove, side armed picklocks with shoulder injuries, and men like Jimmy McCauley that worked the pickax like a meat cleaver. He was absolutely unique. He swung the pick with the power of a dozen men and he never tired."

"That's what your thesis was about?"

"Sort of. I did an economic comparison of miner productivity, 'mechanical' now vs. 'manual' then."

"What are you saying?"

"Your grandfather dug these shafts. I am positive." He tapped the wall for emphasis and pointed down the shaft. "His cuts and fines are as unique as his DNA."

"So, he worked this mine as a young man."

"He wasn't a kid when he scooped out these shafts, Mac. Of that I'm positive. These cuttings are just months old."

"That's impossible."

"You are correct, my friend. It is impossible. Nevertheless, it is the only explanation."

# CHAPTER 64 ~~ Call For Hoop

Cyril Hoop stepped silently amongst the wavering shadows. His exacting footfalls rivaled the shadow's silent caress. He moved past the resting party, listening, wanting to join in, but knew dead men can absolutely kill a party, so he moved on. Kara called to him, led him deeper into the mine, urging him along. "Hoop! My Hoop! Hurry! They are coming!"

\*\*\*

Someone else called to Hoop as well. Cole Kilpatre woke from his dream to a nightmare. Sand and ground glass assaulted a throat that dreamland had soothed with wine served from golden vats and goblets. Caked blood smeared his face instead of dream icing that dripped from nine-layer golden sponge cakes served on golden platters. A suit of unbearable perspiration, human permafrost, replaced a sleeping gown embroidered with golden thread.

The psychotic's plaintive soprano wailed, "Hooooooooooooop! Hoooooop? Hoop. Oh my!"

His calls echoed mockingly throughout the granite tomb, each return more startling. Kilpatre held his breath and listened. He gasped and then held it again for a few painful seconds before his breath escaped with a wheezy whimper.

The darkness was complete. Kilpatre held his hands before his eyes and searched for them as intensely as a sentry using binoculars. He opened his eyes so wide they ached, and when he still could not see his hands, their sausage fingers wiggling frantically "I'm right here!" he thumbed and stretched open his eyelids to the brink of tearing them out. Still nothing.

So complete was the illusion that he was blind, he closed his eyes, stood, and sprinted howling across the atrium. A knee-high boulder prevented him from crashing face first into the granite wall and probably saved his life; though, it did shatter his right tibia when he tripped over it.

Kilpatre flipped, struck his head and rolled limp and unconscious to a stop just twenty feet from his previous crumpling. His season pass punched once more for an excursion to dreamland.

***

Even though Alpha Genesis had never set foot in this part of the original mine, he led his pack through perfectly familiar territory. He sensed another oneness—the humans' presence in the underground world and among them was The One. The One that was all. The One that must be absorbed. The One that possessed a power unparalleled in the human species and once absorbed no species, no power in the universe would stop the Federation.

The pack bounded down the old tunnels, the dead air whispering over their scales. Their claws drew purchase in the stone and launched them forward with little more complaint than a whisper. Their phosphorescent eyes rose and fell in the darkness like barnacles on the backs of pod whales.

Instinct drew the pack and guided it. Hunger and survival were indistinguishable and demanded satiation with every step.

Alpha: The One. Find.

Pack: The One. Find.

Alpha: The defect. Find.

Pack: The Rebel. Find.

Alpha: Kill.

Pack: Kill all Nonbeings.

# CHAPTER 65 ~~ Would the Real Cyril Hoop Please Stand?

Kara gathered herself and dove through the air toward the doorway. Hoop stepped into the opening just in time. He caught and gathered Kara to his chest. He welcomed her, but it was as if he didn't understand why.

James studied the greeting which could only be described as a romantic embrace—a one-and-a-half-sided reunion. Hoop was more than alive. He was young, muscularly chiseled, and handsome. Kara peeled off his cap and a full head of hair fell out. Hoop clearly found great pleasure in Kara's attention but was equally confused by it.

Snatch looked across the table at James George and winked. "I say me Kara has truly missed your Mr. Hoop, aye lad? Look at her, would you?"

"Apparently, but I'm guessing Mr. Hoop has little more understanding than me as to why she is so enamored with him. Just look at him."

Hoop had felt his body and mind changing all night. From living to dead. From dead to alive. From alive to an otherworldly state beyond mere living. Immortality was absolute sensation, a feeling as palpable as any of his other senses that were now amplified.

Hoop could taste the artificial light. He could literally hear the scent of stew cooling on the dinner table. He could feel the seamlessly stitched virtual reality that Snatch had created for James He looked down at Sasha and smiled "hello," and the animal chuffed. He spoke "rat" to the rats that dutifully rose and scratched the air. Hoop cuddled the alien in his arms and felt her beckon him away as surely as might any reunited lover.

"Come… Remember me, my love. Follow me!"

"To where?"

"To us from Golden"

"To us from Golden?" Hoop asked aloud.

Hoop felt himself slipping away as Time tumbled from under his feet, accelerated away, drew him down a deep whirlpool—a memory miasma. At first, he fought the sensation, but with Kara's gentle encouragement to let go, Hoop finally released himself and fell.

"It is safe, my love. Hold me!"

Hoop clutched Kara tightly. The room disappeared, replaced by a swirling barrenness that rumbled an ever-increasing rhythm. Together they watched as time moved in reverse, exponentially faster with each passing second. Yet it was after nearly a minute of tumbling from the great Navistar that he arrived at "us."

***

Hoop is standing on the bridge of an ambushed spaceship that retreats across the universe. He survives the crash-landing on a barren planet alone with his commanding officer. He is a machine, one that seeks and finds sanctuary in the genes of simple life forms. He and the commander secretly pursue their pursuers and carefully recycle the Federation defects. He changes. He evolves within the DNA of the countless life forms that the enemy has plundered. He is in love. He is in love with his commanding officer, and she buries him alive on a nearby mountainside.

Hoop remembers everything! "My Commander!"

***

A pair of karpeleotroceme raced chittering across the forest floor. In the lead was a female. She was slightly smaller than her male pursuer, but no less quick. When she sped up, so did he. When she slowed, he maintained his distance. Over fallen timbers they scampered in and out of tortoise burrows, their occupants ducking and hissing protest post-bellum. They scurried up and down the trunks of behemoth trees, slicing through high grasses, leaving a single

350

swooshing, sensual trail in their wake. Then they disappeared into the shadows, emerging into rare pockets of bright sunlight.

The female was not running from the male. The male was not chasing the female.

She arrived upon a wide stream strewn with boulders and skipped across the stream atop the boulders, zigzagging playfully from one to another and arriving high and dry on the far bank in a single thirty foot, arcing bound.

The male mimicked her every move precisely in perfect synchrony until reaching the last boulder. There, he stopped and stood and awaited to see if the female had chosen him.

Such was the first courtship.

***

"Us, Hoop."

"Us? You and me, Kara?"

"Yes. Feel?"

He did. His cheeks flushed pink. His heart lifted a beat and for a man, who had recently died, sprinted through the blizzard and up a mountain with nary a huff. Cyril Hoop could not catch his breath from anticipation.

"We were...?" he asked.

"Yes. Feel me?"

"Yes, Kara. We were—we are in love. But how?"

Climbing into their burrow, the male dropped a piece of ripened red fruit near the sleeping female and then nudged it closer to her mouth. A cornucopia of nutritious foods awaited the female when she was ready to eat. He deposited fruits, nuts, roots, leaves and grasses into the nest.

James George and Snatch had witnessed the memories with no less clarity than if they had been their own. Snatch spoke, "I'm your answer there, Mr. Hoop."

Hoop smiled as he split-screened his mind's eye between seven hundred million years ago and the present.

"What do you remember about your parents, Mr. Hoop?"

"My parents?"

"Aye, old laddie."

"I actually remember very little about them. I had no..."

"You hadn't a pa, aye? Killed on his wedding night by a drunk driver. Your ma craved a Dairy Queen malted milk that night, she did. And more tragedy, such fate, your ma died on you when you was a wee boy. She worked in a pet store. Folks called her Dr. Doris Little for her love of the creatures. Is this the truth of your life?"

"Yes... I grew up in Denver at St. Michael's Home. But how could you know that?"

"Simplest and strangest of all answers I give you. Our Kara told me long ago. Before you start ciphering more, let me add, not a whit of what I said or what you believe is true."

"Wh... what do you mean? I don't understand."

"Mr. Hoop, sorry, but here be the truth. You see, Mr. Hoop, you never worked for the government. You never attended college, let alone became an inspector of this most recent Kilpatre. In fact, dear Jesus reach down and brand me first for Satan's clique if I lie, but I meself dug you out of the ground where Kara girl had put you long ago for safekeeping, and not ten hours before you arrived in Seer City and presented your official secret letters to me grandson. It's been a fraud, your life, but a necessary one, you see. You are an Orlif Kar."

Snatch's account had an unexpected effect on Hoop. Like in fairy tales when magical spoken passwords reveal and unlock fantastic passageways, or as catalysts transform atomic worlds, Hoop understood that Snatch spoke the truth.

"Yes! I do see." Vivid memories now seemed more like the facades on a movie set. A lifetime of conversations and friendships collapsed, dwindled away increasingly dreamlike. Thirty-five years of knowledge trundled forward in his mind.

A soft light shimmered around Hoop. It stretched and danced about him and then contracted with a shrill buzz. A light ball descended to a spot a few inches above the floor, then disintegrated with a loud pop. A fine white powder remained on the floor. The residue rose and swirled into a tiny funnel cloud. It spun faster and faster. There was a bright flash of light, and then the cloud was gone. Before them, standing next to Kara on his hind legs, was the male karpeleotroceme, Kara's mate.

James turned to Snatch, "Did you know?"

"Aye."

Kara took Hoop's paw and together they transformed for a moment into their true alien form—humanoid except for their eyes that appeared machined, but beautifully blue. Together, the aliens stepped toward James and Snatch and bowed, then reverted to the more familiar karpeleotroceme form.

"A cute couple they makes, don't you think?"

"Cute? Oh, yes. They are indeed," James said faintly. "Sheriff Renner McCauley will certainly be surprised how extremely undercover some federal inspectors might be."

"Aye."

"Snatch. I have one more question. The scene in the burrow where Hoop brought food to Kara. They were mates. Was she...?"

Snatch interrupted James George. "Aye, laddie, I knows what you're a askin'. Yes, Jamesie, she was pregnant. Hoop and Kara had a baby. The Kar have existed for billions of years, Jamesie, but never once have they produced a baby. Theirs was more than just the first offspring. The baby was a new life form. In fact, in their native language, the words *ka'rae* and *h'uupe* spoken separately translates roughly in English as genesis-female and genesis-male. When you say the words together, *k'arae h'uupe*, it means *origin* in English or more accurately..."

"...mother and father. Kara and Hoop."

"Very good, Jamesie."

# CHAPTER 66 ~~ Organics Offensive

Renner's party moved another mile deeper into the mountain before stopping to rest one last time. Tethered together in the dark, their progress was grueling—a seven-man potato sack race. Instinct told Renner the enemy was near and James George was not. Offense now was the best defense. It was time to divide their forces and draw fire.

Renner aimed his flashlight at an opening high on the mine wall. "Erin, Josh, mind checking it out? Will it fit four of us?"

Josh made a stirrup for Erin with his hands. Erin peered into the compartment and nodded down to Renner. "It looks like a good hiding place. Plenty of room for four."

They did not even discuss the plan. It was not necessary. "Who are we leaving behind with Kate and the old professor, Sheriff?" Josh asked.

Renner answered, "Puck and BB. They aren't going to like it."

Chris Jussard shined his flashlight into the opening. "It appears the same person dug this one too. I've counted nine of these cavities so far and never seen anything like it. Beyond the entrance is a chamber. Each is about thirty square feet, I estimate, with seven feet of overhead clearance. The room is clear of any rock debris. There's only a boulder which I suspect fits perfectly over the entrance. It's clearly an invitation, Sheriff."

"How's the air?"

"Our mystery excavator thought of that too. Look." Jussard kneeled and aimed the flashlight underneath two jutting structures below the entrance. There, almost hidden, were several more borings. "These three are the air intakes. Up here is the exhaust. Look at the carved rock formation. Our miner used the Venturi principle and the occupants' body heat to create a natural positive pressure inside the chamber. The relative pressure differential pulls the bad air from the cavity into the mineshaft, while pulling in the cooler fresh air. It's a truly ingenious design."

Doc and Kate stepped next to Renner. The ordeal was finally catching up to Doc. Kate caught Renner's attention and shook her head.

Renner nodded. Doc might be the first to reach the end of his endurance, but likely not the last. "Everyone gather up. Erin, please break out the water and food rations. Puck and BB, a word." The threesome stepped away.

"What's up Mac?" Puck asked.

"We need to split up, boys. Doc is done."

Puck and BB nodded agreement. Truth was everyone was finally showing fatigue, stress, or both on their faces.

"Also, I sense we are being hunted. Our best chance against these creatures is to turn the tables and hunt them on our terms."

"All right then, Mac," Puck said nodding agreement.

"How about you, BB?"

"I'm fine with it. Feels right."

"Okay. Here's the tough part. I'm asking you two boys to stay here with Kate and Doc." He gestured with his chin toward the chamber. "I want you watch out for James George. If he is headed this way, so are the space rats. Somehow, we got past each other." Renner sighed and added, "Not surprising I guess in this maze."

Neither man responded. They just looked at each other and then back at Renner.

"What's wrong, boys?"

Puck answered. "Nothing Mac. BB and me had that exact same feeling. Isn't that strange?"

BB added, "Mac, I've been in some strange situations in my time, but this whole Midas Six experience, well, it's just plain creepy. You know what I mean? Somehow creepier than everything else tonight."

"I do."

BB continued, "This rock is so new I can almost smell the hot iron bits. And, we've already covered more miles than the Midas Six ever were, Mac. We are at least nine miles into the mountain."

"Strangest of all," added Puck, "I've never seen such a clean mine. This thing has been carved with a laser and scraped out with a toothbrush."

Scrape out. Renner recalled the Jimmy McCauley stories handed down to him through the generations. His great-great-grandfather Jimmy McCauley was doing scrape-out duty the day the mine closed.

Dr. Jussard had something to add. "These tunnels are definitely new, and they definitely weren't here last month. Here is proof." He shined his flashlight on the wall opposite the chamber.

### J.M. 145?

Puck exclaimed, "My goodness, Renner!"

"What's it mean, Puck?" asked the sheriff.

"Tell him, BB."

"It's a miner's sig, Mac. His testament."

"A sig?"

"His signature. All artisans do it. Carpenters sign the rafter ridge. Shipbuilders sign the beam. Masons etch a brick. Miners sign the shaft. Sometimes they date it. Sometimes they affix their age to it."

"What's the difference?"

"They use a date, like on a tombstone when they're trapped and about to die and…"

Jussard finished the comparison, "…and they mark down their age when they're finished excavating."

Renner studied the etching for moment and translated aloud, "J.M. circa ?145?… James McCauley, about 145 years old."

Puck said, "It's got to be a hoax, Mac."

Renner nodded and turned to Puck, "On any night but this one, I'd agree."

Josh and Erin had explored the next section of the mine and missed the history lesson. Josh Roe called out from fifty feet down the shaft. "Well, this looks like the end of the road." Together, he and Erin shined the flashlights on where the shaft abruptly ended.

# CHAPTER 67 ~~ Kar Offensive

Alpha Genesis thought "Stop!" and the machines obeyed instantly. Silence replaced whispery flight. The pack stood statuesque—a monolith rivaling the mineshaft itself. None moved. Then, as one, they opened their eyes and focused on Alpha. He turned toward the pack, his scales clicking dryly as he moved.

The enemy was scattering, dividing, and no doubt in search of The One too. There was more. The female Rebel Kar was near, the commander.

"She is here. Find."

"Yes."

"Destroy."

"Yes."

"Find The One."

"Yes."

"Consume."

"Yes."

Alpha also decided it was time to divide his forces, and secondly he sensed the enemy likewise sensed his presence. Stealth was unnecessary. Three creatures leaped onto the ceiling and affixed themselves on the granite. Three more Kars tore into the tunnel floor. Within just seconds, all six had disappeared into the mountain. Alpha and Beta quietly resumed their way down the tunnel.

# CHAPTER 68 ~~ Divide and Hide

"Weapons check," Renner McCauley ordered. "Puck? BB?"

Puck answered, "Ren, we've got sixteen candy-tipped arrows left. Plus, plenty of C4 remaining to make some shaped charges and booby traps. The real question is just how safe is it to use these explosives in tight quarters? I say we go for it. BB figures we can safely snipe from inside the chamber. Dr. Jussard here says the mine structure is dang near perfect, and that it will survive a good blast or six without too much damage. It will be loud as a freight train racing around a corrugated washtub, but Beebs ain't ever wrong when it comes to candy making. Right, Bro?"

BB and Puck tapped each other's fists. Ben Bainbridge said, "Right on, Puck." He turned to Renner and added, "We'll hold, Mac. You can count on us. Just don't forget to come back and get us when you're done having fun." BB and Puck draped their arms over Kate and Doc's shoulders.

Renner smiled at his two old friends' joke. None doubted he would dismantle the mountain if he had to, one rock at a time, to come back for them.

Kate met Renner's eyes. Renner McCauley wasn't fearless. No man is fearless unless he's mad, and Renner McCauley was far from mad. He had fears, and he was looking into his greatest fear right now. Perhaps his only fear. He was in love and entangled wonderfully in all its enchantment. She was so close, yet not his to keep unless they exterminated the aliens. Unless Kate survived. Unless all she loved survived. Killing now. Love would wait. Renner McCauley lingered a moment longer with Kate. She whispered, "I love you."

Renner answered her slowly, emphasizing each word as if it were the last he would speak, "And I you, Kate."

As they embraced and then kissed fully, they might have been lovers drifting down the Seine in France, or huddled under a golden maple tree in New York's Central Park, or anywhere at any moment in time where lovers vow, and where the world shrinks to just two souls.

Their lips parted. Kate looked up and smiled. She stepped back and nodded, mercifully releasing Renner to be once again almost fearless.

Buck Tumulley took a deep breath and willed his hands to stop shaking. He reached for his backpack and managed to hang onto it only after fumbling and dropping it twice. He pawed through the contents like a frantic game show contestant until he found what he was looking for—four packs of foam earplugs.

Buck approached Kate, Doc, BB and Puck. "I've got plenty for everyone."

Kate and Doc glanced at the earplugs and back at Chris for explanation. Buck nervously shook the foam plugs like a pairs of dice.

"Oh, sorry! They're to protect your ears from any explosions. We, uh Resumption, used them in the RV on overnights. Jerry... Jerry snored worse than an earthmover with a bad muffler... he..." Buck couldn't finish. His eyes begged the group for understanding.

Renner accepted the earplugs for everyone. "Dr. Tumulley, I believe there is a 9mm pistol strapped to your right ankle. Am I right?"

Buck looked up. His expression still mourned the loss of so many friends and was beginning to mourn for himself. "That's right, Sheriff. Don't worry. It's legal."

"Good. Can you use it?"

"Oh, yes. I scored 240 out of 250 points on the range when I qualified for my Colorado Concealed Carry permit."

"Better yet."

"How many clips?" Buck shrugged. "Just one, but only half loaded, maybe four or five rounds."

Renner turned to Josh Roe, "I'd bet you're a 9mm man."

Roe tapped the rucksack at his feet with a boot tip, "If four hundred rounds won't do it, Sheriff, ammo won't matter." Roe kneeled, unzipped the pack, removed a fifty-round box, and tossed the ammunition to Renner.

Renner handed the box to Tumulley. The engineer's hands were still shaking. Mac pressed the box into Buck's hands. "Steady, Dr. Tumulley."

"Sorry." Buck nodded and looked away ashamed.

"Erin, Josh, let's see what else you have."

Erin opened her jacket. "I up-armored in town, Sheriff." Under her arm was a Browning P-35, Hi-Power. Around her waist was an ammo bandolier with at least twenty loaded clips. She then lifted her pant leg and revealed an ankle holster with another 9mm pistol.

"Good. Josh, I'm counting on you to have a bit more firepower. You seem the type."

Roe offered the group a rare smile. "Yes, I like to call myself prepared. He pulled from the bag two Colt 1911-A pistols, then the Titan version of the .308 caliber Springfield M1A1A scout bush rifle, and finally, a Mossberg 12-gauge shotgun. Then he opened his coat and revealed one last weapon, a Glock-19. His waist bandolier was stocked with ammo similar to Erin's.

"Did you bring the scope for the rifle?"

Roe reached into the bag one last time and held up the scope.

"Good. Ammunition?"

"Five-by-five. Hopefully, more than we'll need."

Puck and BB stepped next to Renner. "BB and me made you lady and gents a little going away present. See if you can put them to good use." BB pulled open the bundle and Renner peered inside. He found six packets bound in bubble wrap.

"Is this what I think it is?"

BB beamed. "You bet. Six C4 charges, all ready for chemical firing caps.

Puck removed one charge from the bag and handed it to Renner. He carefully unwrapped the bomb and said, "Mac, you can use it like a grenade. There just ain't no pin to pull. Just chuck and duck. Kerplow! Also, with the rifle scope you can use Roe's Titan rifle and nail the cruds from a safe distance, that is, if there is such a thing down here.

"Very good, let's go." Without more discussion, the party of five left.

***

The Midas Six was a honeycomb of new passageways. The searchers had no way of knowing exactly how far they had ventured, but they had spiraled many miles into the mountain, down a great staircase possessing countless switchbacks, long landings and hidden crossovers that with a tap on the rock walls here or there would reveal more of the maze just inches away.

The design protected the humans as much as confused them. The maze leveled the playing field, so to speak, just as Kara and Jimmy McCauley intended. There was yet one more surprise.

The remaining humans waited until Renner's hunting party had disappeared before climbing into their lair. "Up you go, Doc." Puck and BB joined hands and made a stirrup to help Doc climb into the hidey-hole.

"Watch for the dirty backwinds boys. My sails can get quite musical when I strain."

"Doc!" Kate admonished, though she joined BB and Puck in a much needed farts laugh.

"Just being honest, daughter. I'd hate to blind a man."

"We're fine, Doc," Puck said. "In you go."

Doc's boots disappeared into the darkness. A moment later, his face appeared in the opening. "It's perfect. Just as Dr. Jussard said. Come, Katie!"

Kate, BB and Puck joined the professor who was already busy contrasting the mirrored shape of the lone boulder to the entrance. There was no mistaking it—the boulder was a seal.

"Would you look at this, Katie? It is so perfectly hewn, it seems carved from the wall by plasma."

Kate tested the indented handles and ran her hand over the stone. She shook her head in astonishment. "Yes, but why? By whom?"

"Dear, I believe we are expected here." Doc gestured for Puck and BB to place the boulder in the opening.

The men rolled the rock a quarter turn, lined it up and slid it into place as smoothly as a key and its lock. Once set, the boulder's surface illuminated in an electric-blue, arcing light.

"Do you think this might be a trap of some type, Doc?" BB posed the question with little conviction. It just needed asking for no other reason than to get it off everyone's list.

Doc placed his hand on the boulder. The light field turned green around his hand. He smiled and turned to the others. "Goodness! It's warm. I believe this is a force field of some kind! One designed, I believe, to protect not imprison us. This is a sanctuary of sorts. We were supposed to find it and use it."

Puck asked, "Okay, but like Professor Lambert asked, who built it, Doc?"

"Now, I've been giving a great deal of thought to that question, Mr. Ortez, and the only thing I'm sure of is obvious—whoever built this chamber built the others as well."

"Anything else?"

"I just wish our little friend Kara was here. I'm sure she could explain everything. But my current working theory is that this represents some of the ancient technology she brought with her, perhaps part of her spaceship the *Jhim*." Doc gave a Cliffs Notes version of a three hundred millennia civil war.

The group fell silent. Kate shined her flashlight on the four walls, the smooth ceiling, and then on the boulder sealing them in. "Doc! I think you're right. Look!"

"Would you look at that, Puck? If we hadn't set the stone ourselves, I wouldn't believe it."

The foursome kneeled in front of the portal. One by one, they placed their hands on the stone. Although the rock felt unchanged—as solid and impregnable as before—artificial light now passed through it as transparently as if it were plate glass.

Kate understood the next phenomenon. She and Doc had taken several telepathic excursions tonight with Kara including her first few hours on Earth. None was reality. None was illusion either. They were perfect projections of reality. "BB, hand an arrow to me. I think I now know how she drove her spaceship down through three hundred feet of solid ice."

"You bet, Dr. Lambert. Sure thing. Here you go."

"Everyone. Place your hands on the stone." Kate waited until the three had done so. "Now! Watch!" Kate lifted Doc's hand away from the rock and placed the arrow where it had been. She waited a second and then pushed the arrow through solid granite with no more resistance than if it had been an open window. She repeated it for Puck and BB.

She announced, "It's a trap all right. But not for us."

Puck shook his head and smiled. "Literally, like shooting rats in a barrel. We pop them safely from behind our blind."

"Cool, Bro." BB and Puck tapped fists.

Puck turned to Kate and Doc and pointed at the now transparent portal. "Not looking a gift horse in the mouth and all, but how, what is all this?"

Doc answered, "This, my young friend, is ancient alien technology developed far across the universe by a race of machines so superior to us that we are bacterial in comparison."

"Doc, you are forgetting something. Kara was in that jug until just tonight and that Resumption guy, Jussard, says these shafts are pretty recent."

BB added, "Me and Puck don't need no engineer to age these shafts. None's two months old. Three tops. Some are just days old."

Puck nodded and said, "That's the straight skinny, Bro."

"Good point, boys. Then we must conclude she has an ally—someone else helping her."

"If he's helping her, he's helping us."

BB sighed. "This just gets strangier and mangier by the minute. Puck, did we leave the galaxy or am I just drunk?"

"I ain't sure about nothing, BB, except you ain't toasty, and we are definitely in another world."

BB stared at the rock for a moment and asked, "I've got a dumb question. If we can see out, can the space rats see in? Worse, they are machines, inorganic like the arrow. Can they also pass through the stone?"

Doc and Kate looked at each other and agreed. "Probably not. Kara would surely have allowed for that. However, there is only one way we can be sure. We'll have to go back outside."

BB said, "I'll go. I'm the tallest, so if I have to hop back inside in a hurry, I've got the best chance of making it. While I'm out there, I think I'll set out a few surprises."

Puck protested, but he knew two things: BB's logic was correct and secondly, once BB made up his mind, convincing the earth to reverse its orbit around the sun might be easier than persuading his best friend to change his mind.

"All right, I'm coming with you, Bro. You'll need backup, another set of eyes while you lay down the ordnance."

"Won't work." Kate said. "I'll go outside with BB. If we get trapped outside, Puck, you are the only one who can use the bow. Plus, I now know a bit about this entity. Not much, but maybe just enough to save our skins if they show up unexpectedly."

Doc winced. "Kate dear, are you sure that's necessary?"

Kate leaned down and placed her forehead on the professor's. She spoke softly and chose the right word. The one reserved just for times like these. The word that said she loved him, and that he should trust her judgment. "No getting around it, Papa. We'll be fine. Okay?"

Kate waited until Doc nodded, which he followed with a defeated shrug. She turned to BB. "Let's do it. Puck, give me the shotgun."

"Cool. You need a quick lesson?"

"Nope. I had a great teacher." As Kate rechecked the safety and confirmed that the Mossberg was fully loaded, she brushed Doc's cheek and mouthed, "I love you."

"Katie... I wish..."

"She placed her index finger on his lips and said, "Save those wishes for later. Okay? I'll make every one of them come true for you."

Puck said, "BB, you set those charges and get back inside. No dillydallying, Bro. Dig?"

"Dig? My mama was half marmot and half prairie dog. I'm a natural born digger."

"Your mama was a queen."

"Queen of queens she was."

Doc and Puck slid the boulder back. Kate made a move to be out first, but BB anticipated her and squeezed through before her. By the time she reached the mine floor, BB had already propped up two flashlights aiming in opposite directions down the shaft and was setting the first booby trap.

Kate cupped her mouth and whispered, "Seal it up, Doc. Puck!" A moment later, the boulder resealed the entrance. Then magically, as agreed, an arrow passed through what appeared, felt, and weighed like solid granite seal. Kate grasped the arrow and pulled it the rest of the way through. "I'll be damned, Kara," she whispered in amazement.

She turned the point of the arrow against the portal, scratched, tapped, and then jabbed it hard against the granite. Nothing. She cupped her ear and listened to some distant, muffled laughter. The portal was definitely one way.

A moment later BB stepped next to Kate. "I set two charges. The first is a teaser, which hopefully will make the bastards ignore the second. The second charge is shaped and means serious business."

The pseudo granite seal opened and Kate and BB reentered the sanctuary.

***

Three machines tore through the ceiling of the chamber and attacked, spraying their deadly aerosolized venom.

The first chamber was empty.

They dove into the mineshaft and continued their search for The One.

***

Mayor Cole Kilpatre awoke from a nightmare in which he was Robert Shaw, the insane Captain Quint, skipper of the ill-fated shark-hunting vessel the *Orca*. Jaws, the great white shark wriggled onto the Orca's stern and took Quint's leg, then more.

Unlike the fictional Captain Quint's, Kilpatre's tibia was not missing. The mayor's leg bone was self-evident, in fact, two inches of bloody nonfictional tibia protruded through his pant leg.

He bellowed once about his many pains, vomited and then passed out.

# CHAPTER 69 ~~ Hunters Hunted

Chris Jussard and Buck Tumulley studied the sensors and knew what the change in the static meant. "Sheriff, the aliens are definitely near, and they are on the move."

"Can you determine a heading?"

"Negative, well, at least not yet." Buck answered, pessimism evolving to optimism by sentence's end.

Chris Jussard added, "Something else. I think they've split up, just like we did."

Roe and Rogers took up defensive positions. "They are hunting us, Sheriff," Roe announced matter-of-factly.

Buck looked up, closed his eyes and made several mental calculations. "Sheriff, they have indeed changed. If I'm recalling accurately the signature of their accent earlier tonight, their mass has roughly sextupled."

"Then can you tell how many we are dealing with?" Renner asked.

The Resumption scientists conferred for a moment. Jussard answered, "No. We have to assume that like earlier tonight they did not commit their entire force. Nothing survived our trap, but clearly they avoided extermination. However, Buck and I feel a strong probability that their attack force consists of approximately six machines."

Buck exclaimed, "I have their heading! Three are headed this way."

"And the others?" Renner asked, already sensing information he would soon regret. He dropped to his knees and planted the first C4 explosive.

Buck looked up from the cobbled-together seismic reader and shook his head. "They are heading toward Kate, Doc and the demo boys. Sorry, Sheriff."

\*\*\*

Doc Karl slumped against the granite wall of the chamber and continued to marvel at its design. Absently scratching a day's worth of gray beard stubble, he asked, "Katie, my love, how many of these chambers did we pass before arriving at this one?"

"I'm not sure, Doc. Maybe or eight or nine."

Puck confirmed it, "Yep, it were nine. Me and BB counted 'em. We are in number ten. The last one."

Doc continued, "I wonder what the others are for."

"Good question, Doc. Kara does nothing unnecessarily. There has to be a purpose."

Doc nodded. "Yes, but what is it? A shell game?"

\*\*\*

James George, Snatch, Kara, Hoop, Isaac, Newton and Sasha. A genius, an immortal, an alien, a shift-changer-male alien and three common house pets. Together, they departed Snatch's granite castle.

The path they took was unlike any James had witnessed tonight. It inclined about an inch every ten feet and spiraled downward through an arching hallway. Its curves eluded the eye like a rainbow's end. The walls on either side were as smooth as glass and about ten feet high.

Etched in the surface a quarter inch deep and on practically every square inch of the wall was a form of writing that appeared to be hieroglyphic, Cyrillic, Mayan, and dozens of ancient cuneiform iterations. All of it had an unintelligible mathematic theme.

"Mr. Snatch. What is the meaning of this and who carved it?" By James's calculations they had already passed more than a mile of the cipher, and judging by Snatch's pace, more was to follow.

"Me wrote it all, but for the love of the Tar Nation, and all her good souls, I haven't a clue what it means. Ask me sweet gal from Golden."

"Kara?"

"Good."

"Good what?"

"Just 'good.'"

"Are you telling me that this is the concept of 'good' reduced to a mathematical formula?"

"No."

"Kara, I don't understand."

"Then see!"

The plane of Time once again emerged in James' mind. An infinite maze revealed every permutation and consequence of every act and event that the cosmos allowed. Two paths rose up from the myriad: In one, humankind and all other life on Earth perished. Kar's numbers multiplied geometrically. The Federation restored. The predator consumed all organic and inorganic material on the planet. Possessing man's intellect, curiosity, tools and now the knowledge to use both, the immortal machines left Earth and returned to the stars, rendering all in its way. The second path included humankind and the Kar.

What Kara showed James staggered him. He was once again in Maine riding his father's shoulders, gazing into the summer night sky at the stars and fantasizing space travel.

"Would you like to go see the stars, Jimmy McCauley?" Kara asked.

"Yes! I would like to very much, Kara. But how?"

"Can you learn the formula for Life, the precious creation?"

James stared at the wall. A snippet of a pattern emerged. Nothing as immense as the tip of an iceberg, but something infinitely smaller, the scant hint of a lone molecule of truth. It was enough, though. "Yes, I don't care how long it takes me, but I will learn this equation."

"Then you must stay here and begin immediately," Kara said. Kara no longer spoke in her handicapped English, but to his mind in her native Kar.

"Stay here by myself? No! Why?"

"Because fate has placed you, and only you here. Dear child, we must leave you now. I cannot help you again until the Exterms are dead. Humans must fight them alone."

"But, Kara! We are counting on you! We... we can't fight them! They are too powerful."

"It is the ten-eighty, James George. You have taken us onto a different path, a different fate. If Hoop and I confront the Exterms now, you and the big man will die. Hoop and I cannot bear losing you. We must hide and only watch. Open your mind and see."

Time's plane emerged, pulsed, floated in and out of the wall like a cloud. On every path into the future except one, James George watched his life wink out. On that lone course, Kara and Hoop were absent. James George opened his eyes and looked up at Kara. A tear rolled down his cheek. He reached out to her and nodded. Life was on its own.

Kara transformed into her natural humanoid form. She kneeled and embraced James George. Kara closed her eyes and pressed her forehead against his. "The past cannot be changed. The present is complete. The future is yours to determine. You will find a way. You must. The battle for the Creation is now, dear child."

Kara rose and transformed back into the giant rat. Snatch kneeled in front of James. "There are ten more floors below us, Jamesie. Walk with us to the bottom. That is where the code begins. If all goes according to me wee girl's plan, we will meet you soon and Life shall prevail."

***

The machines penetrated the second and third chambers and sprayed the lethal gas. The vessels were empty. The trio dropped into the mineshaft and continued their search for the One.

***

Alpha Genesis observed telepathically as his six offspring continued the search for the One. He must be found. His genes must be acquired. His kind must be advanced.

Find, he commanded.

Yes, the pack answered.

***

James George watched with great unease as his party passed through a granite portal at the bottom of the long ramp and disappeared. Kara was the last to leave. She turned toward the child and helped him recall a memory—a distant, possible future memory.

James George is no longer eight, going on nine. He is twenty-nine years old, an age that does not change as he travels to the distant stars. He commands a vessel created from his own design, crewed by this very party as well as some new friends added along the journey. His memories are alive, literally. His adoptive parents, Renner and

Kate, Doc, the Demo boys, Erin and Josh are all there. Their protective aura never leaves his side. He meets his real parents. Their names are...

Kara abruptly withdrew the vision.

"Kara! Let me see more! Please!"

Kara made her choking, drowned-sounding chuckle, "That is up to you, child. Make it so. Now translate the code of Life!"

Disappointed, but motivated by the oldest manipulation in the universe: Finish your vegetables or no dessert, James turned to the first line of code, studied it and nodded. When he looked back at Kara, she had disappeared. He was alone.

\*\*\*

Alpha Genesis and the matriarch female crept silently through the maze of new tunnels—man-made passageways that defied his recall. He resisted every shortcut, always stayed to the path. It would have been easy for the machines to bore from tunnel to tunnel to speed up the search, but Alpha sensed that the enemy could now detect such acts. He sensed something else, something urgently important about the One.

\*\*\*

The fourth chamber fell. The attack came from above. A coordinated blast of noxious gas. It was empty. The three attackers dropped into the mineshaft and continued the search.

# CHAPTER 70 ~~ Making a Stand

Chris Jussard and Buck Tumulley huddled over the jerry-rigged seismic reader. They conferred for a moment and agreed. Jussard announced, "Sheriff, Buck predicts contact with three of the entities in about five minutes at their current pace."

Josh Roe held out his hand and looked up. "Erin, you feel that downdraft? You thinking what I'm thinking?"

"Yeah. They vented the tunnels using the same principle as the towering termite mounds on the Serengeti."

"Sheriff," Roe said, "Erin and I recommend making our stand here. There is a strong downdraft. They'll have to attack us in a mild headwind."

Buck turned and asked, "Won't that just aid them making it easier to catch our scent?"

Rogers answered. "Yes, but it will also blow their venom back into their faces and keep it off us, maybe just long enough."

Renner agreed with the agents' plan. "Okay, let's establish a defense. He turned to the two FBI agents. Select three fallback positions. Arm and booby-trap each location. We move in threes and twos, providing cover for tactical retreat. Concentrate fire on a single target until it is destroyed."

Tumulley's question was on everyone's mind. He gestured toward the cache of explosives and asked, "Will these things do the job?"

Renner's response was as certain as their circumstances allowed. "Well Buck, we'll soon find out. Let's make it happen."

# CHAPTER 71 ~~ The Code of All

The code on the first floor started with the most basic binaries in the universe: positive versus negative, on versus off, ones versus zeros, singular versus bidirectional, expansion versus contraction. This universal truism was demonstrated dozens of ways, some so interesting, that if only his current situation wasn't so dire, James could have immersed himself for days in the propositions.

James smiled. At the end of the first lesson, the writer gave him the option to select a path of understanding. James chose a simple binary—ones and zeros, and proceeded.

Next was an alphabet of sorts. Not the 26 to 112 characters that reduced human language to the written word, but one that possessed $2^{43,112,609}-1$ building blocks, a number over ten million digits long, representing the largest prime number ever discovered. James absorbed the language like constructing a pyramid floating in space from its apex downward. He did not need to memorize it, though, just use the subtly changing but predictable pattern, one block to the next, one layer stacked below the previous. As he reached the base of this mental construction, he stopped as instructed. He realized that the alphabet could expand in an ever more orderly manner, representing eventually every permutation of every language in the universe.

\*\*\*

The fifth and sixth chambers fell. The attack was so perfectly choreographed, the timing of each machine's movement and footfall so identical to the previous invasions, if videoed, the first six attacks could flawlessly overlay on film.

\*\*\*

"Sheriff, we have contact!" Buck Tumulley announced. "One hundred meters and heading our way at one meter per second."

"Buck, are they in the corridor? Above us or below?"

"Yes, yes in the corridor!"

"Thank you, Buck. Everyone, listen up. Direct our fire only on the leader. Await my order. No explosive rounds, just the 9mm. Empty one clip. Then retreat to our first fallback position. Questions?"

Rogers asked the question to which everyone wanted the answer. "Sheriff, just one salvo with the light stuff?"

"Yes, Erin. These creatures are adapting to whatever we throw at them. They'll expect us to use the C4, so we won't use it. If they see the explosives, and we don't use them, they might move more cautiously. Also, I suspect they will sacrifice one member of their pack to test our strength. We will let loose with everything we've got after they are fully committed to the attack.

The team nodded agreement. Renner sensed that their attackers were as aware of the ambush as he was, so he sacrificed exposing their position in exchange for a better view of the oncoming assault and ordered the passageway illuminated with as much flashlight as possible.

The five stood shoulder to shoulder in the pathway, weapons raised, safeties off, fingers resting outside the trigger guards.

The aliens turned into the corridor, a leader and two wingmen. They saw the humans and stopped.

"Ready!" Renner ordered calmly. He moved his finger from the trigger guard onto the trigger.

Buck Tumulley's teeth chattered. His gun hand trembled, more than his left could steady it. The temptation to bolt was overwhelming.

"Easy, Buck. Await my order."

"Yes, Sir! I'm trying. I just want this nightmare over."

"Sheriff, what the hell are those things?" Josh Roe asked. "They look nothing like Kara."

Rogers speculated, "They must have morphed when they adapted to our weapons. But, how is that even possible?"

The machines' hides were ebony and plated, like an armadillo's, and they appeared to be as impenetrable as an Abrams tank. They clicked and clacked as they moved with the tinny sound of titanium tabs. Their eyes pulsed from red to black to violet to iridescent yellow as they examined their quarry through different wavelengths of light.

Each eye possessed an external second socket that rotated transparently over its orb. Three metallic-appearing claws tapped the granite. A fourth talon, much larger than the three on the forefoot, a Velociraptor's hooked claw on its heel, likewise tapped the granite.

Renner examined the creatures for a weakness and discovered none. The monsters appeared indestructible. "Hold your fire." He hesitated for a moment and asked. "Does anyone smell anything unusual?"

Chris Jussard had noticed the scent too. With the irregular breeze at their backs, it was barely discernible. "Gasoline. I think I smell gasoline, Sheriff. What the hell!"

"Yes, I do too." Rogers confirmed.

The machines prepared to attack and rose onto their hind legs.

Renner saw an opening, literally. "Aim for the mouth. That's how they'll gas us, like a spitting viper. Aim just for the one in the middle. Empty your clip and retreat to our fallback position."

The machines' bodies elongated several lengths. Their bull-sized heads brushed the mineshaft's high ceiling while claws sunk like pneumatically driven railroad spikes into the floor. Their mouths gaped open wide, and they tossed a measure of gas—just enough to dispatch these humans and not the One if near.

"Fire!" Renner ordered.

The pistol fire was deafening. They spent fifty 9mm rounds in four seconds. All of Renner's, Roe's, and Roger's rounds struck their target—the middle machine's gaping mouth. Nine of Tumulley's and seven of Jussard's hit as well.

As Renner had hoped, luck was on the side of humankind, at least for the moment. The draft surged down the ventilation chute and into the corridor just as the attack commenced, safely blowing the poison away from the humans. The other good fortune, ironically, was that the bullets seemed to have no effect.

"Pull back!"

The Federation machines analyzed the humans' weapons and the headwind and adjusted their counterattack. Caution was now unnecessary. The humans' weapons were harmless, and they were unwilling to use their explosives. Secondly, they would chase the enemy, who were now demonstrating their willingness to flee until the poison was more effective.

Renner explained, "Okay, now's our chance. We attack all three with the bows and the C4. Again, aim for their mouths. They'll be careless now. I suspect they have been feeding on petroleum. It's unlikely they recognize the risk it poses. It's in their lungs, and I doubt those organs are as protected. Let's hope we can give them some real heartburn."

The machines advanced and set up for the next attack. The breeze was still in their faces, but to overcome that impediment was only a minor adjustment. They rose up, anchored their claws, and then opened their mouths to release the gas.

Renner, Josh and Erin took aim. The creatures stood less than twenty feet away. "Fire!" They released the crossbow arrows and ducked for cover. This close to the explosions, the shockwave also detonated the C4 booby traps sending all three humans sailing across the mine's smooth floor like hockey pucks.

Renner was the first on his feet with another arrow ready. He surveyed the battlefield. They had neutralized three aliens. Aflame from the inside out and their heads missing, the machines' necks were chimneys of fire. However, the victory came at a tremendous price. Chris Jussard and Buck Tumulley were gone as well, or almost. A few stray molecules of poisonous gas had found both men, who now boiled away to nothing on the mine floor.

\*\*\*

Alpha Genesis felt and witnessed the termination of his three offspring as vividly as if he were present at the battle. He waited for the feedback that would not come. The enemy had killed again by using a weapon that Kar could not appropriate, something not genetically introgressant.

\*\*\*

The unoccupied seventh, eighth and ninth chambers fell to the Kar at about the same moment that their three siblings terminated. They now understood this human tactic—setting traps with bait.

Alpha Genesis adjusted the hunt and divided his forces again. He ordered one female and one male to separate and continue the search in different parts of the matrix. The female tore through the mineshaft's ceiling, the male descended to the lower levels. The remaining alien continued the current search plan.

***

Cole Kilpatre drifted in and out of consciousness. A slab of meaty flotsam slammed onto an inhospitable shoreline only to be snatched by the next ferocious wave.

Nightmares, heightened by his many injuries, hypothermia, shock, and insanity rose with ever-increasing intensity. In one dream, he was trapped inside an insect's muddy cocoon, a paralyzed spider offered to a wasp's larvae as food. In another, he was lynched by a mob, his neck separating from his corpulent body with a sickening snap as the gallows opened beneath him.

In a third, a giant rat stood over him. It was coated in black scales. Its eyes constantly changed colors. The creature tapped its claws on the granite floor as it examined the prey. To Kilpatre it sounded like miners' pickaxes drumming a furious beat.

# CHAPTER 72  ~~  Stop And Think

James George progressed up the ramps deciphering the code on the walls at the pace of a casual stroll through a museum. He had mastered differential calculus in an afternoon, but now rediscovered Sir Isaac Newton's mathematical invention from four new perspectives.

One iteration of Newton's calculus revealed a unique manipulation of Time, another of Matter, and a third of Energy, each as reliably and predictably convertible to the other iterations, as Fahrenheit to Centigrade or dollar to euro.

The fourth iteration was not so easily grasped. It seemed to incorporate a theory that James called Corruption. The formulas were illogical, the calculations irrational, but the results were both logical and rational and dependent on combining the hypothetical principles of dark energy and dark matter with string theory. "This is the mathematics of $k$-energy!" he exclaimed. "Excellent!"

James brushed his fingers over the etchings. He sensed that they represented more than a simple juxtaposition of old, new and irrational mathematics but also the relationship of matter and antimatter particles. Moreover, James had the overwhelming feeling that the creator of the code intended that he pause and contemplate its significance. A foot of clear space followed the last line of code. Its suggestion was unmistakable: STOP NOW AND THINK!

James plopped down Indian style onto the sloping concourse and studied the wall. From his backpack, he retrieved a bottle of water and a Snickers candy bar. He was exhausted, but the need to sleep was overcome by his need to know.

James tore open the Snickers, took a bite and began replaying in his mind the last thirty-six hours. Unlike the merely intelligent, James raced through every event, conversation, observation, and experience with a level of detail and insight that only a camera and philosopher might capture.

He recalled the recent dream journeys.

He recalled his telepathic communications with Kara.

He recalled assembling a casting of a karpeleotroceme's dental work from millions of years ago.

He recalled standing amongst prehistoric creatures, giant insects, and herds of animals.

He recalled the reanimation of a dead man, Mr. Hoop, and a very old but still mysteriously vital Mr. Snatch.

He recalled the lessons on the wall—the fluidity, the multidimensional nature of Newton's expanded calculus of Time, Matter, Energy, and Corruption.

Now James understood. The impossible was now probable. The boundaries of physics were no longer impenetrable borders. Humankind was about to leave its crib. Time, Matter and Energy were mere modes of transportation to places and epochs that expanded like the universe itself.

James recalled the first building blocks of the code, the collection of rudimentary binary propositions on the bottom floor: Action vs. Reaction, and Creation vs. Destruction. That's also when James recalled what Kara had called the code. Suddenly alarmed, he sprang to his feet. Before him was the code for 'Good,' the scientific blueprint for Life. Therefore, unmistakably, the code writer warned that somewhere else in the universe, or perhaps herein, was the countervailing force—Evil, or as better described, the absence of Life.

\*\*\*

In the tenth and last chamber, Doc was asleep and leaning against Kate's shoulder. Judging by his restlessness, the professor was not experiencing a peaceful slumber. Kate silently wrote and rewrote about karpeleotroceme, the most significant discovery ever made, not just paleontologically, but also scientifically. However, the intellectual exercise, even one so fascinating, could not distract her from worrying about Renner and James George.

BB touched Puck's shoulder and gestured toward the portal. He whispered, "Something's out there, Bro."

The Exterm stepped in front of the portal and stood up on his hind legs. It would not attack. It would be cautious. The alien cocked its head from side to side, interrogating, searching for the prize his Alpha required: The One.

The creature communicated with Alpha.

This was a trap.

# CHAPTER 73  ~~  Truths Revealed

The more James deciphered, the faster the code unraveled before him. Stephen Hawking's "brief" explanation of time revealed itself in just six feet of code. However, the permutations of the great physicist's understated "brevity" rolled on for another two floors: stopping time, multiple planes of time, time viruses, time wraparounds, time traps, time loops, time matter exception, time warps, time skips, time levers, bending time and more.

"Oh, Professor Einstein, you would be so fascinated with ren time."

Engineering, medicine, genetics and dozens of other scientific disciplines, some not yet discovered, came to life on the wall on a seemingly infinite continuum of past, present and future.

Across the universe, near its very edge, a sun is born from a womb of gas, delivered to a star nursery a hundred million light years across. Another star dies, collapses, and sends two columns of deadly gamma rays ten billion light years across the universe and... Right before his eyes, a new etching appeared on the wall: two sine waves, a small peak wave followed immediately by a taller peak—the unmistakable signature of the gamma ray.

"Wow. That just happened as I watched. Professor Einstein, your theory on time just got busted by psi!"

***

BB whispered, "Puck, would you look at that thing! Can it see us, Bro?" Both men held their crossbows at the ready. Kate and Doc stood over them with their firearms cocked and aimed.

"Yeah, man, I think so. But I don't know how." The creature's eyes moved from BB to Puck as the men spoke, somehow seeing through the granite.

Kate inspected the machine through the one-way portal with the objective eye of a scientist. The interrogation was mutual. The alien's eyes lifted and looked directly into Kate's. Kate felt a wave of energy wash over her as if she were standing in front of a pair of towering loudspeakers emitting a frequency felt, but not heard.

Kate did not resist.

"Where is the One?"

"The One?" Kate mumbled, dreamily.

The three men turned to her.

"Katie! What is it?" Doc took Kate's elbow and squeezed it, then shook it to wake her up.

The machine mined deeper into Kate's mind. "Where is the... special One?"

Kate's eyes turned white, rolling backward in their sockets. Her body convulsed, slowly at first, then rapidly, violently, lurching as if electrocuted. Her lungs heaved and emptied in a wet burst. Kate's complexion purpled as the alien suffocated her. Blood flowed from both her nostrils and merged into foamy saliva erupting at the corners of her mouth. Her tear ducts emptied into rivulets down her cheeks. The men could do little more than hold her body down to protect it from slamming against the granite walls and floor.

Kate's convulsions intensified. Waves soared through her body. Doc cried, "Katie! Hang on! Hang on, baby girl... BREATHE!" He rolled Kate's body on top of his own, her back to his chest then leg-locked his legs and Kate's together. Doc wrapped his arms around her and hung on as if riding a bucking horse from beneath. Kate's head slammed into Doc's repeatedly, broke his nose, split both lips, loosened his front teeth, but he refused to release her.

Kate felt nothing of the alien's assault. In her nightmare, she sat behind her desk at the museum in Denver. A bright light flashed beyond the desk. Kate covered her eyes. When she lowered her hands, before her stood the humanoid machine. The creature made a fist and shook it threateningly at Kate. The alien then unfurled its index finder and tapped its temple. The warning was unambiguous: Learn or suffer. There was another flash of light and the alien was gone.

Fluttering down from the ceiling like a delicate feather, a yellowed handwritten note landed upright on the desk blotter. On it she read: $S = k \log W$

Kate had double majored in physics as an undergraduate at University of Colorado and immediately recognized Ludwig Boltzmann's mathematical reduction of Sadi Carnot's Principle—the Second Law of Thermodynamics. This pioneer theorized that the release of energy—entropy—is always increasing in the universe.

The piece of paper erupted in flames. It rose on its own thermals and hung in the air before Kate at eye level.

Kate examined the suspended ashes. Instead of falling back to the desk, the ash cloud began to spin on an imbalanced axis, slowly at first, but as it accelerated, the outer ash folded toward the mass's center and began forming a ragged sphere.

Kate leaned closer to study the object. Her nose was just inches from it. The tip of her nose began to tingle as the ball of ash spun faster, more evenly. The ash compacted tighter and tighter, shrinking in size until the black ball was barely visible.

Three tiny rings of dust drew around the suspended speck, orbiting it like the rings of Saturn. The inner band disintegrated and fell into the center. Larger dust belts formed and just as quickly, the rings collapsed to the center. The process repeated itself repeatedly, faster and faster, and it became larger as more rings rose and fell into the black speck.

Another dream within the dream launched itself in Kate's mind even as she continued to watch the first. She witnessed firsthand the Big Bang, the birth of our universe 13.5 billion years ago. She then witnessed the ultimate battle for survival—the ensuing war between matter and antimatter particles in which matter won by a hair. She observed our universe cool and give birth to its first star as well as its death 2.7 billion years later. She witnessed dark energy expand the universe even as gravity consolidated it from within.

The Federation Kar appeared in Kate's dream at her side suspended in space. The alien was in its natural form. The creature took Kate's hand and pointed to a distant point in space. A moment later, they arrived on a battle line where war was imminent. The combatants were mortal enemies: matter vs. antimatter. The alien clapped his hands and Kate watched the two neighboring universes just disappear. The war was over in just two Planck units—just $1/149,896,229^{th}$ of one second—as the matter and antimatter universes collided. The combined energy released by the disintegrated universes equaled their births.

"Why are you showing me this?" Kate asked.

"Because we seek the One, Nonbeing. Surrender the One and you will suffer no worse than what you just witnessed. Your resistance is futile. Your death is certain."

"Go to hell!" Screen two blinked out and Kate returned to her Denver office.

On screen one, the alien nodded as if to say, as you wish. It elongated into a vaporous filament and disappeared into the tiny speck of spinning ash.

A fleck of hair rose on Kate's brow and pointed at the object as if a metal shaving obeying a magnet's call. More hair rose, her eyelashes, eyebrows bristled electrically. Her eyes dried with the desiccation of a salt plain. Kate backed away. The tickling sensation on the tip of her nose was replaced by a bee's painful sting.

She stepped further away. It was becoming increasingly difficult to breathe. The alien black hole sucked the air from the room. She backed into the doorway and watched the office surrender to the speck. Papers rose from her desk, spiraled through the air in hundreds of whirlpools, and disappeared.

"It created a black hole," Kate whispered hoarsely as the air in her lungs was snatched away by the speck that never grew in diameter regardless of the matter it absorbed. There was a singularity, the horizon event.

Books, files, desk mats, and portraits rose from their places and spun toward oblivion. Light from the lamps stretched like wisps of smoke and disappeared. Carpet fibers grew from the floor like mutant bean sprouts and twisted into darkness. The painted walls gave up their properties as a cloud. The gypsum board beneath bubbled outward, buckled and imploded with a roar. The wooden studding cracked, split and sent its cellulose fibers spinning into the storm, dismantled fibrously like a clothes drier's lint. The desk, bookshelves, and office furniture levitated off the floor and began to spin. Their shapes stretched like taffy into an orbital, and then as their molecular cousins had gone before them, they fell to the center and disappeared.

The darkness expanded toward Kate. She gasped for breath. Her feet slid out from beneath her as she backpedaled a futile retreat. She braced herself against the doorjamb, but it dismantled into sawdust. She rose off the floor as much as it fell beneath her and joined the black hole's outer ring, spinning ever faster, stretching, tearing apart, disintegrating...

***

"It's killing her, boys! We have to do something!" Doc cried out with all the authority and hope he could muster. He had no idea where the Kar had taken Kate, but having been on a few excursions tonight with Kara, he knew that anything might be possible. "It's killing her!"

Puck and BB looked at each other and nodded. The men had grown up together and could almost read the other's mind. "Puck? You thinkin' what I'm..."

"Yeah, Beebs. Let's do it. Let's pop this effer through this one-way wall. That's why Kara put us in here, you reckon?"

"Hell yes, makes sense!"

The target was unmistakable. The machine's head was level with the portal and nodding back and forth in an odd figure eight motion. Its mouth gaped wide.

"One... Two... THREE!"

The C4-tipped arrows passed through the wall without resistance and struck the Kar in the back of the creature's throat. The explosion literally shredded the machine. The concussion also detonated the two mines that BB had planted earlier.

Puck and BB braced themselves, but surprisingly little of the shockwave penetrated their cocoon. Satisfied the demo candy had done its job, they turned their attention to Doc and Kate. Her convulsions mercifully ended, but now, something far worse threatened her life. Added to suffocation, her heart had stopped.

"Breathe, Katie! Please!" Doc blew air into her lungs, but her chest did not rise.

"Doc! Let me and BB take over," Puck ordered. In the mountains you can throw a rock and you're likely to strike an EMT. Throw another and you'll hit two more.

"Beebs, you do exterior cardiac massage. I'll get her wind going. GO!"

It was the longest forty-five seconds in Norman Karl's life, every fraction of every moment a torturously precarious tipping point that teetered between the heaven called Katie and an unimaginable hell without her. Tears streamed down his cheeks. Katherine Lambert was more than his student, his friend and colleague. Much more. She was his hope. She was his daughter in every sense other than their uncommon genes. Kate was the dearest, most precious love of his life, his pride, everything a father might dare hope for. "Please, boys, help her," he begged.

\*\*\*

Kate spun faster and faster in the cluttered outer ring, each orbit pulling her farther down into the whirlpool. She called out to Doc and James George one last time, but it was a silent cry, for oxygen had already surrendered to the black hole. She closed her eyes and forced herself to see Renner in the corral yesterday, heart strong, physically exhausted, sitting there on the fence smiling at Kate, then offering her his jacket to stave off a shiver that had nothing to do with winter weather. She tasted his last kiss. She looked into his eyes and heard him call her name. His lips covered hers, and she drew him closer until they were one. Renner then took her hands and pulled her away, faster, powerfully, and the black hole finally lost its influence. Together they tumbled out.

"I've got a pulse, Puck!"

"Come on, Dr. Lambert! Breathe!"

Kate escaped from death with a gasp, but unlike a drowning victim who returns to the land of the living groggy and sick, Kate sat up as alert and alive as the three men and then sprang to her feet. "You killed it! Yes?"

"Popped it right through the one-way wall," Puck reported. "Sent two arrows right down its confessor.

BB added, "You bet, Dr. Lambert! Puck and me blowed that effer straight to hell, and there weren't no complimentary hand baskets neither." Puck and BB tapped fists.

"Katie, you scared us half to death. I was so…"

Kate interrupted the professor and blurted. "Doc! These creatures, they are not what we think they are."

"Easy, my dear! Let's catch our breath before…"

Kate did not seem to hear the suggestion. "Oh, God no! This cannot be. Doc, the creatures are not alive, at least not in the way we define life. They are pure energy, but they are also capable of materializing selectively into almost anything organic or inorganic they choose. They can move at will from an energetic state to matter and back to energy in almost the blink of an eye. They are literally capable of destroying anything in their path. Anything! And their numbers are unlimited."

"Honey, they showed this to you?"

"Yes! They wanted us to know what they are. They also gave us an ultimatum. However, I have no idea what they want, only what's at stake."

"How did they communicate with you?"

"Telepathically. They imparted to me more knowledge in just seconds than any human could learn in a million lifetimes. It was similar to the telepathic trips Kara took us on, only even more bizarre."

"What else, sweetheart?" Kate's hands were shaking badly. Doc took them in his.

"They revealed to me a truth, Doc, something our theoretical physicists are just now unraveling at the most extreme edges of our understanding of the universe."

"Yes, dear. Please continue." Doc examined Kate for other lingering effects as she spoke.

"These creatures are the incarnation not just of energy, but of dark energy. They are the countervailing force to gravity."

"And you experienced this?"

"Yes! Like experiencing a split-screened nightmare. On one screen was a horrific, Kara-like telepathic journey across our universe that took place over billions of years. At the end, the alien demonstrated its power by somehow causing two universes to collide and destroy each other instantly. On the other screen, I watched the alien create a black hole, Doc. It absorbed everything near it, including me, almost."

"The power to create black holes? You say the alien actually caused the destruction of two entire universes? Absolutely amazing!"

"Yes! But I sensed that much of the dream will occur in the future."

"So the annihilation of two universes was a prophecy?"

"No! I sense not. The cataclysm will occur, as assuredly as if it already has happened."

"But how? How could that be done?"

"The destruction of the two universes was instantaneous, Doc. There is only one known event in the cosmos that could cause that."

"Antimatter!"

"Yes. Only the commingling of matter and antimatter could possibly produce such violent destruction. Worse, Doc, I am sure one of the universes was ours. That was why it showed the vision to me."

"So we are to be destroyed by antimatter? That is what they are threatening?"

"Yes. The demonstration was unambiguous. It was clearly a threat. They have mastered both the ability to create black holes as well as possess the ultimate destructive weapon—the ability to manipulate matter and antimatter. Can you imagine the destructive power of that combination if it was unleashed on the universe?"

"No. Humor me."

"First, think about reversing the Big Bang. Cosmologists call it The Big Crunch. The Gnab Gib. Matter, time, light, even space itself will no longer exist. Our entire universe reduced once again to an atom-sized ball of unimaginably dense energy. What Kara called *k*-energy!"

"Katherine, you are saying that's what these creatures are about? Creating the Big Crunch?"

"Yes, but I fear more than that. It's *how* they destroyed the two universes that leads me to believe the aliens themselves possess antimatter characteristics."

"Please explain.

"If my hypothesis is correct—that the aliens are a construct of both dark energy and antimatter—then they are literally the antithesis of us in every manner."

"That part is logical, but dark energy expands the universe. It is the countervailing force to gravity. How can the creatures be both? Gravity contracts the universe. Dark energy expands it."

"Yes, it is an enigma. It's also a problem I fear the creatures have solved."

"Go on, Dear."

"What if our universe is a binary construct?"

"Meaning?"

"Meaning that universes come in two flavors: matter or antimatter. Remember Doc, after our Big Bang, matter possessed a mere one-particle-per-billion advantage over antimatter. But that infinitesimal one point advantage was enough to make our universe a matter-based universe."

"Yes. That always amazes me, Katie. Only one particle in two billion survived after the Big Bang, and yet enough particles survived the conflagration to create our entire universe."

"It was a coin toss—a best of two-billion-to-one that gave us a matter-based universe. Theoretically, though, that means there are an equal number of matter-based and antimatter-based universes out there. Half are matter-based like us, and the other half are antimatter. What would happen if these matter and antimatter universes *were* made to collide somehow?"

"Absolute destruction! Instantly. As great as the Big Bang itself."

"What if these creatures seek to do just that? Facilitate the consolidation of our cosmos resulting in a single black hole powerful enough to draw neighboring universes into it. What if those other universes were antimatter-based?"

"Matter and antimatter particles destroy each other instantly. It would be a cataclysm—the spontaneous, simultaneous freeing of all energy in the multiverse. Unimaginable! Katherine, what you are describing is the terminal universe event—the destruction and death of our universe."

"Yes. The death of our universe, and most, if not all, of our neighboring universes. A chain reaction might occur across the pan cosmos. Independent matter and antimatter would no longer exist. All that would remain in the universe would be free energy."

"These creatures are the ultimate predator, Katie."

"Undoubtedly."

"But they are not quite there yet? They apparently need something to proceed. A catalyst, for lack of a more appropriate term."

"Yes. They seek a mechanism. They called it the One. They have offered us a painless death if we surrender it, whatever 'it' is."

"But two things still bother me, Katie. If the aliens are both dark energy and antimatter, how can they survive here surrounded by so much matter? Secondly, they are of our universe, yes?"

Kate did not answer. It was illogical. If their origin was this universe, they could not have transcended from antimatter.

After a moment of silence, BB spoke up. "Yo Docs, maybe these here space rats is sorta like the bull shark."

Doc Karl and Kate turned toward the demo man.

Puck said, "Shit! Beebs is right. They're just like the damn bull shark. Beebs loves *Animal Planet*. They should hire him as a narrator.

I don't even have to watch the shows anymore. I like how Beebs tells it better."

"Please explain it to us, young man." Doc said, clearing his throat.

"Tell 'em, Beebs."

"Well, you see, Doc Karl, Doc Lambert, Mr. Bull Shark is a freak of nature. Absolutely unique. He's the only shark that has adapted to both fresh and saltwater. He's even born in freshwater. Lives in it for years, too, 'til he bigs out and swims to the ocean. As an adult predator, he hunts inland rivers and the sea alike. As far as he's concerned, grub's grub and water's water. Mr. Bull Shark don't care none whichever. That's what these alien bastards is—like our bull sharks."

Doc laughed and clapped BB on the back, "Very good, Mr. Bainbridge. Very good, indeed. I suppose that makes as much sense as anything."

"Thank you, Sir."

Puck winked congratulations at his best friend.

Kate nodded and exclaimed "Yes! It really does make sense! Thank you, BB. The alien's ancient origin could have been in a neighboring antimatter universe. Over time an extraordinarily improbable crossover symbiosis occurred—a slow contamination on the extreme fringes of two universes. Billions, perhaps hundreds of trillions of worlds perished in the overlap before two lucky mutant entities survived the collision. Their offspring were hybrids, possessing the compartmentalized and safely accessible attributes of both matter and antimatter. Your first bull sharks, Mr. Bainbridge."

Doc studied the chamber walls as he spoke. "Yours and this young man's insight might also explain the destructive power of their venom, and their ability to burrow so fast, so cleanly. They use antimatter as the agent to destroy anything before them. Dark energy, matter-antimatter hybrids, immortality, and according to Kara they are sentient machines. How can we hope to stop them?"

Kate took Doc's hand. "That unfortunately explains their motive and strategy." She hesitated, and then added, "When the antimatter universes collide with ours, all that will survive will be an immune race of hybrid aliens and free energy."

# CHAPTER 74 ~~ Out of Time

Snatch finished the long downward journey into the mountain. The tunnel dead-ended at a smooth wall.

He placed his hand on the granite structure and announced, "This be the arse end of it, Kara. Me stopped the long, long dig here likes you told me. The rest is yours for doin.' What now?"

"Jimmy McCauley and the rest of us wait here."

"Wait for what, now can you tell me, good girl?"

"Now the time to wait. All up to the next Jimmy McCauley now."

***

"Josh, what're the seismic readers saying?" Renner asked over his shoulder.

"Nothing. Counterattack is not imminent. I'm guessing we have stalemate, Sheriff. We nailed three, and that leaves three plus the two they likely left in reserve."

Renner prompted Agent Rogers for her opinion. "Erin, what's your take?"

Rogers surveyed the battlefield and nodded. "I concur. Risk of second attack here is low."

Roe shouted, "Sheriff! I just picked up one hell of a two-stage explosion near the chambers where we left Kate and the others. We

391

detected two Kars break silence and start boring a few minutes earlier. They've split up. I speculate our side killed one more. So, if I'm right, we are down to four hostiles. Two hunting us. Two in reserve."

"Do you have a location on any?"

"Negative."

"Suggestions?"

Erin Rogers had spent what seemed like a dozen lifetimes in harm's way. More often than not, she was the pursuer. On rare occasions, when the odds were bad, she became the pursued. On rarer occasions, she was the decoy. This felt like none of these. "Sheriff, just a hunch, but I sense we are secondary targets."

McCauley lowered his weapon. "Please explain, Erin."

"Their search pattern, the way they are dividing and pursuing is…"

McCauley finished Roger's insight, "Shit! Of course, they are searching for someone or something specifically. Our attack should have drawn them all to us. But it didn't."

"Exactly. We are not their primary target. And judging by the fact that Kate's position is not under counterattack either… I'm guessing Kara, maybe even James George is their primary target."

Renner thought for a moment and said, "We might be able to use that to our advantage. Let's move."

"Where to, Sheriff?"

"Back to the others. Time to reinforce."

*** 

James reached the highest-level ramp. He concluded that this level was something akin to a book's appendix, a listing of its contents. This volume possessed two listings. A final binary. In the first, the universe continued its infinite expansion. In the second, the universe disappeared.

Just as James had earlier witnessed in real time the death of a star and the arrival of gamma rays ten-billion years before they could possibly reach earth, he saw four numbers slowly appear on the wall. The numbers were followed by two words, another binary. The characters etched into the wall like a fingernail on a chalkboard: 1-0-8-0. The First.

James gasped. His inside joke with Kara, 1080 was slang in the pest control business. "Ten-eighty is sodium fluoroacetate—1080 is rat poison!"

He backed away from the wall and began to shiver. James had made a terrible miscalculation.

***

Renner studied the smoldering remains of the alien Kar outside the last "safe room" where he had left Kate, Doc, BB and Puck. Satisfied the area was secure, he motioned Erin and Josh to move forward. He stepped in front of the sealed portal and nodded to those inside. Kate was first to climb out of Kara's hideout. Renner caught her and pulled her close to him.

Kate took inventory over Renner's shoulder. "Where are Buck and Chris?"

Josh Roe shook his head and used a flashlight to survey the mineshaft for evidence of more threats. His voice was matter-of-fact. "They didn't make it, Dr. Lambert."

Erin Rogers added, "We got three of them. How did you do here?"

Puck and BB helped Doc Karl down. Puck answered, "We got one. We was sure they'd all come callin,' cause that one we got had plenty of time to holler for reinforcements. Strange."

Again, Roe, "We are their secondary priority. They are after Kara." He met eyes with Renner and withheld the second possibility, that James George was the intended target.

Kate leaned away from Renner's embrace and looked up into his eyes. "Renner, we need to find James George."

"I know. We'll find him. I promise." Renner pulled her close to him again and kissed her forehead. He turned to Rogers who was studying something on the end wall where the tunnel dead-ended. "Erin, can you take point again? You got us this far."

"Sheriff, I think we are supposed to go this way. Come here and have a look." Roger's voice could not conceal her amazement.

Renner stepped next to Rogers. Erin moved the flashlight's beam over the inscription on the wall like a highlighting cursor. Chiseled in the wall were these instructions:

You'll find young Jamesie just beyond this wall, grandson. Don't think. Don't hesitate. He will be there. Don't try to understand just yet. He's in mortal danger. Have the boys blow the wall NOW! The 'git out' bell has already rung.

— James McCauley, Sheriff, Seer County, Colorado, 1886-1912

***

"Kara, me sweet girl, is it time?"

393

"Yes, Jimmy McCauley. It is time." Kara squatted down in front of the white rats and the bulldog. Hoop, the karpeleotroceme moved beside her. Kara added, "And the animals, they are not to come with us. Must stay here. Too dangerous."

Snatch unbuckled a backpack and removed several items. "Aye, we leaves our little friends the nibble of the good food and some water to hold them until they is found."

***

On his tiptoes James George reached up and touched the wall where the "1080" and "the First" had mysteriously appeared. The numbers were slightly warmer than the area around it. He felt something else too—a connection, a belonging—like finding an old handwritten letter and recognizing the handwriting but not what's written.

James's first warning that he had company was the click of Kar claws on the granite ramp. The movement came from just beyond his line of sight. He had no doubt as to what he heard or what was its source. James held his breath and began backing down the ramp. When he reached the next curve, he turned and sprinted.

An hour earlier while investigating these ramps it all seemed so right, even somehow safe, like he was protected. What a cruel illusion! For a child whose greatest foolishness was mere social faux pas, he had really messed up this time. He descended one more level and was beginning to believe he'd escaped the monster unnoticed.

James rounded the curve just as the second Kar entered his level on the long ovular ramp. The creature stopped and studied the human. James retreated a few steps. Then from above, more click clack of claws and metallic scales. It was a trap. He was literally surrounded. The monsters closed in slowly from above and below.

"Crawl like me, Jimmy McCauley! Crawl like sweet gal from Golden!"

James recognized Kara's voice. He turned and searched for her, but of course, the voice was only in his mind.

"Crawl! Now! Close eyes!"

James did as she instructed. He closed his eyes and fell onto all fours and then onto his stomach.

***

Renner wedged a flashlight between two rocks and aimed the beam on his grandfather's message. "Puck, how thick is this wall?"

BB tapped the wall with a rock and nodded to Puck. "Me and BB think it's no more than an inch or two, Mac. Lord knows what's on the other side. We've trimmed one arrow down to about a half ounce of C4. Should put a nice three-foot see through dent in the wall without hurting Jamesie, if he really is on the other side."

Josh Roe stepped next to Renner. "Sheriff, I don't have a clue how that message got on the wall, but I do smell serious trouble waiting on the other side."

"Me too, Josh. Go on."

"I think we have to assume that we are facing a serious rat problem, and that we need to be prepared to go in hot to save the boy."

"Agreed. What are you proposing?"

"Let's make a big enough hole that three of us can enter together—you, Erin and me. Most likely the maximum rats we'll face in there is two. You grab the kid while Erin and I draw their fire. My gut also tells me they have not adapted to our last trick. Two lucky headshots is all we need. In and out. If we fail, BB and Puck can blow the tunnel. It won't stop them, but it will slow them down enough that Kate and Doc can, well, you know."

Puck and BB had listened to it all. Renner turned to the demo men and said, "Can you do it? Make a hole big enough for three without injuring James if he's on the other side?"

Puck looked and BB and then Renner, "Shit, Mac, my Beebs here could open up a barbershop with nothing more to trim hair than a comb and C4."

Puck and BB conferred for a moment and reset the charges on the wall and on the arrows. "Everyone else, get behind the bend and take cover. Puck, BB you drop those bows the instant you release. Don't wait around to see the show." The two men nodded and aimed.

"Fire!"

***

From the curve in the ramp, James could now see both attackers clearly. One Kar descended the ramp while its mate ascended. They rose onto their hind legs just thirty feet away. Their mouths opened together, in perfect synchrony, choir-like. James saw the fluttery spasms cross over their abdomens as they lifted their antimatter venom.

"Jimmy McCauley, close eyes, cover ears! NOW!"

The wall behind and above James exploded, shattering outward in a deafening roar. Tucked within the lip of the curve and below the detonation, none of the rocky shrapnel found the child. Renner reached in and snatched James by his waist and retreated while Roe and Rodgers stepped through the opening to engage the enemy.

The creatures oriented on the humans and prepared to release their gas. Their jaws opened. Roe fired his arrow, followed by Rogers a split second later. However, the creatures *had* learned. Instinctively, they closed their mouths and ducked, avoiding certain death. The C4 exploded harmlessly against the mine wall.

Erin and Josh retreated a step and dropped the crossbows. The chamber filled with dust and smoke. The FBI agents drew their side arms and began firing. The bullets bounced off the Kar machines as if mere rocks thrown against a battleship's hull.

Josh Roe screamed into the mineshaft, "Sheriff! Run! Blow the shaft! Now!" The agents reloaded and retreated until their backs were against the chamber wall, but they kept firing. The firefight filled the corridor with gun smoke and dust.

Through the haze the Kars emerged, closing to within twenty feet. Their mouths opened once more and readied to deliver venom. Their abdomens clattered like metal washboards as the poison rose. Their jaws spread open further with a ferocious hiss.

Puck and BB ducked in and out of the newly created portal. That's all it took for them to obtain their targets. Puck nodded once and the demo men leaned through the portal a second time and took aim. Two arrows blurred through the air. This time the C4 found its marks. The arrows plunged into the backs of the two aliens' throats. A millisecond later, the chem-caps broke open and the creatures' heads exploded. The rest of their petroleum-based flesh soon caught fire.

Puck looked down at the two FBI agents. "You ladies okay?"

Rogers answered for both, "Never better, lover. Let's get the hell out of here."

The entire episode had taken just fifteen seconds. Kate and Doc did their best to smother James with love but it would have to wait. He pushed Kate and Doc away and ran to Renner. "We have a problem. They are not after Kara or any of us. They are after Mayor Kilpatre. He's the One... the one they need."

Relieved that James was not the Kars' target, but likewise now confused, Renner asked, "Kilpatre? Why Kilpatre, son?"

"I'm not sure."

"Can you guess?"

"I'd rather not just yet. It might sound crazy." James studied the adults and added, "But I will ask this. We have all seen some things tonight that don't make sense in the context of this world and this time. Am I correct in this assumption?"

Kate, who had nearly been killed by a black hole and witnessed the future annihilation of our universe answered, "Yes, James. Tonight only makes sense if we first rewrite the rules for this time and this world."

"I believe that is the answer. All of this is about the future. And the Future, at least one Future has returned here and is on our side."

# CHAPTER 75 ~~ The One

"Awake!" Alpha Genesis ordered The One. The creature stepped closer to Kilpatre and sifted through the mayor's mind, lifting a recent memory and a familiar voice.

Cole Kilpatre opened his eyes, and as if that small act alone was in the pain misery league of being thrown under a twenty-ton steamroller, the mayor shrieked.

"Boss, you okay? You must've had a nightmare."

"Hoop? You don't sound like you so much."

"Right here, Boss?"

"Where? I can't see you."

"Follow my voice, Boss. Just follow my voice."

"Hoop, my leg. I think I busted it."

"Nah, Boss. You just barked it up a little bit. It's fine." The machine reached telepathically inside Kilpatre's brain and began switching off the pain receptors.

"Hurts!"

"It's all in your head, Boss."

"It is?"

"Yep. Just a negative thought. What you need is something positive to think about. Something like gold. Now there's a positive thought. Shit pots full of gold, Boss! You coming?"

"Gold! Wait! Hoop, wait! Please."

Pain eased, drained over a psychotic waterfall, starting with the head wounds. The frostbite, the torn flesh that ranged proud from crotch to teat, and eventually even the agony of the compound tibiofibular fracture faded away. Kilpatre sat up and then stood. Bone ground against bone. More bone shards broke through the skin. Blood ran down the mayor's leg.

But Kilpatre felt nothing. He heard nothing except Hoop's distant, no longer familiar voice. His thoughts were of nothing but gold.

"This way. Follow my voice, Boss. You are The One."

"Damn right I'm the One! Numero Uno. The big cheese. Mr. fucking Mayor I am." Kilpatre lunged forward and found the wall in the dark with his face. His nose broke in two places, but he felt nothing even as blood surged over his lips onto his chin. He placed his hand, then his shoulder against the wall and then braced himself against the mineshaft as if it were a crutch.

Kilpatre started the long march down the yellow brick road. "Oh my..." Gasp. Shuffle. "Oh my..." Wheeze. Shuffle. "Gold..." Gasp. Shuffle. "Mine..." Wheeze. Shuffle. Oh my!"

Kilpatre scraped his way along the mineshaft. A bloody streak marked the path. He gambled one more step and busted. The ground disappeared beneath Kilpatre. He plunged into the pitch dark, landing on his back on a long incline. Gravity got hold of him next and rolled him down a long, circular granite ramp, end over end, careening like a pinball off the walls, depositing a rag doll mass of broken bones and bloody flesh at the bottom three levels later.

*** 

"Kara, me sweet, what be bothering you?" Snatch asked. The two Orlif rebels and the immortal human stood in the center of a cavernous, cylindrically shaped auditorium. The walls were about ten stories high and were perforated with thousands of boreholes—each eight feet deep.

"Jimmy McCauley, Hoop cannot find the Kilpatre human. Cannot speak to his mind."

"Maybe the fat bastard be dead, Kara."

"No!" Hoop-Kar objected. "Not dead! I left him at the new mine entrance in the dark. He was injured and immobile. I assumed we could find and collect him later. I cannot see him now. He is not sleeping. He is gone! The Federation Exterms must have him."

\*\*\*

Alpha Genesis and his mate joined Kilpatre, The One, at the bottom of the ramp. "You are here, Boss. Gold!"

Kilpatre's breathing was a gurgling fountain, sluggishly spewing a foamy red stream. He was literally drowning in his own blood. His eyes were open and fixed. The tumble down the steep ramp had removed most of his clothing as if he'd been undressed by a power sander. More than half his skin had third-degree burns. His joints were a reticulation of abnormal angles resulting from the numerous bone fractures.

As bad as his injuries were, one trumped all the others. The auditorium was brightly lit—a curiosity that Cole Kilpatre would never consider. Before him was the pyramid of gold built by Jimmy McCauley over the past decades.

"Gold! Mine!"

"The One. Ours!"

Nothing in the millions of years of adaptation, no species, no plant or animal, no mineral or element or any natural mutation that Kar had experienced compared to the innate ruthlessness possessed by The One. His genes must be incorporated into Federation's, completing the ultimate introgression—the perfect lifeboat.

Kilpatre's view of the golden pyramid was replaced by the Kars' jaws closing on his throat. Human tissue separated and lifted from his body as smoothly as a ladle of soup. Kilpatre's flesh blackened around the wound from the machines' venom. The necrosis spread throughout his corpse, but he did not dissolve.

The change in the monsters was immediate. The benefaction known genetically as Kilpatre soared through their bodies much like the poisonous gas that dissolved their prey. They died from the inside out, tearing at their bodies, ripping their flesh away and throwing it aside as if on fire. Their last act of destruction was toward each other.

Alpha Genesis and Beta ended their self-dismantlement on some cue. They circled each other, hissing, challenging, and then in a perfectly timed attack, each reached out with a scimitar-like claw and slashed the throat of its mate. Nearly decapitated, dying, two pairs of shark's eyes watched its mate fall.

The One. The 1080. The possessor of genetic rat poison ended the current reign of the Exterm Federation.

\*\*\*

Renner led the group cautiously down the long granite ramp. Roe and Rogers were at his sides with weapons at the ready. BB and Puck brought up the rear, with Doc, Kate and James George in the cradle as they say. Kilpatre's blood pointed the way like crimson breadcrumbs.

They entered the vast cavern and stopped. Josh Roe's flashlight followed the blood trail and was the first to find the dead Kars. "Sheriff, over here."

Renner and Erin aimed their crossbows at the machines and approached warily. Roe kept the light focused. Renner studied the Kars for a moment and announced. "They are dead. Throats slashed. It looks like they killed each other."

"Mac! It's Kilpatre!" BB shouted.

Puck kneeled next to the mayor and examined the injuries.

"Is he...?" Doc asked.

The Ortez and Kilpatre clans had been at war for more than a century. Seeing Kilpatre literally in the blackened flesh, Puck decided to bury the hatchet. Kilpatre had somehow saved their collective skins. Puck reached down and gently closed the mayor's eyes for the last time.

BB, feeling the same emotions as Puck—a mix of gratitude, awe, even guilt asked, "How do you suppose he did it? Got them to turn on each other?"

James George studied the mayor and the Kar's corpses. Genius does not rationalize. It does not make excuses for mistakes. Genius dwells not in the land of doubt for long. The last two Kars were dead. The mayor was dead. The mayor must have been rat poison after all.

James George Spencer was perhaps the most intelligent human who ever walked the earth. He had soared naturally through calculus and physics like other children learned to crawl. He could recall content verbatim from the tens of thousands of books he speed-read like normal people recalled their own names. He discussed matters routinely with Hawking, Einstein, Gamow, Duane and Thorne: black holes, infinity, time and universe, though he had never met or spoken to any of these great men, living or dead. He was still just a child—a child who had gone without adequate food, water and sleep for nearly two days. The room began to spin.

Something was wrong. "I don't think it's over!" James mumbled. He staggered and then passed out in Kate's arms.

The adults hurried to James's side. Kate cradled him like a baby as Renner and Doc pressed a bottle of water to his lips. The child accepted a few drops and slumped more deeply into Kate's embrace.

Erin Rogers gently pulled back an eyelid and waved the flashlight beam near the child's eye. She clicked off the light and said, "I am guessing exhaustion. I don't know how the little guy made it this far."

"Are you sure, Erin?" Doc pleaded.

Renner and Rogers looked at each other. They'd both been trained in the art of sleep deprivation. Erin allowed Renner to assure Doc and everyone else.

Renner nodded and tenderly brushed away a lock of James' hair. He smiled and said, "He's fine. Just one extremely tired little trooper. We'll just let him sleep."

Everyone except Doc and Kate stood up. BB asked, "Say, Mac, what did Jamesie mean when he hollered, 'I don't think it's over!'?"

From the base of the ramp deep in the shadows a voice called out, "I believe I can answer that."

Kara Kar bolted from the shadows and sprinted to James. Hoop-Kar was at her side. Doc and Kate looked at the second karpeleotroceme and then at each other in amazement.

"Who's there?" Renner shouted then ordered, "Show yourself!"

"Aye, lad, we both will. It's time. The 'git out' bell has done rung its last. We've rose up the scupper together, seen the light and breathed the Maker's fine air free we have. You've shown yourself a fine McCauley, you has! I'm proud of yuz, grandboy. Our secret kept safe and the mountain too." Snatch stepped into the light.

For Renner it was like looking into a mirror. "Grandfather McCauley!"

"Aye."

"But how?" It was a question that could not be answered in a hundred lifetimes, and Renner regretted having asked it.

"Like the boy said, it's not over, my good grandson."

"I don't understand."

"Oh, you will, boy. Soon. Our Kara and her fine mate, Mr. Hoop have more in their magic sack to share." The name 'Hoop' stunned not just Renner but everyone.

Snatch laughed and held up his hands. "Forgive me, grandson. I'm in the middle of this very strange pie meself, and even I has not an idea from lardy crust to buttery batter most of the time what this wee, good creature has cooked up. Hoop was her mate, long ago. Don't know how long ago. She brang him here, somehow. Made him human to your eye, somehow. Even hid his Kar self from his human self somehow. Very strange. Lovable, but strange she is. Look at her loving over Jamesie!"

Kara and Hoop probed James's sleeping mind. "Jimmy McCauley! Wake up! What did you mean 1080? Please wake, child."

James was slipping into deep sleep. His mind slurred to her... the rats... poison... and Kilpatre is the rats' poison... He then closed his mind to her, the statement left ambiguous.

Renner could not take his eyes off his grandfather even as Snatch examined the dead Kars and Cole Kilpatre. He smiled and understood Snatch's disgusted expression as he looked upon Kilpatre.

"A sad state of affairs when I have to look on any mother's Kilpatre with pity, like now, aye. Does you know how the fat bastard waxed the creatures, lad?"

Renner sighed and scratched his neck, "No idea."

"Well, doesn't matter. Time for a bit of undoing."

"Undoing?"

"You read me letters, lad. Time to put things back to right." Snatch lifted Kilpatre as easily as he might an infant. "I lied to all yuz McCauleys about the Midas Six. She was a real payer, lad. Became one, that is. None's placer paid out better before her. And it's yours, grand lad, for keeping our promise, for keeping our mountain safe."

Snatch took the flashlight from Renner's hand, aimed it at the base of the pyramid of gold bricks, and then slowly aimed the beam to its top. "It's all yours, son. Rebuild our town, make a new future, put everything properly right again."

Renner lowered his eyes. There was enough gold stacked before him to rebuild New York City, but no amount of gold could replace Gus and Maggie Augustus, or Skip, Chooke and his wife, or even a pair of no-account poachers.

Snatch handed the flashlight back to Renner. He placed a hand on the sheriff's shoulder and smiled. "Look at me, boy. No need for sadness, now. Our little Kara has yet one more surprise. Your wish is about to come true."

"My wish?"

"Aye. Your wish and one of me own, too."

"Your wish, grandfather?"

"Aye! A simple thing. I wished for some warm vittles, amply stocked, and a long, long nap whenever me so chooses. And me sweet Kara has promised me both. So leave us go. Come, Kara. More of your goodness I implore."

Snatch stopped and kneeled beside Doc and Kate. He kissed his fingertips and touched James's forehead. "Sleep, lad. You've done mighty good, you have, and so very far you have to go. Many adventures you will take."

Snatch covered Kate's hand with his. "Thank you, good daughter. Thank you for trusting the McCauley secret. I look forward to your wedding, child, and me giving me grandboy away to yuz. To have and to hold forever as the good Reverend Cooke would surely say."

Kate smiled and whispered, "Thank you." She leaned forward, embraced Snatch and gave him a kiss on the cheek.

Snatch turned to Doc Karl. "And you, Professor, you be giving this fine lass away on her wedding day, I presume."

"Yes, I will indeed." Doc extended his hand to shake and added, "It's been a pleasure meeting you, Grandfather James McCauley, Sheriff of Seer County, Colorado from 1886-1912."

"The pleasure's been mine, Professor. May I ask a wee favor, Professor?"

"Of course! Anything."

"When young James wakes up, he'll surely ask about the pets. I stashed them in a safe place. He will know where it be. Give him his mind and let him go fetch them alone. Should make a fine reunion, lift his spirits. He'll be safe. Yuz has my word."

"Certainly."

"Very good! Someone bring our boy, and now off we go everyone to finish this devilish nightmare. Everyone follow me. Kara! Hoop! Come now. One last affection, please favor us with, me sweet gal from Golden."

# CHAPTER 76 ~~ The Newborn

"Grandfather, what is this place?" Renner focused the flashlight on the far inward-curving wall, then up ten stories to the top of the cylindrical hall. Within the lowest boreholes, he could see an assortment of objects inside but not well enough to identify any.

"Yuz will see soon enough our Kara's plan. Trust a bit more, grandson, and she'll put everything back in place. Come." He took Renner by the elbow and led him outside the chamber. Kara and Hoop remained inside.

Snatch spoke over his shoulder as he reentered the chamber, "You did fine, grandson. Goodbye."

"Goodbye? What?" Renner stepped forward.

But it was already too late. Snatch lifted a one-ton boulder effortlessly and sealed himself inside. The stone was sculpted perfectly to within a millimeter to match the portal. Renner and Roe tried to pry it open, but soon gave up. As she did earlier tonight, Kara opened her mind and allowed the humans to watch what was about to happen. The stone was a foot thick, but as transparent as window glass.

Snatch deposited Kilpatre's corpse into one of the lateral boreholes. The mayor's girth made it a bit of a challenge. Snatch made a show of shoving it into the crypt for Renner's benefit. The

Kilpatre weight issue was a matter of historical consistency. He turned to Renner, winked and smiled. Even Kilpatre, Seer City's reprehensible mayor was to return to life. Renner placed both hands on the "glass" and smiled back.

Kara went to six empty chambers and touched the floor of each with the shard which was coated with the blood of five Resumption Mining scientists and one State Police detective. Snatch walked to the center of the chamber. The aliens took up positions on his left and right. Kara handed the shard to Snatch. He placed it between his teeth. Hoop and Kara returned to their natural android forms with Day-Glow blue eyes. Snatch took their hands.

James George woke from his brief nap and slid between Kate and Renner at the window. He'd been in this room before. He knew what was in the boreholes and what was about to happen.

"Kara! Hoop! No! There has to be another way. Please don't die!" James screamed.

Kara reached into James's mind searching for all the right words. "Don't be... silly! Kara not die. Kara cannot die. Jimmy McCauley and Kara have too much digging to do... no, not digging. What's word? Exploring! Jimmy McCauley and Kara Kar explore."

"Exploring?" James said aloud. The adults turned toward him and looked at him curiously.

"Yes. But, you must wait a while, just until you get a little bit bigger."

"Where will you be, Kara?"

"Close to you, Jimmy McCauley. Always close. Find the pets. They have a surprise for you."

"I love you, Kara."

"Kara love Jimmy McCauley, every one of you! Yes, I call everyone Jimmy McCauley! Hah! Kara make joke! Good bye!"

Snatch nodded goodbye. A green ball of energy appeared and surrounded the three. The orb grew in size and intensity and began to rise with the three inside, slowly at first, then faster and faster it spun, leaving in its wake a double-helix energy field.

The window into the chamber became opaque. A deep rumbling passed through the wall. It lasted for several seconds and then passed. The immense stone that Snatch had placed in the portal crumbled and fell as sand.

Renner was the first to enter the chamber. Snatch, Kara and Hoop were gone. The boreholes were now sealed with a substance similar to the mysterious shard. The only other evidence left behind was a letter. The paper was yellowed and brittle. The handwriting was Grandfather McCauley's.

Composed this date, October 31, 1912

Well, McCauley child, since you are reading this here last letter, I get to say, well done. We did it. The mountain has been set right. The monsters have lost their bidding. Thank God Almighty for that! My Kara and her mate Hoop are safe. At long last I eat and sleep, which I hope and pray I'm doing right now.

Kara said, and how she can foresee such things, child, I cannot say, but she said my best friend Pasqual Ortez's longest grandson is here with you now. Also with you, Cornelia Bainbridge's longest grandson. Cornelia was our midwife. Delivered many McCauley kin. Two professors too, one is your dearest friend, the other your wife-to-be. You have two peacekeepers with you also. A man and a woman. They will be mates. You all owe each other your lives. You are to never break the bond. You are now brothers and sisters, husbands and wives for eternity.

There is a special child with you. She does not know his name. She calls him my very own Jimmy McCauley, but she calls everyone Jimmy McCauley. He will go on a great adventure, and you all will go with him. Sorry. She will not say more. Kara is a delight, but she can be as stubborn as a Crosby mule.

The last is a miracle. The good folks of Seer City will be returned to you. The good men and women who died along the way on this nightmarish night, all will be born again. They will return just as Kara returned me when the cougar took me life. The Ortez and Bainbridge boys are to open the cocoons in exactly one week. How they'll do that, I do not know. Kara says "see-for." And I say, see for what? Me girl talks in riddles. Bring blankets and clothes from their homes. They will all believe that the town was in peril from sour gasses, and you brought them here to be safe. None will question you. None will see their nakedness or any changes in their town. Kara will make sure.

Now go find our special boy before he gets himself into any more trouble! He's with the pets.

Written as told, not as understood, my very best wishes and hope,

James McCauley
Sheriff (retired this date 1912) Seer County, Colorado

Kate was the first to look down and realize that James had disappeared. "James! James! Renner, he's gone!"

Doc Karl took Kate by the shoulders and said, "Don't worry, dear. He's fine. We'll find him. Mr. Snatch assured me. He can't have gone far. He's looking for the pets."

\*\*\*

James sat cross-legged in front of Isaac and Newton's cage. He yawned and studied the rodents. After a moment, he smiled. Sasha rose, finished the water in his dish and plopped down next to James George. The white rats alternately nibbled their snack and sipped water.

Newton stared at James for a moment and reared up onto her hind legs. James laughed and opened the cage door. "Hello, Kara Kar. How about a big hug?"

"Hello, my Jimmy McCauley!" she squeaked.

James gathered up the three reborn machines into his arms and said "Hello, Hoop! And hello Snatch!"

# CHAPTER 77 ~~ Washington D.C.—One Week Later

"Good morning, Mrs. McCauley."

Kate did not open her eyes. She awoke snuggled under Renner's right arm, their bodies pressed together. Their marriage could not wait for Reverend Cooke's return. She found his lips with a kiss and said, "I love you, Renner McCauley."

Renner returned the kiss just to the point of no return and pulled away. The couple giggled softly at the narrow escape. The honeymoon was just beginning, but a bit of official business awaited them. "I love you too, Kate, with all my heart."

Kate cuddled, pressed her body against Renner and felt him answer in kind. "So, how's progress going in Seer City?" she asked dreamily.

Renner smiled and said, "Better than expected. Puck and BB said that every security agency in the government showed up with armies of engineers, electricians, carpenters, plumbers, medical experts, scientists, and the town has been completely restored. The president asked representatives from over fifty countries to observe. NATO invited Russia, China and even Cuba to join forces to assess the

409

intergalactic threat, and they all accepted. It took an alien invasion to unite Earth."

"The rebirths are today, right? The catacombs will open and Seer City will be repopulated. Strange."

"Yes, that should prove interesting. Should make for some rather remarkable dream accounts. I don't think we will ever fully understand how Kara did it. The government spooks and NASA are competing for questions."

Renner changed the subject to something less speculative, "So, my love, what's on your agenda today?"

Kate loved the way Renner so easily improved the mood to the safe present. She kissed his chin and said, "Well, after I pick up James' final adoption decree, Doc, James, and I are going to Georgetown University to see a colleague who has just returned from Montana."

"Let me guess. Something to do with multituberculate fossils?"

Becoming overly melodramatic, Kate covered her mouth with Renner's hand in feigned awe, "Oh my gosh, how could you have ever guessed!"

"An old fossil named Doc told me. Started with a search for our friend Kara long ago." Renner kissed Kate again.

"Yes, our sweet gal from g'Hhol-deune. I miss her."

"I do too. Hoop and Snatch too. Just to think that old bum was my grandfather. What a hoot! Seer City will never be the same without its phantom."

It was Kate's turn to change the subject. "So, Sheriff, what's on your agenda today?"

"I'm having lunch with Erin and Josh. Grandfather Jimmy's instructions were rather specific, but completely mysterious."

"Tell them hello, please."

"Will do."

Kissing for punctuation, Kate said, "Perhaps we should liven things up, just to make sure today does not end boring, before it gets started…" Kate kissed Renner deeply, way beyond the tipping point called 'not now.'

***

Puck Ortez and Ben Bainbridge studied the changes in the catacomb. The CIA, FBI and NSA had performed a miracle. Rising from the floor were ten stories of scaffolding that encircled the cylindrical catacomb, one for each row of sealed boreholes. Several heavy-rated freight elevators had been installed to bring down Seer City's disoriented citizens.

"You say it, Bro." Puck offered the honors to his best friend.

They tapped fists and BB shouted, "Fire in the hole!"

Puck depressed an ignition button, and from outside the chamber it sounded like an interminable automatic weapon firing as the C4 broke open the sealed boreholes one after another. Giant fans removed the smoke and dust. Other fans brought in fresh air.

A hundred medical specialists rushed into the chamber. More followed with blankets and clothing. Within thirty minutes, more than eleven hundred fully mature newborns began to awake. By late afternoon, busses began taking the survivors home. As Snatch had promised and Kara had somehow enabled, their ordeal soon became dreamy fragments, memory bits that over time even the tiniest details were forgotten.

Seer City's population returned, except for three individuals who few would ever miss.

Ol' Snatch.

Cyril Hoop.

Mayor Cole Kilpatre, who somehow slipped away unseen. While the rebirth of an entire town was witnessed by thousands, no one saw the rebirth of the Exterm Federation.

# EPILOGUE

That night James George McCauley dreamed he was aboard and commanded a planetoid-sized spaceship, the star victor *Jhimmy*, the Patriot Kar fleet's McCauley-class flagship.

He was no longer a child. In fact, today was his twenty-ninth birthday, but the small celebration had ended abruptly with the delivery of some very disturbing news. James George stood before a great porthole overlooking deep space and reread the intelligence report. The closest stars beyond the great window were in the Orion Nebula, and ironically, marked the very site of the long ago Rebel Orlif massacre.

Standing nearby were Kara and Hoop, appearing in their natural, android forms. Sasha awoke in a command chair, plopped to the deck, yawned and disappeared under the helm's central control computer panel.

Kara and Hoop stepped beside James. Kara rested her head for a moment on James' shoulder and looked out into space. She wrapped her arm around his waist and spoke to him in her native Kar language. "We cannot allow Kilpatre to finish reconstituting the Federation, James. He seeks the end time. He will not stop until the multiverse is destroyed."

James turned and placed both hands on Kara's shoulders. He too spoke in Kar. "I understand, Mother. We will stop him." James turned to Hoop and nodded, "I promise you and Father that our precious sacrifices will not have been in vain." The three huddled for a moment in an embrace.

James then turned to Josh Roe and Erin Rogers, who strangely had not aged at all. "Commanders, contact Kate and Renner. Warn my human parents that the treaty is another Exterm double-cross! Tell them we are now at war with the Federation and to order the evacuation of the Summit."

James George's expression grew graver. "Josh and Erin, my wife and children are with Doc, as are your twins. They are on their way to Earth to visit BB and Puck. Take two battle platens and twelve saber squadrons to intercept and provide them safe passage to Earth. Once there, organize a defense of the planet. Kilpatre will return there. I'm sure of it. Do not allow Earth to fall."

"Aye, my Admiral!"

"You have our word."

Admiral McCauley then issued one more dream order. He spoke directly to his spaceship, the most modern warship in the restored Orlif fleet. It was a Subnanomech XII, a living sentient machine. Powering its synthetic brain, heart and soul was a well-rested and well-fed former sheriff and one-time Dumpster diver.

"Grandfather Jhimmy, please take us to hyperspace. Make our speed psi-$_{100c}$. Set a course through the Orion Nebula to our ancient homeland g'Hhol-deune. We have a universe to protect and it must start there."

"Aye, Laddie! It be Ol' Snatch's great pleasure to stretch our legs a wee bit by kickin' some Kilpatre arses once again. Ready for psi jump to hyperspace on your mark, me Admiral."

"Mark!"


To be continued with…

*Inorganics Rise*
*~The Second Machine War~*

# ABOUT THE AUTHOR

MIKE TINGLE is a freelance writer, novelist and short story writer, and is the WRONG WORLD® creator. His next science fiction novel is entitled *Dreadnought City Limits*, scheduled for release in 2013, followed by the *Organics* sequel, *Inorganics Rise*.